PENGUIN BOOKS

THE GROUNDS

Cormac Millar lives in Dublin, where, as Cormac Ó Cuilleanáin, he teaches Italian at Trinity College. He is the author of *An Irish Solution*.

http://www.cormacmillar.com
http://www.kingscollegedublin.org

The Grounds

CORMAC MILLAR

PENGUIN BOOKS

PENGUIN BOOKS

Published by the Penguin Group
Penguin Books Ltd, 80 Strand, London WC2R 0RL, England
Penguin Group (USA) Inc., 375 Hudson Street, New York, New York 10014, USA
Penguin Group (Canada), 90 Eglinton Avenue East, Suite 700, Toronto, Ontario, Canada M4P 2Y3
(a division of Pearson Penguin Canada Inc.)
Penguin Ireland, 25 St Stephen's Green, Dublin 2, Ireland
(a division of Penguin Books Ltd)
Penguin Group (Australia), 250 Camberwell Road, Camberwell, Victoria 3124, Australia
(a division of Pearson Australia Group Pty Ltd)
Penguin Books India Pvt Ltd, 11 Community Centre, Panchsheel Park, New Delhi – 110 017, India
Penguin Group (NZ), 67 Apollo Drive, Mairangi Bay, Auckland 1310, New Zealand
(a division of Pearson New Zealand Ltd)
Penguin Books (South Africa) (Pty) Ltd, 24 Sturdee Avenue, Rosebank, Johannesburg 2196, South Africa

Penguin Books Ltd, Registered Offices: 80 Strand, London WC2R 0RL, England

www.penguin.com

First published by Penguin Ireland 2006
Published in Penguin Books 2007

1

Copyright © Cormac Ó Cuilleanáin, 2006
All rights reserved

The moral right of the author has been asserted

Printed in England by Clays Ltd, St Ives plc

ISBN: 978-1-844-88028-7

In memory of
Eilís Dillon
(1920–1994)

Contents

Prelude

Waking was a kind of fall. Finding himself once again in her empty bed, seeing the long white nightdress folded on her pillow. Pale scrubbed wood, clean painted walls, threadbare curtains fired by sunlight. The cold air. Her feet in the kitchen. The fridge door closing. Things shifting into place.

There was the food. Morning fare was thin slices of cheese, black rye and pumpernickel bread, syrupy coffee with sticky grit at the bottom of the cup, Apollinaris water. She drank no poisons from the tap, ate no meat. Stacked fruit in wooden bowls, thrown in the compost when it started to spot. The forest all around them.

There was the outdoor life. She believed in walking, not just on gentle slopes. Clad in khaki shorts and brown ankle-boots, she marched him up mountains, along woodland paths, provisions stashed in her knapsack. She swam in cold-water lakes. (This in February.) He watched from the shore, allowed himself to be tempted, tried one foot in the icy water. In that element, she was perfect.

There was the sex. She trapped him in the dark, ambushed him in the morning, invaded his bath, dragged him from his paper-strewn desk to the creaking bed, the wooden floor, the sofa, the starved patch of sunlit grass (snow still on the ground), straining into new shapes, reaching for happiness. He began to sympathize with the sculptures of Henry Moore.

There was the language. He was writing a memoir of past trauma, losing the battle with words. Orphaned of secretaries, he faced the screen alone, tapped, deleted, stared at the blank window. His English was drying up. Absurdly, he found himself thinking in gapped German. No longer a genuine foreigner, he was a stumbling man recovering from brain injury. Words and meanings resisted fusion. Hence his incapacity to say what was on his mind.

There were the doubts, hedging him in. His former wife had proved to be compulsively promiscuous, yet their sex life, before it had faded, had been at best a sporadic, safe routine. What was the meaning of Heidi's feral energy? He was too reticent to ask. Heidi did not invite questions. He sometimes confessed selected aspects of his past life. She did not reciprocate. Once, when he woke up, she was in tears. Thinking of home, she said, but would not elaborate.

There were no mirrors in the woodland cottage where they spent those first weeks. When they moved back to her apartment close to the Permanent Liaison Committee headquarters, he found himself rougher, leaner, with a weathered face that reminded him of his brother Daniel, not seen in seven years. Home from work, Heidi took him shopping, kitted him out in Harris tweeds and denim trousers, Indian cotton shirts, waxed jackets, Birkenstocks. Too much, really, but she liked the effect. She made him grow his hair longer, bought him razor blades to shave his face clean. He put the clothes on his credit card, but Heidi was paying for everything else. His lump sum had not come through, his pension had yet to be approved. She put away his smooth Italian suit. Now he looked more Irish, less neutral than when he had worked in Dublin.

To his surprise, there was hate mail. Letters from Ireland, typed and handwritten, signed and unsigned, forwarded by the Department of Justice. He was accused of being a criminal, a drug baron, a communist, a secret supporter of the opposition. The trick he had played to bring down his Minister was construed as part of some deep Masonic plot. In the same batch of forwarded post came handwritten letters of praise, even a declaration of love.

Weeks later came a single brown envelope, posted in London, containing copies of press cuttings about Richard Frye, his disgraced Minister. Frye claimed to have been singled out for special treatment, complained that dark forces had worked against him to undermine Ireland's drug-free policies and sabotage the anti-drugs policy that Frye had planned to lead in Europe. The brown envelope also contained the photocopy of an unsigned letter, received in the Department of Justice, protesting that Séamus Joyce, a known associate of international drug rings, was about to receive a state pension. The Criminal Assets Bureau should look into his property portfolio, the letter-writer argued, before any money was paid over. The typing was impeccable, the writing coherent: not the work of a crank.

He thought of demanding an explanation, insisting that the Department cough up his overdue payments. He did nothing. He could not ask Heidi's advice.

As in his former life, once again he was being moulded by his surroundings. Floating in limbo, he was losing his knowledge. It was a good life. Why did she love him? What had he done to deserve that? He loved her, in so far as he could love anything in the world. So why the resentment, why the unease, why the despair he had felt in the forest?

2

Of course there was the music. Having left his jazz collection in Ireland, he searched for sounds to fill the silence. On the radio were jazz stations, others specializing in bland classics and monotonous oom-pah-pah, but Heidi's apartment had shelves full of old twelve-inch discs: symphonies, concertos, chamber music, choral works. She owned no CD player. She had once enjoyed the gritty sound of vinyl, she said, but nowadays opted mostly for silence. He started to explore her collection. During his solitary hours of reading, cooking, writing, her apartment resounded to the dazzling gloom of Shostakovich, Rachmaninov, Kabalevsky, Vainberg. Enough to make you want to cut your throat.

He was too much alone. She went to the office during the day, doing unspecified administrative work for the German secretariat of the Permanent Liaison Committee. She had a special badge to get her into the Policy Division. Séamus had never been inside that particular bunker. She sometimes came home late, after her exercise nights. Heidi was sharp and fit, despite weighing so very little. In the city, she wore black, melting into the drabness of the streets. Covering her hair with a black corduroy cap, she looked like a Victorian child setting out to sweep chimneys.

There were overnight absences. Servicing a PLC delegation, she explained, but didn't say who was in the delegation, nor even where she had been. What services had she provided? Word-processing, interpreting, that sort of thing. She made it sound tedious, but her eyes lit up.

Once, having gone into town in search of shaving foam, he saw her walking with a thin, bald man, moving faster than she ever did with Séamus. They walked close together, in perfect synchronicity of stride, her slight limp barely discernible. Séamus turned away. At home that night, nothing was said.

Out for an afternoon stroll, he recognized a senior Irish policeman alighting from the bus near the PLC headquarters. He greeted the man by name, was rebuffed with a blank stare. 'I don't think our paths have crossed.' But they had, many years before, on a working party examining the protection of the rights of suspects. Obviously, Séamus was a man whom it was no longer politic to remember.

He mentioned the Irishman's name to Heidi. Was he visiting the PLC on behalf of the Irish government? There was no official Irish representative at the moment. Perhaps they were thinking of sending a policeman rather than a civil servant? Heidi made enquiries, drew a blank.

He joined an evening class on Central European history, held in an upstairs classroom at a local high school. His pedestrian German failed to track the lecturer's loftier flights, but he managed to get the gist; and mugged up the material with the help of English textbooks ordered from Amazon. With the aid of two dictionaries he drafted an essay in simple German. The lecturer asked him to do a longer version in English, and declared herself pleased with the result. He read what he had written. It was dead on the page. She set him another essay. He ground to a halt.

Too many years had gone by since he had last been a student. Going back to education should have been a release. It was a normal thing to do in middle age. In a sense, it was easy. He brought the skills of a working lifetime to the task. The assemblage of data was easy enough, but he no longer felt able to risk the sort of grand intuition that had sustained him in his first year at university. Then, he had sometimes felt he could almost reach out and grasp the truth. His teachers were not so sure. Now, it was not the truth, just the facts.

He returned to his own memoir, spent days polishing phrases, revising paragraphs, striking out whole sections. Everything he wrote was true, but the composite result was false. Besides, it took far too much time. It ought to be easy to write about oneself. It is not.

He felt like the burned-out shell of a country house.

He bought a biography of Stan Getz, the gentle jazzman whose nervous melodic lines had nursed him through the worst days of his life. Getz, it transpired, was prone to out-breaks of rage and domestic violence. He stopped reading the biography, switched to books about recent history and contemporary politics: a mixture of sense and delusion. Man cannot live without faith in impossible things.

People still knew him at the PLC. The place was quieter than it had been, as other agencies with better connections were taking up questions of European security, and the Americans had withdrawn their observers from Aachen, leaving the Washington line to be pushed by wannabees. Ritual debates rumbled on, as former democracies and former autocracies competed in adapting their public images to the crudely drawn comic-strip world that followed upon the still unbelievable destruction of the Twin Towers.

Séamus received invitations to PLC events, which Heidi persuaded him to accept. People seemed pleased to see him. Visiting securocrats, politicians and academics liked to have a well-informed audience to debate their views, and Séamus had a store of thoughtful questions.

There was a brief blush of fame when an American news magazine surveyed the state of narcotics distribution in the world, and cornered Séamus to comment on his Dublin experience. He appeared in a lime-green panel of his own, incongruously headed 'Fighting Irish'. His role in the drugs wars was dramatized, and he was made to seem wise and farsighted. Captioning him as 'Modest Hero Who Made a Difference', the article rewrote in positive mode his disastrous stewardship of the Irish Drugs Enforcement Agency. When he read of his manifold triumph, he had the odd sensation of turning into a fictional character. Some of his acquaintances in Aachen, who should have known better, seemed to take this stuff seriously. He was invited to dinners with important people. Heidi enjoyed those occasions, producing a wardrobe of strappy gowns and flimsy shoes. He loved her flickering smile in the candlelight.

He was growing poor, though comfortably so. Still no money came from Dublin. Theresa, his ex-wife, had had tenants in the Donnybrook house that she had assigned to him as part of their separation settlement. The tenants had moved out, retaining the last two months' rent to offset the deposit Theresa had collected from them three years previously. Séamus would not write to Theresa to reclaim the money. He knew what she would say: it was up to him to collect his rent, and besides, the deposit had been spent on maintenance and improvements. The people in the property management agency were unwilling to find another tenant before the house had been refurbished. They said its decor was out of date. Unbelievable, he knew: the frantic Dublin rental market meant that any property, no matter how derelict, could easily be rented out. The letting agents could not take the responsibility of engaging decorators; they demanded detailed instructions.

They could, if he wished, find him a buyer; investors were always happy to snap up houses, however small and dowdy, in good Dublin locations.

Séamus found his key to the house, clipped it on his key ring, booked a cheap flight to Dublin through Stansted. Then he got a nagging head-cold and postponed the trip. He dropped out of his evening class, took to spending too much time on the Internet.

In the mirror, he had begun to shrink. Not wasting away: just becoming less portly. Either Heidi's healthy food was curing his middle-aged spread, or else Theresa must be burning a wax effigy over a slow flame.

Retirement did not suit him. And he had to admit that he was becoming retired, not just momentarily unemployed. In his own eyes, and in those around him, he was a man with time on his hands. He went into a coffee-house one Monday afternoon, carrying an English Sunday paper, which he leafed through at leisure, in all its various sections. The colour supplement had an article on immigration in East Germany that he thought might interest Heidi. He ordered a second coffee, read the book reviews, paid his money and left, then remembered that he had forgotten to take away the colour supplement. When he went back for it, the woman at the

7

cash desk handed it over with a sympathetic air, and engaged him in aimless dialogue for a minute, membershipping him as a sufferer from the incurable disease of loneliness. Séamus had not, so far as he could honestly say, left the colour supplement behind on purpose, as the pretext for additional social intercourse, but in the cashier's eyes he could see that men like him were prone to do that.

Still Heidi loved him. He caught her looking at him, with shining eyes, as though he were a treasure dearly bought.

He could not sleep.

3

She brought him to one of her relaxation classes, and left him alone with the counsellor, a scrawny woman with an earnest frown who informed him that he was perhaps mildly depressed and questioned him sotto voce in hypercorrect English as to his anxieties. She assured him he could speak with utter confidence; she was bound not only by the ethics of her profession but also by the security requirements of the Permanent Liaison Committee Staff Welfare Scheme. Séamus did not find this double assurance doubly reassuring. Since Heidi had brought him here, he made a decent effort to recreate some snippets from his dead marriage and loveless childhood. The counsellor fixed her sympathetic gaze on the bridge of his nose, her ditchwater eyes glowing as each cliché slotted into her checkerboard brain. She urged that he should try to be more of a protagonist, not allow himself be over-shadowed by minor characters in the story of his life. He wondered, silently, how she reconciled this heroic doctrine with her own carriage-wheel role as a pedlar of patent beliefs. She crossed her painfully thin miniskirted legs, flicked thin fingers through her dyed brown hair, pulled back her shoulders, fingered the top button of her dusty pink cardigan and suggested that he was perhaps a little repressed in his reactions to people. He was attempting to be always urbane and sophisticated. It might be perhaps a little better to be basic, no? She advised him that he must struggle to find his own unique identity. Séamus smiled at the memory of a Sempé cartoon in which hundreds of identical people standing at identical windows of identical apartments in identical apartment blocks all exclaim simultaneously how dreadful it would be to live in a world where everyone was exactly the same. He was going to tell this to the earnest counsellor, who was tilting her skull to one side while wetting her glossed lips with the tip of her tongue, but he reflected that to do so might sound cruel.

She instructed him to jot down his dreams, using a small notebook and a ballpoint pen. The important thing was to do this first thing each morning, before any distractions presented themselves. He could be frank: there was no obligation to report his dreams and fantasies to her, or to anyone else.

'Find opportunities to be proactive, occasions of self-assertion,' she instructed him. 'You will feel all the better for it. A man has got to do what a man has got to do. If you will give yourself permission to relax, your life will be more fun and you yourself, as a personality, will become more interesting.'

Séamus had spent a lifetime trying, with some success, to be dull. He made an excuse and left, but found he had agreed to another appointment.

Afterwards, he had to admit that the session had done him some good. We must always be ready to learn from fools. And under the barrage of banalities he had in fact come up with one useful reflection of his own. Over the past few months he had switched from an ageing wife to a younger woman. Tabby cat to alleycat. Could that be what was making him feel so damnably old?

But why had he been trapped by Theresa in the first place? What had gone wrong with his youth?

Why was he hurt by Heidi's spontaneity, her speed? Theresa had anaesthetized him. He was waking up to pain.

His head-cold was persisting into the spring.

4

There was a doctor, a gangling fellow from Bavaria. His office was festooned with diplomas. His name was August Wallenstein-Heinemann. A master of elocution, he spoke American English, Germanic French, Spanish and Italian. These accomplishments were regularly displayed as the great man emerged into his waiting room to summon each new patient with a personalized phrase of greeting. It was not an unpleasant wait. There were glossy magazines and exotic fish. After an hour, Séamus was summoned into the inner sanctum and subjected to various indignities, accompanied by a steady stream of interrogation. Some centilitres of his blood were siphoned into a plastic vial, to be analysed at cut-price rates by the clinic accredited to the Permanent Liaison Committee. The visit concluded with the doctor's preliminary diagnosis that Séamus was carrying far too much weight for his frame, and would shortly pay for this failing in cardiovascular and other disorders. For a start, he should eliminate all alcohol from his diet.

Séamus was discouraged. He had shed so many pounds in the past few months that he could almost discern the shape of his ribcage in the bathroom mirror. He was never going to rival the doctor's plucked vulture profile, but for the first time in years he had been starting to feel more compact, no longer swimming in a circle of useless fat. The skin-and-bone doctor, judging by the dates on his degree certificates, was much the same age as himself, but looked ten years older and closer to the grave.

More than discouraged, he felt insulted. Almost decided not to go back for his next appointment. Ten days later, he was vindicated. The same doctor, test results in hand, reluctantly read him the all clear on a host of diseases and addictions. Cholesterol levels were within tolerable limits. The doctor was clearly crestfallen. Although he ended the consultation with renewed advice on exercise and weight loss, his tone betrayed a certain lack of purchase.

Walking home through afternoon suburbia, Séamus was light on his feet. He felt like ordering cream cake with Schnapps to celebrate his good health, but instead kept walking, and enumerating corpulent men in public life who had lived to ripe seniority. Chancellor Helmut Kohl, for one, was built on an epic scale, and it was quite a few years since his retirement. Hans-Dietrich Genscher, Foreign Minister at the time of German reunification, was no sylph. In an earlier age, Chancellor Ludwig Erhard had been substantial from every angle. Who knows how long the Bunteresque Hermann Goering might not have survived, had the second war worked out the other way? Ranging further afield, Charles Pasqua, Romano Prodi, Kenneth Clarke were living proof that the fuller figure can cut a dash on the European stage. Heavy drinking Boris Yeltsin and well-rounded Mikhail Gorbachev had survived pretty well. In Chile, ex-President Augusto Pinochet was an ambulant advertisement for the good life: the declining path towards his eternal reward was proving slow and stately. His old associate Henry Kissinger, still surviving, might have some difficulty in passing through the eye of a needle. Generalissimo Francisco Paulino Herm-enegildo Teódulo Franco y Bahamonde Salgado Pardo de Andrade (whose full name had been taught to Séamus during his sojourn in secondary school) had hardly been taller than circumferential. The expansive waistline of Ariel Sharon, freely chosen leader of the Israeli people, had clearly been nourished on more than lettuce all these years.

In short, why worry?

5

Late one afternoon in darkest April, as he was being tormented by a global bore at a reception following a Turkish lecture on the joy of human rights, someone tapped Séamus on the shoulder. It was Guido Schneider, flanked by Heidi and by dark-eyed Lieselotte from the firearms secretariat. Guido and Séamus had not met since Guido's visit to Dublin, shortly before Séamus had self-destructed. Guido was still vaguely attached to the German delegation at the PLC, although he was never there.

Lieselotte told Séamus how terrific he looked, hoped he was getting plenty of rest. She launched into a flirtatious greeting of the bore, while Guido took Séamus by the arm and massaged him into a far corner of the room. Séamus had forgotten how tactile Guido was.

'You are enjoying your retirement, Séamus?'

'My new life.' He tried to smile.

Guido narrowed his eyes. 'How do you employ your time?'

'I'm a houseboy.'

'Among other things,' Heidi said. She had followed them.

'It has been four, five months?' Guido asked.

'A little more,' Heidi interjected.

'The world is deprived of your talents, Séamus.'

'Talents like mine the world can stagger on without.'

'You are a good man,' Guido persisted. 'You have experience. You know when to speak, when to keep silent. Which is no longer so common in the world we inhabit. Some people, some groups could benefit from these unusual

12

gifts. I want to ask you about an occasion to deploy your talents.'

'I haven't quite finished with him,' Heidi said.

'A short assignment,' Guido sweetly continued. 'Do not overreact, Frau Novacek.'

'I am not overreacting.' A little too clipped.

'Not yet, Frau Novacek. But we know your dangerous temper. I promise that you have no cause for jealousy here. We are speaking of a temporary loan for an exhibition.'

'He is not a museum piece.'

'That is what he may become, unless you let him work,' Guido smiled. 'Man needs employment. Even the finest brains are subject to stagnation. I have a mission that will suit you, Séamus. My clients would be interested to see you in action. If you do not enjoy it, you need not come again. You can slip back into the twilight world of being Frau Novacek's houseboy.'

'Which is not such a bad deal,' Séamus said.

'Where do you wish to take him?' Heidi asked. They were talking across Séamus, speaking in English for his benefit, but quietly, like a couple in bed. He had the sense of some long-standing intimate quarrel.

'Just across the Atlantic,' Guido said. 'We have an urgent need in the coming days. This will be a private hearing at an institution. Somebody dropped out because of illness. Men of sound judgment are required. It will be brief.'

'I have heard that before.' Heidi scowled like a small child.

'His advice would be valuable.'

'On what exactly?' Heidi insisted.

'Ethical problems, so to say, confronting an international body. Our clients require an external view. Séamus will be part of a high-level delegation from Consultancy International. He will have not too much to do. It does not even require a working visa. The groundwork has been laid. The facts are available. We merely need to reach a judgment. Just a few days, Frau Novacek, and we shall give him back to you, in perfect condition.'

'But where will he have been, Herr Schneider?'

'New York,' Guido said. 'Indeed, dear Frau Novacek, why don't you come too? As our guest?'

Monday

After a sleepless night, he was walking alone in Central Park. Dawn light shone on mountainous buildings. He had left his hotel suite in search of his woman, now presumably lost among the joggers circling the reservoir. How could he feel alone amidst these crowds? How on earth did they manage to be up and about so early? She had escaped while he dozed. The doorman had seen her go, in a pink one-piece.

His head was filled with images from his broken sleep. That blasted psychologist had opened a floodgate. He had stuck with her advice for a week, before ceasing to record his dreams, but he had somehow learned the trick of recalling them, and could not unlearn it. This particular dream went back to his schooldays, and involved the one book you must read to understand everything. He finally found it in a corner of the school library. It was a heavy hardback bound in green buckram. The pages were yellowed, their edges singed almost black. The print was so faded that he could barely make it out. The text was in Latin. *Conticuere omnes*, it began, but when he held it to the lamp the faded letters sank into the paper like minnows diving to the bottom of a stream.

Wide awake, he climbed a grassy bank into the sunlight, and was confronted by an indeterminate number of large dogs on many leads, dragging a tall dark woman. They surged at Séamus: a husky, a Dalmatian, a lean jackal who snapped and chewed the air, smaller curs twisting and growling in the background. He kept walking quickly across the grass. The jackal broke free from the pack and ran in front of him.

The dog-walker, following with the rest of her canine crew, barked her apologies. The jackal circled at a diminishing distance, showing its fangs. He wished he had brought an old-fashioned umbrella to ram down the animal's throat. And he recalled a great black hound who had knocked him down into a ditch when he was only three, and his father looming down to pick him up, and his father's smiling friend Joseph, kicking the dog, which yelped and ran and grew suddenly small. Probably just a friendly Labrador. Not like this slavering beast, snarling and trying to drive him back down the slope into the shadow.

Heidi appeared, catching the dog by the collar. It cowered by her side. She hauled it back to the embarrassed dog-walker, reattached it to its lead. 'I am so sorry,' the dog-walker said. 'My first time out with these guys.' She was wearing a brown uniform. Probably a concierge from one of the mansions on Fifth Avenue.

'No harm done,' said Séamus, and set off across the sward, arm in arm with Heidi. Her snow-white Velcro-fastened plimsolls were lightly stained with grass.

2

The panelled boardroom of the Trade Bank was dark and airy. Séamus sat farthest from the windows, shuffling his papers and forgetting the names of the people to whom he had just been introduced. His nagging head-cold had never quite been shaken off, and he had developed the additional hint of a sore throat on the transatlantic flight. Now he felt distinctly fluey, as well as being jetlagged and out of sorts. The sequence of the past eight hours was fragmented in his head. He had spent part of the night sitting up in the hotel suite, trying to assimilate the thick dossier he had been given, while Heidi slept like a baby in the enormous bed; then he had dozed in his armchair, awakening to find her gone. Later, returning from Central Park, he had gone down to the hotel's Business Center and used a computer to assemble, from notes, a timeline of key events in the case to be decided. Lastly, he had used the Internet to check a three-month sequence of stock prices.

The limo had called at seven fifteen and driven them down towards the seaport in the morning rush. At least he looked the part. Heidi had conceded that he should get a respectable haircut, which had been quickly executed in Frankfurt. The New York office of Consultancy International had sent a loose-fitting blue blazer and a pair of charcoal grey trousers, together with a supply of white Oxford shirts and sober silk ties, which Guido had delivered to his bedroom at six thirty. A navy-blue squall jacket, trimmed in red, managed to convey the impression that Séamus spent his weekends in yacht clubs. He felt a childish sense of new identity, as when he had put on his first boarding-school uniform long ago. 'Working gear,' Guido said. 'Tax deductible. You can dispose of them in the East River if we fail to meet your expectations.'

It was cold in the boardroom. American air-conditioning, or just the lingering cold of early morning? He was going to be glad of the wool blazer. Everyone fell silent. Ceiling lights were turned up to a sullen glare. Jay Lee, the Chinese banker from London, began in her careful British accent:

'Acting on the request of Senator Hinckley, Chairman of the Supervisory Board, we have carried out a preliminary investigation of the complaint made by Mr Hart Stephen. Given the restricted timescale, and because our brief is just to see whether or not Mr Green has a case to answer, limited weight should be attached to our findings.'

Hinckley, Stephen and Green. All three somewhere in the room. The presider, the accuser, the accused. Séamus had not fully assimilated the introductions, which in any case had been incomplete. These people knew each other. There was the Trade Bank's Head of Treasury, whose name he had not quite heard. Then there was the Life President, and the Vice-President for European Loans. His own team was easier: Guido Schneider, Jay Lee, sombre mustachioed Mr Escobar, and Séamus himself. At the far end of the long table sat other senior functionaries of the bank. Séamus gave generic names to the men opposite him: Mr Scrawny, Mr Saintly, Mr Bilious, Mr Bullfrog. The latter two considerably heavier than Séamus. Hence, in the view of Dr Wallenstein-Heinemann, in imminent danger of spontaneous combustion. Hart Stephen was the one he had dubbed Mr Saintly.

Hinckley cleared his throat. 'Committee knows the parameters, Ms Lee.' He was a heavy man, with silver hair worn a little too long for his conventional dark suit. A former Senator, Guido had said, retaining the title. One could picture him in a toga. 'The facts, Ms Lee, as you found them. Ready, Mr Green? No record will be taken of these proceedings today. You have the floor, Ms Lee.'

Hinckley spoke with somnolent authority. When he said a thing, that's how it was. His courtly tone implied no favour.

Jay Lee gave a respectful nod, and proceeded to trace the history of a $17 million loan advanced by the Trade Bank to WATA, the West African Trade Agency, a body largely funded by governments, having its head office in London. The loan, arranged by Mr Green, was to help a number of WATA's client companies to market a new brand of cocoa within the European Union. Instead of passing the money to the client companies in France and West Africa, WATA's chief executive had diverted it to a shelf company of his own, which had then purchased, on the New York Stock Exchange, $17 million worth of shares in an oil prospecting corporation with offshore drilling platforms in the Caspian Sea. Six days later, following the announcement of disappointing results from their latest explorations, those oil shares had collapsed to a value of less than one-half of what had been paid for them. WATA's client companies were calling for their money. Without it, their marketing campaign was doomed to failure. Even if WATA mounted a successful lawsuit and seized the oil shares, their collapsed value would leave the client companies $9 million short. The WATA chief executive was currently unavailable. The Trade Bank would ultimately have to carry the loss.

Furthermore, the Caspian oil shares had been purchased through a brokerage firm in New York headed by the wife of Mr Green, the Trade Bank executive who had arranged the original loan to WATA. There was thus, it had been suggested, the appearance of a possible conflict between Mr Green's official and private interests. His wife's brokerage firm had earned fees of $510,000 from the sale of the oil shares.

Insomniac Séamus had managed to sketch the broad sequence of these events and numbers while sitting in an overstuffed armchair at three o'clock in the morning.

Jay Lee fell silent, looked expectant, turning her narrow head like a seabird waiting on a rock. Mr Hinckley trained his slow gaze on Mr Green. Lewis Green was a small, baby-faced man, and sat hunched in his seat as if he had been waiting for years, or decades, for this moment to arrive. The ceiling lights glared on his shining head and shaking hands. 'I knew nothing – nothing – of that shyster's intentions,' he protested. 'The paperwork was perfect. WATA have been planning that marketing campaign for more than a year. The CEO was new, a whiz-kid with an MBA. They hired him three months back. He thought he could play the market, used our money to do it. African farmers are going to suffer. WATA is financially damaged. When this gets into the public domain its reputation will be shot to pieces. The thing is unforgivable.'

'What exactly led this whiz-kid to consider the merits of oil exploration?' Guido Schneider asked politely. As the leader of the visiting team, he was entitled to cast the first stone.

Mr Green blinked. 'How would I know? Ask him, sir – if you can find him.'

'Was it coincidence that he should choose to deal in over-valued shares which were being handled by your wife's firm?'

'Ask him! Ask him!' Mr Green was leaning towards hysteria. 'It's a free country. I didn't recommend the shares, if that's what you're implying. I never touch a thing my wife handles. We operate a Chinese wall. That schmuck wanted to sink his money in the Caspian, that's his affair.'

Beside Guido, Escobar coughed. 'Mr Green, you say you operate a Chinese wall. How do you ensure that there is no overlap of your professional interests with those of your wife?'

Green looked at him with amazed contempt. 'Sir, that's the point with a Chinese wall. You don't know what's on the other side. Could be Mongolians. Or Colombians.'

'I am chileno.' Escobar was glacial. 'Now, Mr Green, there are established mechanisms for handling Chinese walls. You can have a neutral party checking that there are no conflicts.'

'Just two of us in this marriage, sir. No kids, no cats, no consultants.'

'But would it not have been wiser,' Escobar pressed on, 'to have submitted a list of your activities to an outside party who could cross-check them with –'

'No! And I'll tell you why.' Green jabbed a forefinger in the air. 'First, the Trade Bank doesn't have any policy requiring such a step. Second' – another finger – 'the person who stole the money did so without my knowledge or involvement, so how was I to know what he was planning?'

'Your second point is not an adequate answer to my question,' Escobar said. 'On your first point, we may consider to recommend that the Trade Bank should introduce a policy of monitoring the interests of the associates of its executives. This would, however, be difficult to police.'

Mr Green stared at him with mute disdain. Escobar stared back. Guido nodded at Séamus. It was his turn to speak.

Séamus shuffled his papers, found the page.

'Mr Green. Your wife's company sold those shares at three forty-nine. I have checked the price on the day they were sold. The shares were trading at three fifty-three. Can you comment on the difference in price?'

'Sir, I can!' Green's face lit up. 'My wife's client was losing money by selling to that man. My wife was losing commission. He had an option to buy at the lower price. He'd held the option for two weeks. That's why he needed to steal the cash from the loan. Shares were rising. He thought he had a sure thing. If the Trade Bank hadn't given him the loan for the Agency, two other banks were prepared to do so. I can get their sworn testimony. I told Ms Lee. The schmuck bargained with us, forced the rate down one-quarter of one per cent. Everyone thought he was legit. Including our lawyers. Ask them, why don't you.'

Séamus spoke to the ceiling, addressing nobody in particular. 'So what is the problem, exactly? Mr Green is accused of having favoured his wife by lending money to a man to buy shares from Mrs Green – shares that Mrs Green's client could have sold at a higher price if the man hadn't exercised his option. Is that really the charge we're considering?'

He wondered if he was incubating a fever. Jay Lee was whispering to Guido. Silhouetted against the wide window, Senator Hinckley seemed to have fallen asleep, his eyes hooded under puffy lids, the corners of his mouth downturned in a moue of disdain.

'I'm afraid we're drifting a little from the point here.' A regretful murmur came from the distinguished man of ascetic bearing who was seated directly opposite Séamus. His tone was kind, understated but relentless in its patient pursuit of truth. An Americanized Britisher, or the other way around? This was Hart Stephen, honorary Life President of the bank, who sounded as though he had spent a lifetime in virtuous conversation, with little need to raise his voice. Mr Saintly, indeed.

Green was clenched in his chair. Still one of the set, but marked to walk the plank.

Outside, taller buildings formed a frail stalagmite formation above the huddle of Manhattan, standing against the blue of the morning, probing a peaceful sky.

'The difficulty is that this man,' Hart Stephen continued, 'this trusted colleague, my good friend Lewis Green, after decades of faithful and selfless service, in what was perhaps a unique lapse of judgment, deliberately advanced an unsustainable loan which was then used for the unfortunate speculation. It's a little too close for comfort.' Hart Stephen peered gently at his target. 'We are not vindictive, Lew. We are offering you generous severance terms today. Everyone acknowledges that the ethical position is not black and white. We have the greatest respect for you personally.'

'Coincidence,' Lewis Green pleaded. 'Can't you see, Hart?'

'An unfortunate coincidence,' Hart Stephen said. 'But I am afraid it makes your position, how shall I say, awkward.'

Green was silent.

'You accuse him, Mr Stephen,' Séamus cut in, 'of dishonesty, although he neither misused the money nor profited from its misuse. I'd like to ask you a question.'

'Yes?' Hart Stephen turned his gracious smile on Séamus.

'Do you trust Mr Green?' Séamus was conscious that his voice was hoarse. His question sounded more aggressive than he had intended.

Hart Stephen took no offence. 'Personally, of course, yes, I do trust Lew Green. I feel no compunction about having nurtured his career thus far. Lew is a good person.' He stared sadly into Séamus's eyes. 'In banking, however, especially in development banking, we are subject to a sort of Caesar's wife syndrome. In the sense that excessive purity is a constant requirement.'

'You suggested' – Séamus kept his voice low – 'that Mr Green might have acted dishonestly. Why?'

'I merely flagged the need for an investigation. With the deepest regret.'

'And your fears have proved groundless.'

'Nobody will be more pleased than me if that proves to be true. We would then all of us be out of the woods.'

'Not all of us, Mr Stephen. It would leave serious questions in my mind.'

Hart Stephen looked quizzical. Séamus felt himself falter, but persevered: 'No action is without a cause.'

'Agreed.' Hart Stephen gave him a warm smile of encouragement, a kindly teacher drawing out the dimmest student in the class.

'Over the years' – Séamus steadied himself – 'I have noticed that groundless accusations sometimes occur when people accuse others of doing what they themselves have done. This being so, and given that your accusation of Mr Green seems to lack credible grounds or other plausible psychological motivation, it strikes me that your own conduct might be investigated with equal rigour.'

Hart Stephen merely raised an eyebrow, like a civilized man at a cocktail party, buttonholed by a drunken cockroach whom he is too well-bred to squash.

'On the basis of your unjustified allegation,' Séamus heard himself saying, 'I wonder whether you should consider resigning from the bank.'

'Resigning?' This was a new word.

'Let me explain,' Séamus said. 'Trust is the basis of your working life with Mr Green. You have withdrawn that trust, without apparent justification. To make matters worse, you called in an outside agency before first taking any responsibility for investigating your own suspicions. In my book, that's malpractice. At the very least, an abdication of management responsibility. Being at the top of the pyramid, as I understand it, you have no possibility of sideways movement in the Trade Bank. The only way for you to move is out.'

That was it. He had spoken. He looked around the room. Nobody caught his eye.

Hart Stephen was turning red. He inhaled. Séamus braced himself for an onslaught. Senator Hinckley coughed into life. 'Inadmissible. Hold it right there.' He spoke loudly, as if lecturing a losing sports team. 'That's a whole 'nother subject. We're not assembled at this time to question Mr Stephen. Mr Green is the one and only person whose position is under scrutiny today. Mr Joyce's comments exceed the scope of our brief. If we were keeping a record, which we are not, I'd order those comments struck from it.'

Guido looked pained. Jay Lee and Mr Escobar glanced away.

Séamus rearranged his papers in a neat pile. 'Senator, I have spoken my mind, and I now propose to keep quiet.'

He slipped the papers back into his folder. There was a moment's silence in the room. Guido sighed. Séamus could feel his new persona beginning to evaporate. Clothes do not make the consultant.

The Senator, in courtly tones, called a brief recess, thanked everyone for their participation, announced that the visiting group of consultants would take coffee with him at his club, and promised to contact the management of the Trade Bank with further questions or possibly even some preliminary findings before noon.

They rode down in a fast elevator, piled into a limousine and travelled less than a hundred yards to an imposing neo-classical entrance. Over coffee, Senator Hinckley introduced them to a pair of ancient men with whom he swapped brief political pleasantries. After coffee, he led the way into a private room, pausing to pick up a sheet of headed paper on which he scribbled fluently for a minute. 'I think we could sign this today,' he said, sliding the paper across the table. Séamus read over Guido's shoulder: *The investigative committee finds no evidence that Mr Green has acted improperly, and questions the judgment of Mr Stephen in raising groundless allegations against a trustworthy colleague, given that a cursory investigation of the facts would have exonerated Mr Green. The fitness of Mr Stephen to continue his leadership of the organization must therefore be called into question.*

'My goodness, Senator.' Guido was astonished. 'You are taking the Séamus Joyce line here.'

'Certainly not,' Hinckley barked. 'Mr Joyce proposed we investigate Mr Stephen. A scandalous suggestion, sir. One hundred per cent improper.' He paused, dropped his voice to a basso drawl: 'Now, I happen to have established in the past two days, from independent sources, that Mr Stephen has been running a pretty neat fruit scam in Central America. Wheel came off it last month; there's a better than even chance of it leaking into the public domain. Which is why Mr Stephen was hoping to dump the blame on Lew Green, after getting him shafted over the WATA deal. Our little note will give Mr Stephen the opportunity to resign at this time on a point of high principle. If he does not take that opportunity, I will have to fix it so he gets what he deserves. Which I will do with pleasure. Mr Joyce, you have stumbled on the truth. Indiscretions find discretions out.' He punched Séamus playfully on the upper arm. 'No credit to you, sir. It's early in the day, gentlemen, but after the showdown, if you will have lunch with me, I have some fine Tennessee whiskey.' He turned back to Séamus, as to a favourite son: 'You have fully lived up to Guido Schneider's description, Mr Joyce. Fighting Irish: exactly what we need.'

Séamus felt empty. They were driven back to the Trade Bank, where Senator Hinckley led Hart Stephen into a room and motioned them to follow. He handed Stephen the statement he had drafted in the club. 'End of the road, Hart.'

Hart Stephen read it, blinked, reflected for a moment, shook his head. 'What do you propose?'

'No pain,' said the Senator. 'No scandal. Twice the golden handshake you offered Lew Green. You retire with honour.

We find ways to lose the money that's gone missing in Central America. Just so long as you co-operate.'

'We can't afford to harm the bank,' Hart Stephen said.

'That's right,' the Senator concurred. 'We can't afford to harm the bank. Discretion is the better part of valour. You're a little bit young to retire. Question is, where do you go? You get a job in another bank, we could be liable for whatever you steal there. We can't have you jump out the window, because bankers are like lemmings. Sidewalks wet with financial entrails. No, Hart, your punishment is you're going to be Distinguished Professor of Corporate Governance in Penrith College. Two hundred per, plus the handshake. Teach one semester. Retire after five years, claim your bank pension so long as you've kept your lip buttoned. How's it sound, Hart?'

'I don't know, Senator. Being a professor is not much, not unless it's Princeton. Two hundred per is frankly peanuts. Penrith is the boondocks.'

'Thirty miles upstate. Still close enough to get to the Met. Better than the Tombs, Hart. That's the other way we could play it. Two hundred? That's modest. Help if we said three?'

Tuesday

Now he was suspended in a soft chair 34,000 feet above the dark Atlantic, going home to Ireland. Darkness had fallen swiftly on this eastward flight. Comfort was all around. Slender women proffered food, wines, hot towels. Outside the windows, two huge engines sucked thin air, churned in a frozen vacuum, maintained an almost steady note. There was a movie, set on solid ground, but he was not listening to the soundtrack. His rational mind accepted that he was being kept aloft by the laws of physics, without having to know what those laws might be. A form of twenty-first-century faith. Perhaps the captain understood how the trick was done.

This was the last seat in business class. Heidi was staying on for a day or two. She would join him in Dublin. The Trade Bank assignment had ended earlier than planned. Originally, time had been left for a longer hearing, with questioning of witnesses and provision for Lewis Green to mount a defence. The sudden ending had been due to Séamus's crass intervention. Equally sudden had been Senator Hinckley's infatuation with Séamus's powers of divination, and his lunchtime offer of an additional consultancy assignment as his personal representative to look into the corporate affairs of King's College Dublin. Hinckley had some involvement with FSC, an American-owned chain of private universities – the full name being Finer Small Campuses of the Western World™ – and there was talk of FSC making a strategic alliance with selected colleges in Europe. First they needed to snake-check their prospective partners, starting with King's

College, where there were issues to be clarified. King's had the potential to become a key partner of Finer Small Campuses, given that several million American students identified themselves as Irish and might therefore be susceptible to the Irish manifestation of FSC's Roots to Education™ program. Séamus had accepted the commission even before speaking with Heidi. She was visiting museums on Fifth Avenue. Her phone was switched off. Guido had booked the overnight flight.

They were still reeling from Lewis Green's reaction to the news of his redemption. Green had always looked up to Hart Stephen. Hence his blank shock, his grey face, his fingers splayed across his chest. Other faces too were fixed in Séamus's mind, particularly Hart Stephen's as he contemplated five years of internal exile in the academic world. Green was in Bellevue Hospital for overnight observation, and his wife was threatening litigation.

Finding some time on his hands, Séamus had made a lightning foray to Fifth Avenue, hoping he might find Heidi. The Metropolitan Museum was even bigger than he had imagined, a monstrous cavern of infinitely receding corridors. Sculptures, paintings, photographs, even musical instruments. No Heidi. He patrolled the place like a soldier in a jungle, seeing nothing. *Heroic Women*, said a poster leading to a special exhibition. Amazon queens, martyrs being tortured, Judith and Salome, heroines of ancient Rome and Egypt: Portia, Lucretia, Cleopatra. The paintings had been lent by galleries all over Europe and America. Despite himself, Séamus paused to look. One composition was by an Italian woman, Elisabetta Sirani, who had worked in Bologna in the seventeenth century and died in her twenty-eighth year. Her painting showed a dark-haired young woman pitching a bearded man down a well. *Timoclea*, said the caption, *punishes an officer in Alexander's army. See Plutarch's Lives*. The bearded man was portrayed suspended in thin air, at the precise moment that his startled face was about to disappear down the well. He had violated Timoclea, the note explained, and doubtless deserved to die. Alexander, his commanding officer, would forgive Timoclea for taking his life. She had caught him off guard as he searched for treasure down her well. The calm determination on her face, and the neat composure of her clothing, suggested that she would quickly recover from her violation, whatever form it might have taken. Séamus's sympathies were mostly with the man, partly because he was a loser, and partly because the surprise on his face reminded him of a moment in a television documentary that he had been too slow to switch off, some years previously. A group of Siberian peasants and their dogs had trapped a young snow tiger and were killing it with sticks, and the little tiger had suddenly realized that despite his genetic superiority, this was a fight to the wrong death. Another year of growth, and he would have eaten those dogs by way of a light snack. They had caught him too early in his life: too early, and too late. His fierce baby eyes had flashed with one awful moment of awareness. In the tiger's cruel death, and in the punishment of this brash invincible captain, Séamus read the tragedy of over-confidence. We must believe we can do everything, but we may be wrong.

The saddest feature of the nameless Macedonian captain, however, was his outsized salmon-pink bloomers, exposed to view by his unexpected upending. If he had known that his legs would be splayed to heaven like this, and that he would be exposed in glorious colour as he left the world stage, he might have opted for sober leggings.

Séamus ran down the great staircase of the Metropolitan Museum, hurried out into afternoon sunlight, descended the stone steps, hailed a yellow cab for JFK, where an impatient Guido met him with his ticket and an overnight bag.

There too was Heidi. She had looked through the Goethe-Institut and the Jewish Museum, and called Guido at the end of her visit. They shepherded him through the check-in, watched him being frisked by security guards, walked away, heads close together.

How close were they? He knew so little about Guido, not much more about Heidi. He damned his own reticence. Guido looked like a man who had been married: it was something in the plump decisiveness of his gait, his way of occupying space, the sense you got that he expected his interlocutor to gratify his reasonable requests. One could imagine a weak woman being oppressed by such self-satisfaction. Or a strong woman enjoying it.

Swept forward on a wave of flattery, Séamus had accepted the vaguest of commissions. Finer Small Campuses would be sending other consultants to Dublin, but the first thing that Senator Hinckley wanted was Séamus's personal appraisal of King's College.

There had been changes at the College. The previous President, a man by the inauspicious name of Maxwell, had taken early retirement and had been instantly replaced by an ambitious can-do social scientist called Cregan. A German professor had been dismissed, a History professor was missing, believed to have drowned along with his research assistant. A previous FSC nominee had effectively resigned from the College board back in March, and was not returning Senator Hinckley's calls. FSC had sent a cohort of Junior Year Abroad students to King's College, and there were disputes about fee payments. The College's financial procedures were not entirely clear. Time was short: a contract for the next academic year would need to be signed soon or not at all. Senator Hinckley wanted to know what he was buying into. Should he talk to one of the other Irish universities instead? There had been approaches. Or should FSC set up its own independent Dublin campus? These were questions that Séamus might consider in his draft report. He would be further briefed by telephone. Supporting documents would be sent by courier.

In short, a half-baked assignment. Séamus wondered if the private sector always proceeded like this. Flying by the seat of the pants. He winced at the thought, listened to the steady drone of the engines, admired two willowy stewardesses bending over a recumbent businessman, reverently settling a blanket around his shoulders, like nurses shrouding a corpse. They advanced on Séamus with servile solicitude. He recognized an oddly familiar sensation as they approached, having experienced something similar when accompanying his Minister at international meetings. The difference was that this time the fuss stopped with himself, as though he were a real grandee rather than an imposter. Trapped in the role, one had to be gracious.

Guido had handed Séamus his own mobile phone, having learned with surprise that Séamus lacked this basic item of equipment. It was a tri-standard phone, capable of working in Europe and the United States. At least in theory. Its PIN was easily remembered: 7777. It was fully charged, and a replacement charger could be bought over the counter. Guido had also shuffled a sheaf of banknotes into Séamus's fist. Advance payment for the Dublin assignment, or a fee for the Trade Bank meeting? The money made Séamus feel valued, and cheapened. Which was why he had not counted it. He did so now. Four thousand euros. Was it legal to carry so much currency across borders? Better not to think about that. Where would he pay tax on it? He would take one day during the coming week to chivvy the pension authorities in Dublin, who were still stalling on his payments, blocking his promised settlement. If they continued to string it out, he would sell the small house in Donnybrook. He could not become dependent on Heidi. She was already lending him money, and was displeased with him for keeping an account of it. Séamus disliked being a rent boy. Besides, his enemies had to pay up.

It was time to fight back, take control. Just as the stupid

psychologist had urged. Be a man, his father used to exhort him when he was a small boy. The meaning of the exhortation had changed over the years. Back then, a man had had obligations to his fellow creatures, particularly if they were platinum blondes tied to railway tracks. Nowadays, a real man was one who fought for himself alone.

Séamus was tired of being a loser. He smiled at the thought. Anyone looking at him might see him as a success story: vindicated in his professional life, starting on an exciting new career, matched with a vibrant younger woman. Was it George Orwell who said that any man's life, seen from within, is a succession of defeats? Séamus's defeats were conceivably drawing to a temporary close.

He divided his €4,000 into two equal batches, stood up, placed half the money in the waterproof inside pocket of the squall jacket which was neatly bundled inside the overhead locker. Somehow this act of shrewd precaution made him feel entitled to the money.

Resuming his seat, he drained his glass, extended his footrest, reclined. A passing stewardess, dark-haired and serious, poured more wine as though it were a painless duty. This must be how the best people lived. And why not? Life was too short to worry about.

As if to illustrate the point, the plane started to buck. A dull ping, and a calm voice announced a patch of turbulence, requested passengers to fasten their seat belts. The plane crashed into air pockets, bouncing back with a sickening shudder. Upright walls shifted against the curved ceiling, as though the airframe were trying to split apart. Outside, blackness had given way to flashing mists. The flash might be merely a reflection of the lights on the wings, but the mists meant that storms and clouds could reach even up here, in the unchangeable heavenly sphere.

Séamus restored his seat to the upright position, tried to make a joke of what was happening. Would the crew come for him, announcing that they had found the Jonah who was endangering their ship? Would the stewardess be wearing a nameplate saying *Timoclea*? But they could hardly throw him out. Not at this height.

Thirty-four thousand feet below, the freezing North Atlantic churned and heaved. Mythological fish snapped their jaws.

As abruptly as it had begun, the turbulence ceased. They resumed their smooth progress. In the darkened cabin, passengers settled back to rest. Mostly men. All white, so far as he could see. Mostly middle-aged. Most of them more portly than Séamus. Plump inheritors of the earth.

He tried to sleep. It was not possible. He was too tired to relax. Somebody had to stay awake. The very smoothness of the flight kept him on edge, for what seemed like hours. In the end, boredom came to his aid. Vague fears began receding, loosening their grip on his muscles. The sights of the past day returned to haunt him. The drained faces from the bank meeting were blending in his mind into an unreeling of Manhattan streets seen from the back window of the limousine: great chimneys of glass and concrete enveloping him like the landscapes of a dream. Faces of swiftly striding men and women dressed in working black. Columns of a broad monumental building from earlier times, exceeded but not dwarfed by the height of later constructions, swimming by in traffic. A compressed anthology of images that he had known for twenty years without ever having been there. A deceptive sense of homecoming. The only part of the United States he had previously visited was Florida, where he had been sent by his Minister to speak at a private-enterprise anti-drug conference organized by a Christian foundation. That was during his first weeks at the iDEA, when everything he knew about the drug trade could have been written on one side of a Rizla paper. He had spent three days cooped up in a lurid holiday complex and seen nothing of America.

New York was a different story. Although he had been

there for less than a day, it was strangely familiar. He remembered his early visits to England, when he had first seen the Anglo-Saxon originals of buildings and streetscapes and social attitudes that he had always taken to be native Irish: he recalled the sudden loss of identity when so much of Ireland appeared to be a fossilized carbon copy of English ways, then the gradual recovery of distinctness, the reassuring sense that similar surfaces may hide different depths. This first visit to New York, although it looked nothing like home, had shown him, unexpectedly, an aspect of the new Ireland, where the mental circuits of the rising generation were partially reprinted from beer advertisements and television serials set in Manhattan, where being Irish was just one more interesting possibility, like being Jewish or Jamaican. He himself had first and second cousins in New York, whom he had never met. Had they passed him in the street? And now he really was asleep, and standing in an over-furnished drawing room with deceased and separated members of his family, rendered in sepia rather than normal flesh tones, while Ariel Sharon sat in state on a broken armchair, smiling blindly at their conversation. Sharon had lost quintals of weight: his face had withered into fissured rock. Séamus left the room and wandered through a shopping mall that led into a retirement home where cheerful women raised scarred wrists and quietly sang of better times. In a courtyard Ariel Sharon again, restored to obesity, sat in a wrought-iron seat, tilting a teapot to fill a china cup for raven-haired Mrs Leah Rabin. A scene of domestic calm. Down the monumental staircase was a great iron door standing open to the empty street, unguarded. In another courtyard, boys with big dark eyes were crowded like poultry behind wire netting.

The engines changed their note, and Séamus awoke. There was natural light. A smiling stewardess was offering orange juice. He wanted to warn her of the open door, the massing of dark-eyed boys, the certainty of divine retribution when

34

they were killed. Recollecting himself, he smiled weakly and let her drape him with a damask napkin.

They were losing altitude, drifting down. The pilot announced their approach to Dublin, his voice undimmed by night work. Shimmering worries clustered at the back of Séamus's mind: his outburst at the Trade Bank; the shortage of clean clothes in his overnight bag; the lack of a full explanation, or any written authority, from Senator Hinckley; the slight possibility that some of his former adversaries might find out that he was in town. Beyond all that, the vague miasma of doubt about returning to his old university, King's College Dublin, the place where his youth had finally been spent.

For a moment he had the hallucinatory feeling that Senator Hinckley did not exist, that he had invented him. He had never heard of an American politician named Hinckley. A would-be assassin, yes. But the somnolent white-haired man he remembered from the previous day seemed more of a ham actor than the real thing. Did that make him genuine?

The natural green of Ireland's grasslands showed below in the early-morning light. Incredible. They were sinking into their final descent. Six o'clock already. He needed more rest, between clean white cotton sheets. Even the reclining seats of business class had left him stiff. The engine note changed again. All perfectly normal. No need to be petrified. At least he had a place to stay. Guido had promised to contact the King's College authorities. There would be a message, or someone to meet him.

2

The raw bustle at Dublin Airport created its usual illusion of a world metropolis. New York was provincial by comparison. Still sleepy, Séamus stood in line for the immigration check, was duly recognized as a member of the master race, switched on his mobile phone, retrieved his overnight bag from the baggage hall, emerged into the main concourse. A silver-haired man in a royal-blue suit was holding a card with his name on it.

Séamus approached him. 'I'm Joyce,' he said. 'King's College?'

'Welcome, Mr Joyce. I'm Hynes,' said the silver-haired man in a voice of throttled dignity. His eyes were red, his teeth yellow, his skin close up a patchwork of pinks. Within his old ferryman's skull, a younger face struggled into Séamus's memory. Had there been a Hynes in the Science Department? If it was the same man, would he not be long past his working life? The man gave no sign of recognition, and Séamus said nothing.

'I'll bring you to the College straight away, sir. You're staying in the President's House. Did you have a good trip?'

Hynes wrestled the overnight bag from Séamus's hand. Outside the door was a shiny blue Mercedes. Hynes made him get in the back, hung his new squall jacket from a hook, handed him the seat belt. Almost before he knew it, they were flying along the motorway towards the city. Hynes switched on the radio, at a low, comforting volume: news of tribunals investigating ancient Irish planning scandals, hearings on war crimes at the Hague, a woman's body found in a house in Carlow. No drug stories. An excited voice previewed sports events. At the gargantuan roadworks for the Dublin Port Tunnel, the carriageway was channelled into narrow switchback lanes which Hynes negotiated like a slightly unsteady contestant in the Monaco Grand Prix.

Séamus sank back into the leather seat, reflecting on his new-found status as a person for whom all ways must be made smooth, and who therefore could not protest at speed and discomfort. Now they were threading through fast early-morning traffic, spring sunshine gilding sleepy suburban houses. Séamus remembered the violence of the sunset out of New York, its colours squashed by the start of his flight against the sun's track. Hynes was taking a circuitous route. The towers of Ballymun hovered on the horizon, Dublin City University flashed by, they crossed the Tolka. Why should the name of a stream in Dublin sound like some mighty Siberian river? And every few hundred yards, the cranes. Why had he not remembered these? Dublin, the old blowsy city, was being reshaped, remodelled along cleaner lines. The cranes clustered like surgeons above the emerging shapes of new buildings, or old ones having their frontages enhanced by cosmetic procedures. White plaster, sheets of Kingspan insulation, panels of nubbled brick and double-glazed windows were surging from torpid suburban streets where long ago there had been nothing much to do but sit and wait for the sporadic arrival of the number 13A bus. Institutes, agencies, offices, flats and the tiniest of townhouses were being dotted around the city in a bacterial pattern. Soon the whole place would be inflamed with economic intercourse. At this ungodly hour of the morning, the mighty heart was mostly still, but there were disturbing signs of life, as if new Dublin suffered from insomnia, could not settle down in bed, spent her nights fencing with intestinal pain. They were passing through Glasnevin, through Phibsboro, by the King's Inns, across the Liffey – an unnecessary diversion, unless perhaps new traffic flows imposed it – along the southside quays, past Calatrava's flamboyantly truncated James Joyce Bridge, smelling the whiff of malt from Guinness's Brewery, weaving through trucks to cross the river again close to Kingsbridge railway station, and up into the Phoenix Park. A quick left turn past the Wellesley monument, several sharp bends through curving banks of green grass, and they were at the College gates.

Hynes accelerated up the beech-lined drive, turned a corner and crunched to a halt on the gravel in front of a glowing red-brick Victorian mansion. 'The President's House,' he announced. 'We've put you in the guest quarters. President Cregan is returning from France tonight. He knows you're here. He'll be seeing you tomorrow. Meanwhile, you can ask for anything you want. Your key to the door. We're bang up to date.' The yellow teeth were bared. The key was an electronic card.

Séamus stood on the gravel, surveyed the grounds with sleepy eyes. He had forgotten just how handsome King's College could look. The President's House, framed by monumental trees flecked with young leaves, stood at the end of a range of red cloisters that caught the morning light. Green leaves against old brick: Séamus thought of the fresh generations of students that had been herded through since his day. In the background, dormant cranes signified that here, too, a building site lurked in the background behind the tall beech hedge that blocked his northward view. Beyond the cloisters, acres of grass ran down towards the river, shaped into tennis courts, a bowling green, a croquet lawn. He saw the shape of soccer goalposts, a plebeian institution that would hardly have been tolerated in former times. Gaelic games had always been favoured, as had rugby. Tall goalposts for those manly sports were clearly visible in the distance.

Most of all, there was the glow of old red brick. Not in itself a beautiful building material, but somehow suggesting an idea of beauty when deployed across ranges of buildings.

'Just a tick.' Hynes left him standing in the hallway, looking at rows of monochrome photographs: gowned professors, students in sports gear, views of the original College buildings. Séamus looked for his contemporaries, then realized that most of these students dated from even further back. One or two stirred vague echoes of elderly lecturers he had known.

Something else fell into place. Hynes had been a technician in the chemistry lab. There had been an accident.

Strange being back here, at a new crossroads. The long

and latterly disastrous marriage from which he was now recovering had been incubated during his student years. This was the place where he had lost Fionnuala, begun to drift into the soft arms of Theresa. The branching paths of his future had forked in the grounds of King's College, where the ghosts of possibility still hovered.

His life, properly considered, was a landslide of retrospective decisions. Even Heidi had been reached through inertia. He remembered Fionnuala, her tantalizing beauty and his anxious pursuit, a quarter-century back. He had been so sure about that – his proactivity and assertiveness would have earned warm approval from his German psychologist – but Fionnuala had been two-timing him with a married professor. When last seen, she was starting to worm her way into the lower reaches of academic life.

Hynes reappeared, accompanied by a mangy boy in a security man's uniform. 'Now, Jamie,' he said. The pale boy seized Séamus's bag and trotted up the carpeted staircase. Hynes, with a sort of virtual obeisance, conveyed Séamus in the boy's wake, ushered him through a doorway on the upper landing and announced, 'Here we are, sir. Guest quarters. Thank you, Jamie.'

This room felt newer than the rest of the house, although the furnishings were old. The boy dumped the little bag on a suitcase stand and withdrew. A dark-haired maid carried in a heavy silver breakfast tray, which she positioned on a mahogany hunting table, Victorian or even Georgian. 'Good morning,' she murmured. 'Tea or coffee?' Her soft enunciation sounded Eastern European. 'Coffee, thank you.' She bobbed her head. Hynes followed her from the room.

Séamus looked around. The guest quarters were undeniably comfortable, with several concessions to good taste. There was a glass-fronted bookcase in the Edwardian style, filled with respectable volumes, some in extended series – including an entire set of *The Field Day Anthology of Irish*

Writing, which Séamus had always intended to read. There was a kneehole desk with a finely tooled leather top, and a prie-dieu by the window. Lace table mats and a Waterford glass vase rounded out the impression of established comfort. The ceiling, however, was marginally too low, the nineteenth-century landscape paintings a touch too shiny, the lace bedspread a shade too white, the shamrock-green carpet a bit too fluffy, and on closer inspection a blank television screen was shyly visible through the imperfectly closed doors in the lower half of the bookcase. This was the brand of yesteryear luxury which consists in the obvious concealment of the obvious. The bathroom, by contrast, was high-tech. There was a choice of toilet flush volumes, and when he went to wash his hands, an optical sensor directed warm water from a mixer tap.

The maid returned with coffee, poured him a cup, made a quiet exit. Having eaten on the plane, Séamus was not hungry, but nibbled what he could out of Irish politeness. He lay on the bed, but could not rest. His mind was racing, without any thought content that he could make out. Why so restless? Jetlag? He'd barely been away two days; could his body clock have settled into Eastern Standard Time already? Exhaustion? The stimulus of new things, and old? Fear of falling asleep and failing to perform some unknown task?

The house had gone quiet. He stood up, left the room, closed the door, went downstairs and slipped into the open air.

3

It was cold. That was reality, of a sort. His throat was still sore.

He realized that he had left Guido's phone in the pocket of his squall jacket, draped across a chair in the guest quarters. If Heidi and Guido wanted to talk to him, they would be unable to reach him. Of course they would not want to talk; it was still deepest night in New York.

There was time. Time to reconnoitre, to case the joint, to update his ingrained knowledge of this grand old Dublin institution. Sunlight poured down between gathering clouds. Another unpredictable Irish day.

He wandered across the College grounds, crunching gravel underfoot, then passed under the great arch and along the cloisters darkened by long morning shadows, skirting the side of the great quadrangle, in the centre of which grew a single arthritic chestnut tree. Here, at least, nothing had changed. He was back in his student days, padding through vaguely impressive spaces devised by nineteenth-century architects to simulate the conditions of a medieval monastery. Genuine fake. He read a noticeboard littered with personal messages, raunchy advertisements for student entertainments, regulations and tattered threats issued by the College authorities, dates of examinations and conferrings, offers of help and pastoral care, of part-time work and freelance grinds. *Colourless Green Ideas Sleep Furiously*, announced a poster for a public lecture; the subtitle was *The Transmission of Republican Ideology in Southern Ireland, 1932–66*. PROTEST GLOBALIZATION, said another poster. SAVE OUR GRANTS – MARCH TO THE DÁIL, urged KCDSU, which Séamus inferred must be the King's College Dublin Student Union. Some of the events announced in these posters had already taken place.

A young man hurried towards him at speed, brandishing a sheaf of leaflets. He positioned one of these on the noticeboard, fished a drawing pin from his pocket and jabbed it through the leaflet. Then he hurried on, without catching Séamus's eye. The leaflet was advertising an English teaching course with guaranteed employment for successful participants.

A thin old man in a security guard's uniform was stripping posters from the cloister wall. He tore down the young man's leaflets, while looking at Séamus with suspicion, then indifference. His Adam's apple bobbed up and down as though he had swallowed a rat. His uniform was of the same design as Jamie's. It was green, and bore the name of a commercial firm on its collar. Interesting that King's College should opt to import an outside security service.

Another noticeboard was headed STUDENTS UNION ELECTIONS – Séamus wondered how one goes about unioning an election – and featured mugshots of various candidates. One poster, sponsored by *The King's Chronicle*, had no photographs, but invited students to support the Homosemantic Party slate: for President, Bianca de Faoite; for Welfare, Dolores Payne; for Entertainments, Theo Devine; and Executive members Max Biggar, Minnie Little, Saoirse Freeman and Pete McCarrick.

There was a glass-fronted refrigeration unit offering soft drinks and bottled water. No cigarettes, but the evil-smelling student toilets featured condom vending machines and crude slogans threatening him with gonorrhea should he venture forth without one.

Further along the cloisters were staircases, and little traffic signs in royal blue pointing the way to *Staff Toilet's*, *Art's Faculty Office* and *Account's*. Séamus wondered if the redundant apostrophes were part of a deliberate policy of modernization. He was hyper-observant this morning: probably a physical reaction to displacement.

There was a board displaying departmental names on strips of coloured metal: English, Modern History, Medieval History, Irish History, Social Studies, Languages, Genealogy, Irish Heritage Studies. The last three strips were new. He paused by office doors bearing academically titled names, none of which he recognized.

A couple of doors flanking the cloisters stood open. He glanced into an untidy office where a frantic young man in shirtsleeves scrabbled through piles of paper. In another, two women whispered while a portly white-haired man swigged from a small flask. Séamus added him to his collection of corpulent men who had lived to tell the tale. Through a closed door came the babble of high, weak voices, and a slapping sound such as might be made by an old Gestetner.

Another outsized figure loomed at the end of the cloister: a smooth man, of about Séamus's own age, enormously broad. Cased in fat like a bulletproof vest. What would the Bavarian doctor have said? The man looked healthy despite his girth. Hardly an academic, unless King's College had opened a Department of Sumo Wrestling. There was something of the country squire in his clothing – flat tweed cap, waxed jacket, green wellington boots – but rimless spectacles and a document folder suggested that this was a man at work. Scrutinized through the lenses of the big man's spectacles, Séamus felt an impulse to pull his waist in as they passed. He did not do so.

There were more election poster sites, and an abstract granite sculpture. Then came an open arch, framing a vista of green landscape, currently being traversed by a squadron of students in royal-blue sweatshirts, running behind a youngster who trailed a royal-blue banner. Some new-minted College tradition?

Where was the chemistry lab? He supposed it had been moved, for safety reasons. The fire during his own student days had not been the first.

4

As he wandered on, Seamus was accosted by a bent, crabbed man who conveyed an impression of coiled energy, all of it directed inwards to sustain the tension in his twisted skeleton. If he had stood straight, he might have been tall. He was wearing scuffed brown leather shoes, twill trousers and a threadbare tweed jacket over a green cardigan and frayed blue shirt, while a maroon bow tie spotted with cream-coloured blotches proclaimed his status as a gentleman. The egg stains on his cardigan were worn like honorific medals. His right elbow was filled with books.

'Looking for something?' A challenge, not a welcome.

'Just looking,' Séamus replied. He had recognized this ghost from the past, and hoped for a moment that recognition might not be mutual.

'Another inquisitor?'

'I wouldn't say that.'

'Shamus?'

'Yes.'

'Not your name,' the twisted man snapped. 'Your profession. Shamus, as in private eye. Peeper. Snooper. Pinkerton man. As in dime novels. Penny dreadfuls.' He took a step back, peered at Séamus again like a photographer lining up a subject. 'Why do I know you, Shamus?'

'Joyce,' Séamus admitted. 'I was a student of yours, Mr Quaid.'

Jeremy Quaid took a step back, like a bad actor miming an unexpected encounter. 'Little Jimmy Joyce,' he declaimed in sing-song, 'of whom great things were expected, particularly by himself, but who went on to become a camp follower in the civil service. Ho my God,' he sighed. 'You've aged, old man. Before your time.'

Séamus hardly knew how to reply. Quaid himself looked not so much like an old man as a very old boy. He pulled a grimace that Séamus had once known well, and put his hand on Séamus's elbow.

'Could almost have been a don, if you hadn't escaped. Shem the Pen-pusher. You did well, eventually. A certain notoriety. Drug Enforcement. What brings you here? Have our dealings in illicit substances caught up with us?'

'I'm out of that business.'

'True. You resigned. So what brings you here? Planning to retrain?'

'No, I'm a consultant.'

'For?'

'A group of American universities.'

'Ah.' Quaid looked at him more sharply. 'Finer Small Campuses? Yes? Replacing the lost Connolly? Yes? What's your angle? They want to know about our vanishing professors? Suspect us of kidnapping? Barratry? Fraud?'

'They asked me to look around.'

'Around what?'

Séamus recited Senator Hinckley's checklist: 'Faculty, students, resources, governance.'

'"Governance"?' Quaid was intrigued. 'That happening word! Then you really are come to shame us! Can of worms, our governance, I can tell you. My colleagues will have reason to fear you. They might have been better sticking with Connolly, instead of scaring him off. He came creeping around, you know, tried to be our friend. Seemed quite taken in. Particularly fond of bogmen. Come with me. I shall tell you all.'

He set off, not looking back. Séamus followed. 'Hup we go!' Quaid scuttled up a stone staircase. Séamus had the odd sensation of repeating his actions of half an hour previously, when he had followed old Hynes upstairs in the President's House. Quaid moved along a bare corridor, flung open a brown door and ushered Séamus into a room where books were piled from floor to table, table to ceiling. There were shelves in the background, overwhelmed by books. One broken bookcase tilted over, propped by another set of shelves tilting in the opposite direction. The books were covered in dust, as was the carpet, and the desk, and the windowsill.

In the galley kitchen, a gas cooker stood beside the stone sink. Quaid half-filled a plastic kettle and made a show of washing two mugs under a trickle of water. Indoors, there was a whiff of cigarette smoke about him, coupled with other scents of masculine sweat and damp wool. On a makeshift shelf piled with tattered books – not cookery books – stood a packet of tea bags. Quaid dropped two into the damp mugs, soused them in hot water. 'Sugar? Milk?'

'Neither, thanks.'

In the study, Quaid moved some plastic boxes to reveal a broken sofa. 'Sit,' he commanded. Séamus sat. Quaid remained standing. 'Have to keep student assignments in these boxes,' he explained, 'because the little dears will insist on writing them in ink, and sometimes they don't get corrected for some time, and they do tend to get ruined when the rain comes through the ceiling.'

'Roof problems?' Séamus asked, superfluously.

'Only for the past eight years. Our college authorities, as they charmingly style themselves, are more interested in throwing up new buildings. Governance, you say. Do you recall little Ollie Cregan from your undergraduate years?'

'Is that the same Cregan?'

'Don't sound so surprised,' Quaid said. 'Our new President was always leadership material. Manipulative little sod. Hasn't he done well? Everyone looks up to him, he being the sort of plastic Führer that appeals to the brain-dead consultants and failed civil servants who determine our destiny these days. Oops! Present company excepted.'

'Too kind.'

Quaid uncorked his full height, towering over Séamus on his sofa. 'There have been three infestations of inspectors this year alone, picking over the carcass. Another firm of scavenger gurus is currently reviewing the whole higher education sector on behalf of our dear government. They will be recommending that King's College should be merged or closed down. So your Americans may find that their joint venture lacks a counterpart.'

'I'm sorry. I hadn't heard.'

'Poorly briefed? Hmm. The other Dublin colleges are trying to keep their distance. Nobody wants to carry a dead weight. We are an albatross. And yet!' Quaid raised a finger. 'All is not lost. Cregan's going to reconstitute us. Big Bang. Year Zero. "Exciting" innovations abound. Faculties to vanish. No more deans. A large tranche of our annual budget to be controlled directly by Cregan and his cronies. We're to be boiled down into four centres of excellence ("excellence" being the currently accepted term for loud mediocrity), complete with directors and deputy directors and leaders of teaching and resource allocation managers, each paid twice the going rate, each appointed directly by cretinous Cregan and his sycophantic sidekicks on the new-look board. Already, image consultants are slaving over such essentials as new College sweatshirts, new signage (which you may have seen) and a College mascot. We are truly thrilled.'

The almost liturgical timing of this expository harangue suggested that it had been frequently rehearsed. Still, to Séamus it was fresh, and he might as well become familiar with the local soundscape. He settled back, sipped his tea. Quaid changed tack:

'Yes, Cregan's become a great man, and something of a babe magnet. Kisses the girls and makes them cry. Cregan goes through lecturettes like a slug through lettuce, while not neglecting the older woman. Even the odd male minion, they do tell me.' Quaid narrowed his eyes at Séamus. 'You, little Jimmy Joyce, as I recollect, used to be ever so eager' – Quaid paused for effect, fixing Séamus with a glittering eye – 'to get into Miss Fagan's pants.'

The rules had been broken. That was not how he had thought about Fionnuala. Nor had he been aware that people like Quaid were observing the sad lives of students.

'Long time ago,' he mumbled. As indeed it was. He had never been back. 'A long time,' he repeated. 'I was no match for Dr Gaskell.' He wished he hadn't said that.

'Gaskell!' Quaid lit up as though Séamus had answered a taxing quiz question. 'Great man, Gaskell.' Pivoting on the name, Quaid launched into another monologue, like a stream temporarily diverted through a mill race: 'Gaskell: he believed in the hands-on approach. When Gaskell decamped to Canada, leaving ruptured hearts etcetera among the bluestockings, Fionnuala followed him at once. Started a quick-and-dirty PhD under his paternal guidance. And what else did she do? We always wondered. Gaskell shoved her into Medieval History. Physical remains. Back she came. Five years as temporary tutor, four years as temporary junior lecturer, then got a permanent junior lectureship and even made it to acting senior lecturer when Cregan was Dean, for services rendered, it may be supposed, although that quick-and-dirty PhD had never been actually awarded. Now she is acting assistant director of a centre, which is one of the plum posts created by Cregan to reward his little groupies.'

'You've taken quite an interest,' Séamus said.

'What's that supposed to mean, Jimmy Joyce? We are all fascinated by questions of career progression. I could cite you chapter and verse for a dozen colleagues. Not that Fionnuala was entirely unqualified. Wrote a handful of ball-breaking articles. Attached herself like a limpet to the hulls of great men. Then along comes' – Quaid stepped back, drew a hand across his face like a theatre curtain, paused – 'the love of her life: Andrew O'Neill. Yes? Famous?'

'Not to me.'

'Good. Professor of History. False pretences. Amateur archaeologist. And a spoiled priest. You know what they're like. Making up for lost time. Andrew loved excavating the ancient remains of King's College Dublin. Starting, it goes without saying, with the delightful Miss Fagan, but also including St Malachi's Abbey and all that crap.' Quaid gestured vaguely out the window. Brightness shone through dirty panes.

'St Malachi's Abbey was hereabouts?' Séamus asked.

'Here-very-much-abouts. *Herr Professor Doktor* O'Neill claimed he could trace the history of the abbey within and without these very cloisters. He was writing it up. So all day long the sound of typing rolled from behind the doors of his boudoir. Punctuated, *ça va sans dire*, by the twang of bed-springs. There was said to be an enormous manuscript, over which the publishers of London and New York would do battle. President Maxwell was bewitched and bewildered by the thought of so much history buried beneath his feet. You've heard of Maxwell, I take it?'

'Yes. His resignation was mentioned.'

Quaid pointed vaguely in the direction of his study window. 'There went Andy O'Neill with his trowel,' he continued, 'digging up the cricket crease, buggering the rose beds, gouging the gas mains, chipping at the chapel foundations. Six months' sabbatical on full professorial salary, free housing in College rooms, Fionnuala to plump up his pillows. Took over her post-doc research assistant, Ronan Gannon.'

'The one who drowned?'

'That's the one. Brilliant young fellow, Ronan. He'd got his doctorate at only twenty-five, under Fionnuala. In the sense that she wrote it for him, because he needed that PhD to get the post-doc. *Post doc, ergo propter doc*, as we Latinists like to say. She took a strong interest in the young man. As indeed she does with all young men. You'll see.'

Séamus said nothing.

'Andrew sails on,' Quaid continued. 'Announces the birth of the King's College Centre for the History of Medieval Dublin, generously funded by little Ollie Cregan in his new incarnation as bursar, and featuring Andrew and Fionnuala as Director and Deputy Director respectively. Introducing Dr Post-Doc Ronan in the role of rank and file. Lovely boy. Good at remembering facts, which always tended to elude our Andrew. Ronan could recall entire piddling dynasties and so-called royal families from around Ireland, stretching over hundreds of years. Also, he was a technological wizard, could set up databases and websites. Hence the very fancy website of our Medieval Dublin Centre. Other universities were a tad miffed, actually, because their chaps had pioneered studies on Medieval Dublin some decades before King's. Some of them, I am given to understand, even know a thing or two about it.'

Séamus gave a non-committal nod.

Quaid took a dramatic sup of tea, drew breath. 'And still our Andrew digs and digs,' he said. 'Stumbles on a pile of bones, claims he's found a charnel house. President Maxwell looks up the word in his big dictionary, and sees that it is good. Maxwell retires, Cregan seizes power. Andrew keeps digging, trowelling through the rugby pitch, tunnelling under the tennis courts, burrowing along the College boundaries, scratching his way out into the Phoenix Park where he has no right to be. Almost breaches the borders of the American Embassy, risking immediate and terrible war. Stiff letters of protest from Dublin City Council. Threats of legal action. President Cregan, the new broom, finds himself with this pile of trouble on his desk just when he has realized his lifelong presidential aspiration. There's talk of prosecuting the College for criminal trespass, talk of writs and restraining orders, all conveniently dropped when Andrew goes swimming off Portmarnock Strand quite early one morning, and sinks like a prehistoric flint. Unless he was abducted by Martians, which is always possible.' Quaid drained his remaining tea before declaiming: 'Full fathom five our Andy falls; of his bones are coral made. Those are pearls that –'

Séamus interrupted. 'His body wasn't found?'

'Not so much as a scapular. Which greatly increased the range of theories concerning his death, assiduously put about –' Quaid smiled – 'by malicious folk. Andrew was murdered, claims one faction. Andy lives, according to another. Andrew will come again. Poor Andy was drowned in a tragic swimming accident, say the unimaginative among us. Which may of course be true, although the sea that day was not rough. They did at least find his swimming companion. None other than post-doc Ronan. Faithful to the last.'

'Drowned?'

'Ten miles out' – Quaid wiped a theatrical tear from his right eye – 'with the tides running east. Picked up by a trawler, brought back to Howth. Great scenes of ululation. Widowed mother, kid sister, the works.'

'It must have been terrible,' Séamus said.

Quaid refused to register distress. 'A great loss, Cregan lamented at the memorial service. A dead loss, he might have said, as far as King's College was concerned. Andrew's great typescript, if it ever existed, never came to light. Insurance men and cleaning ladies scoured his rooms for weeks. Anyway, Cregan wasn't into medieval remains. To Cregan, the idea of a university is a valuable piece of property. That's why we have malodorous business types on the board. Forde and Connolly, real-estate moguls. Two house-builders, both alike in dignity. Of course, you know Connolly.'

'No.'

Quaid raised an eyebrow in apparent disbelief. 'Forde's men have moved in with their heavy machinery, throwing up apartment blocks around the campus. We call it a public-private partnership, because it privatizes public goods. There will be rooms for overseas students, and tourists in the summer, complete with bathrooms and Internet connections. There's talk of refurbishing the slums where we currently house our students. There will be split-level mansionettes for favoured professors and super-administrators and favoured young researchers, because otherwise we can hardly expect to recruit international stars, what with Dublin housing costs the way they are. Connolly tried to argue that we don't need better instructors, and the space would be better used building multi-storey car parks, but Cregan, like Maxwell before him, loves quality and excellence above all things in the world. He is installing power showers and walk-in fridges and In-Sink-Erator waste-disposal units. He can already envision hordes of Nobel Prize-winners abandoning Yale and Berkeley and beating a path to the Phoenix Park. Meanwhile Seán Forde, the developer, is pocketing his profit. Shouldn't wonder if Cregan himself isn't getting a cut.'

Séamus finished his tea and glanced towards the door. Quaid's ability to switch topics was wearing him down. He realized how much of his life nowadays was spent in ruminative silence, and what a blessing that could be.

'I'm boring you,' Quaid said. The idea seemed to please him.

'By no means,' Séamus protested. He was appalled by the digressiveness, by the random venom, but most of all by the sheer length of the tirade. Civil servants could be bitter too, but rarely gave such voluminous vent to their feelings. Quaid had been an engaging lecturer in Séamus's youth.

He had not finished. 'Fionnuala never changed, you know.' He took Séamus's empty cup. 'As an undergraduate, she persuaded herself that Gaskell was about to leave his horrid rich wife. In the event, all she got in exchange for her virtue was a sneak preview of the degree paper and a place on his graduate programme in Canada. Where she learned the value of patronage. In all her years back here, she has attached herself to alpha males. Professors, deans, bursars and the like. Even Cregan had her for a few years, on and off. Now she wants to become Director of Equality, on a full professorial salary. I hope you don't think less of me,' Quaid said coyly, 'for being so frank about your old friend.'

'Don't mind me,' Séamus said.

'I won't.' There was a fixity in Quaid's eyes, like a small child having a tantrum.

Séamus tried not to let his annoyance show. 'I haven't seen Fionnuala in years.'

'Now's your chance,' Quaid said. 'She's on campus today. I spotted her Deux Chevaux in the car park this morning. Lazy girl. She could easily walk it. Her office is downstairs. Why don't you nip along? It's early in the day, but you never know. You might strike it lucky at last. Don't tell her what I've been saying, for goodness sake. She might be offended.' Quaid seized some papers from his desk. 'Must teach,' he said, throwing open the door of his room. 'My classroom is not far from her office, as it happens. I'll point out the way.'

Séamus followed in Quaid's wake down the corridor, up a short flight of steps, through a swinging door and into a modern lecture room, a bold cube of semi-finished concrete. There were plate-glass windows, but they were smeared with mud. Daylight barely pierced the gloom. Séamus paused on the threshold. Quaid had not yet told him how to find Fionnuala's office.

'*Introibo!*' Quaid proclaimed. 'If that's not infringing any-body's copyright. Has God been dead for seventy years? Come, Mr Joyce, watch me gladden these youths.'

Not knowing where he was, Séamus hesitated.

'Our latest inspector, boys and girls,' Quaid went on: 'Séamus Joyce.' A dozen students, male and female, sat slumped at Formica-topped tables under pulsing fluorescent lights. 'Dearly beloved' – Quaid dropped his books on a desk, flung his arms out in an ecumenical gesture – 'we are gathered here today to study "The Sisters" from *Dubliners*, by the alternative Joyce.' His voice boomed under the concrete-coffered ceiling. The room was designed to baffle verbal communication. 'One of the more lamentable productions' – Quaid continued – 'of that overrated writer.' The students looked puzzled. 'You will remember, won't you, that –'

'This was to be our Michael Farrell tutorial,' an American girl protested.

A deafening burst of machine-gun fire and rocket bombardment filled the room. 'Oh, dearie me!' Quaid was delighted. 'Must be ten past nine already. Enhancing the teaching environment. See!' He took Séamus by the arm and hustled him over to the window. Séamus peered through the filthy glass. Outside, in what might once have been the cricket pitch, a concrete palace loomed, shaped like a Byzantine shopping centre. Men on the roof wielded pneumatic drills, while a cement mixer churned below. Overhead, cranes circled lazily. 'Forde's Education Emporium,' Quaid shouted. 'That's Forde with an "e". We'll be allowed to hold classes there, when it's not being used for the bingo. The basement will have language labs for drilling Chinese students in American. We're calling it the King's English School. Isn't that nice? There will also be a Fern Valley minimarket. Forde happens to hold the Fern Valley franchise for the Republic of Ireland.'

'Does this racket last all day?'

'Only during lecture hours,' Quaid shouted. 'Forde believes that his munificence will make him look good in the planning tribunals. When you leave this room, turn right, follow the corridor around to the right, go down the next staircase and you'll find Fionnuala. See you in the common room for coffee. I may have additional information for your American friends.' Quaid turned back to the students. 'Forget soggy Farrell, my lads and lassies. Forget Joyce with his scrupulous meanness. We need something more emphatic to render the form and pressure of the age.'

As Séamus made his way to the exit, Quaid's rapid patter sounded at his back, punctuated by the monstrous stutter of building machinery:

Cannon to right of them,
Cannon to left of them,
Cannon in front of them
  Volleyed and thundered;
Stormed at with shot and shell,
Boldly they rode and well,
Into the jaws of Death,
Into the mouth of Hell
  Rode the six hundred.

5

Séamus closed the door behind him and walked along the echoing corridor, taken aback by his own discomposure. For years, he had repressed most of his memories of that sordid time, the pursuit of Fionnuala. To have the story dragged out again, in such a torrent of bitterness, was more than he had bargained for.

The back of his neck had gone dead. Nothing to do with feelings. Bits of his body going on strike. His throat was still sore.

He could not face Fionnuala. Not now. Not straight after Quaid. He turned on his heel, retraced his steps, found a staircase and descended to the lower floor, then another staircase that led into the cloistered quadrangle. Here one could glimpse the mirage of academic peace that had probably animated the builders of this secluded campus. There was fresh air in the shadows, and sunshine on the foliage of little bushes; the sound of building works was partly masked by the bulk of the surrounding walls. Séamus walked over venerable flagstones, back towards the main arch, passing the entrance to a canteen. *Ocras Mór*, it said over the door. Plastic triangles of sandwiches were being stacked on glass shelving. A queue was forming: students and middle-aged lecturers. Some were deep in conversation; some clutched books and papers. He might have been one of these. Should he be grateful for not having chosen the academic life? Or was this cloistered world an opportunity missed?

He had been a good student, by the standards of his time. Indeed, it had been said, an excellent one. In his middle years, he had revised that early sense of achievement, concluding that reports of his life had been greatly exaggerated. His degree, after all, had amounted to a mere smattering of knowledge: a glance at history, a nod to English, a touch of pious philosophy, a superficial introduction to political science and social studies. As he progressed through his civil service career, he realized that graduates of other Irish universities had received a more rounded education. They could discuss cultural questions, matters of public policy, historical controversies with a fluency and confidence that he never felt. Cursed with a tenacious memory, he sometimes noticed known facts taking on strange shapes in their polished discourse, yet he also recognized that the skill of marshalling those modified facts into a persuasive argument was something that King's College had left undeveloped in himself. He had done his best to make good the deficiency, by reading, listening and occasionally speaking. By middle age, he had at least developed enough intellectual confidence to know when he was out of his depth.

Back in the guest quarters at the President's House, the bed looked strangely inviting. It was broad enough for three. A short rest, and he would be ready for the world. He drained a bottle of water, drew the curtains, slipped off his jacket and trousers, lay down between crisp white sheets.

There came the sound of sprightly elfin music. Exasperating, repetitious, like the ringtone of a mobile phone. Which was precisely what it was.

He had slept far too long. In his latest incipient dream he had been scaling a ladder to board a plane that hovered precariously fifty feet above the ground. He recognized the blue and yellow livery: Ryanair, cutting back on landing charges. His father was reaching down to pull him up.

The clock radio said 12.25. In New York, therefore, hardly daybreak. He climbed out of bed, found the squall jacket and the ringing mobile phone, and managed to push the right button first time.

'Good afternoon, Séamus.' Guido was allowing for the time distance. 'What answers have we found?'

'To what questions?'

'We consultants only ask the questions to which we have answers. Senator Hinckley was going to fax your briefing documents, but there has been a takeover bid in a software company of which he is a non-executive board member, and he has flitted away to Los Gatos.'

'Central America?'

'No, no, near San Francisco, California. We may hear something later today from his deputy chairman at Finer Small Campuses. Or we may not hear. It is uncertain, like everything connected with Mr Hinckley. You must prepare for the possibility of being interrogated, by telephone, at any moment during the coming days, probably from a miniature jet over the Rocky Mountains.'

'So what will he want to know?'

'Whether the college is financially and academically sound,' Guido said. 'How many students he should agree to send to Dublin next year, what exactly happened to the professor who died, how the new President is performing, where his board nominee Mr Patrick Connolly is hiding –'

'Why should Connolly hide?'

'That is what Hinckley will wish to know. Connolly has ceased communicating. Hinckley wants to know his plans.'

'How much time is he going to allow me?'

'Maybe one week, but he will want first impressions sooner. When will you meet the President?'

'Tomorrow.'

'What will you be doing today?'

'Looking around.'

'You must demand information and documents. As FSC representative, you will find that people will wish to do what you say. It is sometimes best to create a certain pressure. How is your jetlag?'

'Under control. I think. Though I am rather tired. May I speak to Heidi?'

'Frau Novacek is on her way to see a colleague in Washington. I myself have an appointment now.'

The line went dead. In the background there was the steady sound of a gong. Then a discreet knocking. He answered the door. It was Hynes.

'Almost lunchtime, sir. The dining room is downstairs, or if you prefer we could send up a tray.'

'Actually, I'd prefer to eat in the campus canteen.'

Hynes's face fell. 'Cook has been preparing a soufflé, sir,' he said, crestfallen.

'I'm not hungry,' Séamus said firmly. 'A sandwich will do. Thanks for waking me. And could you get somebody to bring me a current prospectus of courses, a staff list, a recent set of accounts and the President's Reports for the past three years?' He was about to test Guido's theory that he could demand information.

Apparently so. Nodding his head respectfully, Hynes withdrew. Séamus got dressed, smoothed his hair and went downstairs. There was indeed a tempting smell. Half-rested from his sleep, he still felt disembodied. The sore throat was beginning to fade. He slipped outside. It was a pleasant springtime day, not too hot. A light breeze ruffled the trees.

As he walked across the gravel, he juggled the few facts he had learned. The College was to be reorganized, or abolished, or taken over. The new President was Cregan. The old President was Maxwell. The drowned professor was O'Neill.

The developer was Forde. The missing board member was the FSC representative, Patrick Connolly. The gossip was Quaid. So many stories. So much blather.

6

As Séamus passed under the archway, he heard the rumble of building works in the distance. He repeated his early-morning trajectory, finding the staircase, then Quaid's room, then the lecture hall where he had met the students. The sound of building work was overwhelming. Farther along the corridor, he came to a carpeted stretch, with dismal plaster busts of sawn-off dignitaries, some Irish landscapes and a clutch of dull portraits in oils. Rounding a corner, he found a sign printed on yellowing paper: *King's College Centre for the History of Medieval Dublin*. An arrow pointed diagonally down.

He descended a nearby staircase, two flights into a dark basement. No light switches to be seen. He tapped on a glass-panelled door saying 'Conservation Area'. No answer. He pushed the door and went in. Another corridor, tinted in ancient two-tone institutional paint, green and cream. 'Fionnuala Fagan' was lettered in yellow ochre on a brown door, with 'Acting Director' added in fresher paint. Again, he tapped.

'Come in.' The voice was familiar, but deepened by time.

He pushed the door. A middle-aged woman was hunched at a desk, reading a letter, with other unopened mail piled neatly on the desktop. Light poured around her from a standard lamp. For a moment she did not look up.

Fionnuala had aged well. The ground plan of her youthful beauty was still clearly visible, although the texture had changed. Her features had lost their chiselled shape, her long neck was scored with lines, but the set of her head was the same. In her youth she had fixed on things and ideas with intensity. He had loved her absorption. Youthful sharpness was now faded to what looked like wounded puzzlement in her soft eyes as she noticed him, gestured vaguely that he should sit down, then glanced up again with wonder. 'It's not Séamus?' She rose, turned, stepped forward. 'It is? Yes.' Blinking while she spoke, as if simultaneously signing her message in Morse code. And kissed him on the cheek, softly, as though they had parted some days previously, on the friendliest of terms. There was a slight tremor in the hand she placed on his forearm.

He looked at her again: dark hair streaked with henna, soft eyes rimmed with fine-hatched wrinkles, long hands beginning to be mottled by advancing age, amid the indelible traces of her youth. She was dressed in a dark trouser suit, with a blue cotton scarf flowing over her left shoulder, and still wearing boots, as she had done when barely emerging from childhood. There was the same gallant abandon in her stance. Fionnuala was a lovely fish half out of water. For some unfathomable reason, he had the momentary image of a salmon hauled in from the river, droplets glistening and falling back. Flooded with pity for her life story as recounted by Quaid, filled with the memory of worship and affection, Séamus was back at the crossroads of his life, that path he had never taken. If he had, this is where he might have fetched up. He would have been a different man.

'What brings you here? Where have you been?' Her voice was slightly husky, unlike the blackbird clarity that he remembered.

'New York. Germany, before that.'

'Yes, I heard you'd moved.' She must have read about him in the newspapers. He realized that she, too, was looking at him with something like pity. He saw himself reflected in her gaze: a fading middle-aged man. She flashed him a quick smile. 'How have things been for you?'

Exactly as when they were young, she made him feel as if he were the only person left in the world.

'Not bad,' he said. 'I have a new life now. It's fine.'

'You've been through the wars. I read about it. Your wife and so forth.'

'Yes. We were a long time together. Or so I'd always thought.'

Fionnuala took his hand. 'Is the drugs agency settled?'

'Yes, except they don't know what's happened to Billy O'Rourke. He could be waiting in the long grass.' Billy was his deputy director, who had done sweetheart deals with drug-pushers, using the money to care for his brain-damaged son. 'And I seem to have made obscure enemies in the Civil Service Pensions Authority. Also, I've turned into a flying Dutchman. Apart from all that, yes, it's survivable.'

'What brings you back?'

'I'm doing consultancy work for an American –'

'FSC. They're going to take us over.'

'How could they? King's is hardly for sale.'

'Everything's for sale, Séamus. The old ways have gone.'

'That sounds pessimistic.'

'It's true, though.' She searched his face for signs of sympathy. 'We're living through a sea change. Partly economic: prosperity depends on low taxes, because Ireland competes for global investment, yet at the same time our population is ageing and tax money will be needed for health services, not education. Medics can get more resources by treating their patients as hostages –'

She broke off. He was disappointed at how quickly she had slid from intimate conversation into lecturing mode, and she had sensed his dismay. Was this to be his role: a target for speeches? If they were really going to talk about the College, he would have liked to ask her about Andrew O'Neill's disappearance. Yet this would be too tasteless a topic, if she really had been the man's lover, as Quaid had claimed.

'Am I talking too much?' she asked, with an anxious smile that rekindled the old look in her eyes.

'Of course not.' He forced himself to smile back. 'Tell me more. It's what I'm here for.'

She took him at his word. 'The change is more than economic,' she continued. 'The culture has shifted.' Like a careful teacher, she kept eye contact to check that he was following. 'The government no longer believes in education or free enquiry. Long ago, people respected universities. Back then, we didn't deserve respect. Today we can do nothing right. They measure us against institutions that perform three times better by consuming twelve times our resources. They demand that we be original, while prescribing every step we are to take. They're suffocating us. Our work is being destroyed. We can either wait to be chipped to death, or we can choose to go back to –'

'The Big Bang?'

Fionnuala looked wounded. 'You've been talking to Jeremy Quaid.'

'Listening.'

'So you've heard what he says about me.' She was blushing. He wondered if she knew the extent of Quaid's denunciations. She shook her head again, like a horse, and placed her trembling hand on Séamus's arm. 'Jeremy can't help himself. Anyway, this is not about me. If President Cregan's reforms are blocked, we'll be sold down the river.'

'To Senator Hinckley?'

The telephone rang. She picked it up and a look of babyish distress swept her face like a radar scan. 'Yes? I am. Oh, please! It's not like that. For goodness sake, Paddy, what is this about? All right. Stop. Don't. No, I'll come over. Yes. Now.' She slammed down the receiver. 'I'll be back, Séamus.' She slipped past him.

He sat in her orderly room for what seemed like an age. Between the pair of bookshelves hung a brooding photograph, framed in black, of Fionnuala in her tall slim youth, and others showing details of Gothic statuary. On her desk was a small colour photograph of a rough-hewn outdoorsman smiling amid classical ruins. Andrew O'Neill? And an old back-and-white photograph of a young man in shorts standing on a rock with two little African boys. Also Andrew O'Neill? And a larger colour photograph of the rough-hewn man, photographed with a smiling Robert Mugabe in a beautiful suit. Definitely Andrew O'Neill. There was an old green metal filing cabinet, with one drawer open, filled with neat files. On a side table sat a small mound of what looked like student essays, and a handwritten personal note which he studiously refrained from reading. Only the faint hint of a clean lineny scent conveyed Fionnuala's absence. Otherwise, the room could have been that of a monkish male scholar from an earlier time. On closer inspection, he guessed that the bookshelves were standard issue King's College furniture, related to the broken ones he had seen in Quaid's room. Hers were polished. In a corner of the room was a glass case with what looked like combs made of bone.

He glanced at the titles of books on the shelves. Some he recognized. The end of one shelf was filled with tall dissertations bound in royal blue. The one with the most recent date bore the title *Strongbow and Globalization*.

The telephone rang. He let it ring.

After three rings her recorded voice cut in: 'This is Fionnuala Fagan at extension 1527. Please leave your message after the signal.' Séamus noted that her extension number was the year of the Sack of Rome. A high squeak was followed by a husky male voice: 'Lookit, Doctor Fagan. Listen here.' A rural accent. Tipperary? Calm, self-satisfied. 'It's up to you to control the fella. Get a grip. We're trying to keep things steady here.' The sound of an asthmatic breath. 'We don't need another barney. Call me back.' The message ended in another prolonged electronic squeak.

Séamus sat in silence. His head was echoing with Fionnuala's soft voice. They had said very little, yet he felt as if he had fallen back into an earlier time.

The telephone rang again, and this time the voice leaving the message was Fionnuala: 'Séamus, are you there?' He picked up the receiver. It reeked of her scent.

'Sorry.' She sounded as if she had been running. 'Something has come up. I'm leaving College now. Hope to see you in the next few days.'

'I'll look forward to –'

She was no longer there.

He stood up, went out into the corridor, wandered along, following a bend to the right, then to the left, in the shadows. No light switch that he could find. An absolute maze. In the gloom barely relieved by refracted shafts of outdoor light, he came face to face with a bull-necked young man in a white linen suit.

'Hello.' The young man switched on some lights. He seemed trapped in his clothes. His head was large, his shoulders bulged. A button on his navy-blue shirt was hanging by a thread. On his feet he wore expensive-looking boat shoes, no socks. The effect should have been sporty and relaxed; instead, the young man looked as if he had forgotten to finish dressing. 'Who are you?'

'I'm Séamus Joyce. Visiting the College.'

'You can't. Not here. This part is closed to the public.' His eyes were clouded, his voice loud but lost. His accent was Irish, overlaid with slight American twinges, as practised by many young Irish people who have spent very little time on the far side of the Atlantic.

Séamus wondered whether or not to cite his FSC credentials, explain that he was here by the authority of an omnipotent will. Looking at the young man, he could see that this was unlikely to work. He retreated, found a staircase, climbed to the next level. There was a bathroom. He used it. When he emerged, the young man was standing in the corridor.

'What were you doing down there?'

'Visiting Fionnuala. Miss Fagan. I'm staying in the President's House. On official business.'

'She didn't mention it,' the young man said. He was halfway between a student and an adult. His hands hung loose.

'It was a surprise visit. Why would she mention it?'

'I'm in charge of this area,' the young man said. 'I'm her research assistant, and I look after the safety of the artefacts. That's why. Please don't be offended.'

'I'm not. Not at all. I just wanted to talk to her.'

'You can't, not now,' said the young man. 'She's had to leave.'

'I know. She told me.'

'There's a way out, over there.'

'Thank you,' Séamus said. The young man made no move to follow him.

7

He was shaken by the encounter with the bull-necked young man, for reasons that he did not understand. Perhaps it was the sensation of competing with other acquaintances of Fionnuala. Competing for what? This young man seemed almost to be asserting rights of ownership in her territory. He moved along the upper corridors, passed by Quaid's lecture room, heard him inside again, still yapping through the din of building work, presumably not to the same group that had been there at nine o'clock in the morning. He caught some fragmentary words: *Critics. Discredited.*

He was at ground level again. At the end of another corridor, a door to the open air stood ajar. Séamus looked through the gap. There was mud, and the tracks of earth-moving equipment, with the mass of the new Forde Centre rising in the background. Cranes overhead. Beyond the Centre, broad green lawns stretching away to a distant line of tall trees. The day was no longer as summery as it had seemed. Over there beside the new building was Fionnuala, a figure diminished by distance, walking fast, followed by a worker in orange overalls.

Closer to the main university building, not far from where Séamus was now standing, cars were parked on a patch of gravelled ground on a slight rise beside what he now recognized as the Temple of Remembrance, a small neoclassical building erected to commemorate the College's sons who had fallen in the Crimean War. In his own student days, it had been used for storing sports equipment. Now it looked semi-derelict, with boarded-up windows. Some builders' Portakabins were placed beside it. Fionnuala had already skirted the sea of mud that surrounded the Forde Centre, and was making her way through the line of young trees that flanked the path to the temple. He could see a Deux Chevaux among the cars in the temporary car park. Nostalgic and impractical: the perfect vehicle for transporting Fionnuala Fagan. She was moving swiftly, her blue cotton scarf floating behind her. Séamus called her name through the noise from the building works.

He pushed the door fully open, looked for a path through the mud, called her name again. A fresh outburst of pneumatic drilling drowned his voice. He waved his arms, stepped forward through the straggling remains of a low hedge, took another step, starting to lose his footing, stumbling forward, catching his ankle in a jagged branch of the uprooted hedge. He saw himself starting to fall in slow motion into a deep ditch cut through the mud, saw the sky reflected in dirty water at the bottom.

A grip of iron grasped his arm. Another hand encircled

his waist. He was lifted off the ground, hefted like a baby by its mother, deposited on a patch of dry land.

'You all right, man?' His rescuer was the outsized man he had seen walking through the cloisters in the early morning. What he had then taken to be flab was mostly solid muscle. This person was as healthy as an ox.

In the distance, beside the temple, Fionnuala was opening the door of her car.

'How can I get over there?' Séamus gestured towards her.

'Afraid you can't.' The conclusive though regretful reply was accompanied by a burst of white noise from the squawking walkie-talkie that he brandished in his enormous fist. 'No way through.'

'Can I go along the side of the building? Is there a way across?'

Fionnuala's car was starting to move.

'Restricted access to this part of the site.' The accent sounded English, with an undertone of something sharper. Australian?

Séamus watched Fionnuala's car stopping to pick up a passenger: a man with a huddled walk, wrapped in a heavy overcoat. The Deux Chevaux whirled around in a circle and disappeared behind the Temple.

'Restricted access,' the voice insisted at his shoulder. 'This is a hard hat area.'

'Where's your hard hat?' Séamus was surprised at his own ingratitude. But for this man's help, he would be sprawling in the ditch.

'Fair comment.' A genial display of teeth. Built like a tank. Miraculously clean, even to his boots, although he had trodden in the same mud that soiled Séamus's shoes. His face and hands were pink, as if scrubbed with a household detergent. His rimless spectacles glinted hygienically in the sunlight. 'Can I ask you to step inside,' he continued with bright restraint. 'We're not insured for visitors.'

'You're the site manager?'

'That's me. And you?'

'Visitor.'

Fionnuala's car appeared again on the main driveway, a distant blob rolling away. Séamus thanked the large man and withdrew to the safety of the building.

Hynes was hovering in the corridor. 'I see you've met Mr Stanihurst, sir.'

'Very helpful. In spite of my trespassing.'

'That's good, sir. He can get quite territorial. Now, I've been asked to conduct you to the senior common room. Dr Burren is most anxious to meet you.' Hynes bustled along the corridor. It would have been rude not to follow. 'Mr Stanihurst is a very serious man,' Hynes called over his shoulder, 'where health and safety are concerned.' There was an oddity about Hynes's walk, a comically three-legged gait, as though he were about to break into a dance step. Séamus could barely keep up with him. A bunch of keys jangled from his waistband, as though he were the elderly housekeeper in some Gothic novel. It struck Séamus that Hynes could probably open every door in King's College. But then, Séamus's own trouser pocket bulged with keys for which he had little or no use. His old house in Dublin, his new house, the key to his old green filing cabinet at the iDEA. He rounded a corner, flung open a door, and there in a parquet-floored comfortless room was a man whom Séamus had once known.

8

'You do remember Dr Burren, don't you, sir? Coffee, gents?' Hynes slipped into faithful retainer mode, solicitously filling white china cups from a silver coffee pot.

Séamus had been retrieved, prevented from wandering around on his own. Burren was to be his minder.

A thinner, hairier version of Burren had tutored in the German department when Séamus was a student. In middle age he was gravity-bound, bird-eyed, with a downturned mouth and hunched shoulders. Back then he had been the life and soul of the party, a mainstay of the student bar. He had a melodious high singing voice, was handy with a guitar, knew dozens of songs by Cole Porter and Harry Warren, could do a perfect rendition of Marlene Dietrich yearning for *einen richtigen Mann*.

As a student, Séamus had warmed to him instinctively. Burren, however, had shown an aversion to him, for no reason that Séamus could discover. Gratuitous dislike had once bothered Séamus, until he had noticed, later in life, that he too was capable of loathing worthy people, whom he could approve in the abstract but whose company made his flesh creep. Burren's visceral distaste for Séamus was another of the repressed memories from his King's undergraduate days. He braced himself for distant exchanges, but Burren's face flashed a rictus of welcome. 'Satchmo!' His voice quivered with delighted bonhomie. 'Long time no see! How have you been?'

'Rocky!' Séamus echoed dubiously. 'Good to see you!' And yes, his memory had not let him down. Burren's nickname really had been Rocky. Only Séamus's closest friends had called him Satchmo.

'Heard you were back,' Burren said, still smiling. 'Afraid you won't find much for your musical tastes these days. The Jazz Society is a basket case.'

'How's Marlene Dietrich?'

'Never better. We have a new broad cultural programme, compulsory for all students. I do German history and politics, George Grosz, Brecht and Weill and, of course, the immortal Lotte Lenya.' Burren's voice was high and clear. When he spoke, you could imagine him singing.

'Not through German, though,' Quaid counterpointed

through the open door. 'Nothing through German. President Cregan doesn't approve of them barbarian tongues. Hynes, I'll trouble you for some of your coffee.' He was carrying a large batch of papers under his arm.

'Finished your lesson already, Mr Quaid?' Hynes raised an eyebrow at a wall clock, which seemed to have become congealed at a permanent midday, or midnight.

'My students had absorbed their fill,' Quaid riposted, holding out a cup. Hynes trickled coffee into it. A large tray of sandwiches appeared, carried by the same Central European girl from the President's House who had brought Séamus his breakfast. 'Real food!' Quaid exclaimed. 'Never before seen in the common room. To what do we owe this miracle?'

'Mr Joyce's visit,' Hynes replied, taking command of the tray. He held it for Séamus, then Burren. Then, reluctantly, Quaid, who took a fistful of sandwiches, jovially remarking, 'Ah, Hynes! Age cannot wither you, nor custom stale your fifty-seven varieties.' Nobody was amused. Hynes deposited the depleted tray on a side table and stood guard in front of it.

'Nothing through German,' Quaid repeated. '*Deutsch streng verboten*,' he insisted with his mouth full. 'Languages are passé. French is for the tumbril. Spanish is holding on by her long red fingernails.'

'German is temporarily suspended,' Burren conceded.

'From the gallows!' Quaid crowed. 'By the neck!' He turned to Séamus, holding centre stage, his manic energy undiminished since the early morning, if not indeed since Séamus's youth. 'Let me tell you' – he fixed Séamus with a grandstand stare – 'about Cregan's campaign against the Hun.'

'Jeremy,' Burren said quietly, 'you talk too much for your own good.' There was a measured nasal quality to his voice, as if he were speaking ironically, although in the present case it appeared that he was not.

'Burren has been the chief casualty of Cregan's *Blitzkrieg*,' Quaid insisted. 'He has in fact been redeployed, and is now attached to the pastoral office as our Student Experience Officer (Temporary), or as the student acronym has it, SExpOT.'

Burren shot him a murderous glare. 'A title and acronym devised by yourself,' he observed through gritted teeth.

'And none the worse for that,' Quaid allowed. 'Widely used, they do assure me. It goes schwimmingly with your Marlene Dietrich shtick. Even if so far you have refrained from doing her in full drag and falsies. Burren has a special show' – Quaid turned ostentatiously back to Séamus – 'for incoming sophomores from the US of A. It is grandly titled "Innerjuicing Yerp". Señorita Lola Sanchez of the former Spanish department joins Burren for the flamenco demonstration. He strums, she stamps.' Quaid snapped suggestive fingers. Séamus kept a straight face.

'Loyal as ever, Jeremy,' Burren said. There was resignation in his voice. He clearly knew the Quaid line, and did not expect it to change.

Quaid grinned. 'We old-timers, Rocky my lad, must stick together. One day soon I may be reduced to your condition. Meanwhile, Séamus will want to hear how you were shafted by Presidents Maxwell and Cregan in turn, despite having served the College fitfully for nigh on thirty years, to say nothing of your father's long service before you.'

'More coffee, Mr Joyce?' Hynes was still hovering.

'I'll have some too,' Burren said, 'while we wait for Quaid to talk himself out.'

'You'll be waiting, sir,' Hynes said, filling his cup.

'Good of you to stay on, Hynes old fruit,' Quaid said, 'while the television channels abound with greyhound-races and horse-races. Isn't this your siesta time?'

Séamus put down his cup. 'I must get back.' With most of

a day to wait before the President's return, he did not wish to waste it listening to Quaid. He felt like a man who goes walking through a Gothic cathedral, only to find familiar gargoyle faces popping out from behind every pillar, ready to spout. The trouble was that most of the gargoyles so far were turning out to be Quaid. And Quaid's range was limited. Senator Hinckley would want to know more than the fact that King's College was dysfunctional and partly staffed by logorrhoeic neurotics. Time to read some official documents, make a few phone calls. Even go and visit his house in Donnybrook. Why not? He was a free man.

'The documents you wanted, sir,' said Hynes, as though reading his thoughts, 'will be in your room. By the way, Professor Millington, the Vice-President, has left his telephone number in case you need any further information. Dr Burren has kindly agreed –'

'Thank you,' Burren cut in. 'I'll speak for myself.' Hynes inclined his head and stepped back. Burren turned his fixed smile on Séamus: 'Given that we used to be pals in the old days,' he said in his nasal voice, 'President Cregan has asked me to act as your guide.'

Hence, Séamus inferred, his forced bonhomie, and his forbearance of Quaid's teasing. Quaid added in a stage whisper: 'Burren has been told to talk. Others have been warned off. Secret tape recorders store everything we say.'

'Nothing up my sleeve,' Séamus said.

'The rules do not apply to Jeremy,' Burren said. 'Would you like me to show you the new lecture theatres?'

'Later, thanks.'

'Burren might even be able to explain' – interjected Quaid, the alternative guide – 'what happened to Connolly. Honest Paddy Joe from Tullamore. For months he sat on the board, representing your Yankee friends. Recently began to demand financial information. Dared to question our building boom. Claimed the College was not receiving a fair deal from Forde.

Talked of tribunals. Then he vanished. There he wasn't. Rumour has it he sent a letter of resignation. Do you suppose he might have been drowned, like poor Andy O'Neill? Or is he buried in the concrete pylons of the Forde Conference Centre? One is simply dying to find out.'

'You talk too much,' Burren said again, 'for your own good.'

'Are those the essays you were marking for last Easter?' Hynes pointed to the bundle of papers under Quaid's arm.

'Good of you to remind me, Hynes old fruit.' Quaid turned to Séamus. 'I shall leave you for a moment. The chief examiner is pining for results.' He swept from the room. Hynes closed it after him.

'Let me walk you over to the President's House,' Burren said to Séamus. 'The back way is quicker.' He put down his coffee cup and made for the door. Séamus followed. Burren led the way along the corridor. At the foot of a staircase, notices pointed upwards: EMIGRATION STUDIES, GENEALOGY CENTRE, NEW LIBRARY. Séamus remembered the dark library of his youth, where dead light bulbs were rarely changed, readers were regarded as a necessary evil and the Angelus was proclaimed at six o'clock by a quaking gentlewoman from Cataloguing.

'Could I see the new library?'

'If you must,' Burren said. 'It will look better in a year or two, when we get some books out of storage.' He led the way up a short flight of stairs, into an echoing antechamber equipped with turnstiles like an underground railway station. Burren parlayed them through the barriers, and Séamus found himself in a long grey room subdivided by grey metal shelving. At long tables, a few students were hunched over books and papers. Séamus approached one of the Sociology shelves, on the gable end of which was inscribed a depressing list of contents:

This sounded like the story of his own life. The grey shelves were almost empty.

'Anything in particular you'd like to see?' Burren enquired. 'Our card catalogue, perhaps? Computerization of library records is not yet quite complete. Staff cutbacks. Which is also why the issue desk is only open in the mornings. Hence the sepulchral calm. What else can I show you?'

'Nothing, thanks, I've seen enough for the time being.'

Burren nodded grimly and left the room, followed by Séamus. He led the way downstairs and out into the open air.

They were on a path through a slightly overgrown parterre. The Forde Centre loomed in the background.

'What exactly happened to the German department?' Séamus asked.

Burren hesitated, looked around. His lips twisted into a smile. 'It's a long story,' he said at last. 'Professor Dunkley retired three years ago. You do remember Dunkley?'

'Albert Dunkley.' Séamus did remember. 'He lasted that long?' Burren nodded. Neither of them mentioned Dunkley's universal sobriquet: Adolf Dummkopf.

Appointed in the far distant past, Dunkley had proved to be an egregious mistake. By Séamus's student days, he was reduced to giving one lecture at the start of each academic year. It was called 'Prolegomenon to German Studies' and came from a little brown copybook in which Dunkley kept lecture notes from his own undergraduate years. In the following week he delivered the same lecture, verbatim, on the grounds that there might be some students who had missed

74

his first performance. On the third and subsequent weeks, he put up a notice announcing that he was unable to lecture. Which was the gospel truth.

'Albert retired after suffering a stroke,' Burren said. 'I continued to run the department. When it came to replacing the chair, however, President Maxwell made a stand for standards. Brought in assessors from Great Britain' – slight emphasis on the word *Great* – 'and they duly appointed a prolific scholar, a German lady who had worked in America. Prolific in every sense, with a remarkably large family and a string of books on subjects unmentionable in polite society. Brilliant lady, but, as it turned out, barking mad.' Genuine amusement was creeping into Burren's voice. Although this was a painful topic, he had clearly succeeded in distancing it through quiet but corrosive humour.

'How did her madness manifest itself?'

Burren looked around, dropped his voice. 'Her first action, before she even moved to Ireland, was to draft a mammoth memo to the Academic Council, denouncing the existing staff of the department as incompetent. She demanded that we all be sacked. She proposed to appoint a whole new department of brilliant young persons, productive in research and assiduous in teaching. President Maxwell sat on this memo for months. Meanwhile, Dr Gudrun Mardersteig (for that is her name) arrived in Dublin and requisitioned a house. President Maxwell was succeeded by Oliver Cregan, who quickly concluded that the only hope for King's lay in attracting Americans, and the last thing Americans want is German. He therefore wrote a curt note to Professor Mardersteig, thanking her for her mega-memo, which he accepted in every detail. The current department was indeed hopeless and beyond repair. He would therefore sack them all except for myself.'

'How did you escape?'

'Permanent contract,' Burren said. 'The others were all

short-term. Two of them were trying to get our ineffectual staff association to join one of the academic trade unions, which was another reason for dismissing them.'

'Was there much resistance to that?'

'None. We don't like troublemakers. Or at least we don't support them. King's has a large cohort of precarious academics, hired by the hour; these include some of our best teachers. President Cregan's letter to Mardersteig went on to explain that, since the College had no money to engage new staff, it would regretfully be obliged to suspend its German operations following the dismissal of the current incumbents. This being so, Mardersteig's chair was automatically redundant, and she was welcome to clear off home to Oberammergau or wherever took her fancy.'

'An extraordinary position to adopt.'

'Yes. It has attracted some press coverage in recent months.'

'I've been away.'

'So you have. La Mardersteig threatened to sue President Cregan, but when the College's lawyers saw the memo she had written, they advised him that, even by the usual standards of academic expressivity, her stylistic excesses were such that no court was likely to find in her favour. She then resorted to physical menaces. President Cregan got a restraining order and imported some rather alarming security men. Mardersteig still lives in Dublin with her numerous offspring and, according to Quaid, she takes in washing – although this may be an exaggeration on Quaid's part. She is currently engaged in writing a book to expose us all.'

'Including yourself?'

'Oh, yes,' Burren said. 'I am, apparently, part of the enemy. She has gone so far as to write an article impugning the validity of my rather well-received book on German Catholic lady novelists. This article has been submitted to several reputable and disreputable journals. So far, it has not found a home.' He led Séamus out beyond the parterre and into another part of the muddy building site. A workman in a hard hat approached, looking concerned, and tried to redirect them back into the main building, but Burren cited his presidential authority, after which the workman led the way, shifting planks for them to cross the mud-filled trenches. After a minute they found themselves on a curving path, reasonably dry, that led around the far side of the Forde Centre. The noise of machinery, grinding and churning, grew as they rounded the corner of the building. Men stepped aside to let them through. High above them, pneumatic drilling still went on unbroken. Bricklayers were covering the concrete façade with fine red brick. A vast wall of plate glass was already in place.

'Quite an achievement, to get a building this big,' Séamus remarked to Burren. 'Your President must be a good fund-raiser.'

'Oh yes,' Burren said. 'That, certainly. President Cregan thinks on the grand scale. The original approval for a lecture theatre and assembly hall had actually been secured by President Maxwell, with a government grant and modest private funding. Cregan brought in Forde and quadrupled the size of the project, redesignated it as a conference centre with various ancillary bits. We're to have a multi-purpose indoor sports hall, a little museum, some shops and a state-of-the-art language teaching facility.'

'Language? I thought Quaid said you were moving out of languages.'

'This will be for teaching English to Asian students.'

'So President Cregan is a global strategist, not just a scholar.'

'Not just a scholar, indeed.' Burren cast a sharp look in Séamus's direction, before proceeding with grim circumspection. 'Cregan's scholarship is, of course, impeccable. His name appears on the spines and title pages of several books, and he has been remarkably successful at landing fellowships and funding of all kinds. Back in the Cold War, he helped to organize congresses and colloquia of leading Western social thinkers, on both sides of the Atlantic. He was a leading light in the Grand Rapids Group. When he got his personal chair of Social Organization, he spent years touring campuses in the American Midwest. Eventually he raised the funds for an Institute for the Study of Business Culture.'

'Most impressive,' Séamus said. In truth it was extraordinary that Oliver Cregan had risen to any eminence, even within King's College. Prompted by Quaid's diatribes, Séamus's memory was beginning to fill in patches of the past. Cregan he recalled as a drab young lecturer, always eager to make an impression. This was gratifying for the first-year students, although even they had grown restive at his compulsive self-advertisement. For his senior colleagues, it must have been irritating in the extreme.

'Most, as you say, impressive,' Burren concurred. 'I was his contemporary here. We started as lecturers on the same day. I failed to detect his future greatness.'

They were clear of the building site and moving through open parkland, with trees fluttering with green leaves. The President's House came into view, seen from the back. Séamus thought he could recognize his own bedroom window, in a newer extension attached to the side of the house. 'Are those the guest rooms?' he asked.

'Indeed,' Burren replied. 'And that low building on the far side is the Servants' Lodge, so-called. Hynes is the only resident. You might remember it as the tool shed.'

'Formerly the stables, I think. Didn't the College gardener live there when I was a student?'

'That's right.'

Séamus remembered neat borders full of marigolds, petunias and wallflowers. These had been replaced by concrete cobbles on which a small jeep-like vehicle was parked.

'Our President has had the whole complex remodelled,' Burren said. 'Adding a new wing and clearing out the servants' rooms from the President's House means that it now contains not only the guest suite but also a billiard room, a small gymnasium, a sauna and a double garage for the official Mercedes and official Land Rover. I'm sure Hynes can show you how to use the sauna.'

'Most impressive,' Séamus said again.

'Quite.'

They were rounding the corner of the President's House, by the kitchens. Through a window he could see gleaming expanses of stainless steel. The scale of the installations seemed suitable to a medium-sized hotel.

Stalking from the President's House towards the Servants' Lodge was an enormous cat, as broad as he was tall, with ginger hair fluffed out in a great halo. His expression was one of angry disdain. He placed his paws with great care. It was not that the ground actually trembled as he walked, but his ponderous gait suggested that he was distributing his weight with due regard for the fragility of the earth's crust.

Burren noticed Séamus's admiration. 'That's Major Tom,' he said. 'Undisputed College champion, heavyweight division. They feed him gallons of milk.'

The ground-controlling cat reminded Séamus of those men who dominate their fellows by sheer bulk: a docker he had seen once at a political demonstration, a weightlifter in Duffy's Circus, a wrestler vaguely remembered from black and white television at boarding school and, most recently, the sure-footed man who had saved him from his muddy plunge into the trench on the building site. Were all of these powerful men milk-drinkers? Séamus's own status, such as it was, had never come from muscle power. He was not a physical man, except when cornered. He had hated tests of strength ever since the day when, as a very small child walking home from school, he had been challenged to a fight by a toddler standing at a garden gate, and had won, and the toddler had started to wail, and the toddler's father had appeared on the horizon, blocking out the sky, and had caught Séamus and threatened to break his face.

With a lazy sway of his ginger rump, Major Tom disappeared around the corner of the Servant's Lodge.

The front door of the President's House was standing open. Burren ushered Séamus inside.

There was an air of contained panic in the hallway, with the sound of feet. Hynes was scurrying down the stairs in a state of agitation. 'Was it young Nadia?' he called out.

A worried woman entered from a side door, followed by the same pale boy who earlier that morning had carried Séamus's bags upstairs. 'There's never been a hint of trouble,' she protested.

'I'm going to contact the agency,' Hynes declared, 'have them catch –' He saw Séamus, turned, red-faced. 'I hardly know what to say, Mr Joyce,' he faltered. 'It seems one of the maids is after making off with some things.'

Séamus wondered what had caused Hynes to switch codes from stage-butler to stage-Irish diction. 'What sort of things?' he enquired.

'We're not entirely sure, sir. I was leaving the documents you wanted in your room and I noticed your effects strewn across the floor and money littered on the carpet. A whole raft of money, sir. Could I ask you to check, please, and see what's been taken. Nobody likes to make trouble for these people, but we can't have them doing the likes of this, so we can't.'

Séamus climbed the stairs, followed by Hynes, and entered the guest quarters. The pile of College documents he had requested had been placed on the mahogany hunting table, in a clear plastic folder. His squall jacket was draped across the bed, with a fan of €50 banknotes neatly arranged on top of it. He counted the money quickly, turning away from Hynes. One thousand, nine hundred and fifty: a single banknote short of half of what Guido had placed in his hand yesterday afternoon. The other €2,000 still remained in his blazer pocket. 'All present,' he lied to Hynes, before searching through the other pocket of the squall jacket. 'My phone has disappeared,' he said, trying to sound surprised.

'Are you sure?' Hynes was appalled. Burren hovered by the door.

'Unless I left it somewhere else.' The hideousness of false accusation flashed into his mind. He could picture himself as one of those ghastly upper-class twits who go around persecuting hotel workers with gripes and suspicions. It would be unspeakable to put everybody through the wringer, only to find that the thing was in his overnight bag. He searched there, and under the bed.

'It looks as if the girl must have taken it,' Hynes said sadly. 'Of course we'll replace it for you. She's just after finishing her shift and she has two days off, but we'll catch up with her, you can rest assured of that. Meanwhile, the house phone is not blocked in any way. You could phone Moscow from this room.'

'Thank you. I'll make one call,' Séamus said. Hynes ushered the others from the room. On the threshold, Burren remarked quietly, 'Strange that she should take a phone and leave all that money.'

''Tis indeed,' said Hynes, embarrassed.

Stranger still to take just one banknote out of forty. That was what gave Séamus his sense of certainty. If one wants to leave a bunch of notes to delay detection of the phone theft, why not remove five or six of them for verisimilitude? This had the look of a person disobeying orders.

The removal of his mobile phone offered one obvious advantage to its perpetrator. From his previous existence, he knew the value of being able to tap landlines and monitor conversations.

New York time was approaching nine-thirty in the morning.

He got the hotel number from directory inquiries. The switchboard put him through to Guido's room.

'Schneider.' There was the sense of a voice already in use, another conversation momentarily suspended.

'Séamus here. I'm afraid your mobile phone has gone missing.'

'Ah. Where are you?'

'Guest room in the President's House.'

'You are using their phone? Please give me the number.'

He read it from the card beside the phone.

'We cannot talk now,' Guido said. 'I must be downtown in half an hour. Can you buy another cellphone? We like to be able to reach our people twenty-four seven, so to say. Just like that relaxing weekend we took in Leipzig – you and me and Mrs Novacek – when Frankfurt kept calling us with their tedious requests. Let me know your number, please, when you get it.'

The line went dead.

They had never been to Leipzig.

He sat on the edge of the bed, closed his eyes, took a deep breath.

9

He needed to get out.

It was no big deal, being burgled. Losing a mobile phone was not like burying a childhood friend. But he was feeling the classic effects of theft: edginess and aimless anger. Someone felt entitled to monitor his calls. His instant assumption had been confirmed by Guido's response.

He suspected everyone. Burren had walked him by a circuitous outdoor route, and delayed him still further with his endless talk, which explained why the ubiquitous Hynes got back before them.

Séamus's need to escape was another stock reaction to burglary, he knew. One is supposed to feel soiled and violated, and indeed he did. Comfortingly normal.

He hoped the maid would not get into trouble. If she came from the European Union, she would have some rights, but if she came from a country outside the club, dismissal could mean ruin, as the Irish government had engineered a form of licensed servitude for lesser races, by the simple expedient of assigning immigrants' work permits to their current employers rather than to themselves.

He would give his own statement to the Guards, saying that he knew no reason to suspect the maid.

He used the house telephone to call a taxi firm. The number surfaced in his memory: he could usually remember numerical patterns, although calculating with figures was of no interest to him. He arranged to be picked up at the door of the President's House in ten minutes.

Coming downstairs with the College documents under his arm, he found Burren hovering in the hall. 'I'm so sorry about that phone,' Burren said, as though he had stolen it himself. 'Where can I drive you?'

'Nowhere, thanks. I've ordered a taxi.' How had Burren known he was going out? Of course: he was wearing his squall jacket.

The taxi came. Burren escorted him, held the back door open. 'Where are we off to, boss?' asked the grey-haired driver.

'Westin Hotel,' Séamus said, and then, as they rolled down the driveway, 'I've changed my mind. On second thoughts, I'll go straight to Donnybrook.'

'OK, boss.' The driver was indifferent. He turned up the volume on his radio, which featured soft porn mewling and puking by starlets affecting baby voices, backed by a sewing-machine beat. Popular culture, like progressive ideology, is devoted to the proposition that women are sexualized infants. Which is not always the case.

The air in the taxi was freshened with a sharp fragrance that caught in the throat. It was like travelling in a chemical toilet.

As they crawled through the traffic, Séamus twisted in his seat from time to time to see if Burren was following. He noticed no sign of pursuit. The driver was amused. 'Fugitive from justice, are we?' he enquired, turning down the music. 'Fuzz breathing down our necks?'

'No.'

'Would you like me to try a few side streets?'

'No, thanks.'

'Suit yourself,' the driver said, switching his radio to a sports phone-in show, all throaty bluster.

Séamus asked to be dropped on the main street in Donnybrook, a hundred yards from his house. The driver was displeased at having to change a large denomination euro note. Séamus tried to compensate with an over-generous tip, using up half the coins from his trouser pocket. 'Working for the Germans, are we?' said the driver, surveying the small change in his hand.

Only after watching him move away did Séamus retrace his steps and walk up the little street. Still there seemed to be nobody following.

He remembered the number. The key worked first time. At least Theresa had not had the locks changed.

He had visited the house only once before, shortly after his separation, to meet the tenants and assure them that their maintenance needs would continue to be met. He had felt awkward then, intruding on other people's space, and he felt awkward now, intruding on his own. This, a place where he had never been at home, was now his property. What remains is not what existed.

It was dark. He raked aside a pile of junk mail with his shoe, found the light switch, pulled heavy red curtains and looked around a surprisingly spacious living room, which had obviously been knocked together from smaller spaces by a deconstructive architect. He must have seen this room on his previous visit, when he had called to see the tenants, but he had managed to erase the memory. The place was a sort of stage set, finished and furnished in yellows and reds, and featuring a rather elegant black marble fireplace flanked by shining brass fire irons. Upholstery and cushions were new, with a hint of times past. Lighting came from recessed spotlights. The black and white tiled floor contrasted with a scarlet curtain half-hiding the door to the kitchen. Sharp papier-mâché Venetian carnival masks were ranged around the yellow walls, each picked out by its own spotlight. There was an antique mirror in a gold-leafed frame.

The place had an empty smell, but the living room at least was in good condition. If there were a fire in the grate, a bunch of flowers on the coffee table, it would be eminently desirable. So why had Duke Street Properties failed to find a tenant?

Because it had been created by Theresa, this room conjured up memories of his former home in Glenageary, which it in no way resembled. Here, she had created the illusion that the cramped little house was part of a larger space; there, she had contrived an intimate scale within the frame of an oversized building. By such illusions, Theresa had shaped a good life for him. She had given so much, and what she had taken – his soul – had at first been invisible. Had she not declared herself his enemy, he would have stuck by her to the grave. His or hers.

Coming straight from King's College to Donnybrook was like stepping from early manhood into his wasted middle years. From Fionnuala into Theresa. Misplaced hope, misconceived acceptance. First he had wanted too much, then too little. What he had got was too little, then too much. What an ungrateful wretch I am, he said to himself, and tried to smile into the mirror. Well-fed disappointment peered back at him.

He climbed the stairs and inspected the two little bedrooms, decorated in clean white paint, expertly lit and equipped with mirrored built-in wardrobes that doubled their apparent size. They were fully furnished, with a king-size bed in one and a narrow double in the other. There was a small bathroom, featuring a hip-bath that doubled as a shower. The mattresses were mildly stained. They could all be replaced for less than half the cost of a month's rent.

The kitchen too was fully equipped. He opened the refrigerator door: perfectly clean. The tenants, he recalled, had seemed like decent people: a young couple with a business, recently moved from Galway.

Behind the kitchen was a scullery. In a corner beside the washing machine, spiders had woven a killing ground for other insects, and had clearly enjoyed some success. The shells of tiny bodies clogged the floor.

The large kitchen window gave on to a tiny back yard, paved in concrete slabs and surrounded by high plastered walls painted in dazzling white. It was barely big enough to slaughter a goat.

The place was worth fifteen hundred a month. More, perhaps. He would sue the property agency for lost income. Six thousand euros at least. He was tired of being taken for a fool.

10

First things first. He spread the King's College documents on the kitchen table. That was the room with the largest window. He switched on the ceiling lights. Almost too brilliant to read by, they would have been adequate for a dissecting room.

He found the tap for the water mains, twisted it on, rinsed one of the tumblers on the draining-board, poured himself a glass of water and settled down to read.

The calendar contained lists of academic departments, which he scanned for names he might have known from his student days. Almost none. The College telephone directory listed staff members alphabetically. Here, again, few names rang a bell. Odd, then, that he should have spent large parts of the day in the company of Fionnuala, Quaid and Burren, old acquaintances of varying degrees of intimacy: two of them encountered by chance or destiny, and Burren presumably selected after a hurried trawl.

After the day's exposure to a slightly freakish gallery of College characters, looking at documents should have come as a welcome relief. And indeed the papers did help him to gain a little distance from his immediate impressions and fill in more of the factual framework. They showed the College's profile as being strongly slanted towards the humanities, the only full science department being chemistry. There was no law, no medicine, no engineering, no business school, though social studies offered some commercial-sounding courses. All of which meant that King's College should be relatively cost-effective. It would, on the other hand, be politically weak, as Ireland's new mandarins tended to see the humanities as cheap and therefore valueless.

He noticed also that the present configuration of King's would make it an almost perfect fit for an American liberal arts college. Expensive professional subjects could be left for later study, in graduate courses at another institution. No wonder Finer Small Campuses was interested in making a link.

When he looked at the financial information Hynes had given him, annual running costs, as expected, proved to be quite low, at a little over €30 million, largely made up of staff salaries and covered by government grants in lieu of student fees. Maxwell's final years had seen little capital expenditure. There were references to borrowings mortgaged against the value of existing buildings. President Cregan's first report noted that a public-private partnership had been set up for capital projects; this would be reported on in the following year.

How stringent were the rules on borrowing? Were universities obliged to maintain their annual accounts in balance? Who would know? He thought of a sharp investigator called Lennox, who worked in the Fraud Office or thereabouts. Lennox it was who had cracked the mystery of Billy O'Rourke's finances. Séamus instinctively trusted Lennox – not because he liked him, but because of the man's dry obsessive style.

In the phone book he found a number for Garda headquarters. They might know where Lennox was to be found. He picked up the house phone. The line was dead.

There was no reason why this should affect him. He had grown used to isolation in Germany. Mostly, it was a relief.

11

He searched the same phone book for Patrick Connolly. Although he could not reach him by phone, he could visit him in person if Connolly lived somewhere accessible. He could find out more of what Senator Hinckley wanted to know. But there were so many Patricks, Paddies, PJs and Pats with the surname Connolly, even in just the Dublin directory, that it was clear he would never locate the correct person without at least being able to call the numbers listed. Even then, there was no guarantee. Hinckley's particular Connolly could be ex-directory.

The College prospectus gave descriptions of undergraduate courses, evening classes, postgraduate diplomas and Master's degrees including a new course in Irish Genealogy. From the President's Reports he learned, inter alia, that his old professor of English had recently died, and that Professor Gaskell, formerly a distinguished member of the College staff, had been selected to head a review group evaluating 'quality' in UK higher education.

The untimely disappearance of Professor Andrew O'Neill was covered in a panegyric that outlined his early career as a missionary priest in Malawi and Zimbabwe, his commitment to political justice across southern Africa, his abandonment of the priesthood, his brilliant postgraduate work at Oxford and subsequent academic career in England and Scotland, ending with his plans to revolutionize the study of medieval history at King's, now, alas, unrealized. A second notice, apparently written by a personal friend, added further details. O'Neill's interest in liberation theology had earned him the suspicion of his ecclesiastical superiors while still a student. A keen sportsman, he had organized football teams during his missionary years. His doctorate, on the links between military, economic and religious colonialism in Colombia, had been published by Leveller Books under the title *Not Peace But the Sword*. He had worked as a political activist for pressure groups for some years after completing the doctorate, and had continued to serve as a council member of Justice Watch Africa. His interests, in life as in academic research, had always been eclectic and adventurous. While teaching in Edinburgh he had written his most challenging work, *The Sociology of Invasions*, and gradually moved into medieval history after becoming fascinated with the history of Viking settlements in the British Isles. This had led to his application for a chair at King's College Dublin. Dublin was to be his last posting – he was only five years away from the official retirement age – but he had brought all the energy and enthusiasm of a younger man to his research. A keen walker, swimmer and mountaineer, he had revelled in the natural beauties of Ireland. KCD students were sadly deprived of the benefits of his infectious lecturing style: his presumed demise at sea had occurred just weeks before he was due to finish his sabbatical research and launch his new course on Medieval Remains. He had also announced his intention of holding a series of public seminars on liberation struggles in Africa. This had brought welcome publicity to the College in Irish republican circles. His inaugural lecture had already been announced at the time of his disappearance in a tragic swimming accident. It was to be called 'Digging up the Past: Confessions of an Unrepentant Historian' – a defiant and witty title that summed up the gaiety and energy of the man.

It sounded like an interesting life, and the notices gave the hint of things left unsaid, changes unaccounted for. Yet Séamus had read equally glowing obituaries of dusty old bores whose paucity of achievement was exceeded only by their personal nullity.

There were no photographs in the obituary section. He must try to get his own picture of Andrew O'Neill.

The death of O'Neill's young research assistant merited fewer words, and was padded out with an account of his funeral in Fife. At least he had had a funeral.

Afternoon was wearing on past five o'clock. Evening light, still clear, was visible above the rooftops. Séamus's work in King's College might have made little headway, but this visit to inspect his property was putting concrete shape on his inward reflections. Staring out the kitchen window, he thought of the choices he had to make. To move back to Dublin, or sell this house and cast in his lot with Heidi. Once he formulated the question, the answer was clear. As the psychologist had so percipiently pointed out, a man has got to do what a man has got to do. Besides, he would die without Heidi.

Meanwhile, he could see that the best way to make rapid progress in producing his report for Hinckley was to prepare a strong set of questions for President Cregan, and flesh out his information with details prised from Burren and Fionnuala. Even Quaid's voluntary contributions, taken with a pinch of salt, might be useful. A talk with Connolly could speed up the task. He looked through the President's Reports once again and found a short paragraph welcoming Patrick J. Connolly to the board in the last year of President Maxwell's reign. Mr Connolly had built up an extensive contract-catering business in Ireland, Britain and the United States, including a number of campus restaurants. His corporation managed fraternity houses in more than a dozen American colleges. His Irish holding company, Padcon, was mentioned in the President's Report. Séamus found Padcon listed in the business section of the Dublin phone book, with an address at Clarendon Lane. It was probably about to close at this time of day.

The first requirement was a new mobile phone. He gathered his papers into a neat pile on the kichen table, let himself out of the house, moved briskly away, leaving the ghost of Theresa trapped inside. There was no traffic on the narrow street.

He walked along Morehampton Road, looking for a taxi, and found a bookshop where he bought a little black notebook. Standing near a bus stop, he wrote down some questions for President Cregan, a few section headings that might go into his report. How would he get it typed? If he was going to continue working with Consultancy International, Guido might provide him with a laptop computer.

Each passing taxi contained a shadowy outline beside the driver or in the back seat. At this rate, he was going to be late for the city-centre shops. A double-decker bus pulled up quietly beside him and three students alighted, two athletic boys and a muscular girl jabbering into her mobile phone. Probably coming in from University College Dublin at Belfield. They looked exactly like the King's College students he had seen in the morning: square-shouldered, casually dressed. Not like the squirrelly folk with their crooked teeth who had been the Dublin students of his day. Today, the young people of Ireland believed the world was at their feet. Because of this misplaced confidence, they could achieve far more than his generation. He had read somewhere that mildly depressed people (such as himself) had a more realistic view of their true capacities than people with the normal dose of optimism. The catch was that, given their depression, these admirable realists were incapable of extracting any advantage from their keen awareness. Best to be deluded, then?

An old lady struggled to board the bus, dragging a shopping bag on wheels. Séamus helped with the bag, then stepped up beside her and the bus pulled out. It was years since he had last been on such a vehicle. He bought a ticket and climbed upstairs, as he had done on his first visit to Dublin as a child. The bus swayed in mid-air, avoiding at every curve or change of lane what seemed like certain impact with the upper branches of trees. Séamus sat at the front window, getting the full benefit of the rush of scenery, the succession of ironwork and gardens and tall Georgian windows. Around him were the voices of other young people, speaking the new languages of Ireland: Spanish, Polish, Russian. Also an Asian language spoken by a small, neat, black-haired young woman, containing at regular intervals the interpolated English word 'certificate'. If he lived to be old and stayed in Ireland, she would be his nurse.

He climbed off at Dawson Street, where the first telephone shop he saw was already lowering its shutters. The second one had posted a bouncer to repel tardy customers. He gave it up as a bad job. Marks & Spencer, at least, was still in business on Grafton Street. He invested in socks and underpants, and a grey cotton shirt.

He presumed they might be planning to feed him back at King's. He could imagine Hynes fluttering around the President's House. Let him flutter: Séamus was his own man tonight.

Walking down to Temple Bar, he passed through narrow

cobbled streets nestling under the incongruous vertical reach of the Central Bank tower: a pleasing clash of styles and centuries. Hunger plucked at his stomach. In Elephant & Castle they brought him an omelette with cheese and spinach, and a glass of earthy Australian wine. He had a mug of coffee to fortify him against what might lie ahead, and a couple of minutes later had found a taxi on Aston Quay.

12

'Fact is,' Quaid said, 'Cregan has a grip over everyone. Keeps doing favours, issuing little decrees. As bursar, he showered everyone with cheap sherry, while conducting forensic audits of departmental accounts in search of improprieties. Cregan knows where the bodies are buried. Perhaps literally.'

'You talk too much,' Burren said sadly. 'Too much for your own good, and too much for the common good. What if Séamus believed you?'

'What indeed?' Quaid grinned.

They were sitting at a curved bar in a corner of the senior common room, drinking Cointreau. This was apparently Burren's favourite tipple, stocks being laid in for his benefit by the Bar Committee. He had been lying in wait – more precisely, he had been standing under a tree – on Séamus's return to King's College. Unable to persuade him to come out for a second dinner, Burren had pleaded with Séamus to join him just for a little drink, and Séamus, realizing how desperate Burren was to entertain him, had acquiesced. He had hoped at least to discover why people on campus were so concerned about Senator Hinckley, and overawed by his harmless representative on earth. But once Burren had secured Séamus's company, he had relapsed into sodden incommunicability. Séamus guessed that he had been drinking alone for much of the afternoon.

At first it had almost been a relief to be joined by Quaid, who proved as talkative as Burren was taciturn. Quaid was wearing a dirty silk scarf around his neck like a priestly stole; otherwise, his attire was the same as in the early morning, right down to the egg stains and the spotted bow tie.

'Little Ollie Cregan knows we hold him in contempt,' Quaid went on, seemingly oblivious to the stoic presence of a weary barman. 'But he also knows how easily we're bought off. Dons, you see, are basically stupid.' Quaid's sleepless energy seemed undiminished since the dawn.

'Have you been bought off?' Séamus asked.

Quaid looked at him sharply. '*Au contraire*. I've been let down. Cregan promised me promotion when he was Dean, but I'm still a common or garden "lecturer". They won't count my reviews, you see.'

'Amazingly,' Burren counterpointed, blinking at Séamus from the brimming brown depths of his koala eyes. Burren was one of those brooding drunks who look sincere and harmless. He was beginning to smell rather pleasantly like a small orange grove.

Quaid pressed on: 'For years I've analysed contemporary literature in the English language. Stuck my neck out. Dared to say what's good, what's bad, what should never have been published. I deserve a knighthood for services to literature, if only for the fakers I've stopped in their tracks. Do you read me in the *Gazette*?'

'I've seen some reviews,' Séamus replied. 'But I hadn't read the books.'

'Now you'll never need to.'

'Why couldn't Cregan swing your promotion, if he's so influential?'

'"Objective Criteria".,' Burren interjected, with a broken snigger, tracing double quotation marks in the air with the index and middle fingers of both hands, as though scratching the eyes of a committee.

'During the last years of Emperor Maxwell,' Quaid explained, 'the College Promotions Committee brought in a set of "objective criteria", which objectively happened to favour their favourites. Not that criteria matter when it comes to the crunch. Dons being by nature complacent and corrupt, and having an almost unlimited propensity to self-deception, they always feel free to skew their own perverted rules in order to reward their clones and catamites.'

'Jeremy,' Burren interposed, 'you're talking like a book again. What have I said to you about talking like a book? Nobody in Ireland says "dons".'

'One does so apologize,' Quaid replied, seemingly chastened.

'So some people get ahead,' Séamus said, 'while others are overlooked. Doesn't that happen in every institution?'

'Who cares about every institution?' Quaid demanded with a certain *hauteur*. 'This is King's. Of course there are natural corrective factors. The nuisance factor, for example. They would probably promote me if they thought it would keep me quiet, but they fear it might not.'

'They know damn well it would not,' Burren confirmed. 'You would merely become even more insufferable, take to writing letters to the *Irish Times* as well as the *Gazette*.'

'I already do!' Quaid exclaimed. 'Pusillanimous wussies just won't publish them.'

'Unaccountably,' Burren said. 'So beautiful as you write an' all.'

'Then there's the fear factor,' Quaid continued, as though planning a full-length lecture on the iniquities of the promotion system.

'Fear?' Séamus asked. 'You mean physical fear?'

'Not physical. Dons are easily scared – by loud noises, for example – so they promote vociferous members of victim groups, such as women and halfwits. Then there's the sympathy factor. I too might have been bundled through under that rubric, despite all, merely to alleviate the distress caused by repeated disappointment. I was perhaps the perfect sympathy case, set to rise to relative stardom, except for one tragic flaw.' He paused for dramatic effect.

'Do tell,' Burren intoned, morosely extending his empty glass to the attentive barman, who replenished it from the almost empty Cointreau bottle. Séamus modestly covered his own glass with a hand. 'Do tell,' Burren repeated. 'One of us has never heard it, while the other two' – he gestured at the barman – 'are always pleased to hear it again. We may even join in the chorus.'

The barman nodded, stopped polishing his glasses.

Quaid gleamed, fixing Séamus with his boyish blue stare. 'President Maxwell had written a book! A novella, or so he believed. Ninety-eight pages long. The work of a lifetime! Exquisitely crafted. About a Big House, and three generations of doomed grandees. It was called *The Greener Grows the Grass.*'

'No, it wasn't,' Burren said.

'All right, it wasn't,' Quaid admitted. 'It was called *Emerald Acres.*'

Burren began to bubble with silent mirth.

'Maxwell had published this God-awful swill,' Quaid continued, 'under a pseudonym, so it was quite proper for me to review it, all unaware of its authorship.' He laughed out loud. 'I gave my frank appraisal: "The themes and rhythms of this carefully constructed novelette" – he recited from memory, and Burren's lips moved as though in silent prayer – "reverberate and resound with all the compulsive force of semi-digested scrambled egg rising in the gorge of a queasy spinster on an ill-advised day trip to Holyhead." Of course, if I'd known who'd written it, I would never have put it that way. Would I?' Quaid giggled gleefully, on a high girlish note. 'And if Maxwell hadn't in the meanwhile received a glowing review from his cousin in the *Granard Advertiser* –'

'No, it was not the *Granard Advertiser*,' Burren said.

'All right, it was *Prospectus*, that sump of intellectual sewage. Be that as it may, the review in question caused poor Maxwell to start quietly boasting to his friends, which made my little contribution to literary history all the more wounding. Not even the great Oliver Cregan, then Dean of Humanities and acting bursar, could shield me from the presidential wrath. So I live in hope. I rely on my dear friend Cregan to see that Justice is finally done, as she certainly deserves to be after her provocative behaviour.'

'To Justice.' Burren raised his glass. 'Not to mention Revenge.'

'Cregan made such wonderful promises,' Quaid mused. 'Promises with a certain poetry about them. He was going to transform us into a hothouse of lavishly funded research, with nubile assistants to do our teaching for us. He babbled of greenbacks. He even dispensed them, right and left. Did I mention he was bursar? Yes, perhaps I did. We were given to understand that Cregan had unlimited access to Yankee gold.'

'Crocks of it,' Burren counterpointed. 'Known as "matching funds".'

'You see,' Quaid said, 'all Irish universities get research funding from the government. And for years the sector was showered with largesse by a crazed philanthropist. Now the money's getting tighter, and in recent years there has been a catch. You have to be halfway competent. Mostly, we're not. So brave new Cregan has to obliterate inglorious decades of mediocrity. We're to be rebranded, repositioned. We're sprouting research institutes. My pathetic Head of Department, Paddy the Stoat, author of a slim compendium entitled *A Reader's Guide to 'Thy Tears Might Cease'*, is setting up the Irish Bildungsroman Research Institute. Our historians are launching a Centre for Irish Heritage Studies. Three deranged old biddies who fifteen years ago founded a samizdat rant called the *Journal of Women's Liberation Studies*, nearly losing their jobs in the process, are now being centrally funded as the Irish Gender Institute, and *JOWLS* is published by the King's College Press, with a distinguished advisory board headed by your old friend Fionnuala Fagan. None of these worthy ventures, sadly, has won a government grant. We need American money, and even Cregan can't get enough of that.'

'Jowls?'

'*Journal of Women's Liberation Studies.* You are slow, Jimmy Joyce.'

Burren had subsided once again into torpor, swaying gently on his barstool. It would have been time to go to bed, but Quaid had mastered the art of speaking without drawing breath between paragraphs. Séamus tried to tune out as Quaid rabbited on about the Higher Education Authority starving universities of day-to-day funds, undergraduate degrees being dumbed down, graduates shovelled out semi-educated, then brought back to do gimcrack postgraduate courses. Burren nodded from time to time, either in agreement or because he was about to fall definitively asleep. Irish universities, Quaid proclaimed, were being funded on a fur-coat-and-no-knickers basis. 'Except that in our particular case,' he concluded triumphantly, 'we don't get to wear the fur coat.'

Clearly, these were themes that buzzed around his head, and it gave him a certain pleasure to formulate them in a striking manner. Like many bitter men, he assumed that his personal gripes would be of immediate interest to all who heard them.

'They're scared of you,' he added, staring into Séamus's eyes.

'Who are?'

'The crooks that run this place. They think you're plotting to plant drugs in the President's flowerpots. To say nothing of the mace.'

'Mace?'

Burren woke up, blinked like a traveller whose train has reached its destination. 'You're becoming boring,' he told Quaid. 'Time for bed.'

'I am a little tired,' Séamus said. 'It's been a long day.'

'Nonsense!' Quaid snorted. 'The night is young. I haven't yet told you why Andy O'Neill had to die.'

'I read his obituary in the President's Report,' Séamus said. 'Very nicely written.'

'It didn't say why he was killed,' Quaid said.

'Shut up, Jeremy!' Burren groaned. 'Go to bed.'

'He Defied the Will of His President,' Quaid said in sepulchral tones, like the voice-over on a movie trailer, 'and Paid the Ultimate Price.'

'Do stop ranting, Jeremy,' Burren pleaded. 'You talk far too much.'

'Closing up, gents,' said the weary barman.

13

Séamus drank all the bottled water from the silver tray in his room, and still it was not enough. There were vending machines in the cloisters, he knew, but walking around the quadrangle might expose him to further encounters. Quaid could still be on the prowl, and his previous recital was more than enough for one night. Séamus switched on the television and watched late-night news reports of famine and repression in distant lands, and a continuing campaign to capture old war criminals from conflicts in Bosnia, Kosovo, Burundi, Rwanda and beyond, dragging these monsters to face trial in the civilized surroundings of modern Holland. There were reassuring shots of modestly imposing civic architecture, neon-lit courtrooms, attentive judges, well-behaved guards, compliant prisoners. None of which could wipe out the memory of the 600 Dutch troops guarding the safe haven of

Srebrenica who in 1995 abandoned 7,000 Muslim boys and men to be massacred by the Serbs, instead of fighting to the last, or indeed the first, drop of Dutch blood.

The human race was doomed to infamy. Recent years had brought an obsession with control, with containment, with the discovery and documentation of past mistakes and misdeeds, not so that new ones might be avoided but in order to distract the hypocrite world from its unrelenting cruelty. Just as Séamus's own past continued to surface uselessly before his eyes. Time to put the past to bed. It was over, wasn't it?

He slept rather well, dreaming of endless porticoes in Morocco or Bologna, along which Quaid advanced and retreated like a country dancer, yapping little eddies of incomprehensible gossip, while Fionnuala Fagan, young again and shining with hope, wove in and out among the pillars in the Roman baths recently excavated under the President's House, singing ancient Irish melodies, out of tune, while wearing one of Heidi's white cotton nightdresses, buttoned to the throat. The water in the Roman baths was a dark raging sea, soundless against marble cliffs.

Wednesday

I

He woke late. Nobody had cared to disturb Senator Hinckley's man.

Descending the grand staircase with its new and fluffy carpet was like walking on recently deceased Persian cats. His head hurt, but not excessively. His throat was distinctly improved, and jetlag was certainly not a factor.

There was nobody about. He struck out across the gravel, skirting the buildings around the quadrangle, went down a grassy slope and walked along one side of the first rugby pitch. The little copse of trees that he remembered was still there, at one end. Passing through, he crossed another sports field and made for the boundary fence. Again, he had remembered correctly. An open doorway in the fence led out on to a public road, which he crossed and looked down into what had been the sleepy hamlet of Chapelizod, now seemingly transformed into a bustling Alpine village, with new apartment complexes and the latest in modern traffic jams.

Around King's College, the world was changing. Even within the College, generations of students had come and gone since Séamus's day. There was no need to feel haunted. His one-man tribunal of enquiry into his own past did not need to remain in permanent session. He should look to the future.

Walking back through the grassy grounds, he managed to identify the source of the inner peace that momentarily pervaded his mind. It was not the foliage shifting in the springtime breeze, or even the lazy twittering of birds in the branches. It was the merciful absence of Quaid that made life seem good this morning.

Entering the President's House, he followed the smell of coffee. It led him to the large dining room, with its bow windows, against which three men in crisp white shirts sat at one end of a long table.

'Ah! Morning! Do join us, whoever you are,' one of them greeted Séamus in a hearty Yorkshire accent. This was clearly the father figure of the group. His grey hair and craggy face looked as if they had been sculpted in granite. 'You're not the chap from Finer Small Campuses, are you?'

Séamus admitted that he was. The Yorkshireman was suitably impressed. He produced a business card. 'I'm from the Leadership Forum. Head of Mission. My two colleagues are educational technology specialists, working with AI.'

'Artificial intelligence?' Séamus's first thought had been artificial insemination.

'No no no no no.' The other man seemed unsure that Séamus might not be feigning ignorance as a joke. 'AI: The Academic Infrastructure Group, Britain's leading ed-con company.'

'I'm sorry,' Séamus said. 'I'm new to the field. And what areas do you work in?' he asked the other men.

'e-knowledge adaptability standards,' one of the two replied. 'Pastoral systems,' said the other, waving at his computer screen, which contained a bulleted list. Séamus made out a few phrases — ANSWER BY THE THIRD RING; LINK CUSTOMER RECORDS TO DISCIPLINARY DATABASE; PREDICT POTENTIAL PROBLEMS BY POSTCODE — and glanced away, but not before noticing the banner at the top of the screen: UNIVERSITY OF STEVENAGE — MOVING UP THE LINE.

The three men returned to their informal discussion. Séamus poured some coffee and sat down at the long table, listening to their evaluation of the qualities of King's College staff. The new administrators were good: they had vision. The new President had come late in the day. The teaching staff were a mixed bunch: some exciting young researchers among them. A good early retirement scheme was essential.

Séamus had met consultants before, and knew the breed. They were a little too loud, too nasal in their judgments. Their position depended on an assumed superiority and a level of conformity with each other's views. Their reports, by definition, would support authoritarian power, and would recommend a raft of expensive structural changes, so that the energies and resources of the institution would be engaged in tedious window-dressing, the results of which could not be evaluated until well after the consultants had been paid. Who was Séamus to sneer at their bandwagon, now that he seemed to have boarded it himself?

'Your people,' said the Yorkshireman, and Séamus realized that he was talking to him, 'FSC, had a nominee on the board. Man by the name of Connolly. Prominent business-man. Good chap. Just the sort of external input a niche university needs, going forward. Why did he withdraw – any idea?'

'I haven't spoken to him yet.' Séamus tried to convey an impression of discretion rather than complete ignorance.

'Connolly's knowledge of traded services would be spot-on for a university. It's vital to think in terms of traded services. You've got no language barrier, have you? Dublin's nicely positioned, if the deal's attractive. You could imagine a whole heap of institutions willing to buy into the King's College thing. It's a nice brand – the royal nomenclature and so forth.'

Hynes entered, bearing fresh supplies of coffee and crois-sants. Séamus was mean enough to enquire whether his mobile phone had been found, or the missing maid. Hynes, red-faced, muttered that enquiries were proceeding. A new phone would be made available, courtesy of the President.

They were joined by a bustling senior citizen who wore a pin-striped suit and sported King's College cufflinks. 'Séamus Joyce!' His voice was a perfect ruling-class growl. 'The man who broke the Dublin drug rings! Good to see you, Séamus!' His handshake was vigorous, though his hair was white as snow. 'Derry. Ring a bell? Derry McKinley, chairman of Trustees. Purely honorific, I'm afraid. Sort of fundraiser and general factotum, if that's not a tautology. Remember me from the rugby pitch?'

An image surfaced in Séamus's mind. He tried to match this man to the ludicrous old boy in the College scarf who had sponsored the team, shrieking encouragement from the touchline, paying for drinks when they lost, even including those in the bar who had been nowhere near the rugby pitch, thereby earning the heartfelt contempt of all and sundry. Disreputable rumours had circulated on his account.

'How could I forget?'

McKinley seemed to take this as a compliment. He peeled a business card from his wallet and presented it to Séamus, making no comment on Séamus's lack of a similar card to reciprocate. 'That's my special limited edition card,' he said. 'Home number included.'

'More than we received,' the Yorkshireman said.

McKinley ignored this interpolation. 'We must get together, Séamus, and I'll tell you all the gossip. Doing anything this evening?'

'Free, so far as I know.'

'Modicum be all right?'

Séamus was no longer surprised at being treated like minor royalty. 'Sounds good,' he said, as though Dublin's finest restaurants were his normal stamping ground.

'We'll have an old chinwag,' McKinley said. 'Who have you been talking to?'

'Dr Burren, Mr Quaid, Fionnuala Fagan, Hynes, of course, and I bumped into the manager of the building site. Literally.'

'Ah. Stanihurst. Not quite one of us. He's Forde's project manager for the Forde Centre building. Very sound fellow in actual fact. But rough around the edges, you know. What did Stanihurst tell you?'

'Nothing. He saved me from falling into a ditch. Then cleared me off his site. Understandably.'

'Rough and ready, that's our Stanihurst,' McKinley said heartily. 'Not, as I said, one of us. The others we must acknowledge. Burren and Fagan and Quaid: King's men and women through and through. Like ourselves, Séamus, like ourselves.' He smiled and dropped his voice. 'I won't ask what they've been saying to you. No doubt they all spoke highly in praise of our new President.'

'Oh, yes.'

'What, all of them?' McKinley smirked. 'I know what you're thinking, Séamus. The younger Cregan used to be a bit of a dork. He's improved over the years, though. Been around the block. Knows what needs to be done. See for yourself.'

3

The door opened and a handsome, well-groomed man entered, treading like a puma. He was not physically large, but his demeanour radiated a sense of well-proportioned power. Cregan had indeed improved out of all recognition, Séamus thought. One would have to look very carefully, and with foreknowledge, to discern the old greenhorn lurking under the oiled-back coiffure, the lantern jaw, the bronzed skin and sharp, appraising eyes. Even under his chalk-striped suit, Cregan's fitness and strength were apparent. He was light on his feet, firm in his movements. He advanced on Séamus and took him by the hand, covering it in two muscular hands of his own, shaking and holding not too long, but long enough. 'Séamus!' There was a halo of aftershave. Séamus could feel the power. Cregan's royal-blue silk tie was a tasteful reminder of his institutional allegiance. The matching blue eyes were smiling, not too much, but in a friendly way that suggested that Séamus and he shared some secret joke at the expense of the rest of the world.

Séamus remembered a story that he had been told as a child about an alligator in Dublin Zoo. This reptile had been imported while still young, and had eventually grown to be exactly the same size as the large bath in which it was lodged. After some years, the administrators of the zoo had decided to rebuild the alligator house, considerably extending the length of the creature's bath. Whereupon the alligator had promptly grown longer by a yard. He had no idea whether this story was true. As a child, he had accepted it as gospel. In middle age, he tended to assume that everything he had learned in his youth was mere fable. But that was foolish. One must not throw the alligator out with the bath water.

Cregan, in short, might well have grown into his job. As Séamus had grown out of his.

'Home is the hero,' President Cregan was beaming at the company. The three consultants looked on politely. 'Séamus Joyce, one of our most distinguished alumni, the man who tackled the drug barons and almost brought down the régime. Be not deceived, gentlemen. Under that mild exterior lurks the brain of a shark. Séamus is weighing us up as a potential partner for Finer Small Campuses. It's make or break for King's. And Séamus knows us inside out!' Cregan burst into good-natured laughter. 'We are properly nervous.'

Derry McKinley beamed. The Yorkshireman coughed. 'Finer Small Campuses would fit rightly,' he observed.

Cregan was nodding. 'Good for us, good for them. Dublin is Europe's most happening city. We've got the space to develop the residential facilities. Through no merit of our own, be it said. This college stagnated for years. We lived a quiet life. No expansion, no innovation. We slept through the boom. The result is that now we've got less than one-quarter the number of students they have in Trinity College, yet our campus is nearly as large. So this is our opportunity. We've got to grow. We have the old tradition; let's build on it. We can become a special place for Senator Hinckley's students.' All of this without raising his voice or relaxing his dimpled smile.

At least the rhetoric was less luxuriant than Quaid's, Séamus thought.

'How many bodies is Hinckley talking of sending you?' the Yorkshireman asked, to launch the President on the next stage of his discourse.

'Hundreds,' Cregan proclaimed. 'Junior Year Abroad, summer semester, even full degree students. We're happy to appoint a special liaison officer, and to welcome a new FSC nominee on to our College board at any time. Our new structure of governance is open and modular. People who want to be partners simply plug into our management systems. All above board. Performance monitored at every stage. Full reports on entry points, retention rates, grade averages, inputs, outputs. Or at least there will be, when our computer system recovers.' A self-deprecating laugh. Then, seriously: 'Stakeholders set the agenda here. That's the new compact.'

'Who's been setting the agenda up to now?' Séamus asked despite himself. The other consultants were clustered around, listening respectfully, but it seemed to be Séamus's privilege, and duty, to act as the principal interlocutor.

'Committees,' Cregan shuddered. 'Endless committees. Department committees, school committees, faculty committees, deans' committees, safety committees, planning

committees, staff committees, and all their tangled conclusions floating up to the Academic Council, the College
board and the trustees. Meetings that go on by the hour, by
the day, by the week.' A note of rueful sincerity had crept
into his voice.

Séamus nodded. 'Sounds familiar.'

'The same people sitting around the same tables. You
could hear the same issue chewed over in identical terms at
your department, your school, your faculty, and on and on
and on. Great for those who love the sound of their own
voice. I've listened to learnèd colleagues make the same
twenty-minute speech verbatim three times in succession
during the course of a single month. Or suddenly change
their minds and adopt the opposite point of view, forcing us
to trash weeks of preparatory work on urgent items of
business. And then they tell me they can't find the time for
their research. My new system is going to let the academics
do their work, and give us all something to celebrate going
forward.'

The contagious phrase 'going forward', used at the end
of a sentence, denoted a positive mental attitude and was
obligatory in all statements and interviews given by manageri-
ally minded persons. Which was not to say that the rest of
Cregan's speech had been entirely unconvincing. In fact,
Séamus was beginning to see him almost sympathetically.

'What's going to happen to those committees?' he asked.

'Oh, there'll be plenty of monitoring,' Cregan assured him.
'We're not going to have free-wheeling managers imposing
their theories on the working man or woman. Academics are
too bolshie to go along with that. Wouldn't wash. So we'll
hold a regular forum, not cutting into the working week but
meeting at eight thirty on a Saturday morning, when those
colleagues who are genuinely interested can come in and hear
my management team explain and defend their proposals and
decisions. The forum will be open to everybody, including

cleaners and gardening staff. I'm tired of the coterie of great academic bores trying to strangle each other in the coils of their eloquence.'

'You'll need some pretty good managers,' Séamus said.

'Top of the range.' Cregan shot him a sharp look, as if he knew exactly who had been talking to Séamus. 'I'll source the best for my team, by fair and open competition. No nepotism here. And I'm going to reward them properly. If you pay peanuts, you get monkeys.'

You can also pay cashews and still get monkeys, Séamus reflected. Some of the most dismal decisions he had seen in his civil service years had been taken by overpaid chimpanzees. He nodded politely, nonetheless.

The President stood in close, like an Elizabethan battleship, and dropped his voice: 'So what do you want to see, then? What does Senator Hinckley need to know?'

Unexpectedly, Séamus sensed Cregan's nervousness. Was Hinckley so powerful?

'Just an overview,' he replied softly. 'How the place is organized; how it stands in the local setting; what it can offer students.'

'These are the very things we're improving,' the President assured him. 'I'll be sending all our current discussion papers to the Senator. Would you like copies?'

'Yes, please, but what I'd most like is simply to wander around, talk to people.'

'Absolutely. You know the campus. You've seen the annual reports. What other documents do you need? How long can you stay?'

Séamus knew the answers to none of these questions. He would talk to Guido once he had his own telephone. Did Cregan know about the theft? Could he really be as friendly as he looked? Séamus took refuge in vagueness: 'Just a few days, if I may. I have to thank you for your splendid hospitality. Could we make an appointment to talk sometime tomorrow?'

'Why don't we do lunch?'

'Perfect.' By then, Séamus hoped that he might have a definite list of questions to put to the President.

Cregan patted his arm. 'Meanwhile, you're at home here, Séamus. Dr Burren will introduce you wherever you want to go. You'll find plenty to criticize, I've no doubt, although nothing on the scale that you were used to in the drugs industry. At least, we hope not!' Another quick, vulnerable smile. 'For a start, just so that you can see us at our best, I want you to come to our honorary degree ceremony, and join us for lunch. Your timing is perfect.'

'We didn't receive an invitation to the lunch,' the Yorkshireman grumbled cheerfully. 'All they give us is beer and sandwiches.'

'That's because you're not as important as Séamus,' the President smiled. 'We might send you some trifle if the VIPs don't scarf it all.'

4

Hynes put his head around the door. 'They're here, President,' he hooted in an altered voice. 'Will I usher them in, or will you come out to greet them?'

There was something schizoid in the contrast between Hynes's normal self and his new butler persona. Perhaps all servants have to learn the art of self-division. Séamus wondered if Hynes was aping an earlier major-domo from the days of Presidents past.

'I'll come out,' Cregan said quickly. 'Can you show Mr Joyce into the main drawing room? And can you find Dr Burren, to be on hand?'

'Already done, President,' Hynes said in an almost offended tone. 'Dr Burren is fully primed. The other graduands are robing. We are set to go in forty-five minutes. Mrs Forde's robes are upstairs, with her stylist.'

Cregan smiled. 'What would I do without you, Hynes?'

'Thank you, President.' Hynes quivered with gratification.

Séamus followed Hynes out of the room, across the broad hallway and into a high-ceilinged parlour. Comfortable sofas were disposed around a marble fireplace in which an unconvincing gas fire blazed. Burren was warming himself unnecessarily at the fire. Derry McKinley, chairman of the trustees, followed them in, closing the door on Hynes.

'Here we are,' Burren exclaimed, heartily if superfluously. There was no hint of his alcoholic stupor of less than twelve hours previously. 'You are about to meet our most important benefactor. Seán Forde is a real friend of the College. Never got a third-level education himself, but he's doing great things for us.' Burren was speaking unnaturally loudly, as though dictating a language test to foreigners.

'Quaid was telling me that Forde is responsible for that exceptionally large new building,' Séamus said to McKinley.

'Which is going to transform us, both academically and economically,' McKinley said. 'For the first time since the foundation of the College, we'll have a hall big enough to accommodate 400 students in one lecture, and facilities to bring the finest conferences and concerts and plays to King's College. The Forde Centre is going to put us on the map. All Quaid can see, of course, is the inconvenience of its construction. Petty myopia or what? Academics insist on self-governance, then they behave like children.'

This seemed to require no answer. The door opened, and President Cregan entered with a powerfully built old man in grey tweed, flanked by a young woman with dark, dark hair and heavy-lidded brown eyes. Her beauty was such that it created a blaze that engulfed the room. She stood in quiet glory.

'Seán Forde,' Cregan purred, 'and Mrs Lucy Forde. Séamus Joyce, former head of the Irish Drugs Enforcement Agency, now an international consultant advising universities world-wide.' Séamus tried not to wince. 'Mrs Forde is here to receive her honorary doctorate.'

'Congratulations,' Séamus said.

Before she could reply, her husband cut in: 'Joyce! You're the man who brought down that bastard Frye.' His Irish countryman's voice had been strained through urban England. 'If only we had more like you, to sort out the crook politicians. They're all at it. Try to move in this country, and you'll find they're on the take. Tripping you up. Standing with their baskets at the ready.' He seized Séamus's hand in a bone-crushing grip. 'Though, mind you, I suppose selling your soul to the drug-dealers is worse than what most of them get up to. You put a stop to Frye anyway. Pleased to meet you, Séamus.'

Once again, Séamus found himself adjusting to the epic scale. Forde was taller than Séamus, older, broader, with a halo of white fluff around his globe-shaped skull. His eyes were light green and piercing, his face red with broken veins. He was an over-bright restoration of an Old Master painting, a ruddy apostle taken out of context. His excessively beautiful wife looked on silently like a sad madonna.

Séamus's hand felt like a chicken whose neck had been wrung. He tried to ignore the pain.

'Mr Forde is a straight talker,' Cregan put in. Standing beside Forde, even the President was a faint shadow. 'He believes in getting things done and he doesn't suffer fools gladly. Which is, of course, what brings him to King's, where we have no fools.'

Burren emitted a loyal bark. Hynes floated into view, reverently approaching Mrs Forde: an unlikely Angel Gabriel. 'Would you care to accompany me upstairs? Your robes are waiting.'

She followed him like a lamb well used to the slaughter.

'I've been admiring your new building,' Séamus said to Forde. 'It looks impressive, even at this stage of construction.'

'Never mind impressive,' Forde said. 'Useful is the thing. I made President Cregan tell me exactly what they needed to develop this place, and when I had it clear in my own mind, I went off to the best architect I know, a man who has done me halls and malls and megastores up and down the United Kingdom, and I told him what to do. Five months later we hit the site. I've got my own team managing this thing. My logistics man, Stanihurst, is taking it as a full frontal assault. Because it's urgent.' His eyes blazed with excitement. 'The young people need more education than we ever got. And we know what it costs to give it to them. I never went to college. That was for the next generation. I went to the technical school and did surveying. For more than forty years, I've built up my business, working with ordinary men and women, rough and ready, the salt of the earth. I'm proud of that. The men I've worked with – up at six in the morning and out in the rain and the wind, transforming the cities of Ireland and Britain with their work – very few of them have ever gone near a university either. But they and their like built the colleges, the churches, the railway stations, the offices, the roads, the sewers, the services. The thing we're building here is a monument to them too, and maybe some of their sons and daughters will come here to study and better themselves.' This sounded like a speech made many times before. A good one, though. Séamus was impressed.

'We won't let you down,' Cregan said. 'We'll make this place hum.'

'Of course you will,' Forde said. 'I have complete faith.'

'Even if I've got my hand out?' Cregan smiled.

'I know you have to,' Forde said. 'We can't expect education to pay its way. I'm as idealistic as the next man. If a thing should be making money, be sure it makes plenty. If it has to be subsidized, subsidize it right.'

'Music to my ears,' Cregan concurred, still smiling.

'Who sent you here?' Forde asked Séamus.

'Consultancy International. Our client is Senator Hinckley's organization.'

'The Small Campuses crowd. Our new partners, if all goes well. I'm joining the board of trustees here, you see. Small Campuses sound like pretty good operators in their own country.'

'What do you think of them coming in here?'

'I'm for it,' said Forde. 'It's the way forward. As long as they don't try to push us around. There's room for everyone. We can teach English to the Russians and Chinese, and bring Americans over as well for their own classes. That'll give us the money to put on good courses for the Irish students who need them. There's no reason why we can't do it all. Too many things in this country are compartmentalized. People don't want to mix. That's all wrong. You can't have snobbery dictating what gets done in a place. It doesn't even have to be the same staff. Plan it right, and you can get two extra months' work out of the same plant. We're building flats around the edge of the campus. Tasty little blocks that will add to the look of the place and allow us to house the workers and the students that we have to bring in. I'm not making a penny out of all that, though my firm is doing the building. Do you believe me?'

'Why wouldn't I?'

Forde gave a short guffaw. 'I'm a developer. A builder. Builders are crooks. Whatever I do is all done for the money. I'm up before the tribunals. Guilty till proven innocent. And you can't be proved innocent if you're a developer. Well, Séamus, you probably know what's eating Senator Hinckley. A property tycoon getting involved in a university. Investigate, then. Bring in whoever you want. Go through the books. If you find anything wrong, let me know. I'd be interested.'

'Nearly time to be moving?' Cregan suggested.

'Is she ready?'

'Yes.' Mrs Forde appeared in the doorway, wearing her gown with celestial poise. 'Under starter's orders.'

5

After much shuffling, they found themselves in the old Assembly Room, where Séamus had once taken annual examinations at rickety desks, in an atmosphere of sweating anxiety. Now the room was augustly panelled, lit by chandeliers, flanked by formal portraits of haughty men, some with side whiskers. Had those portraits hung there in his day?

Long tables had been ranged against the walls, and the space between was filled with rows of collapsible chairs, occupied by well-dressed guests and gowned academics. Séamus attempted to slip away and sit at the back, but was captured by an orderly, who frogmarched him to the front, where he was placed on a plush chair near the side of a platform splashed with bouquets of gladioli, red and white. The flowers looked out of place. Imported from where? Holland? Kenya? In the seat to his right, a minor politician was coiling and preening.

'What's your connection?' asked the politician.

'Consultancy.'

'I'm a trustee,' said the politician. 'Former Lord Mayor, you know.'

'I know.'

The politician nodded his little round head vigorously, pleased to have been recognized. He had a receding hairline and the features of a hungry rabbit.

A burst of electronic organ music filled the air. From the back of the hall a procession advanced along the centre aisle, led by a slow-stepping Hynes in black hat and gown, wielding a large metallic bludgeon. St Malachi's mace, not quite as threatening as Séamus remembered it from his own graduation. Behind Hynes shuffled President Cregan like a well-groomed macaw, resplendent in reds and greens and a soft blue velvet cap with trailing peacock feathers. Next came a gaggle of ageing academics, none of whose faces were familiar. All wore expressions of paralytic solemnity. Three women, none of them Fionnuala. Hynes stood aside, allowing the academics to troop up on to the podium, then headed off the recipients of the honorary degrees and channelled them into their allotted seats in the front row. All except Mrs Forde were men, a little older than Séamus.

He looked again for Fionnuala. Nowhere.

Mrs Forde sat perfectly poised, her brown eyes taking in the scene with just the right degree of calm pleasure. She saw him admiring her, glanced candidly into his eyes for a moment before slowly turning back to survey President Cregan rising and calling on the registrar to read out the citation for the first degree. After the registrar's emphatic peroration, delivered in the style of a sermon, there was a parley in Latin before the candidate stepped forward to receive his scroll and a warm episcopal handshake from President Cregan, followed by a barrage of flashes from press photographers.

The first graduands were clearly men of honour. John D. Provenzano had been chancellor of two small universities in the Boston area, both affiliated to the Finer Small Campuses chain, and now served on the board of Lucania Inc., a private prisons conglomerate. Alexander Murphy had marketed Irish dairy products, notably Lo-Liter Long-Life Milk for the Asian teenage market. Trevor Grace, an ex-boxer, was a Dublin-born sports commentator on British television. Pat McCollum, a native of Sligo, had built up a chain of language schools in Ireland, Britain and Hong Kong. Together, as Cregan repeatedly pointed out, these people reflected the new international outlook of King's College.

Last to step forward was Lucy Forde, whose praise took

twice as long as the rest. Of mixed Lebanese and Irish parentage, she had graduated from the National College of Art and Design and worked briefly as a model, before giving up her career to marry the distinguished entrepreneur Mr Seán Patrick Forde. She had then dedicated herself to charitable work, notably the provision of dowries to destitute girls on the Indian subcontinent, and was one of the most important fundraisers in Europe for this deserving cause. Mrs Forde listened to the registrar's speech with what appeared to be equanimity, then walked forward as cameras flashed like summer lightning to accept a scroll and a handshake from President Cregan. They stood side by side, like a celebrity couple announcing their engagement. One photographer crouched at their feet and snapped their ready smiles over and over again. At last Mrs Forde detached herself. As she stepped down from the stage, she posed with patient professionalism once more for the press photographers, carefully extending one high-heeled foot to a lower step in order to shape the perfect vertical image. Her face, while she went through these motions, held an archaic smile, saying everything and nothing.

'Jeepers,' ejaculated the politician to Séamus's right, 'I wouldn't mind that. Trophy wife, what?'

'I hope the others don't feel left out,' Séamus said. The men who had preceded Lucy Forde, having resumed their seats in the front row, were smiling and applauding politely. Their pictures would not be in the newspapers.

Seán Forde, sitting on the far side of the platform from Séamus, wiped a tear from his eye and clapped his hands like a child at a party. Beside him bulked the figure of Stanihurst, the site manager, his face wreathed in smiles as he grasped Forde's left shoulder and squeezed it affectionately, before removing his spectacles and polishing them on his tie, as though they had misted up with emotion. For one moment, Séamus had a hallucinatory vision of the two big broad men as the proud parents of Lucy. Stanihurst was wearing a bright blue suit which, given his dimensions, must have been hand-tailored. Into Séamus's mind came the unbidden image of a great ship about to be launched, and tiny workmen finishing the painting of the hull. That would be Stanihurst being fitted by his tailor. Gulliver in Lilliput.

'Forde's first wife was a right old bag, by all accounts,' the former Lord Mayor continued. 'Drank like a feckin' fish, or so they say. Had to be carried out of the Mansion House once, between two Guards, they tell me.'

'Is that so?' Séamus rejoined politely.

''Tis. Fell over a cliff, I believe. Your man didn't marry again for years. Grief-stricken, to coin a phrase. Then along comes Lucy, and bingo! Lucy in the sky with diamonds on the soles of her feckin' shoes. Nice move. The guy has ten years to live, max. What did you say your name was?'

'Séamus Joyce,' said Séamus.

'The iDEA?'

'The same.'

'Thought so. It's you should be getting an honorary degree for breaking up them drug rings.'

'They're not broken up,' Séamus said. 'Just displaced. Supply follows demand.'

'Do you tell me so?' The former Lord Mayor thought for a moment. 'Do you know what Richard Frye's up to now?'

'Thankfully, no.' His former Minister. Exposed and disgraced by Séamus, triumphantly re-elected by his doting constituents. 'I don't follow his career these days.'

'You ought to keep abreast, all the same. For your own good, like. They tell me Frye has a parliamentary question down about you and your pension. Did you know that, did you? He wants the Dáil Finance Committee to get a report on you off of the Criminal Assets Bureau, so he does. Won't take a written reply to the PQ, either; he's going for the full production. Wants to get on TV. That boyo's got his knife in you.'

'Understandably,' Séamus said. Strange, not to know you are the subject of an attack. He should have been grateful to the little rabbity politician, instead of which he felt degraded.

6

President Cregan was wrapping up proceedings in his sonorous voice, displaying a full set of white teeth that contrasted with his tan. There was no sign of his former mediocrity. Oliver Cregan was the 'after' picture in an advertisement for self-reclamation. He had acquired the gift of speaking banalities with an air of significance. All he was doing was announcing that the next honorary degree conferring would take place in the new Forde Conference Centre – gowns and hard hats would be worn, he grinned – and inviting his guests to lunch in the dining hall, but he managed to convey these points as though he were unveiling the structure of DNA. He would have been equally impressive, Séamus thought, pointing the way to the over-wing exits.

Hynes reappeared, bearing the mace aloft, and led the assembled dignitaries in a slow conga through corridors, around corners, down steps and into the dining hall. As Séamus shuffled along, he was joined by Quaid, whose tattered gown made him look unexpectedly handsome. 'What did you think?'

'Not bad.'

'Cregan's good on a stage. When you meet him one to one, he's even better. You always come away reassured. Even if he cheated you the last time. I've fallen for it myself. There's an innocence about Ollie Cregan. He genuinely forgets the promises he's made. Did you notice the mace?'

'Of course. The College's weapon of mass destruction.'

'It's a fake.'

'Keep your voice down,' muttered Burren, who had come

up on the other side. 'What does Séamus care about our pathetic phallus?'

'As a private dick, he will wish to be conversant with the local scandals. To us they may be old hat. To him they are fresh and new. Don't yawn, Séamus. Admit it. Had you heard about St Malachi's mace?'

'Since I saw it paraded at my graduation some decades ago, I have to confess I haven't given it much thought.'

'To be sure, it was never a genuine medieval artefact,' Quaid began. 'Produced in the seventeenth century, rather than the twelfth. Even the seventeenth century is nice and old, if you're looking for a centrepiece for the so-called museum over the supermarket in the Forde Conference Centre. Which, by the way, is also to house, inter alia, a video games arcade, an off-licence and a gift shop selling Celtic kitsch, with parking for thirty tour buses packed with Yanks. The mace will have its own illuminated showcase. Cregan was getting it restored in Switzerland, at an astronomical cost, but one couldn't help noticing that what came back was a replica, rather than the original restored. Question is: how much did little Ollie get paid for the original?'

And Quaid fell silent, as if content. They had reached the dining-room door, and the welcoming face of President Cregan.

7

The refreshments included a ready flow of Sancerre and Châteauneuf-du-Pape. Did they always entertain on this scale? Séamus made his selection from the buffet, which was impeccably staffed by squads of Chinese waiters, before becoming embroiled in a discussion of the medical ethics of stem-cell research with a philosophy lecturer who turned out to be a part-time priest. Next came a brief exchange with

John D. Provenzano, who was aware that Séamus had been sent by Senator Hinckley and assumed that Séamus would have heard of his own connection with Finer Small Campuses. He wanted to know how the Senator was doing. How was that pacemaker? Séamus could not enlighten him on this point. Chancellor Provenzano expressed disappointment that Pat Connolly was not on hand. Great guy, Pat, real maverick, one of the deep thinkers in college catering. Séamus confessed that he had yet to meet the FSC nominee to the board of King's College Dublin. 'Track him down,' Provenzano urged. 'Hear what he has to say. Tell him we want him back on the team.'

'He's out of contact at the moment,' Séamus said.

'Track him down.' Provenzano turned away.

Séamus's glass was full again. His head felt delicate, either from an excess of alcohol or from the after-effects of too much travelling. Stanihurst was drinking water. President Cregan urged him to try something stronger. Stanihurst replied that he never drank alcohol on Wednesdays, which caused the President to laugh and punch Stanihurst lightly on the upper arm. Stanihurst smiled behind his spectacles.

Séamus would have liked to ask about Fionnuala. Why was she not here? Too junior, or persona non grata? He went to the buffet, helped himself to cheese, and got pinned against a wall by the beautiful Mrs Forde in person and questioned earnestly on the economics of banning opium poppy production in poor areas of the Third World which depended entirely on the crop. She knew about his work with the iDEA, and worried about poor farmers in Afghanistan going hungry if the West gave up its love affair with heroin. He tried to tell her that there was no chance of the poppy being removed from cultivation. The most one could achieve was displacement. She listened with rapt attention, and her concentrated beauty led him to continue at greater length than he had intended. The Western powers which claimed to be undying enemies of heroin production tended to be willing, in practice, to tolerate opium-growing in exchange for other favours. The CIA, in the 1980s, had spent billions of taxpayers' dollars funding and training drug-dealing warlords to overthrow the modernizing Russian-backed régime in Kabul, thereby consigning Afghan women to renewed slavery and illiteracy and helping the spread of fundamentalist terror worldwide. Just a few months before the attack on the Twin Towers, the Bush administration had paid a further $46 million to America's former allies, the Taliban, as a payment for destroying Afghanistan's opium crops. Three years later, the warlords of the Northern Alliance, who had become America's new military allies in overthrowing the same Taliban, had re-established Afghanistan as the world's leading supplier of heroin. Profits from drugs produced by the West's military allies now funded the terrorist organizations which were threatening the West. It was a game of mirrors. Nobody was willing to legalize drugs and cut off the terrorists' funds. Nobody truly believed that the heroin trade could ever be stemmed.

As she listened attentively, Lucy Forde's brown eyes welled with tears. He had not meant to sound so sour.

8

He sank an extra cup of coffee, his drug of choice. Nearby, Quaid was standing close beside Stanihurst, talking eagerly into the big man's ear. His demeanour was friendly, even affectionate. This was surprising, given his stated antipathy to Stanihurst's building efforts. Stanihurst looked long-suffering, but apparently tolerant of Quaid. Séamus thought of the little bird that cleans the crocodile's teeth. Quaid was a parasite. Parasites have to be inherently useful to at least one other creature, larger or more powerful than themselves. Otherwise, how could they survive?

Cregan was at Séamus's side. 'Some light reading material,' he said in his ear. 'For your eyes only.' He produced a large white envelope stamped *Confidential*, and thrust it into Séamus's hands. 'The document in here will give you some idea where we're headed and, more importantly, how we're going to get there. My personal thoughts. I'll be interested to know what you think.' All the while patting Séamus on the upper arm, as one might caress a faithful spaniel.

Séamus thanked him solemnly and set off, with the white envelope under his arm, to find the accounts office. Getting there involved circling the cloisters and descending a flight of stairs not far from Fionnuala's room. Dr Burren trailed along behind him, drunk but determined, and put him right when he got lost.

The door marked *Account's*, when he finally found it, was locked. Séamus knocked and waited, being finally admitted by an elderly lady with blotchy skin, threadbare tweeds and a regretful voice in which she identified herself as Miss Agnes Lambe. The chief accountant, buildings officer and university assets manager, otherwise known as Mr Hanratty, was unavailable. He was ill, and had been ordered by his doctor to take a complete rest. She was his assistant. Mr Hanratty might be back at the end of the week. Then again, maybe not. She had no authority to show the accounts to anybody. As she told him this, she twitched as though being nibbled by poisonous insects.

Dr Burren vouched for Séamus's status and plenipotentiary powers. Reluctantly, the threadbare lady picked up a telephone and whispered into it. Séamus looked around. The walls were lined with large metal cabinets with their doors standing open, revealing cascades of disordered paper. Ledgers were piled on an oaken desk. There were computers and printers, but they were not switched on. Surfaces were dusty. The barred window was grimy and ivy-encrusted. The antiquated atmosphere was accentuated by the fine Turkey carpet that took up the middle of the floor and the wooden desk lamps that provided the only illumination.

Doing her best to smile, the careworn custodian placed a printout of the most recent monthly accounts on the corner of a crowded table and watched Séamus worriedly as he turned the pages. The cause of her worry was not clear to Séamus, but obviously she believed the worst of all new-comers. He tried to give the impression that he knew what to look for. Expenditure so far in the current year had been just over €14 million, half of which had been met by capital grant income, contract research payments and current grants in lieu of student fees. There was no record of any payment from Finer Small Campuses. Perhaps the FSC transactions were kept in a separate account? She could not answer that question off the top of her balding head. One large payment she could identify: it came from a major bank in connection with the remortgaging of the sports hall. Séamus enquired about this, and Agnes Lambe confirmed that the new Univer-sities Act made it awkward for King's College to run a deficit. The government had been cutting back on basic running costs across the sector, and moreover the grant for each year was announced long after financial commitments had already been made. The result was a series of random cuts carried out wherever gaps appeared, combined with a constant jug-gling of assets. Most of the new buildings in King's College had been refinanced more than once.

Séamus had already seen something of this from the sum-mary accounts presented in the President's Reports. He com-mented that it sounded like a recipe for chaos. Agnes Lambe gave a convulsive shrug and replied that it was government policy. 'No contradiction there,' Burren remarked.

Séamus asked if he might see the College bursar. Burren

explained that President Cregan had only recently ceased to act as bursar, the post he had held before becoming President. He had relinquished his post at the end of the transitional period, and the new bursar had not yet fully entered into his office. Hanratty was the man with all the answers.

9

They left the accounts office. Séamus announced that he was going into the city to buy some clothes. Burren offered to accompany him as soon as he was free, but Séamus was determined to go on his own, not least because he intended to buy a new mobile phone for secure communications with Guido Schneider. 'You must have other things to do with your time?' he said to Burren.

'Plenty,' Burren said gloomily. 'We're all multitaskers now. A new batch of visiting students arrived this morning from China. I've got to place the little dears in the classrooms of my reluctant colleagues. I have my orders, but not the authority to carry them out. Hence, negotiations will ensue. I'm to meet the Chinese in five minutes.'

'Well, go and meet them. I'll wait for you in the senior common room.'

'Thanks.' Burren sounded positively grateful. 'I'll be there in twenty minutes. We'll get a taxi into town.'

The moment Burren turned the corner, Séamus was out of the building. As he hurried across the grass towards the driveway, he saw Mrs Forde again. She was standing under a tree at the car park closest to the main avenue, holding the hand of the bullish young man who had challenged Séamus outside Fionnuala's room. As he watched, she planted a fervent kiss on the young man's cheek, gripping his shoulders. He reciprocated nervously. Behind her, Stanihurst climbed out of a blue Ford Transit van and approached, walking quickly. The young man pulled himself free of Mrs Forde and lumbered away across the grass in the direction of the College buildings. He passed close by Séamus without seeing him. His face was blank. Mrs Forde ran her fingers through her dark hair. Stanihurst was carrying a yellow work jacket and helmet, but was still wearing his formal suit and looking, if anything, even larger and broader than he had when Séamus had first encountered him on the building site. Stanihurst engaged Mrs Forde in close dialogue. Séamus felt that the events of the past two days were being reprised in some sort of mimed tableau, in which he was required to understand things that had not yet been explained. He reached the drive and walked quickly towards the College gate.

There must be taxis to be had outside the College. He would walk as far as Parkgate Street if need be. The trees were whispering in a light breeze. The light green grass, spreading over little hummocks and larger rises in the ground, suggested that the pastoral peace of the Phoenix Park had invaded the campus. Not pastoral: there were no sheep, although he knew there were herds of deer in the vicinity. Not so peaceful, either: apart from Dublin Zoo, the park was home to Garda headquarters, the American Ambassador, the President of Ireland and the remains of the Magazine Fort. Once the Papal Nuncio had also resided in the park, but dry rot had driven him out, the Roman presence being currently marked by the mammoth papal cross standing on the spot where John Paul II had said mass in 1979. Séamus could see the tip of the cross through the trees.

A diesel engine slowed beside him. 'Heading into town?' It was Lucy Forde. Her shy smile flickered like a light bulb with a loose connection. Rather than the usual BMW or Mercedes coupé favoured by rich men's wives, her car was a dusty black Citroën Picasso. The degree citation had mentioned her training at the National College of Art and Design; Séamus wondered if she had bought this Picasso as a homage to the great Malagueño, or whether she herself produced artworks of such dimensions that they filled the available space with the back seats down. Somehow he guessed there were no children to be transported.

'That's very kind of you.' He went around the front and got into the passenger seat. They started moving, not very fast. She had taken off her shoes, and worked the pedals with stockinged feet. 'Thank God that's over. I didn't enjoy it.'

'I've been at worse.'

'My husband insisted. He wouldn't accept the degree himself. What I do isn't worth a degree.'

'It sounded good.'

'Oh, yes. It's good. Only thing is, the money I raise, you know, comes mostly from Seán and his friends, but he wants me to take the credit.' Her voice rose at the end of each phrase, like a teenager checking the comprehension of her listener.

They passed through the College gates in silence. She was still driving slowly, in a wandering style, remaining in second gear. Then, as she came down towards the river, she said casually, 'You're here on behalf of the Americans, aren't you?'

'Yes.'

'Because my husband is the main benefactor of the College. He's going to be put on the board. It means quite a lot to him, for personal reasons. If the American partnership is going to work properly, they'll have to talk to Seán. Sooner or later. He won't let the place be taken over, you know. And he can't just be pushed around.'

'I'm sure there's no intention –'

'People have tried to push him around, you see. And it hasn't worked. He's generous, but he can be touchy. He won't say this to you himself, but it's true. Twelve years ago, when we were first married' – she caught him looking at her and frowned – 'yes, I'm older than I look. Twelve years ago, people tried to blackmail my husband. Two men he had fired from his building company. He had them arrested, but they were released, and one of them made a threat to kidnap me. I'm sure he didn't mean it. Just letting off steam. Anyway, he was injured. A back injury. This was over in England.'

'Who hurt him?'

'I don't know.'

'And the basis of the blackmail?'

'I never heard.' She half-closed her eyes, as though shielding them from sunlight. 'Now Seán has to face the planning tribunals. Of course he has nothing to fear, really. His hands are clean. He made his money in England, and the work he's done here in Ireland is all above board. He never paid bribes. He's been dragged in, all the same. He had to make a statement about a minister, years ago, who tried to squeeze money out of him and then blocked his plans for a poor area in the city centre, where people really needed jobs at the time.' The injustice of it smouldered in her gentle voice.

'I'll be happy to talk with your husband,' Séamus said. 'He's certainly under no threat from me. My job is simply to report how the College is run.' He hoped this was true.

'You've dealt with drug people, gangs and so forth.' She shot him an appraising glance. 'You know how these people behave. We could ask your advice.'

'About what?'

'People taking advantage.' They were moving along the Liffey quays. Although the traffic was unusually light, Lucy Forde drove well within the speed limit, almost as if she were deliberately lengthening the journey time. She drew a deep breath. 'Defamation. And threats. Violent people. It started a couple of months ago. One of my husband's site security men was injured last week. Not here. In Kinnegad. That's Seán's other big building project in Ireland. The man is out of danger. The Gardaí won't take it seriously. They say he owed money to a drug-pusher. Which may be true. Stanihurst, my husband's site manager, says he's been stepping up security, but that's giving in, I think. You can easily put yourself in the wrong. We need professional advice. Do you know an honest policeman?'

He found the question irritating. His reaction could be dictated, he realized, by lack of sleep, or by the fact that she sounded prim and sanctimonious while remaining so very beautiful.

'Yes, I do. Honest policemen, honest gangsters – in fact, I've even met some honest public servants.'

'Honest gangsters?' She looked at him sideways. 'In what sense?'

'Loyal to their friends. Selfless. Making no claim to be virtuous. I suppose that's a kind of honesty.'

She drove in silence for a moment. 'I could've been a painter for a living,' she said. 'Not an awfully good one. I won't show my work any more, because people buy it to flatter my husband. Even the charity work makes me uncomfortable. There's so much humbug, so much fraud, so many people like me raising funds for tear-jerking causes, doing more harm than good. Ladies who lunch on other people's misfortune. My committee consists of five women, two of them in Birmingham and three in India, who won't take a penny for their work and refuse to appear in public. Everything we do is audited by a retired accountant who doesn't believe in charity. He thinks all our money is wasted. India is changing, he says, and our little aid programme is irrelevant and superfluous. He doesn't trust my five women and questions every penny spent by the local staff in Delhi. How do I know they're honest, or that he is? I don't. I can't trust anybody. But you have to trust people to get things done. We take our chances. It's all we can do.'

Séamus said nothing.

'So,' she continued, 'you do know an honest policeman?'

'Yes. Declan Dowd.' Decko, who had worked against drug gangs and racketeers. Who had taken over the iDEA after

Séamus had wrecked it. Who hadn't blamed Séamus for being stupid.

'Will you introduce me?' she asked. 'Confidentially?'

'I can try. I'm out of those circles now, but I could make a phone call.'

'Here.' She handed him a visiting card. 'It's got my mobile number. Where did you want me to leave you?'

'Dublin Woollen Mills would be fine.'

'It's a haberdashery now,' she said, as though he might have been planning to buy a length of tweed.

'Everything changes.'

Without warning, she fell silent, concentrating on her driving. Her silence was a barrier that he did not feel welcome to cross.

He tried to remember making this same trip in shuddering green double-decker buses during his student days. As indeed he had, over and over. Especially on quiet Sunday mornings when Dublin had been moribund and devout, and a bag of chips from Forte's on O'Connell Street was the height of debauchery. In those days, dereliction seemed just a step away, as plaster peeled from respectable old houses and grey stone tilted out of true. Today there were the angular landmarks of a new opulence, finished in sharp synthetic colours. The remaining older buildings had been tarted up and refashioned, some sprouting penthouses along their rooflines. Crowds surged and bustled. Asiatic bicyclists wove through the traffic in death-defying arabesques.

He got out opposite the Ha'penny Bridge, waved his thanks to Mrs Forde's indifferent smile, strolled along the boardwalk like a tourist. It was a fine spring afternoon, and sunshine warmed his back in the cold air. He loved the city's openness to Liffey water and ever-changing sky. He liked the pasteboard reproduction style of the new apartments on Bachelors Walk. He was even prepared to tolerate the tinny millennium spike that had lately sprouted into the upper atmosphere above O'Connell Street. However pointless in itself, this null installation had prevented even sillier eruptions of civic pride.

Walking south towards Grafton Street, he went into Brainwave to buy a new phone. The hyperactive young man behind the counter lost interest when Séamus explained that he needed to be able to make calls to the United States. No such phones were immediately available over the counter. It would take several hours to unblock the international facility.

In Pócafón on Chatham Street the problem did not exist: he simply paid an extra deposit and got a phone that was ready at once to make transatlantic calls. They allowed him to leave the packaging behind.

Standing in the noisy street, he got through immediately to the hotel reception in New York. Guido Schneider had checked out two hours previously. He wanted the details of Mr Joyce's new cellphone and had left a number for him to call. Séamus tried the number, got a voicemail service, left a message, then called the hotel again, got a different operator. Mrs Heidi Novacek had left, approximately two hours previously. There was no forwarding address.

He took Lucy's card from his pocket and fed her number into the address book on his new mobile phone. He did not call the number, as he had nothing yet to report.

On an impulse he called Sal O'Sullivan, Secretary General of the Department of Justice, Equality and Law Reform. He could remember her extension: names and figures tended to stick in his mind. One of her personal assistants answered the call, took his name. Then Sal herself came on the line.

'What can we do for you, Séamus?' Businesslike as ever.

'Pay me my pension?'

'Not my decision. You agreed that direct with Roinn an Taoisigh, remember?'

'What's holding it up?'

'The real answer? Somebody's putting out a rumour that

you were in cahoots with Billy O'Rourke; you let him get away, and you warned off the Crow before we could catch him. In other words, you already got paid off by drug-suppliers, so why should the Irish taxpayer be contributing to your retirement?'

'And what do you think, Sal?'

'I'd say you've annoyed a few people, starting with our ex-Minister, who still has good enough connections to make life difficult for you in the short term. He has his friends in the media, his public relations advisers. They're saying similar things about me, incidentally. Even about Decko. Naturally, once rumours get started, they must be looked into. Especially by the nervous nellies in our pensions outfit. It all takes time. Are you starving?'

'Not yet. Could you put out a rumour that I'm getting impatient?'

'You don't have the reputation.'

'Who should I be talking to in the pension authority?'

'Nobody. It's gone to the special cases commissioner. Diarmuid Muldoon. Retired from the Department of Defence seven years ago. They gave him an office. He's slow because he's senile.'

'Why is nobody keeping me informed of the progress of my case?'

'Because there isn't any. Where are you calling from?'

'Dublin. Where's Diarmuid Muldoon's office?'

'Bowen House, Upper Mount Street. What brings you to Dublin?'

'Consultancy work at King's College. I think I'll pay Mr Muldoon a visit.'

'Enjoy. Just don't expect results. Nice to hear from you, Séamus, but now I've got to go to a meeting.'

Next, Séamus tried Decko Dowd's home number, got no answer, but left a greeting on his answering machine.

10

Sauntering down Clarendon Street, past restaurants and fashion wholesalers and 'adult' shops in higgledy-piggledy houses left over from past centuries, he saw nobody that he knew. Nobody noticed him. He was a ghost, back where he'd never belonged.

That was how it should be. He was a man born for quiet mediocrity, who should never have been placed in charge. If there was one lesson to be learned from his debacle in the iDEA, that was it. He had been made director of the drugs agency precisely because he was seen as a man of straw. The fact that he had been forced for a moment to rise to the challenge, that he had acted out of character, with violence and cunning, bringing down his enemies and destroying his agency, did not change his essential nature: a bystander, not an actor.

And yet he had been decisive once, for a brief moment, or a little longer. He had precipitated events. He saw himself reflected in a café window. Could this be a man of action? If not, why not?

Sal's cool voice had put him in his place. His civil service career over, his moment of notoriety past.

'Look who thinks he's nobody!' That was the punchline of the old joke about the rabbi, the cantor and the humble shamus who swept the synagogue floor.

Being nobody, properly considered, is a job for great men. Which Séamus was not.

If he was a ghost, would he be able to find other ghosts, such as Andrew O'Neill, lost at sea? Had O'Neill's excavations led to his disappearance, or had he vanished by accident, or for other reasons? Perhaps he had simply come to the end of things and could not face starting to teach in his new university. Perhaps he had been found out, or found himself out, in some way that he could not live with.

Séamus looked at other drab men in suits bustling along the narrow street, at foreign students sitting on the steps of Powerscourt Town House, at a tired middle-aged woman contentedly lugging a shopping bag, and he wondered what wild invisible dreams might fill their heads. What could they see of his thoughts?

He vaguely remembered an episode from a solemn poem that Quaid had forced him to read as a student, in which a great poet – T. S. Eliot? – sits on his stern in an Underground carriage that has stopped in a dark tunnel, thinking superior thoughts about his fellow passengers as they wait for the train to move on to the next station. Eliot (if indeed it was he) believes he can see into their mental emptiness, or some such grand assonantal phrase. Presumptuous bollicks. Why should other people's minds not be filled with thoughts just as engaging as those buzzing about in Mr Eliot's brilliantined skull? Isn't that the whole point about people's appearance? You can't tell what lies behind it. No art to find the mind's construction in the face. Take serial killers. Their mugshots show a slightly bothered, inoffensive normality. Or those winsome mass murderers with their sad, twinkling smiles who lead humanity into war. We keep looking naively for danger to be signalled by visible difference, while all the time it nests within us.

This stream of semi-consciousness came to an abrupt end when he was struck on the shoulder by a bicycle courier rounding the corner from Exchequer Street. No harm done.

Time to call on Patrick Connolly's company, Padcon. He remembered the address from the phone book.

Clarendon Lane was lurking under an archway, more or less where he had guessed it might be. More of a yard than a lane. He ventured in, squeezed past some parked cars and followed the curve of the dirty laneway. Brown brick buildings were propped up by rusting girders. There was a second-hand bookseller, a little printing shop and a doorway with a cracked glass panel that read *Clarendon Investigations*. At the end of the lane was a dingy concrete fortress with barred windows and a black steel door. Fading plastic plaques announced that this cramped building housed the registered offices of Padcon Holdings and four other companies.

Séamus had expected something more imposing. He pressed the plastic bell, which bore the name FRIEDLAND: a name well known to him from his early years with Theresa. Friedland made plastic bells. Tenants were expected to insert their own names in the clear plastic slot. Many did not bother doing so.

'Yeah?' The intercom projected a woman's voice. 'Who is it?'

'Is Mr Connolly in?'

'Nope. What can I do for you?'

'I was looking for Mr Connolly.'

'And you are?'

'Séamus Joyce.'

'From Finer Small Campuses of the Western World?'

'Not exactly. I'm advising them on –'

'Drop dead.'

He breathed in. 'Excuse me?'

'Be missing. Pat Connolly will not see you. He is not available. You can tell them. We do not appreciate being taken for a ride.'

11

In Wicklow Street sat a broad-nosed man with a small hat and stubby fingers, squeezing the life out of a wheezy accordion. Séamus loitered, pretending to price watches in a jeweller's window. After a few minutes he moved to another window, closer to the performer. Romanian folk dances, slow laments, popular tunes half a century old were coaxed and sucked deep inside the lungs of the instrument and lost in its troubled airways until flying buttons launched them brilliantly into the faint babble of surrounding commericial noise. The man was expressionless, blind to the indifference of his surroundings, playing for himself and the music and the echoing street. His music accelerated, then dragged to a climax, but strangely, instead of gaining volume, it grew quieter and quieter and then still quieter. He lifted his heel, less than an inch, and brought it down on the main rhythmic accent like a conductor giving the downbeat to a great symphony orchestra. Nobody noticed. The authentic musician stood up, packed his instrument and walked morosely through the crowd, passing fashion shoppers, fake performers with backing tapes, and a string quartet scrawling through the first arpeggios of *Eine Kleine Nachtmusik*.

Séamus bought an *Evening Herald* from the vendor at the bottom of Grafton Street. The main story concerned planning tribunals: the amnesia epidemic showed no sign of abating. New sufferers were being infected every day. On Suffolk Street he slipped into Nude and bought a small bottled smoothie. The high-ceilinged room pulsed with percussion recorded in a stadium acoustic; the clientèle ranged from young students to middle-aged matrons almost as old as himself. He took his drink and sat at a high stool inside the plate-glass front window, watching the world go by: Dubliners of varied shapes and colours, visitors from many lands, flowing to and fro between the Molly Malone statue and the old Anglican church on the corner which now served as the headquarters of Dublin Tourism. He remembered long ago, shopping for records in the tall building opposite, McCullough Pigott, a multi-level shop with everything from sheet music to grand pianos, and a band instrument section where hopeless young hopefuls plucked at what they could not play. Recently the shop had become a jeans emporium, then a general fashion and design store, Avoca, with a restaurant purveying tasteful nourishment to the chattering classes. Including himself, because Theresa had approved.

He remembered the scene he had witnessed one year earlier, looking through this same window: a boy and girl playfully embracing on the pavement, directly outside Nude, watched by all four of their parents. The girl twisted away. The boy reached his long arms around her. But they weren't embracing, and those weren't their parents. The boy was trying to throw her to the ground, trying to wrest her iPod from her grasp. He was tall and gangling; she was strong and compact. She planted her feet firmly and hunched against him. The predator had picked the wrong victim. One of the older couples took a faltering step forward. The boy gave up in disgust, pulled away with a jeering gargoyle's face, loped slowly across the roadway, pausing to fling back at her the earpieces and leads that he had yanked from the iPod but now disdained to keep. Calling out something inaudible, the boy ran in slow motion along the opposite pavement, his awkward movements suggesting weakness, motor impairment or the action of narcotics in the body. Nobody moved to follow. The girl stood indignant, being patted and reassured by the older people. She walked away firmly in the opposite direction. It was over in seconds, and it had all happened in silence for Séamus, marooned behind his plate glass. He had sipped his coffee, saddened by the cruel futility of the failed mugging, by his own inability to react in time to help. What he had seen on that afternoon was a spin-off from the drugs industry that caused weakened young men to harass their fellow citizens in the hope of raising money for tainted supplies. That was what the Irish Drugs Enforcement Agency had been set up to prevent. That was the larger disease that he had failed to stop.

'Don't blame things on yourself,' the stupid counsellor in

Germany had said during their second session. 'It is unfair, and it is also a form of self-engrossment.'

'Should I feel guilty about that?' Séamus had asked.

'Feeling guilty is just another method of claiming to be better than in effect you are,' she had replied, deadpan.

12

Having told Burren that he was buying clothes, he treated himself to a blue shirt and green silk tie in Kennedy & McSharry. It reminded him of the understated drapers' shops of his youth. They gave him a paper shopping bag big enough to fit Cregan's large white envelope, which he was still carrying around unopened, and which was beginning to look a little grubby. Carrying the shopping bag by way of justification, he hailed a taxi on Dame Street and returned to King's College through heavy late-afternoon traffic. The driver's taste in music ran to easy listening, but Séamus was glad of the distraction. They went by Christ Church and Kilmainham: another version of dear old tumbledown Dublin now tarted up and reconstituted. It was a dusty afternoon, unrelieved by rain.

Once again he travelled up the beech-lined drive of King's, turning and crunching to a halt on the gravel in front of the President's House, shaded from the sinking sun by the mass of the main buildings.

He looked into the cloisters, hoping to see Burren and apologize for having given him the slip. Instead there was Quaid, talking animatedly to a lanky young man, craggy but thin, clad in worn denim, old-fashioned tortoiseshell spectacles sliding down his prominent nose. The young man seemed too old to be an undergraduate, yet he appeared to be excusing himself for the non-delivery of a term essay. Quaid was agreeing with him that the essay in question, being on a popular poetaster of the 1940s, was not worth doing, despite which he was insisting that it must be done. Séamus slipped away, but not fast enough. Quaid summoned him to his side, introduced him sonorously: 'Fergus Kilpatrick, Séamus Joyce. And vicey versy.' The younger man blinked vaguely through his glasses; he looked like a weedy middleweight boxer who has fought one bout too many. 'Mr Joyce is an inspector sent by Finer Small Campuses of the Western World to report upon our arcane practices. Burren was detailed to keep tabs on him. Joyce gave Burren the slip. Burren's in the doghouse!' Quaid turned to Séamus. 'Nobody knows where you've been. Blessèd Oliver Cregan is climbing the walls, like Dracula.'

'I nipped into town,' Séamus said. 'I needed a tie. McKinley is taking me to dinner.'

'Burren's in the boozer, licking his wounds. Come on.'

Quaid led the way around the cloisters and escorted them out through the far door into what Séamus realized had once been the farmyard where the College's daily meat had been slaughtered and sliced. He remembered it as a squalid unhygienic precinct. The blood had been washed from the cobbles and the stables turned into something bearing a passing resemblance to a country pub. Over the door was a sign: KING WILLIAM III. There were horseshoes and saddles by way of decoration, and even an old-fashioned glass case containing a deceased Liffey salmon. Students were crammed around the bar. The noise level was high. There was no sign of Burren.

'Let me introduce you to some of our leading lights,' Quaid shouted, reeling off the names of six students, male and female, whom he described as the committee of the Rational Society. Séamus remembered the Rational Society, known in his day as the Rat and Mouse Club. Rationality had been far from its practices.

'Liquidating the assets,' Fergus Kilpatrick shouted into

Séamus's ear, a little more loudly than was necessary. 'We've got to talk to Séamus Joyce,' he called out to the company in a real-Dub accent that sat slightly awkwardly with his creaky voice. 'He's an inspector. Wants to know all about Quaid's teaching.' Kilpatrick's eyes were bright, but lacked a clear focus.

'Teaching?' Quaid was scornful. 'What teaching? I don't *teach*.'

'That's so true?' said an American girl. 'I been to your classes three times and they were like *cancelled*? Then I stayed in bed this morning and you taught *poetry*?'

'The money we're paying,' another American girl said, 'there ought to be teaching.'

'If you want to be taught,' Quaid riposted, 'try my illustrious superior, Professor De Soto.' He gestured to a broken man with bloodshot eyes, hunched over a whiskey glass. 'Whether Paddy the Stoat knows anything worth knowing may be a matter for debate, but he's ever so willing.'

'I do know something,' the red-eyed man objected. His was a sonorous voice, English-accented, which carried through the loud babble. 'I know the difference between scholarship and journalism. I know what it means to earn one's wages honestly. I know the difference between doing the job and bellyaching about it.'

'Not mutually exclusive,' Quaid said.

'And when you are reporting to your paymasters' – De Soto fixed Séamus with a sullen stare – 'you might mention that some of us are still devoted to the pursuit of knowledge like a sinking star, and its transmission to the younger generation.' He might have made a good actor.

'However misguided the attempt,' Quaid put in, to egg him on.

'That's the point,' De Soto insisted, still glaring at Séamus. 'Misguided. That's what academic freedom means: working without guidance. Being your own guide. Some of us think what we do has some value. We do not need to whore after new gods. The old orthodoxy got everything arseways. Or so the new orthodoxy believes. But why should the new orthodoxy be any more infallible than the old?'

This was mere ranting. Séamus made no effort to respond. 'Your pint,' said the barman, placing a glass of Guinness in front of him.

Séamus had not ordered a drink. He smiled vaguely around, trying to identify his benefactor, and raised his glass, as did the two American girls beside him. They appeared to be drinking Coke. A photographic flash went off. The camera was held by a smiling lad with a shaven head, whom Kilpatrick introduced as the chief photographer of the *King's Chronicle*. 'Known as the *Chronic*,' he explained. 'Published whenever there's news. I'm the editor, actually.'

Séamus sipped his pint and parried the students' questions about his time with the Irish Drugs Enforcement Agency. Somebody had been spreading his fame. The American girls told him that there were drugs on the campus, cheaper and better than back home.

'You went away,' called a mournful voice. Burren had fought his way through the crowd and was closing in on Séamus. 'You promised you'd wait.'

'Didn't want to take up your day.'

'Bad Burren!' Quaid chided. 'Left his post on the burning deck. Neglectful, derelictious Burren!'

'Time to go, Satchmo,' Burren said wearily. 'Finish your drink. Derry McKinley is waiting to take you to dinner. I'm to bring you in handcuffs. We will not have our hospitality evaded.' Despite Séamus's escape, Burren seemed to be in better humour.

The shaven lad flashed his camera again, this time including Fergus Kilpatrick in the picture beside Séamus. 'It's digital,' he said. 'We keep the best and do away with the rest.'

Séamus put his unfinished drink on the bar, picked up his

shopping bag and followed Burren meekly. As they crossed in the courtyard they passed a tall bony man dressed in black, bent double, spewing vomit on to the cobblestones while holding a whiskey glass upright with outstretched arm.

'Is he all right?'

'Allow me to introduce you,' Burren said. 'Condy Moran, writer in residence. Séamus Joyce, consultant. Sorry we can't stop.'

The writer nodded politely, without raising his head.

'What does he write?' Séamus asked as they moved away.

'Fiction.' Burren was hurrying, pushing doors. He elaborated without slowing down: 'More precisely, three short stories and an autobiographical novel, all about coming of age in rural Ireland. The novel is almost ready for publication, after twenty-eight years. Eagerly awaited. Extracts appeared, in the form of the three short stories, but he lost the typescript in the Ringsend floods. He's trying to reconstruct it during his residency here.'

'Three stories? One unpublished novel? That makes him a writer?'

'Of course. It's like being a murderer. You don't have to keep doing it to retain the title. Writer in residence is a new position invented by President Cregan. Who chose the first incumbent himself. They attended the same secondary school, apparently, though not at the same time. Condy Moran is much admired in some quarters. Not all. De Soto is not pleased. According to him, the man's illiterate. Even in an age when "artist" is a synonym for "failed craftsman", he can frequently be heard to say Condy does not cut the mustard. On this particular point, Quaid agrees with his Head of Department. Mediocrity, masked by incontinence, is the Quaid verdict. Personally, I find Condy rather poetic. Mind the step.'

They rounded a corner, passed under an archway, and were greeted by Derry McKinley, smiling with broad indulgence.

13

McKinley drove a leather-bound Jeep Cherokee with music from the vibraphone of Gary Burton. On the way into town he talked about his visit to the jazz festival in Montreux. Next year he hoped to go to Newport, Rhode Island.

He had invited Fionnuala to join them, but she was tied up. Might make it later.

He found a parking place quite close to Modicum. The restaurant was furnished in a stark style, featuring bright lights and cheap veneers, as though to suggest that its food was decor enough. Séamus was not in the mood to enjoy an evening out. He was edgy after his overcrowded day. McKinley ordered a bottle of Californian Chardonnay, fielded the homage of another diner, placed their order with a convincing French waiter and gossiped sotto voce about the internal politics of the Department of Justice, the demise of the Irish Drugs Enforcement Agency and the subsequent career of the disgraced Minister for Justice as a backbench TD. McKinley was exceptionally well informed on each of these points.

It emerged naturally from the one-sided conversation that McKinley was a major player in Dublin's business world, with an interest in some notable high-tech ventures. Although never an 'A' student, he had always rated his undergrad experience as the happiest time of his life, which was why he needed to put something back – a phrase that always conjured up in Séamus's mind a dinner guest who has been caught pocketing the spoons.

It was Derry McKinley's desire to make a difference that had led him to join the College trustees. 'The problem, put simply, was cash. *Radix malorum*.' The Latin tag jarred.

Séamus sat back to listen. King's College needed serious money, McKinley explained, if it was to hack it as a niche research university, but it had been cash-starved for so long, its staff so degraded, that it had simply forgotten how to compete. KCD grant applications got turned down by return of post. They lacked credibility when compared with the superb standards of other Irish institutions. 'I'm going to level with you, Séamus,' McKinley said. 'We may go back to William the Third, but King's College, to be frank, doesn't measure up today. At best, we're mediocre. We don't fit the category. And it's chicken and egg. You don't get the grants, you can't get the staff. Under President Maxwell, the place stagnated. That's why Cregan had to go for complete regime change in his first hundred days. He hit them hard, but they're beginning to respond. To achieve excellence, we need to start with regeneration. Senior guys have got to perform. *Hic et nunc.* Talk the talk, walk the walk. *Facta non verba.* Back to the drawing board. Year Zero. That's why we're training them. Sending them on seminars, on bonding weekends. Teaching them how to eyeball the donors. We've got to raise the cash to hire the next generation. That's why we need Oliver Cregan in the hot seat.' He stuffed another forkful of hors d'oeuvre into his busy jaws. 'Where do we go from here? That's the question.'

Séamus nodded politely. 'And how do the staff take to their new President?'

McKinley snorted. 'Knee-jerk academic resistance to authority. Professors make the elementary mistake of thinking the smart guy should be running the shop. He that is good with a hammer tends to think everything is a nail.'

'Who said that?'

'Abraham Maslow. What's more, it's true. Those professors were clever boys and girls at school. They were "A" students in college. That's their stock in trade. Can't handle real life, where being smart is not enough. There are exceptions, of course.'

'Of course.'

'You know what they say: changing a university is like moving a cemetery. You don't get much help from the residents.'

Séamus tried to probe beyond the sound bites. 'How do you deal with the established figures in the various faculties? Deans, heads, professors? Surely they dig their heels in?'

'The solution is childishly simple,' McKinley smiled. 'We go around them. Set up task forces, change management teams, consultation channels, working parties. All very informal, all appointed by us. Status unclear. A good mix of respected elders and ambitious mid-career guys. They tend to do what we want. Coalition of the willing. And their colleagues tend to trust them. You know the old Turkish proverb? "When the axe came into the forest, the trees said, 'At least the handle is one of us'".'

'Never heard that.'

'De Soto sent it around College on an email, and somebody copied it to Oliver. Gave us a good old laugh at the team meeting. We traced it back on the web to a lefty intellectual. Dunlop? Some such name. An Australian.'

'You're part of Cregan's management team?'

McKinley laughed. 'No way, José! Trustee, non-executive board member. I have my business to run. I'm an advisor. *Amicus curiae*. I give Cregan the benefit of my experience. Actually, it's starting to work. We're rebranding King's. Raising the cash for exciting capital projects.'

He extracted a sheet of paper from his pocket, unfolded it. A colour photocopy, it showed an artist's impression of a mall of glassy buildings leading up to the Forde Centre. 'Preliminary plans,' he said. 'Come up and see my etchings tomorrow morning, and I'll show you the whole thing. We're doing a complete design job. Buildings, colour schemes, signage, livery, stationery, serviettes, guest packs, the lot. No detail too small to receive the magical King's touch.'

'What's that circular building at the end of the row?'

'Interfaith centre, to replace the chapel. The old Gothic Revival chapel becomes the new King's College dining hall. A thing of beauty, to rival Harry Potter's hall in Christ Church, Oxford. Having a decent hall with a high table and stained-glass windows will enable us to market the "King's Dublin Experience" to American retirees in the summer season. A residential course, creating added value for our accommodation offering. We'll have leading lecturers from Irish and British universities, covering all aspects of European culture. It'll pay for itself inside five years.'

'Do you think you'll get planning permission for all those buildings, and even for changing the original chapel?'

McKinley laughed his confident laugh. 'Oh, we think we'll manage that.'

'And how are you going to pay for the works?'

'We've brought major donors on board. They're excited by our development plans. Some very substantial endowments are in the offing. Cregan's own Institute for the Study of Business Culture is already well-funded. It's about to launch its own MBA in Entrepreneurial Change and Innovation. A first in these parts. Top young researchers from stateside. We're pitching for a partnership with the Milan Business School, one of the finest in south-east Michigan. Now, what's Jeremy Quaid been saying to you?'

'Quaid hasn't changed.'

'Quaid has long been a disappointment,' McKinley agreed. 'What was he telling you?'

'Much the same as yourself.'

'No need to be cagey, Séamus. You're among friends. What was he saying?' McKinley chuckled. 'Did he mention a fur coat?'

Séamus admitted that he had.

'Thought as much. Quaid has his routines. He does them word for word, for all who will listen. He didn't say anything else?'

Séamus changed the subject. 'Those consultants – why so many?'

'They have to eat. We have to hire them. When the Blair government put up sixty million pounds sterling to boost teaching standards in British universities, consultants pocketed one-third of that money. Twenty million! Our government is going down the same road. It's about transparency.' McKinley refilled Séamus's glass. 'They waste our money in public, lest we might waste it in secret. Same principle as the planning tribunals.'

'Tell me about the people I met this morning. AI?'

'Top men in their fields, Séamus. They've done reports for some of the up-and-coming universities of Britain: Winchester, Newmarket, Harwich. Very perceptive chaps. We've had visits from other eminent consultants. Apart from yourself, I mean. Let me tell you the real trick, though.' He leaned forward. 'Commission a raft of reports, then pick the bits that suit.'

The second course arrived with a flourish, accompanied by the grilled pumpkin crisps for which Modicum was justly famed. McKinley switched to an unexpected topic: 'Your dad, Séamus. Gentleman of the old school. We were acquainted, you know.'

'Really?'

'You were young when he died.'

'How did you know him?'

'I played a bit of Gaelic for a while with some lads in the Department of Agriculture, after I left the seminary. Your dad was a keen supporter. Didn't play himself, but loved coming to the games.' McKinley took a small photographic print from an inside pocket. There was the tall figure of Séamus's father, clad in a dark suit, wreathed in smiles, flanked by sunny young men in old-style sporting gear. 'Snapped in Claremorris,' McKinley said. 'Being an Inspector, your dad had a car. One of our steadiest fans.'

Séamus had never seen that photograph. His mother had destroyed all images of her late husband. After his death there were none to be found, not even from the wedding. Later, Séamus's elder brother Daniel had made prints from a few negatives he had salvaged. Nothing so happy as this picture, though.

'Which one are you?' he asked.

'None of the above,' McKinley smiled. 'I'm the genius behind the camera. Kodak Brownie 127. You can keep that copy. It's just a sample from the old collection. Terribly sad, his passing. We know not the day nor the hour.'

Séamus remembered the funeral, his mother's silence, the grimness of his aunts, Daniel in awkward new clothes. His father had died in Dublin and his body had been brought home for the funeral. Interminable rain.

'Your dad would have been proud of you,' McKinley continued, pouring more wine. 'Taking your degree while holding down a civil service job. And what a result! Still talked about in King's. They don't often get students as good as you. Pity there was so little postgrad done *in illo tempore*. Your English professor used to say you were the one that got away.'

He shuddered at the thought of that lugubrious fool, author of *The Catholic Message of Christopher Marlowe*. Postgraduate research under his aegis would have been a dismal prospect. Young lecturers mocked him behind his back; Quaid mocked him to his face.

'Of course there was the problem with Fionnuala,' McKinley went on, joining his fingertips like the buttresses of a Gothic cathedral. 'Her uncle was an eminent churchman, so it was hushed up. Gaskell got out while the going was good.'

Séamus was not quite following. He said nothing. No doubt there was some rationale to McKinley's habit of skipping from topic to topic, but it made him an uncomfortable host. Séamus was reminded of wrestlers circling each other, reaching out hands and retracting them, looking for the grip that would decide the contest.

'It wasn't just Gaskell's peccadilloes,' McKinley continued, unasked. 'Fionnuala was vulnerable too. Apart from the strait-laced morality of the day, there was the rumour that she'd been given a quick peek at the final exam papers. That would have called the quality of her degree into question. To say nothing of her suitability for postgrad. Way back then, a word from the Monsignor was enough to nix it. Nowadays we'd have a tribunal of enquiry and senior counsel and I don't know what-all. If anything had been proven against Fionnuala, then all her friends would have been suspect too. Which would have been tough on the guys who'd played by the rules.'

Séamus had seen no previews of examination papers. He had done undeservedly well in all three of his subjects, owing purely to his youthful talent for memorizing and regurgitating agreed facts and received opinions. He had not been attracted to postgraduate research. In any case, his scholarship had required him to return to full-time civil service work.

McKinley shook his head, as though responding to another intervention by Séamus. 'It's hard on Fionnuala, you know, that allegation still knocking around, decades later, without ever being properly tested. Admittedly, standards were lax in those days. Few of the staff were research-active. Some of them wasted their time on aimless reading. Some played golf. One man ran a flower stall in Smithfield.' He refilled Séamus's glass, pushed back his chair, went into expository mode, like a television presenter walking towards a camera. 'Today we've got quality assurance, quality improvement and a standards committee chaired by President Cregan himself. Everything is metered. An objective system for research appraisal, based on what they publish and where they publish, how many students they supervise, and the precise amount of grant money they personally attract. Nowhere to hide any more.'

He paused to allow Séamus to speak. Séamus, resigned to being talked at, said nothing. McKinley resumed: 'On the teaching side, we have student surveys, observation, statistical tracking, regular audits, not to mention departmental reviews and benchmarking. Everyone's got their ten hours of admin. Not that they have to do well under every heading. We allow for individual variability. *Non omnia possumus omnes*, as the man said. I've read the guidelines laid down by Finer Small Campuses, and let me tell you, Séamus, we already meet those standards.'

Séamus held his peace.

'The likes of Gaskell,' McKinley continued, 'wouldn't get away with it today. They know they're being watched. Your American friends have nothing to fear. They can send us their sons and daughters and they'll get them back in the same condition in which they reached us. Whatever that might be.' Complicit smirk. 'We'll provide the security levels, we'll deliver the facilities for religious practice, Internet access, whatever. We'll go the extra kilometre. And there's no worries if they want to nominate staff to our pastoral care services. We're going to get a dedicated official for Asian students, no reason why we shouldn't have one for the North Americans. That said, we're not to be pushed around. There's a proud independent tradition here. We've got support in the community. King's College has the best PR company in the business, by which I mean' – he paused for effect – 'my own. The Billings Advertising and Public Relations Partnership. Senior partner: you're looking at him. How's that for a declaration of interest? Plus we've got friends. You saw Seán Forde here today. One of the most influential men in Ireland. Anyone thinks King's College is a pushover has another think coming.'

'I'm not aware of anyone trying to push you over.' Séamus drained his glass. He was drinking too much. 'There seems to be a certain paranoia afoot.'

'Well, you know what they say. Just because you're

paranoid –' He was interrupted by the chiming of his phone, which tonight was set to play 'Take the "A" Train'. He listened for a moment, smiling. 'Yes, pet, we're still here,' he said. 'Don't worry about double yellow lines. Traffic wardens are tucked up in bed.'

He waved his fingers like a man playing the concert harp. A waiter materialized. 'Dessert menus, please! Now, what have we here?' McKinley recited a list of delicacies in lamentable French. The waiter kept a straight face.

'Nothing for me, thanks,' Séamus said.

'Do try the cheese. And a little cognac, perhaps? Or a single malt? Spot of Calvados? Oh, who's come to join us for a nightcap?'

Séamus glanced up to see Fionnuala, looking strained in a tight black dress.

14

When they parked outside the President's House, it was not far short of midnight. Séamus had drunk a considerable amount of chemically enhanced Chardonnay during McKinley's monologues, followed by two generous measures of Armagnac after Fionnuala's arrival. He was suffering from a slight pressure headache.

McKinley, citing a dawn meeting in County Kildare, had asked Fionnuala to drive Séamus home. Fionnuala opened the front door of the President's House with an electronic key of her own. She had to collect documents from Cregan's study. For some reason, Séamus did not believe her. He said goodnight. She took his hand in her faltering grip, walked away carefully across the dark hall.

The house was quiet. He climbed the stairs and let himself into the guest quarters. Somewhere in the overnight bag was his supply of paracetamol. The drinks tray had whiskey and gin, but the supply of bottled water had not been replenished. Hynes was falling down on the job. He found the paracetamol and knocked back two pills with a glass of tap water. It tasted like poison. He had forgotten the sour taste of the King's College pipes.

He used the bathroom, started to get undressed, put his watch and tie on the bedside locker, hung his jacket on the back of a chair.

Why was he so wide awake? Was it the effect of coming home to Ireland after exile, or being back in his old university and the disaster of his youth? Or the after-effect of the jangling stories he had heard during the course of the day?

What had he learned? King's College seemed to be living under condemnation, but with hopes of reprieve and signs of frantic but meaningless activity. Something similar to what had allegedly happened in Saigon hospitals towards the end of the Vietnam war, where purposeful treatment was suspended and patients died, aimlessness being a rational but fatal response to uncertainty. Always supposing that Séamus had not been misinformed by cunning propagandists. The syndrome was not confined to lower ranks: witness McKinley's praise and condemnation of the College in the same breath.

Fionnuala had drunk two large measures of Talisker in quick succession. She had been ill at ease, joining awkwardly in McKinley's modified stream of gossip. This was probably because the subject matter was uncomfortably close to herself. Even in her declining years, she was still central to the jealousies and tensions of the place. Where had she gone after meeting him on his first morning? Why had she told him to wait? Why had she changed her mind? He should have asked her in the car, but it would have seemed intrusive. Where was she now?

He forced himself to think back over the whole two days since his arrival in Dublin, and tried to retrieve his first impressions without allowing them to be coloured by other people's hindsight. Quaid's hatred of Cregan was predictable enough. He had articulated it with unusual venom, but others probably shared it. Séamus knew the mechanism. Anyone receiving a favour from the top man would accept it as nothing more than was due. Those failing to receive a favour would take it as a personal slight. Over time, therefore, any President is likely to become unpopular, especially if a facile impression of future largesse has been propagated, and if money is being spent on luxuries like good wine and cars.

Cregan's unopened white envelope was still in the shopping bag. He took it out, opened it. Like the envelope, the document that it contained was marked *Confidential*. Titled A FUTURE FOR KING'S, it presented the personal thoughts of President Cregan on the state of the College (mediocre), its future (brilliant) and the path towards that future (authoritarian). From a cursory glance through the pages – there was no executive summary – Séamus noticed some extremely unflattering appraisals of departments and even individuals within the College. If Cregan was to achieve his stated objective of positioning the College as Ireland's top liberal arts institution and a world leader in social and cultural research, a number of these unproductive colleagues would have to be induced to take early retirement. Others would be demoted from positions of responsibility and redeployed to service functions. Four of the proposed victims were identified; the only name he recognized was Professor De Soto. A new system of sponsored chairs would infuse the College with new blood at the highest level. There would be a new system of probation and tenure. There would be random audits of teaching quality, and individual inspections of academic output modelled on the UK Research Assessment Exercise. There would be new state-of-the-art facilities and dedicated buildings. But only the best would get to work in them. Cregan had appended a handwritten note on the final page:

Séamus — As you can see I've been very frank here. I wanted to share my private thoughts with you, so that you can appreciate what is at stake in your old college, and advise Sen. Hinckley accordingly. Naturally, I rely on your discretion not to reveal any of the details or names contained herein. One does not want to cause unnecessary hurt. I'd value your views. Best, Oliver.

This seemed to be little more than the fantasies of regeneration and excellence lately proclaimed by McKinley in the restaurant. Nothing extra worth adding. All dependent on money from fairy godmothers. Of whom there were indeed some to be found. He folded Cregan's private thoughts and slipped them in the inside pocket of his blazer. Banal though it was, the document could provide some useful ammunition for the following day's lunch with the President. He washed his hands, switched off the lights, took off some of his clothes, lay down, closed his eyes. The beating continued between his temples: an empty message transmitted on tribal drums, travelling no distance at all, inside his own skull. There was no way for the message to escape. Sender and recipient were too close together.

He had drunk far too much. Weakness of character, duly and swiftly punished.

Another thought came from nowhere. McKinley had spiked his drink. He was poisoned. He was going to die.

Nonsense.

How long he dozed he could not tell. He went from thinking over his meetings at the College to running around silent cloisters, searching for the source. Of what? Nobody could tell him, but it was essential that he find it, and drink deeply of the antidote. Fight his way towards it, if that was what it took. In his dream, he was parched.

He opened his eyes. In the penumbra a soft shape was circling. A bedside lamp flicked into light. Fionnuala was frowning as she closed in, perched on the edge of his bed, leaned forward, extended her arms like a swimmer, encircled his neck. Delicate scents of lavender soap and malt whisky.

Unhelpful thoughts shuffled slowly through his mind. Did she keep her soap in Cregan's bathroom? Was Cregan particularly fond of lavender? Where was Cregan now? How long had he been asleep? He was buzzing all over. The headache was crouched in the background, waiting to spring.

'What brings you here?' A superfluous question.

'Don't ask.' She nibbled his ear lobe. He wished he had washed it.

'Where's Cregan?'

'Don't worry about him.'

'Who are you supposed to be controlling?'

'What?' She paused, puzzled.

'The voice on your answering machine. While I was waiting in your office. Am I the one you're to keep quiet? Stop me foostering?' He wanted to shout. His words were barely audible.

She sighed, resentful at the distraction. 'I haven't been back in my office. Something came up. I haven't heard the message.'

'A man's voice. Country accent. Giving you instructions. Not the President. Nobody I've met. We've got to talk.'

'Not now.' Fionnuala's lips pressed on his. She had brushed her hair, just for him. He was back in the last century, the intervening years fading silently away. She held his head and kissed him again. Suffocation, punishment for past desire. 'About time,' she whispered.

'But you never,' he managed to say, 'had the slightest inclination –'

'You didn't know me. I was innocent.'

'Despite Gaskell?'

She shrugged her shoulders. 'He took advantage. Of me and others. Enough about that.' She undid her dress, pulled it over her head, bore down on him again. He remembered

Theresa, and the paths his life had taken. He was filled with accumulated sorrow like a well of bitter water. He thought of Heidi's thin muscular frame, and plump Guido.

Fionnuala was bigger than he had imagined. Had he imagined? Apparently so. He was thinking now of South Sea islands and Gauguin's paintings, fretting about the extinction of turtles and about faithlessness and contraception and abortion and venereal disease and suitable names for twins. The last of the great romantics. Fionnuala drew herself upright, ran her fingers through her hair. Naked, she looked magnificent, like an African lioness about to consume a zebra. And she knew how well she looked. But he could sense the sadness too, the pressure of regret. She was going through the motions.

An electric bell rang in the distance. She stopped. 'I can't,' she whispered. 'I can't.' The bell rang a second time. She stepped from the bed and was gone, slipping the black dress over her head as she padded barefoot from the darkened room.

Nothing had happened. Not for the first time.

Séamus lay motionless for several minutes, wondering if he had dreamed it. He wanted to ask why.

She was not coming back. That much he knew.

His headache had not cleared. Paracetamol was useless. He had drunk too deep, and it had turned his blood sour. No question of sleep. He sat on the edge of his bed for a minute, remembering another time, when Fionnuala had promised to go with him to hear the Ronnie Scott Big Band, playing in the Examination Hall at Trinity College, and he waited and waited for her at Front Gate, watching the dark green buses go by, and finally went in to the concert three-quarters of an hour late. Ronnie Scott's patter was better than his music.

Meanwhile, Fionnuala had probably been in bed with Harold Gaskell.

He heard a door closing somewhere near at hand.

The room was unbearable.

He filled another glass of water in the bathroom, took a sip, felt poisoned, poured the rest away. King's College tap water was infested with wormwood.

She had left his bedroom door ajar. He pulled on some clothes, went to the door and listened. No sound. He stepped out on to the landing. There were footsteps downstairs, then the sound of the heavy front door, opening and clicking shut.

He thought of summoning Hynes and asking for fresh supplies of water. Did the old rascal know what had happened in the bedroom?

He remembered the vending machine in the cloisters selling drinks. Probably including bottled water. He slipped into his shoes, checked that the electronic key was still in his blazer pocket, found some coins, left the room, went downstairs. No sign of Fionnuala. She must have been the one who had clicked the front door shut. He opened it, saw nobody.

Not that he was looking for her.

Of course not.

No sound anywhere. He shut the front door behind him. There was coldness in the night air.

15

The vending machine was amply stocked with cola, orange squash and Eau'Reilly water. He fed in his coins and retrieved three half-litre bottles.

Fight fire with fire, drink with drink. If he flushed himself out with water, he might be able to carry on. He must find a computer, start drafting the headings of his report.

Why was he fooling himself with thoughts of work? Fionnuala was so beautiful. Still carrying the traces of her youth.

Why should he feel guilty? Women can happen to anyone.

There was nobody about in the quadrangle. Not a soul. Then, as he walked back through the dark cloisters, cradling his three bottles in the crook of his arm, the Mephistophelean figure of Quaid hove once more into view, angular and crabbed as it had been at dawn the day before.

Quaid was the inevitable ghost. If one stabbed him to death, he would rise from the grave, still talking.

'Sleepless as myself? Come and have some tea.' Quaid was finishing a cigarette. Séamus began to construct a chain of explanation for this. Suppose Quaid was given to sleeping in his study, and suppose the study was a room not officially designated as residential, then, under the wise legislation introduced by an enlightened Minister for Health, Quaid would not be legally entitled to smoke there. Or perhaps he himself wanted to keep his room smoke-free, or was trying to quit smoking. Any of these hypotheses would explain his hovering presence. Equally, Quaid might be a man who could not stand his own company, and used cigarette breaks in public places as a desperate expedient for meeting people. Séamus shook his head. 'Tea? No, thanks. I've got water. I'm going back to bed.'

Quaid pointed an accusing finger. 'You've been on the town with McKinley. Did he take you to Laptops?'

'Modicum.'

'More staid than his usual style, then. Derry likes his slap and tickle. Food all right?'

'Excellent, thanks.'

'You missed a good evening here. Rational Society meeting in the old lecture theatre in Centenary Court. The motion for debate was "That We Don't Need No Education". The star speakers were Cregan and the Minister for Finance, both of whom strongly hold with that proposition. Forde was guest of honour.'

Séamus coughed and made shuffling-away gestures, but

Quaid, an old hand at holding an audience, simply fixed him with his piercing gaze and inhaled like a Wagnerian tenor. The trouble with trying to escape from Quaid, Séamus decided, was that you could never be quite sure that he wasn't going to say something interesting. 'Our mad German professor turned up,' he recounted, 'defying a court order that's supposed to keep her seven leagues away, and heckled not only Blessèd Oliver Cregan but also the Minister, including some gross personal abuse in her remarks. I'm afraid she made some rather wounding allegations about the conduct of College business. Gosh, I hope nothing I said provided her with ammunition.' Quaid's eyes were dancing. 'She accused Cregan of nepotism, malversation, false accounting and sexual harassment, particularly of herself. Professor Mardersteig looks exactly like the Red Queen out of *Alice*, which lent an extra layer of hilarity. Students thought they'd died and gone to heaven. She started bellowing about the new buildings, and how Cregan was alienating College lands for private gain. All quite unfair, I assure you. She further alleged that Andy O'Neill had been bludgeoned to death, not drowned, and strongly hinted that Cregan was mixed up in it. Hynes was attending the meeting as a sort of presidential escort, and tried to organize the porters to throw the old bag out. She blacked the eye of McEntaggart, a daft, blameless creature who came here fifty years ago as a messenger boy and has risen to the dizzying heights of deputy head of security. At which juncture the Minister's bodyguards, great big bruisers from the Special Branch, intervened and dragged her kicking and screaming from the hall. She was threatening to have the law on them and making strange and interesting allegations about Cregan selling off the College silverware to a collector on Long Island. Can you believe it?'

'Not particularly.'

'Nor can I! My Head of Department, drunk as a skunk, intervened from the floor with a moving speech in favour of great books and big ideas. He denounced, sadly without naming them, those ambitious academics who tend to publish the same piddling pseudo-research over and over, with minor alterations. He accused them of topic-squatting, salami-slicing, self-plagiarism and rampant ASD.' Séamus looked blank, thereby allowing Quaid to keep expounding: 'Attention Surplus Disorder. Perennial disease of academics. Some of the poor dears spend a lifetime researching things that are worth no more than a few days' casual reading, simply because when they sink their tiny teeth into a topic, they get stuck and can't let go. Like the Amazonian candiru or toothpick-fish. You know –'

Séamus winced. 'I know.'

'Our latest generation of high-flyers deliberately infect themselves with ASD and spin around in ever-diminishing circles. They select some trendy body of crap and chip away at it like a budgerigar with a cuttlefish bone. Their cages are littered with feathers, droppings, husks, all packaged into small bite-sized balls.'

'Well, I must be off,' Séamus said, as Quaid continued further in the same vein, denouncing what he called painting-by-numbers, one-trick ponies, inter-institutional frottage and other pitfalls of the new research culture. Then the cloisters echoed with the sound of feet, and Hynes rounded the corner. His steps were unsteady, his hair dishevelled, his face wild and white, his mouth opening like a drowning man gasping for air. The eyes were empty. Breath rose from his chest like a creaking gate.

'Killed!' he mouthed.

'An age of academic fraud,' Quaid was saying.

'Who?' Séamus asked.

'The President,' Hynes breathed.

'The canon replaced by candy floss, our intellectual teeth are set on –' Quaid interrupted his flow, turned to face Hynes: 'Are you referring to Cregan?'

Hynes stared at him. 'Of course!'

'Dead, you say?'

'Yes!'

'Where?' Séamus asked.

'Downstairs. I've already telephoned for the Guards.'

Quaid's eyes opened wide. He looked at his watch.

Darkness

I

There was to be no sleep. Hynes walked quickly back the way he had come, as if being reeled in by some gigantic fishing line. They followed. Séamus's headache had suddenly lifted. He seemed to hear other feet, out of sight, but that was probably his heart. There was shouting in the distance, voices dropping as they approached. Before they had reached the corner of the cloister, there were blue flashing lights at an arched entrance. Unnaturally quick? No: a rapid response might be expected in the Phoenix Park, considering that the American Ambassador lived within a few hundred metres of King's College. But where were the campus security staff?

Heavy footsteps. A young policeman in a yellow reflective jacket: 'Where is he?'

Hynes stepped forward. 'This way, Guard.' His white face had aged twenty years.

'Who are you?'

'Personal assistant to the late President,' said Hynes, with stentorian dignity. 'Follow me.'

A small group of students had materialized. Where from? Were there student bedrooms in this part of the campus?

Hynes stumbled downstairs, switched on lights, flung open the door marked *Account's*, smoothed his white hair with shaking hands. 'I found him myself.'

The Guard hesitated on the threshold like a swimmer poised on a diving board. A sweet butcher's shop smell wafted out into the corridor.

Hynes reached in and found the light switch. Séamus

glanced into the office. On the Turkey carpet lay the distorted form of a suit, containing the stylized shape of a man, legs obscenely splayed, knees raised, one shoe missing, elbows clenched by his head. Death had reduced him to two dimensions: an empty composition. Séamus felt strangely embarrassed at intruding on the domain of the dead, being present in Cregan's absence.

There were physical traces of his former life: blood spattered in wheeling lines across the papers that littered the floor, strewn in a great curve from wall to wall, mingled with bits of a broken metal lamp standard. The static scene seemed to freeze all the explosive violence that had shaped it, just as a mountain range holds the memory of unimaginable forces clashing and grinding, millions of years back.

'Is there another door out of this room?' the Guard asked, looking at the cupboard doors.

'Not now,' Hynes said. 'There used to be, but it was blocked up.'

The Guard stepped back into the corridor, pushing the door shut behind him. His walkie-talkie was squawking. Help was on the way.

As though he had witnessed every second of Cregan's final struggle, Séamus saw in his mind the flickering silent movie of a man trying to escape, then defending himself from bone-crushing blows that shattered his defences and snuffed out his life.

Cregan's silence, on the far side of the door, was louder than all the growing noise around them, as a swelling group of students, male and female, clustered in the broad passageway. From their conversation, Séamus inferred that they had been drinking after hours in the student bar. Then there were some older people, presumably faculty members. None that he knew. No Fionnuala.

Séamus had almost stopped breathing. In sympathy with the corpse, he supposed. He was still clutching his water bottles. He drank from one, handed one to Quaid, placed the last of the three on a ledge beside the door.

Quaid drank from his bottle. He was uncharacteristically silent.

An ambulance crew was admitted to the office. A second yellow-clad Guard materialized and stood sentry.

Minutes later, a stocky man arrived, holding an old black leather bag. 'Show me,' he commanded, only to re-emerge after a moment, followed by the defeated ambulance men. 'Too late,' he remarked to nobody in particular.

Hynes pulled himself together and stood beside the Guard at the door.

'What's happened?' called one of the watching students. 'Another murder?'

'No comment,' Hynes said.

'It's the President, isn't it?'

'There will be a statement later.' Hynes saw a photographer beginning to take flash pictures, holding his camera aloft. Not the outside media, just the shaven lad from the student bar. 'What do you think you're at?' Hynes demanded, incandescent.

'Photography,' said the student photographer. 'I'm from the *Chronic*.'

'You need permission.'

'You're the man, Hynes,' said the photographer. 'You can give me all the permission I need.'

'But I deny you permission.'

'On what authority?'

'My own.'

'Since when –?'

'Silence!' Quaid's interjection was loud and authoritative. He stood in front of Hynes, facing the crowd. 'As the senior resident academic,' Quaid pitched his querulous voice with calm certainty, 'it falls to me to give instructions. Photography will cease. Mr Hynes, kindly telephone Professor Millington, and request his attendance. Instruct the man in the gate lodge to bar the way to outsiders.'

The photographer moved away, followed by the denim-clad student whom Séamus had met earlier. Fergus Kilpatrick. Editor of the *King's Chronicle*. The crowd parted to let them through. Séamus reflected that they had a saleable story tonight, if the professional media really were excluded.

A face that he recognized from his Justice years loomed above the rest. This was a craggy man of middle age, athletic in build. His square jaw and curly brown hair gave him the look of a comic-book hero. He paused beside Séamus and muttered, 'Joyce. Back from exile. What's your connection?'

'Consultancy. And yourself, Mike, what brings you north of the river?'

'Some of us in Harcourt Square think murder is a serious crime.' Inspector Mike Dineen, of the National Bureau of Criminal Investigation, tapped three times sharply on the door and disappeared into the accounts office.

2

Back in Quaid's room, Séamus crouched uncomfortably on a low stool. He realized that his feet had braced themselves as if ready to spring up. It was impossible to relax, with the image in his memory of Cregan's legs in their unnatural position, and the feeling of danger from the faint knowledge that a killer was at large, and the thought that if it could be anyone, then it could even be Quaid, who now emerged from the kitchen, bearing two mugs of tea, set one down beside Séamus, heaped two spoons of sugar into each mug. 'Shock,' he explained. 'Death. Antisocial. Tiring. Sugar will give you a kick.'

He was right. Séamus was hollowed out.

Quaid leaned against the back of the dirty sofa. 'How

appropriate. Oliver Cregan died by the trappings of authority.'

'How do you mean?'

'Our belovèd President was battered to death with St Malachi's mace. Didn't you notice?'

'I thought that was a lamp.'

'No, no. Our priceless heirloom, recently restored, now tragically vandalized.' Quaid's mouth smiled, but his eyes were blank.

'Who could have done it?'

'Many had cause to hate him,' Quaid said, his face a mask. 'Myself, for example, constantly rebuffed in my quest for advancement, driven beyond endurance. Inveigling the President to a midnight rendezvous, I finally extract a terrible revenge. But no' – Quaid spread his arms wide – 'it won't wash. Academics bitch, but rarely kill. That only happens in Golden Age detective stories, where bodies are found in libraries. Cregan has never been in a library.'

'Who did it, then?'

'Séamus Joyce. Ruthless drug baron, involved in a Yankee conspiracy to take over third-level education in Europe as part of a global plan to reduce the entire English-speaking world to imbecility. Better?'

'Not much.'

'Or Fionnuala Fagan,' Quaid continued, watching Séamus as he spoke. 'Cregan's part-time crumpet. Beguiled with worthless blandishments. Tonight he summoned her to the accounts office, had his wicked way with her on the rug and announced his intention to marry another. Fionnuala, losing her head, seized the first item that came to hand. They can be vicious when provoked.'

'Does that exhaust your natural inventiveness?'

'By no means. Mr Fergus Kilpatrick, whom you met today, has a finger in every student pie. He risks being turned out of College for embezzling the entertainment funds of the Ethical Society, spending them on drink, drugs and dissipation.

Fergus, in real life, served ten months for manslaughter. Fracas at a party. Another upper-class schoolboy died.'

'What do you mean, another?'

'Oh, Fergus is not as proletarian as he lets on. Family disowned him, of course. After his release, he went on to a stretch of homelessness and a well-developed addiction to narcotics. So what happened tonight? Cregan finds out about the missing funds, threatens to expose or expel him, and Fergus, seizing the first weapon that comes to hand –'

Even allowing for Quaid's twisted imagination, this seemed too bizarre a scenario. Still, murder does not invite a normal explanation.

Séamus went along with the game: 'How did the mace come to hand? Is it kept in the accounts office?'

'No, it lives in the storeroom.'

Séamus thought of the bullish young man who had confronted him in that corridor on the previous day. Another possible suspect.

'Who's in charge of it?'

Before Quaid could answer, there was a light rapping at the door. Fionnuala put her head into the room. 'Is it true?' she asked. Her face was white, her voice so hoarse as to be barely audible. Her cheeks were streaked with the marks of tears.

'Here, take my tea,' Quaid said softly. 'I haven't touched it.' Quaid's demeanour had changed to one of tender solicitude.

'Thank you.' She clasped it in her hands, sank on to the sofa, eyes downcast, looking at neither man. She was wearing a loose denim smock, not the black dress. A wild notion flashed through Séamus's head: having bloodied her black dress with Cregan's gore, she had gone to her study to change.

'The mace?' she whispered. 'He was killed with the mace?'

'Afraid so.' Quaid's face was set in its usual pained brightness. 'Ruined,' he added, and winced at his own indelicacy.

She nodded, as though confirming a widespread rumour. Her eyes stared into an invisible darkness.

The door swung open. Inspector Dineen filled the frame. His civilian sports jacket and corduroy trousers failed to cast any doubt on his profession. It was as if his bones were shaped to form a policeman.

'Hynes tipped me off,' he said. There was a menace in the man's physical presence, a feeling of force restrained. He reminded Séamus of a teacher from his primary school: a man of tensed muscular strength, whose moods had to be watched like stormy skies. 'We'll need statements covering the time of death.'

'When was that?' Séamus asked.

'Not long ago,' Quaid interrupted. 'President Cregan was noticeably alive at the Rational Society this evening. The meeting ended after ten o'clock, and he invited the best people for drinks in the senior common room.'

'Including yourself, Mr Quaid?'

'Unaccountably overlooked. I've been sitting here, writing a book review for the *Gazette*.'

'We think he died less than two hours ago.' Dineen glanced at Séamus. 'Where were you?'

'I'm staying in the President's House. I'm doing a consultancy job here. I was getting ready to go to bed.'

'Changed your mind?'

'I came out to buy some bottled water in the cloisters.'

'What was your relationship with the victim?'

'I met Oliver Cregan today for the first time in many years.'

'And you, Ms Fagan, have you been on the campus all evening?'

'Just a couple of hours,' Fionnuala said. 'I met Séamus in town, at the end of his dinner with one of the College trustees. I drove him back in my car, left him at the President's House, then went to my office to check some papers. How do you know our names?'

'I've been taking a healthy interest in King's College since before the O'Neill disappearance. And Séamus Joyce is something of a celebrity in the world of law enforcement.'

Séamus wondered what might have attracted Mike Dineen's interest. The National Bureau of Criminal Investigation had a wide remit: not just murder but also organized crime, theft of art and antiques, paedophilia, copyright and software violations, and several other fields of criminal endeavour.

'You confirm Miss Fagan's story?' Dineen asked Séamus.

'As far as the President's House, certainly.'

'You didn't mention she gave you a lift.'

'No reason to.'

Dineen turned to Fionnuala. 'Where is your office?'

'Far corner of the cloisters, down one flight of stairs into the basement.' Séamus noticed that she was making an effort to speak clearly, like a drunk driver talking to a traffic policeman. Perhaps she was practised in that skill.

'Near the accounts office?' Dineen asked.

'Not far. I had to look over some manuscript records, printed from microfilm. I'm a medieval historian. We have a research centre down there.'

'At this hour of night?'

'I'm revising an article for a learned journal. It's not unusual to find academics working late.'

'Were you aware of any disturbance?'

'I didn't hear anything, but when I left my office I saw that the storeroom was open. Where we keep various artefacts, including St Malachi's mace.'

'The murder weapon?'

'So Jeremy tells me. I tried telephoning the security men, but there was no answer. I came up here to find the night watchman. I was worried about the mace, but of course it fades –'

'Of course.' Dineen nodded.

Quaid interrupted. 'Its use as the murder weapon makes a rather interesting link with the last great mystery at King's College. Do you suppose the ghost of Andrew O'Neill –'

'Please stop, Jeremy,' Fionnuala said. He stopped.

'The O'Neill–Gannon case,' Dineen said, 'is under active investigation. If anyone knows of a connection between those events and tonight's killing, you have a duty to speak out.'

Nobody spoke. A uniformed Guard came into the room. 'Millington's here.'

The Inspector nodded. He included them all in a sweeping glance. 'Come with me, if you please. I'm going to need an office, and I'll be wanting swabs from everybody's hands. Sergeant Kyne will inform you of your rights. You are entitled to get legal advice, if you think it necessary.'

3

Next came a period of unreal calm, as they waited with others to be summoned into the alumni office, not far from where the accounts office doorway was being sealed off behind a white nylon cloche. The group waiting to be interviewed reminded Séamus of Nitelink bus queues that he had driven past in years gone by.

Quaid went in first, then Fionnuala. Policemen and officials passed by, clad in pristine white shell suits and wearing surgical masks over mouth and nose. DNA had turned murder into a matter of obsessive cleanliness.

Quaid and Fionnuala were whispering in the shadows. Séamus did not join in. He had too many questions. Burren stood farther along the passageway, talking confidentially to three female students.

Séamus was summoned at last. Sergeant Kyne was a fragile blonde with ice-blue eyes and a teacher's encouraging smile. She wrote down his movements for the evening into a black-covered notebook, and innocently enquired whether there was a connection between his former employment as director of the drugs agency and his current responsibilities as a consultant visiting King's College. He said there was not. Was there a drugs problem in King's?

'No idea. I'm out of that scene.'

By the time he had finished his statement, Quaid and Fionnuala had gone. He tried to buy another bottle of water from the vending machine, but there was none left. He walked out through the great arch and crossed the gravelled drive towards the President's House. City lights glowed orange against the clouds behind the trees. There was a clock over the main arch, which he had not noticed before. Ten past seven, its hands indicated. The clock too was broken, then. Ten past three might be closer to the mark.

He felt strangely disinclined to go indoors and sleep. He could see strong lights at the end of the drive, near the gate lodge, suggesting that television crews were already encamped.

He fumbled for his card key, opened the front door of the President's House, and was confronted by a Guard who asked him his name, confiscated his key and informed him that nobody was to be allowed into the building. Séamus was to be accommodated in the Servants' Lodge next door. No, he could not have his overnight bag. No, unfortunately he could not fetch his night clothes and washing gear. Nothing was to be touched.

Séamus was too tired to argue. He made his way around the corner to the former outhouse where Hynes was lodged. The front door was open. Hynes was in the hall, swaying like a man who has been through a shipwreck. There was an aura of good brandy in the air. Hynes pulled himself together and enquired whether Séamus would like some refreshment, or would he prefer to lie down in the spare room?

'Some water, please. What time is it?'

'Just gone four, sir. I have left some bottles of spring water in the spare room, sir.' He showed Séamus to a poky bedroom and withdrew. On the bedside table beside the narrow single bed were two little bottles of King's College Water, specially bottled by Carrigdove, two miniature bottles of South African red wine, a half-bottle of pink Mercier champagne, a package of dry-roasted Planters peanuts and a miniature barrel of Pringles. Had Hynes procured these from the President's House, or did he keep his own personal supplies? Séamus opened a bottle of water and sat on the edge of his bed.

Now what?

His work was finished for the time being. There would be no chance of observing the College under normal circumstances. Besides, Finer Small Campuses would be unlikely to sign any new agreements until the scandal had died down.

Perhaps he could return at the end of the week. For the moment, it remained to retrieve his things and go. Which he would do within the next couple of hours, leaving a message for Guido and Heidi, in case they cared to contact him. He would stay in Dublin for a few days, sort out his pension and his house, persist in his efforts to find out why Patrick Connolly had given up representing FSC on the College board. Then he would return to Germany, or New York, or wherever.

He would log on to the Internet in the morning, find some numbers for Consultancy International and Senator Hinckley. If he had not lost the mobile phone that Guido had given him, he would at least have had some stored numbers to play with.

His suspicions about the theft of that phone floated once more to the surface. It was probably a question of secondary importance; he was thinking about it merely in order to block out larger questions. Somebody – probably President Cregan – had wanted to listen to his landline calls. Definitely Cregan, the outlines of whose mortal remains he had last glimpsed when walking past the white nylon cloche outside the accounts office after being interviewed by Sergeant Kyne. He would try to die more decorously when his own turn came.

To block out the image of Cregan's death, he set his mind again to the question of who might have done the killing. Quaid had mentioned a few prime candidates, but the field was wide open, the shortlist promising. Not Fionnuala. Too soft. Quaid himself? His coiled energy could certainly have been bent to assassination. Quaid, however, was so pleased with the verbal wounds he could inflict that the addition of physical harm might have seemed almost superfluous. Burren? Strong enough, and suffering sufficient humiliation. Burren was a man of hidden depths.

Then again, the murderer could be someone of whom Séamus knew nothing. Why should he assume otherwise?

And still he went on churning the meagre facts in his possession. Hynes? More than met the eye. He knew something about the theft of that phone. What had gone on between Cregan and Hynes? Of course, Hynes was old. He had not been young when Séamus was a student. He had looked so shattered when he announced the death that he might well have been suffering from his own exertions, as well as the shock. Being well over sixty-five years old – Séamus had a little flash of delayed insight – then he was well past retirement age and was probably being kept on as a superannuated College servant, at the President's grace and favour. Could Hynes be facing the scrap heap, now that his patron was gone?

He drank more water from the bottle, went on thinking, listing, suspecting. He knew that he lacked information, but his brain could not stop hypothesizing. 'Professional deformation,' his European colleagues would have called it: a brain that cannot stop processing data in its accustomed way. The mad German professor? Séamus had not yet seen her. Perhaps he never would. As caricatured by Quaid, she was an Amazon of redoubtable strength. In the flesh she might be merely mortal.

Fergus Kilpatrick? Had Quaid told the truth about him? And that other young man whom Séamus had met outside Fionnuala's office: if he was in charge of security for the area where the mace was stored, could he have brought it to the accounts office and attacked the President? And Forde, the developer, who had hurt a blackmailer once, whose workers were being intimidated on building sites, whose grip was as strong as a horse's jaw?

There were still sounds of movement in the house. Who lived here? Other domestic staff besides Hynes?

Séamus decided he would move out at first light. If he summoned a taxi now, it might not come, or he could be detained by the police. That would not do. He lay back on the narrow bed and closed his eyes. He drifted instantly to sleep and then after a time was awake again, choking on what he had seen: a vision of old Hynes, in a white nightcap, creeping in with a soft pillow to sit on the edge of his bed and slowly suffocate him. Absurd, but once he had got the vision into his head, it was not to be expelled. If not Hynes, then another. Someone here had a murderous heart.

He sat up again and drank the rest of his water. Hungry after all, he ate the Pringles and the peanuts. Thirsty from the salted nuts, he poured some champagne into his water glass. There was a small television set. He turned it on. Masked men and women were delving in soft earth. This was a mass grave in Croatia, where Serbs had been massacred. Old news films, recycled to lend colour to a BBC News 24 report that some notable war criminals might be yielded up by their supporters to face trial in the Hague, as part of the price for admission to the European Union.

Not much by way of light relief. He switched it off.

There came a soft thumping on the door of his new bedroom, such as might be produced by a cat's paw. Séamus opened the door and took a quick step back. It was a pink, balding man.

'Saw the light on,' he smiled. 'Hope you don't mind. Millington. I knocked quietly in case you might be resting. Millington.' His words were breathy, as though he had a perforated windpipe. 'I didn't want to wake you. Millington – remember me? I joined the staff in your final year.'

Which meant that Millington had looked up his records.

'You're the Vice-President?'

'That's right.' Millington beamed at this evidence of his fame. He produced a business card by way of corroboration and pressed it on to Séamus, who pocketed it politely. 'Normally a sinecure. Largely ceremonial. Apart from chairing twenty-three committees. Now I can see I'm going to have to take an interest. At least until we can appoint a new President. Oliver Cregan will be a hard man to replace. Dreadful loss. You don't remember me, do you? Chemistry? But we're phasing out the department. Can't get the students for Chemistry. Hence my brilliant administrative career.' A self-deprecating smile.

'President Cregan seems to have done rather a lot of closing down departments.'

'As did his predecessor. Classics went a few years back. Then Physics, Chemistry. Now German. The sciences, in all fairness, had stagnated. Uncompetitive. Partly my own fault. Residual staff go to Education. Last refuge.'

Séamus wondered why Millington was bothering to converse with him, and at such an ungodly hour. 'Just wanted to assure you,' said Millington as if reading his thoughts, 'as a courtesy, that you're welcome to stay on, as our guest. The more continuity, the better. As our guest. We'll be hoping to complete Oliver's development work with his American partners. Continuity. If we can get this business cleared up, the link with Finer Small Campuses can still go ahead from next year. I mean, there's nothing to stop us going ahead.'

Millington's habit of repeating key words had probably served him well in the lecture hall.

'I'll have to speak with my principals,' Séamus said. 'They may prefer me to come back when things have settled down.' It would not do to admit his hazy understanding of Hinckley's requirements.

'I must apologize about your change of room. They won't let us into the President's House. I really must apologize. We could book you into a nice hotel in town that we often use for guests. The Washington. At the College's expense, naturally.'

Again the nervous hospitality, the anxiety to please.

'No, thanks. I have other things to do. I'll move out this morning for a couple of days.'

Millington's phone began to chirp, in an ascending chromatic scale. He pulled it from his pocket, and for the first time his smile faded. 'Really? Certainly. Put him on. Yes?' He listened for a protracted moment. 'Thank you so much for letting me know.' He ended the call and turned to Séamus, gulped, fell silent.

'Bad news?' Séamus felt compelled to ask.

'Awkward. Very unpleasant. One of the morning papers seems to be insinuating that you are somehow involved with the incident here tonight.'

'Me?'

'Somebody is bringing the early editions around. You know, the country editions, the ones for the provinces. They print them first, you know.'

'I know.'

'And of course they can change their pages very quickly nowadays. You know, with computer technology and so forth. Very quickly indeed.'

'Of course.'

There was the sound of an engine, slowing down.

4

Séamus followed Millington to the front door, which stood open. A man in motorcycle leathers was handing a plastic bag of newspapers to Hynes, who passed its contents to the Vice-President, who shuffled them one by one into Séamus's hands. The *Irish Independent* used a formal portrait of President Cregan with Mrs Lucy Forde at the conferring ceremony to illustrate their front-page headline, DUBLIN COLLEGE HEAD KILLED. The *Irish Times*, *Gazette* and *Examiner* also led with the story and carried different photographs of the crowd around the accounts office, all taken by the photographer from the student newspaper before Hynes had driven him off. The new tabloid *Dublin Morning Courier*, under a red EXCLUSIVE! tag, proclaimed a different angle: KCD SLAYING – DRUGS CHIEF QUIZZED. There was an old, unflattering photograph of Séamus. He scanned the story: '. . . President of King's College savagely beaten to death . . . detectives on the scene within minutes . . . latest crisis to hit the ailing College . . . alleged scandal of missing funds from overseas student fees . . . top US education group Finer Small Campuses considering an equity stake . . . sent in former drugs chief Séamus Joyce to investigate accounts . . . alleged drug abuse by students . . .'

'Easy allegation,' Séamus remarked.

'Which allegation is that?' Millington seemed mortified with embarrassment.

'Drug abuse by students.'

'Oh, that. Drug abuse. We try not to dramatize –'

The front door was still standing open. Inspector Dineen walked in like a blast of cold air.

Séamus returned to his reading: 'President Cregan said yesterday afternoon, "We have every confidence that Séamus Joyce will do a first-class job. We have nothing to hide.

Mr Joyce is one of our own graduates. We are proud of him. His leadership of the former Irish Drugs Enforcement Agency is an inspiration to us all. We are happy to open our books to his inspection." But last night President Cregan lay dead and among those questioned was former top lawman Joyce.'

'You've seen the *Gurrier*,' Dineen said.

'The *Courier*,' Millington explained.

'New since my time,' Séamus said. 'Is this their usual standard?'

'More or less,' Dineen said. 'Professor Millington, are you aware of any drugs business in the College that could justify this gutter-press story?'

'Certainly not.' Millington pursed his pink lips.

Inspector Dineen said nothing. Behind him, fragments of weak daylight were settling into the foliage of tall trees. Dineen held a natural dominance in the group. In the silence, Millington seemed to fade. He drew breath. 'Surely there's no suggestion –'

'No suggestion, Professor,' Dineen replied. 'But we'll be covering all the angles, now that we're here.' He turned to Séamus: 'Any observations you'd like to share? Anything strike you since you've arrived?'

'Yes. Someone stole my mobile phone.'

'Why do you think that happened?'

'Having been through this before, I'd say the aim was to get me to use the house phones, so that my calls could be monitored. Or is that the sort of thing that only went on in the iDEA?'

'And in politicians' offices, once upon a time, and in certain private companies in Dublin, and Garda stations up and down the country.' Dineen's voice was hard. 'There was a time when you only talked in your car with the windscreen wipers on.' He turned back to Millington. 'Telephone systems were renewed in this College when Cregan came to power. Isn't that so?'

'I believe it is.'

'Where are the tapes?'

'Tapes?' Millington blinked. 'Tapes?'

'Out of the loop? I'll ask Hynes.' The Inspector threw back his handsome head and called, 'Come in, John Hynes!'

A door opened at the back of the little hallway and Major Tom, the cat, emerged, licking his whiskers. Next, white-faced Hynes tottered forth, with the air of a political prisoner about to be purged. 'Can I be of assistance?'

'That was the idea,' Dineen said. 'Where are the intercepts of phone calls? Did Cregan keep them in his own house?'

'What makes you –?'

'I've had people on this campus. I know what went on.'

Millington was outraged. 'You have had people here? Who? Whom have you had? You might at least have told us.'

Dineen ignored Millington's distress. 'People spoke on the phone and their words were used against them. Are you going to tell me where to find the intercepts, Mr Hynes?'

Hynes reflected, trembling. He looked lost. Séamus wondered if he was going to collapse on the floor. At last he shook his head. 'I think the President may have had something on his computer. In his study. He would have had passwords.'

'Which were?'

'He didn't –'

'Don't fuck with me, John.'

Hynes winced at the obscenity, drew a long breath, caved in. 'Do you have a pencil, sir?'

'Use this.' Dineen produced a pocket notebook and a ballpoint pen. Hynes took them in his shaking hands and traced the outlines of a password, containing letters and numbers in an apparently random order. 'Shall I go and switch it on, sir?'

'You will do no such thing. That machine is coming down to headquarters with me. When I get there, I'm going to put in that password, and if it doesn't work, you will spend tomorrow night in the Bridewell, which at your advanced age could be bad for your health.'

Séamus found this threatening manner distasteful. It worked on Hynes, however. 'There's a box of disks,' he volunteered, 'in the wall safe in President Cregan's study.'

'Key or combination?'

'Combination, sir. Here, let me write it out for you.' Hynes jotted the numbers in the notebook. 'Can I go now?'

Dineen nodded. Hynes shrank away behind his door. The cat rubbed its furry flank against Millington's trouser legs, as though deciding that he was now the top man and deserving of homage. Or perhaps he knew Millington of old as a good source of milk.

Inspector Dineen addressed Millington. 'A case like this puts the Guards on the spot. We'll be expected to produce an instant solution to all crimes affecting King's College in recent years. Going back to the O'Neill case, and beyond. That will include washing any dirty linen that might be lying around in labs.'

'Labs?' Millington had found a new word. 'Labs?'

'Where chemical substances get produced,' Dineen explained. 'Normally we'd need a lot of evidence before poking around a place like this. But I'm taking no chances. We'll be searching your nooks and crannies.'

'Why on earth?'

'Because we know that chemical drugs have been supplied to nightclubs through people associated with this College. What we don't know is where the stuff gets processed.'

'If I thought that anyone here were involved in such a thing, I would take strong measures.'

'Strong measures are common in the drugs trade,' Dineen remarked. 'Meaning that people tend to die. Have you ever heard of drugs being produced in this College?'

Millington looked distinctly unhappy. 'You are casting your net widely, Inspector. Very widely. If I claimed I had never heard rumours of drugs being concocted by students, on an amateur basis, for their own use, I would be exaggerating.'

'Did you report your suspicions?'

Millington nodded. 'I mentioned them to one of your colleagues when he came to investigate a break-in at our chemical stores about a year ago. Frankly, Inspector, I don't believe in persecuting students over every last speck of illegal substances that they may or may not have consumed. The laws of this country, in my opinion –'

Dineen raised his eyebrows. 'Whom did you inform, Professor?'

'One of your colleagues. A detective. I don't recall his name. Heavy-set man, quite big, short hair, red face. Rough skin. Don't know if he gave a name –' His voice faded again.

5

Dawn light was staining the campus. Daybreak was imminent. Early-morning traffic made its presence felt, at a distance. Through the open door, a lorry could be heard hooting and sniffing its brakes; it sounded close at hand, although it was probably down by the Liffey quays. There was a hint of church bells. Straggling greenery had regained its colour on the upper branches of trees, while the sky had changed from neon-infested black to a luminous indigo. The solemn bulk of the main College buildings was beginning to take shape, and birds could be heard twittering their litanies of pure sound.

Millington said, 'I'm going to make some tea. Hynes is exhausted, poor chap. Anyone for toast?'

'I'll take a cup,' Dineen said. They made their way through a door and found themselves in the kitchen. Gleaming stainless steel, hygienic tiles, harsh lighting: a miniature version of the kitchen in the President's House. Millington filled an electric kettle, fetched milk from the refrigerator, tea bags from a shelf, mugs from a cupboard, fed slices of bread to the toaster.

'Where were you tonight, Professor?' Dineen asked.

Millington had clearly been expecting the question. 'I went to the Rational Society meeting, looked in at the President's party, then went home, caught the headlines on CNN, went straight to bed.'

'Any witnesses?'

'Just my wife.'

'How did you know there was bread in this kitchen?'

Millington sighed at the Inspector's persistent suspicion. 'Hynes takes the bread from the President's House after one day. Oliver Cregan told me that. Also, Hynes likes to feed the ducks down at the pond. And he shares the President's leftover meat with the College cat.'

A telephone rang in another room. It ceased ringing. Hynes put his head around the door. 'President Millington, sir, Miss Fagan wanted to see you.'

'I'm not the President. Yes, all right, ask her to drop by.'

'No, sir. She needs to see you at once over in the security room.'

'I'll come too,' said Dineen. 'You stay here, Joyce. Don't go anywhere without saying goodbye. I've got men on guard around the grounds. If you want to leave, they'll have to clear it with me.'

'I'll wait here for the time being.'

Séamus sat alone in the kitchen. The kettle boiled and switched itself off. Every time he closed his eyes he saw Cregan: a carnival image of disaster in lurid red. Thinking rationally was better than being mocked by that image. He stood up mechanically and made himself a mug of tea. His brain clanked into action. Things had to fall into a different pattern after Cregan's murder. But there were too many threads in the tapestry, too many possible motives: the academic jealousies, the fears for the future of the College, the drowning of O'Neill, the murder of Cregan with a fake medieval artefact recently restored, the nervous young man responsible for guarding the murder weapon, Dineen's suspicions concerning the production of chemical drugs. Another set of motives lay in the property transactions, the financial deficits attending the new building projects, the role of Forde the developer, his wife's fears for anyone who stood in his way. How had Cregan balanced between Irish and American interests? If he had snooped on his colleagues, closed down their departments, blighted their careers, could this alone have provided reason enough for his elimination?

Everything seemed to be personal; nothing to be taken at face value. Derry McKinley, chairman of the trustees, had tried to put Séamus at a disadvantage with his flurry of gossip and innuendo about Fionnuala. That dinner, in retrospect, had been symptomatic of a wider malaise.

He would be glad to be out of King's College. This visit had cured him of any wish to recover his lost youth, to stand again at that particular crossroads. If he had linked his fate to Fionnuala instead of Theresa, if he had opted for the academic life, might he have fared even worse than he had done?

And the future? Would he always be with Heidi? Could he imagine himself growing old in a German landscape, taking holidays in places where Germans went? Disappearing through the curtains of a German crematorium, with a German requiem ringing in everyone's ears but his? The life of an exile may be hard, but death is the last exile, and that is the same everywhere.

Séamus was a willing exile from the places of his childhood, so why should it matter if he also became an exile from this place, which had merely been the stepping stone to his new life? He had moved on. This visit might yet do him good if, when it was over, he could talk to Heidi. Heal the unhappiness that on some days breasted her skin like a broken bone. The pain that shot through her greyhound body when she moved quickly. The shudder of the past. The limp that on some days was imperceptible, on others came against her like an enemy.

Could these things be spoken of? He remembered a play he had seen in his student days. A man and his servant are marooned in a room. They fill their time with witty repartee, but the emptiness of the universe keeps pressing on the stage from the back, from the sides, from the audience. Who leave the theatre at the end of the evening, pleasantly fulfilled, on their way to a late-night snack.

There had been a ghostly man at his school, a commerce master who traded on two maxims. One was from Keynes: 'in the long run, we are all dead'. The other came from Goethe: 'meanwhile, do what lies nearest'. Combine these principles, the master claimed, and you can live a good life.

Séamus was nodding off. He needed to sleep, specifically with Heidi.

He was asleep, on his own. Then awake again. How many minutes? He had been close to the surface. There were voices in another room. One was so low that he could make out no words. Then Hynes in a falsetto whine: 'How'd I know? You've looked. Maybe he –' The sound of something falling. And falling again.

Séamus had to see. He reached for a heavy cast-iron frying pan, picked it up, put it down again, feeling silly. He pushed through a swing door, following the sound of the silenced voice. No sign of Hynes in the pantry area. He walked through into a little sitting room, with a doorway leading to a small bedroom. An unmade bed, a patio outside the open French window. Dawn still seeping with its attendant echoes of birdsong.

'Hynes?'

Silence.

'Mr Hynes?'

Other voices in the distance: Inspector Dineen coming back?

From the inner bedroom, a rasping intake of breath. Séamus stepped forward.

A heavy footfall at his back alerted him. He tried to shout. A powerful weight struck his head, and he was blundering across the floor, on his knees, almost getting up as the second blow fell, on the back of his neck, and through the blackness he struggled to twist himself and see, but was powerless to do so. He felt himself sinking into the wooden floorboards that rose to meet him like slanting water.

Thursday

I

The weight of his head. Sight breaking like waves inside his skull. Cold air.

Voices. A man barking in an echo chamber. Another reciting a string of words, and a woman he knew, saying clearly, 'You left him.'

'How were we to know?'

'Who was looking after him?' The woman's voice again. 'Where's John Hynes?'

'Can't say.' Feet, retreating.

From another room, an authoritative male voice: 'Hynes? Hynes?' Change of tone: 'Get a doctor.'

Séamus opened his eyes. His temples were pounding slowly, like somebody playing the bass drum. He was lying on his side. On a floor. Beside a sofa. In a small sitting room. There were trouser legs and polished shoes. Fionnuala was there, in her loose blue smock. Where was her bloodied black dress? She saw he was awake, sank to her knees, stroked his head. 'You poor man,' she murmured. 'Are you badly hurt?'

He opened his mouth like a fish, but could only breathe at her until he found the voice hiding in his throat. 'Thanks.'

'Who did this?'

'I don't know.'

She settled a rug around him. He closed his eyes again.

'Get me Sergeant Kyne,' the policeman said.

'You should have protected him.' Fionnuala's voice.

'You were the one who called us away, with your story

about the chalice.' Mike Dineen was angry. Yes, Dineen was the name.

'I'm sorry,' she said, wounded. 'It was only for ten minutes.'

'Fifteen.' Dineen was not mollified. 'How's he doing?'

'Not well.' Millington's voice, from another room. 'Not well.'

The next time Séamus opened his eyes, Fionnuala was bending over him. Beside her stood a slim blonde woman in shades of blue. Sergeant Kyne. Whose first name he had not been given. No damage to his short-term memory.

'Let me see,' drawled a voice from outside the room. A plump man sloped in: purple bruises of sleeplessness ringed his eyes. He stood still, glanced at Séamus, peered through into the next room. 'Yes. Yes. Ambulance?'

'On its way.'

'Warm water, then.'

This was the same man who had attended after Cregan's murder. Presumably the College doctor. Did he live close by? Séamus struggled to his knees, while Fionnuala supported him as though pulling him on board a raft after a shipwreck. He clung to her arms, managed to rise, slowly, to his feet. The room swayed, and he felt a pressing desire to lie down flat once again and close his eyes. He leaned against the sofa, sank into it. The pain in his head switched from black to yellow to black again.

'Take it easy,' the doctor said. 'I'll get to you.'

Inspector Dineen sat down beside him. 'What happened?'

'You tell me.'

'Who battered John Hynes?' Dineen looked into Séamus's eyes.

'I don't know,' Séamus said. 'Somebody hit me. From behind. You said you had men guarding the grounds. There was a French window standing open.' He was swaying on a sea of nausea. The room darkened again.

Inspector Dineen rose, went into the next room. Séamus

got to his feet, with Fionnuala's help, and followed, leaning heavily on her. She was shaking, but strong. Stronger than he had known. In the small bedroom of his living quarters, Hynes was curled on a rug, elbows protecting his head. The room was cold.

Hynes lay still, yet his shape did not hold the artificial pose of Cregan's corpse. He was breathing. The sound was that of a broken harmonium in a windy church. A single note rose and fell. His face was blackened. There was blood on the pale rug, rust in his dirty white hair. His jacket was missing one sleeve, which lay like a severed arm some feet away across the floor. The window, still standing open, was the source of the cold. Outside, it seemed darker than before.

The sound of a diesel engine died as wheels crunched on gravel. Two men came in from the other room, carrying a stretcher. They looked down at Hynes huddled on the floor, and waited for the doctor to tell them what to do. The doctor was kneeling beside Hynes, palpating his head, neck and shoulders with gentle fingers. Hynes made no move. 'Bandage his head for a start,' the doctor said, looking up. 'He'll need a transfusion.'

Séamus stood, unable to help.

'So what exactly did you see?' Sergeant Kyne asked him.

'Nothing. There was a voice. Hynes was answering. Then something falling. I came in from the kitchen. That's all.'

'Whose voice?'

'I only recognized Hynes's.'

The binding of the head was finished. The ambulance men fitted a neck brace, then manoeuvred the old man, still unconscious, on to their stretcher, using minimal movement. The doctor watched as he was strapped down. 'Tell them to admit him straight away,' he said. 'I'll check in later.' He moved towards the door. Fionnuala put her hand on his arm. 'Please. Séamus could have concussion.'

'All right,' the doctor said. 'Loosen your shirt.' Séamus

complied. 'Bit of a bruise.' He felt Séamus's neck and skull. 'No obvious head injury. What's the name on that TV set?'

'Ferguson.'

'Count backwards in sevens from one hundred.'

'Ninety-three, eighty-six, seventy-nine, seventy-two, sixty-five, fifty-eight –'

'Good.' He had lost interest. 'We'd better have you assessed, all the same. The ambulance can fit you in.'

2

Hours later, in the Accident & Emergency department, Séamus was sitting on a plastic chair. The view included a plastic clock, a vending machine and some laminated notices issued by the Eastern Health Board. Out of date already: it was the Eastern Regional Health Authority now. Soon to be something else. All change is good.

This was not called the waiting room for nothing. Its occupants, rightly known as patients, looked as if they had been there for months. Some were sick, some were related to sick people, some were making themselves sick by wandering outside and smoking cigarettes, wheezing pitifully on their return. Several were pasty-faced, carrying too much bulk. They reminded Séamus of the crowds of outgoing holidaymakers at Dublin Airport, patiently awaiting their charter flights. This was their destination.

Neon tubes, stuck to the yellow ceiling, blinked like autumn leaves. Bright daylight was fended off by frosted-glass windows. New patients were arriving, shifts changing over.

If he held his head at a certain angle, it hardly hurt at all. Displaced pain migrated to his shoulders.

Hynes had been shunted into intensive care. Séamus was on his own. He was one of the younger patients here. A white-haired man with severe aquiline features, seated in the far corner, was taking assiduous notes. Not a government inspector, but a gambler with his *Racing Times*. An ancient woman with mousy hair and papery skin grasped her broken wrist with her free hand, describing her fall to a middle-aged mother whose baby cried in a quiet cadence.

Instead of a flight indicator, the television screens dispensed breaking news. What was cracking this morning was the earth's crust, somewhere in Turkey. So far, it seemed to be only a minor quake, but the judiciously excited tone of the reportage implied that there might be hope of greater damage.

Séamus felt uneasy at intruding on other people's distress. He had not been inside a hospital since Theresa's iatrogenic illness. During that time, he had seen the five-star version of Irish healthcare, with boutique wards and prosy menus. His present experience reflected the opposite side of the coin. This indifferent reception facility, into which misfortune funnelled people from their living rooms, was an insult to society. And yet, once they got past no-man's-land, the people waiting here would mostly be well treated.

Should he be taking up scarce resources in Accident & Emergency? He was not exactly dying. As a low-priority case, he had already been briefly scanned by a busy nurse. She had synchronized her eyes with his for a split second, shone a torch into his pupils, tapped his right knee to test his reflexes. A doctor would see him later. They had given him a cup of tea and a sweet biscuit, not as an entitlement but as a kindness. They were doing their best.

It was impossible to relax. An angry corner of his mind was clamouring for answers, without knowing which questions to put.

A gurney pushed through the plastic-sheeted swing doors, carrying a fat man with an oxygen mask over his face. The waiting patients looked at the hurrying trolley as though it were an express train speeding through a suburban commuter station, detached from its surroundings by superior urgency.

He tried reading a tattered tabloid newspaper, left lying on the floor. His concentration kept switching out like a faulty light. The paper was published in London but printed in Ireland, with small adjustments for the local market. It was out of date, but that made little difference. There was a crime wave in Dublin. Some American celebrities drank more than was good for them. A child had been killed in a freak accident. A footballer had pulled a muscle and might miss a crucial match. An English actress found significant parallels between her personal life and the role she had been hired to play. The Zodiac Diet, matching enzymes to star signs, was sweeping all before it.

The television broke into its breaking news to summarize the main headlines, which now included an item from the Irish Republic. Police were baffled by the murder of Dr Oliver Cregan, president of one of Dublin's oldest universities. Stock images of the campus accompanied this report. Another university president, looking statesmanlike, appeared against the backdrop of his own institution and said how shocking it was that such a dynamic leader, with so much to offer in the field of excellence and innovation, should have been cut down so savagely at this point in time. The unfortunate death of President Cregan was not going to halt the reforms presently reshaping the Irish university sector. This was an exciting time for higher education.

Sergeant Kyne came through the emergency treatment area, accompanied by a thin, predatory man. She looked tired under the neon lights. 'Mr Joyce, I have to ask, do you know who opened the safe?'

'President Cregan's safe?'

'Yes. Was it Hynes? They won't let us talk to him.' She was trying to appear friendly. The thin man by her side was silent and menacing. Séamus guessed that this might be his principal talent.

'I was there when he gave Inspector Dineen the combination. When did it get opened?'

'We don't know. Did you see the combination?'

'No.'

'When Inspector Dineen went into the President's House, the safe had already been opened.'

'Hynes was in his own house. The old stables. I doubt he went outside before we were attacked. Dineen had people patrolling the grounds. They would have seen him.'

Her blue eyes brightened with impatience. 'There's a corridor under the stables, leading to the basement of the President's House.'

'News to me.'

'Could Hynes have gone through to the main house while Inspector Dineen was over in the College storeroom?'

'I suppose it's possible. He left me alone for a few minutes.'

'Did he give you anything? Any papers, computer disks?'

'Certainly not.'

The thin man spoke without moving his lips. 'We're under instructions to search you.'

'Do your instructions include a warrant?' Interesting that anger made him feel slightly better.

'No.' Uninflected, unapologetic. 'They don't.'

'Have you brought me my overnight bag?'

'No. If you'll agree to come with us, we can get the doctors here to fast-track you. We'll see about the bag.'

Séamus did not like this thin policeman. He had heard stories of evidence planted, witnesses abused, probably by men such as this. Of course there were good people in the force. He stood up. Sore, but roadworthy. Fighting back dizziness, he picked his way towards the door, the thin man at his heels. People watched with blank curiosity. The porter intervened: 'You leaving with these guys?'

'No. On my own.'

'You should wait for the doctor.'

'How long?'

'Hard to say,' the porter admitted. 'They're busy. Sure you haven't been here three hours yet. It's only gone half past nine.'

The clock was closer to ten.

'Thanks, anyway.'

Outside the door, in the spitting rain, a taxi was pulling up, disgorging a mother and child. Séamus slipped into the back of the taxi. 'Donnybrook, please.'

'We could have driven you there,' Sergeant Kyne said through the open window. 'If you'd asked.' Séamus made no reply.

3

He opened the door of his house. A Garda car was already stopping halfway down the little street.

He pulled the red hopsack curtains against the mid-morning light, went to the kitchen and poured himself a glass of cold water, came back to the living room and sat on the sofa. The curtains were diffusing a crimson glow, like a pizza oven when the fire dies down. He closed his eyelids, leaned back, tried to relax in the semi-darkness, but he was restless and sweating, as if he had a fever. Drinking tap water did not help much. He loosened his tie. His clean clothes were still out at King's College.

No danger of dying, yet.

It was quiet after the noise of the hospital. The strange house felt almost familiar, merely because he was its legal owner.

A crowd of sensations – not just the physical shock of being attacked, but also the memory of Fionnuala and the vision of Cregan in death – had set his brain spinning again, independently of his damaged body.

The killer of President Cregan had gone on to attack old

John Hynes. Séamus himself had been an incidental victim, struck down to stop him from raising the alarm. If the contents of the safe had provoked the later attack on Hynes, could the same contents have triggered Cregan's murder? That was presumably Inspector Dineen's assumption.

What kind of greed or desperation could drive a person to such violence? Had the safe contained money, valuables, documents, or drugs?

Of course people kill for money. Hardly, however, with a ceremonial mace. An amateur job, then. A person planning to kill would have brought a more convenient weapon. It must have been an emotional killing, done by somebody deranged, or disorganized, or drugged.

Séamus lay still, trying to breathe slowly and stretch his limbs, and fell through to another world, neither sleeping nor waking, where President Cregan was walking urgently towards him along a dark corridor, explaining something with conviction and exhaustive detail, in a foreign language that Séamus could almost follow. They were crossing the quadrangle, stepping illegally on the grass, from one cloister to another. He caught one repeated word in Cregan's speech: 'Fionnuala.' It sounded like a foreign word. Scandinavian. No: Finnish, of course. Cregan was finished. They wandered through the kitchen garden. A dead groundsman had come back to do work there, pulling up weeds and planting new lines of herbs: rosemary, sorrel, tarragon, sage. 'Young tullabawns,' the groundsman grumbled. 'They has the soil ruined with the chemicals; they don't know a thing at all.' That man had been decrepit during Séamus's student days. If he were alive today, he would be more than a century old.

It was not that Séamus was asleep. More like hypnotized. Had they given him something toxic?

He was on a boat; the bell was sounding to warn of shallow water. Not a boat: he was on board one of the hundreds of sofas Theresa had bought, for hotels and house properties, in job lots direct from manufacturers in the north of England. Upholstered in velour, soft and inviting. Like Theresa herself. What a tasteful chime she had chosen.

The chiming stopped.

Someone was battering at the door.

He rose to answer. At the front door he put his eye to the spyhole, and finally recognized a friend.

This was Peter Simons, the radio reporter, the man who had helped him once in his hour of need, the man who had driven him away from the hotel after his fight with the corrupt policeman Patrick 'Pimple' Boyle; who had probably saved his life, who had put his clandestine tape on the Internet and brought his Minister crashing down in flames.

Séamus opened the door. The Garda car was still parked down the street. Its occupant was speaking on a mobile phone.

Peter Simons shuffled in, a squat, dishevelled figure, and glanced around appraisingly. 'Nice pad,' he said. 'You look zonked.'

'I got hit. How did you find me?'

'Not through the cops, though I see they know where you live.'

'Who told you?' It hurt him to speak, yet it came as a welcome distraction.

'I put your address in my little black book when you got separation from Theresa.'

'Why?'

'That's how we news hounds work. We hoover up facts, large and small. You never know.' Simons was not in the least embarrassed. 'I was planning a profile. But you faded from view. Yesterday's man. Now you're back in town, a great man bites the dust, and Peter Simons hits the jackpot.'

'What news of John Hynes?'

'He's a-going to die. Five years at the most. Lingering, I hope.'

Séamus was taken aback. 'Why so heartless?'

'I was a student in King's, before they shagged me out. Always found Hynes a royal pain.' Simons plonked himself on the sofa, uninvited, and looked up at Séamus with his round eyes, like a clever small boy planning a prank. 'But enough about me. What's your take on Cregan?'

'I don't have one.'

'Why him?' Simons insisted. 'Why now? Professional rivalries?'

'Implausible.'

'Financial?' Peter Simons asked. 'Family? Jealous husband? Jealous wife, perchance?' He waggled his eyebrows after the style of Groucho Marx, while looking sideways at Séamus.

'So far as I know,' Séamus said, 'Oliver Cregan was as straight as –' He stopped.

'Straight as a die, were you going to say?'

'What would you suggest?' Séamus was amused despite himself. 'Straight as the shortest distance between two points?'

'My own favourite,' Simons said, 'is "straight as a desert highway". That comes from Joseph Hansen.'

'Never heard of him.'

'The loss is yours.'

'Anyway, Cregan favoured the female of the species.'

Simons shrugged. 'Pity. Would have made a better story. Anyway, the sex motive is hardly what did for Hynes. Hynes was not a ladies' man. Still less a gentleman's gentleman. I happen to know who peddled your mugshot to the *Gurrier*.'

'Who?'

'Mature student, name of Kilpatrick. Involved with the student newspaper. He's offered me stuff from time to time. Always for cash. He's fond of cash. Kilpatrick has connections in the gutter press. As have I.'

'I met Kilpatrick yesterday,' Séamus said. 'I first heard of the *Courier* this morning. It's new since I left Dublin.'

'It's not going to last,' Simons declared. 'Every few years

someone brings out a new Dublin paper. If they're lucky, they sell out to the Brits before going bust. Nobody's buying the *Gurrier*. They're getting desperate. Less than two months old. Losses doubling every week. Twice-a-day formula isn't working. Having nothing left to lose, they'll say anything. My sources tell me there may be further Séamus Joyce titbits in this evening's edition. These guys have no scruples.'

'Unlike Radio Free Dublin.'

Simons was pleased with this indirect homage. 'We are a model of respectability compared to the *Gurrier*. I also happen to know that Fergus Kilpatrick has been peddling College information to Trixie Gill of the *Gazette*, who has never forgiven you for nixing beautiful Billy O'Rourke. Trixie will screw you as far as her legal department will allow. She may look stupid – she may even be stupid – but she's pure eighty per cent poison.'

'Whereas you're my friend and ally?'

'Until further notice. Do you know Derry McKinley, proprietor of Billings, public relations practitioners and advertising agents of that ilk? Trustee and board member of King's College Dublin?'

'He gave me dinner last night.'

'McKinley's PR puffs are one of the chief news sources for the *Gurrier*. My spies tell me he's behind this morning's story.'

'Interesting. He invited me to call on him today. Though he may not be back from Kildare.'

'I'll be your chauffeur and bodyguard,' said Peter Simons.

The Billings Advertising and Public Relations Partnership was housed in a Georgian square near the city centre. Peter Simons found a parking spot close by. The receptionist, an ethereal waif with a chemical blonde crew-cut, peered over the parapet of her mahogany bunker, accepted without demur Séamus's claim of an invitation to view Derry McKinley's designs for King's College Dublin, regretted that Mr McKinley had stepped out temporarily (which she pronounced to rhyme with 'airily'), and would they like to take a seat?

'Could you try his mobile?'

'I draw the knot. He hates to be disturbed.'

The panelled wall was hung with oil paintings of old advertising posters in gold-leafed frames, discreetly lit from below. A silhouetted woman with a veil and a long cigarette-holder was captioned *Filter-Tipped Menthol Soubiros – Cool as a Mountain Spring*. Beside her, *Offaly Sausages, Offaly Nice* was the slogan for a red-cheeked colleen wielding a skillet.

They sat in wing-backed armchairs. Séamus's neck was sore. He hovered on the edge of sleep, irritated curiosity keeping him awake. He caught the receptionist's eye and saw himself reflected in her evaluative gaze: an ageing male, not sugar-daddy material, deficient in self-presentation. He was unshaven, although wearing a good blazer and tie, thereby falling between the two stools of creative and executive. He turned deliberately away. Another painted poster caught his eye: *Give Us This Day Our Daly's Bread*, with a jolly fat baker cutting a loaf for a smirking boy. Séamus could remember none of these old advertising campaigns. Perhaps his long-term memory was damaged, after all.

'Help yourself to coffee,' the receptionist suggested. Simons filled cups for both of them. Over the coffee-machine, a painted whiskey bottle, set among wild purple glens, illustrated *Burntollet Blended Malt – the Scotching of the Irish*. He finally got the message. These campaigns had never happened. The paintings were intended as a joke.

On the brass-bound coffee table a brochure proclaimed *The Billings Promise: Targeted Productivity through the Tried and Tested Billings Technique. Minimum Input, Maximum Output*. That was not a joke. Neither was a booklet with a blue moiré cover announcing *The Golden Circle: Your Entrée to the Inside Track*. It appeared to be a scheme for small firms to buy into corporate entertainment facilities at race meetings in England.

Séamus took a closer look at the day's *Irish Times*. Their King's College coverage contained a small item about an oddly similar case in King's College, dating from the 1940s, when a President Bradley had been poisoned by a Professor Fox. This was the first he had ever heard of that case. To lose two Presidents, as Lady Bracknell might have said, looked like carelessness.

People came and went with parcels. The receptionist fielded two telephone calls about unpaid bills with practised ease, and made a private call of her own which involved a great deal of Tibetan-monk droning but almost no articulated speech.

The tasteful grandfather clock bonged midday.

Séamus shook himself awake, went over to the desk. 'Is there a loo?' He hoped his terminology would prove acceptable.

She smiled her understanding. 'I'll bewitch you now,' she promised, and was as good as her word, rising to her feet like a salmon breaking the surface. Taller than she had seemed while seated, tightly wrapped in olive-green muslin, she opened an inner door and ushered him up a narrow staircase.

In the Creative Jakes, lipsticked graffiti were everywhere: *Freedom Is Divisible; Le pouvoir a pris l'imagination; More Is Definitely More; Bondage Freaks of the World, Untie!*

Coming back down the stairs, he saw Derry McKinley standing by the desk, whispering to the receptionist with a carefully cultivated confidential stoop. She was craning eagerly to catch his words, her face transfigured by devotion. He looked played-out this morning, his white hair wisping to that baby fineness that fails to conceal the skin. He did not see Séamus.

Early editions of the evening newspapers were being dumped on the coffee table by a slapdash boy. Séamus sat down and looked through them, passing each one to Peter Simons. The *Herald* led with King's College: EVIL THUGS BEAT KCD OFFICIAL. The story below reprised the previous night's murder, adding the savage attack on Hynes to the broad coverage already carried by its sister paper, the *Irish Independent*. The *Herald* also raised the unsolved disappearance of Andrew O'Neill, and briefly noted Séamus's presence in the College.

The *Dublin Evening Courier* led with a story about the break-up of a boy band, relegating King's College to an inside page, where the report – headed DRUGS CHIEF QUIZZED AFTER NEW ASSAULT – dwelled on Séamus's presence in Hynes's house at the time of the second attack, before outlining his civil service career and his family background. There were two photographs of his father, similar to those shown him on the previous evening by McKinley. One of the pictures featured the smiling young men from the Gaelic football team; the other showed his father surrounded by women in evening clothes. There was a photograph of his childhood home, recently extended and looking far larger and more opulent than in the draughty days of his youth. *Lavish Lifestyle*, said the caption. What was the source of the Joyce family fortune, the article wondered. 'Patrick Joyce was a junior inspector in the Department of Agriculture, but he could always afford the best. Big house, boarding school, good car, the works. His sudden death, which was never explained, left his young family struggling. His son Séamus Joyce, former chief executive of the Irish Drugs Enforcement Agency, is today battling to claim his pension rights in the teeth of allegations about his financial dealings. Five years ago, while working in Aachen, Germany, Joyce was suspended for expense account irregularities. Joyce was living the high life as Ireland's man at the PLC, a top European security agency. Last year, he received sums of money paid from a secret bank account in Vaduz, Liechtenstein. Today he works for CI, the shadowy New York consultancy firm. CI has links to FSC, the American college chain now planning to take control of King's College, Dublin's second oldest university. Séamus Joyce was in King's College late last night when the President, Oliver Cregan, was murdered, and the President's butler, John J. Hynes, was viciously beaten.' The article was bylined 'Frank Barrymore, Crime Reporter'.

McKinley glanced around, blinked, straightened up. 'Séamus, good to see you! This is Séamus Joyce, Vonnie.' The receptionist broke into an ecstatic smile. McKinley's voice was strong and benign. He was wearing a dark necktie, perhaps to signify mourning. Séamus introduced Peter Simons. 'How was your meeting in Kildare?' he asked.

'Cancelled when I heard the news,' McKinley said. 'Drove back to town at six in the morning. Isn't it ghastly? Poor Oliver.' His face was grey, like soft stone. Séamus wondered about first aid.

'We need to talk,' Séamus said. 'All three of us.'

McKinley sighed. 'Okey-doke. Anyone calls, Vonnie, I'm in a meeting. Follow me, gentlemen.'

They tracked along behind him. First, McKinley delivered a portfolio to Jason in graphic design. On Jason's wall, along with clever pastiches of Modigliani and Egon Schiele, was another gold-framed oil painting: a group portrait of worried female faces, vaguely diseased in the style of Toulouse-Lautrec. *Quicklime Counselling – We'll Take Care of Your Pregnancy*, the caption said. This belonged in the same series as the spoof advertisements in the entrance hall, but had obviously been found unsuitable for display in a public area. Jason, then, was the putative author of all those artworks. McKinley laid out the portfolio: a full-page fashion layout for *The Suit Season by Henry Howard*. The client wanted a lighter typeface and two new sketches. Jason and he solemnly assured each other that the new deadline was for the birds, off the wall, and just not on.

Having dramatized this contretemps to its maximum feasible duration, McKinley finally led Simons and Séamus – a slight stiffness in his walk – to a large first-floor office, empty and spotlessly clean, with shaded windows and a light smell of wax polish. Spotlights picked out more paintings of advertising posters. *Make Every Day a Grade A with Lawless's Luxury Hotels*, said one. *Derry Air – the Plane People of Ireland*, said another, presumably in homage to the proprietor's first name.

'Séamus, Peter.' McKinley's voice was catching in his throat. 'Poor Oliver.' He waved them to chairs around a mahogany table, extracted a set of drawings from a map chest, spread a selection in front of them. Séamus recognized the inside of King's College Chapel, transformed into a dining hall with a long top table festooned with silverware, and dozens of venerable portraits. Another watercoloured drawing showed male and female students clad in dark-blue academic gowns, talking to young athletes in royal-blue tracksuits, under a redesigned King's College flag. There was a larger version of the Forde Centre and its surrounding buildings, and another view of tall glass blocks, more like business accommodation than academic buildings, that were hard to imagine in the Phoenix Park. There were photographs of a new College ring, various College ties and tableware. Some of the designs looked soberly attractive. Under normal circumstances Séamus would at least have gone through the motions of considering them politely. Instead he placed the evening edition of the *Courier* on the table, open at the page about his father and himself.

McKinley took a rasping breath, sat down, held up his palm like a traffic policeman. 'Nothing to do with us. That's the *Courier* on a solo run. I'll warn them off.'

'You didn't need to read through the article,' said Peter Simons, 'to know what was in it.' He walked around the table to stand behind McKinley. 'The photographs for this piece were supplied from this building, this morning.' He was standing too close for comfort.

McKinley turned in his seat: 'I have no knowledge of that.'

'One of the Billings Agency's six directors,' Peter Simons observed, 'is Gilbert Covey. Sidekick of Richard Frye.'

'What are you suggesting?'

Séamus leaned across the table. 'Those pictures come from the same batch as the ones you showed me in the restaurant last night. They have been used to suggest that my father and I were both on the take.'

McKinley drew breath, said nothing.

'Is it defamation?' Peter Simons wondered. 'Technically, you can't defame the dead, but this innuendo is clearly aimed at discrediting Séamus, as the man who brought down Richard Frye, the drug dealers' own Minister for Justice. Frye wants to claw his way back into government. So he enlists the help of honest Derry McKinley and his friends at the *Gurrier*.'

'I don't consort with Frye,' McKinley protested.

'Except last Friday, in the bar in Leinster House,' Simons said.

McKinley was taken aback. 'That was a social gathering. There were others present. Just casual chit-chat –'

'Who's holding up my pension?' Séamus asked.

'How should I know?' McKinley demanded. 'This agency works for all sorts of people. Including politicians from several parties. Including adversaries of Richard Frye. Everything we do here is ethical. Chinese walls. *Uberrima fides.*'

'And I'll bury yours,' Peter Simons riposted.

'Total good faith.' Séamus gestured at the newspaper on the desk. 'Your spirits shine through you. Somebody is whispering to the Civil Service Pension Authority that I was in the pay of drug-dealers. Who would be saying things like that?'

'Nobody in this building.' The ruling-class growl was functioning again, but McKinley's eyelid flickered like a hummingbird.

5

'Where next?' asked Peter Simons. They were back at the car.

'I feel guilty taking up your day.'

'Balls. Haven't had such fun since we buried Mother. Cancelled my engagements. I want to be your buddy. You won't mind me taking the occasional note?'

'You're very welcome.'

'I'm not like the *Gurrier*, you know.'

'I know.'

Simons grinned. 'Actually, I am. But not today. Today I feel mature and responsible.'

An ally like Simons would open possibilities. And Séamus needed to do something positive, to take action, whether for Finer Small Campuses or on his own account. That blow on the head marked a boundary. Fight back, or go under? Fight back. Keep going. When he needed to sleep, he would sleep.

'Where next?' Peter Simons repeated. 'Scene of the crime? You might be able to get me into King's?'

'No harm in trying.'

Séamus tried to sound light, but he was weighed down with a nauseating sense of disaster, of something that should have been stopped and had instead been allowed to happen. It was as if the violence of the night were a tangible thing, a high carnival float that rolled majestically over human bodies. Why such an outlandish image? He could see the spokes turning on the wheels.

Traffic was heavy.

'Feeling bad?' Simons asked.

'Yes. I feel I should have prevented it.'

'Common reaction,' Simons replied comfortably. 'Understandable, but stupid.' He risked invading a bus lane, gained a hundred metres with impunity. Then the traffic cleared ahead, and the little Punto snarled like a jaguar. Simons put on the radio. The talk was of the falling price of package holidays, a remarkably soothing topic. The ebb and flow of unconnected life helps to repair the damaged mind. Séamus was glad he was not giving voice to his thoughts.

At Kingsbridge they crossed over into the Phoenix Park, drove around to the front gate of the College. The gates were shut. Simons sounded his horn.

A Guard approached, resplendent in a high-visibility yellow tunic. Séamus explained that he needed to collect his overnight bag from the President's House. The man looked sceptical, but agreed to telephone his superiors. A loud journalist, recognizable from news reports, approached from a van parked nearby. A cameraman followed, filming.

'Séamus Joyce, what do you have to say about the story in this morning's *Courier*, linking the death of President Cregan to your presence?'

'Nothing.' He was annoyed at the intrusion.

'And the coincidence that brings you here as the President is murdered?'

'You said it. Coincidence.'

'Is it true you're investigating the College on behalf of a foreign consortium?'

'No comment.'

'You saw the President after he was murdered?'

'No comment.'

'What have you got to say about the missing chalice?'

'Sorry?'

'After the destruction of St Malachi's mace, it has come to light that other medieval treasures are missing from the College collection.'

'News to me.'

'Are you aware of collectors willing to purchase such items?'

'No.'

'Do you have any comment on media speculation about your pension? And your expense account?'

'No.'

'Thank you, Séamus Joyce.' The journalist turned away, disgusted.

The Guard came back. 'I'm sorry, sir, they can't let you have your bag at the moment. The President's House is still sealed off.'

'Part of the crime scene?' Peter Simons asked.

The Guard made no reply. He went over to pull one side of the gate open and let a Deux Chevaux emerge from the College driveway. Fionnuala was at the wheel. In the passenger seat was the young man who had claimed to be in charge of security for the medieval artefacts.

Séamus stood in front of her car.

Fionnuala noticed him, blinked, pulled over to the grass verge, switched off the engine.

'You know each other?' the Guard asked.

'Old friends,' Séamus said.

Fionnuala got out of the car. He wondered if she was going to offer an explanation for her foray into his bed.

'That's Martin Forde,' she said, gesturing vaguely at her passenger as if to explain why he had to be excluded from their heart-to-heart.

'Anything to Seán?'

'Of course. His son. He's working as my research assistant,

replacing Ronan Gannon, who drowned with Andy. Martin is also doing postgraduate work. He started under Andy's supervision. Now I'm his supervisor.' Fionnuala had steadied herself. She was clear-eyed. She stood close to Séamus, as if measuring her body against his. As if she had really been his lover.

'I didn't notice Martin at the honorary degree ceremony for his mother – sorry, stepmother,' he corrected himself. 'Why didn't he go?'

'He has a difficult relationship with his father, ever since his mother's death. Most of the time, he lives in my house.'

Séamus changed the subject. 'Any news of the investigation?'

'Nobody knows. There are detectives everywhere, and men in white. Classes are suspended. Some buildings are still out of bounds.'

'What sort of questions are they asking?'

'I don't know,' Fionnuala said. 'They've left me alone. Will you be staying on in Dublin?'

'For a few days, anyway.'

'Maybe we'll meet again, then,' she said, without the slightest hint of embarrassment.

A large van approached. 'I'll have to ask you to move off now,' said the Guard on the gate. Fionnuala got back into her car and drove away. Séamus went back to Simon's Punto. It struck him that Fionnuala was too calm, too detached. He remembered her this way before examinations when they had both been students. Outer poise, inner terror.

'Who is that fascinating creature?' Peter Simons asked.

'Former classmate, now a lecturer.'

'Are they all as beautiful?'

'I suppose not.'

'You can tell me more over lunch. Where shall we go?'

'Somewhere central. You choose, I'll buy.'

He was drifting, treading water, marking time in a sinister

vacuum. It was good to have Simons on hand, to create a sense of bustle, the illusion of progress.

6

In the dark, timbered cave of Dunne & Crescenzi, they ordered panini, salads and sparkling water. Peter Simons recalled his student days. Having hoped to get into Trinity, he had dropped out from UCD, and had been accepted at King's as a special case. His parents had died, leaving him too much money, so he went to the bad, failed his exams, neglected to turn up for the repeat sessions. By the time they asked him to leave, he was already working in Leverkusen. Some years later he came back to Dublin, paid his way through a private college, studied at the King's Inns (an entirely separate institution) and was called to the Bar. After two years of genteel starvation as a briefless barrister, he had made a fresh start in journalism. He remembered nothing of the courses he had taken at King's, estimating that he had attended perhaps one-tenth of his scheduled classes.

Séamus ordered more water. He felt a compulsive need to drink, but no appetite for food. He asked Simons about Seán Forde's property interests in Ireland. Simons was aware of Forde's activities on the British property market, and had heard about the King's College project and the Fern Valley development in Kinnegad. The Fern Valley complex was to include a range of artisan shops and services staffed by immigrant craftworkers, with the support of several government agencies. Derry McKinley's PR firm had succeeded in obtaining wide advance publicity for this aspect of the project. It was to open within two months. 'Want to go see?' Simons asked. 'My driving skills are at your disposal.'

Séamus was beginning to wilt. The afternoon was wearing on. His concentration was still flicking on and off. He realized that part of his unconscious brain was asleep, while his senses were working overtime to maintain the illusion of wakefulness. He worked on finishing his panino. Each time he chewed, there were crunching noises in the muscles of his head. Every bite reminded him of Cregan fighting for his life. Survivor guilt?

'You're all shook up,' Simons said. 'Do you need a siesta? Want to go home? Or lie low somewhere?'

'No, I'll be all right. It comes in waves. I'm ready for strong coffee now.'

Simons waved to the waitress, ordered espressos.

As they drank the coffee, Séamus said, 'I have an odd request. A personal score to settle. Would you mind coming with me? Nothing to do with King's College. It's purely personal.'

'The personal is political.'

Séamus drank more water and explained his problems with renting out the house in Donnybrook. 'I want to know what's going on. I want to sort it out. The agency is just around the corner. Am I being selfish?'

Simons shrugged. 'Why not? How can I help?'

Séamus fished out his new mobile phone and tapped in the number for the lawyer who had represented him during his separation from Theresa. This was one tough lady.

'Bridie? Séamus Joyce here.'

'Aha!' Bridie erupted. 'Thought you'd forgotten us.'

'Can I ask you something?'

'Sue the pants off of the *Gurrier*? Don't waste your time. Men of straw.'

'My immediate concern is that Duke Street Property Brokers won't rent out my house.'

'Really? Won't or can't?'

'They said it's dirty and needs to be redecorated. But they refused to get it painted when I was in Germany. I've seen it now, and it's perfectly habitable.'

'Duke Street. Theresa's agents, weren't they?'

'Yes. I didn't change agents when I took over the house. I thought it would work. They had an incentive, after all. They'd get a percentage of the rent.'

'Probably put them up to it, the bitch.'

'You think so?'

'Knowing Theresa. And you've been paying them shysters a management fee?'

'That's true.'

'Ho-ho. Contractual obligation. You can screw them for non-performance. Not that I'm looking for work or anything. We'd have to prove they weren't offering the place for rent.'

'I think I can do that. They don't know me by sight.'

'Aha! You'd need an independent witness, though.'

'That's just what I've got. He even has his own recording machine.'

'You're on the pig's back, then. Bring me the evidence, Séamus my lad, and I'll have their ears on toast. Did you hear Theresa's after finding a new squeeze?'

'No.'

'Investor in Eastern Europe. Made for each other, people say. How does she do it? She's older than me, and not much more appetizing.'

This was untrue. In all fairness, Theresa was desirability personified. And it was improper, though typical, of Bridie to tease him about her.

7

In a pharmacy on the corner near Duke Street Property Brokers, Séamus bought a pair of standard reading glasses; in the mirror, they made him look rather less like the newspaper photograph taken in the King's College bar and published by the *Morning Courier*. Accompanied by Peter Simons, he climbed the stairs to the cramped headquarters of the property agency, where they were received by a velvety man. Peter Simons identified himself loudly as Secretary-General of IBBC, the newly founded Irish Bed-and-Breakfast Confederation, and introduced Séamus as Malachi Mulligan, a tourism consultant based in Paris, who would be visiting Dublin on and off for a period of six months to a year, and would therefore be requiring suitable accommodation. Could the agency offer anything in the Dublin 4 area? A small house would be best. Mr Mulligan was tired of apartments, and found hotels constricting.

Their host produced a list of available properties, including a number of apartments and two small houses in Clonskeagh and Upper Rathmines. Séamus recognized the address of the Clonskeagh house. Theresa had bought it two years previously.

He professed himself interested in the two houses, but asked if there might not be anything available in Donnybrook, as he had grown up on Belmont Avenue and was particularly fond of that part of town. He emphasized that the house would only be for his own use, as he normally ate in restaurants, never entertained at home, and consequently did not require a high standard of decoration. 'Just a place to lay my head,' he pleaded.

'Nothing in Donnybrook. Sorry.'

'Anything coming up in the area in the next few months? I don't need a place straight away.'

'Nothing, as I said, in Donnybrook. I'm sorry.'

Peter Simons then revealed Séamus's identity, and his own. Waving his microphone in a friendly fashion, he enquired why Duke Street Property Brokers had been taking a regular fee for managing Séamus's house property in Donnybrook, if they had no intention of renting it out. Had Duke Street Property Brokers received inducements not to offer Mr Joyce's property for rent?

The velvety man kept silent, but turned bright red. Simons proceeded to read out the company's mission statement, which was framed in solemn black on the wall: *Duke Street Property Brokers: leveraging timely solutions to accommodation needs while meeting world-class benchmarks of integrity, synergy and excellence.* 'Wow!' said Peter Simons. 'Inspiring or what? Did you write it yourself?'

The man still kept silent, but started to scribble furiously on a memo pad, then pushed his piece of paper across the counter: 'I don't run this office. I am a new employee. Please leave now.'

8

As they descended the stairs, Séamus was already beginning to feel ashamed. His mean trick had left a sour taste. Fighting on his own behalf seemed unworthy.

He asked Simons what he knew about the disappearing board member, Patrick Connolly, and about his company, Padcon. He explained that Senator Hinckley, having nominated Connolly, would want to know what had happened to him.

'I don't know much about Patrick Connolly,' Simons said. 'Next to nothing, in fact, but I can find out. Only trouble is, I have to go to work now. Radio Free Dublin is running a corruption show tonight, with a panel. I have to prime them, and then chair the discussion and stop them from slandering us into bankruptcy. Got to be at the office by half past five.'

'What sort of corruption?'

'Infrastructural. Nothing to do with King's College. Much bigger. Outrageous, in fact. This stuff would dwarf the scale of previous scandals, if anyone could be bothered to pay attention. Now, can you amuse yourself for the next few hours?'

'I'm a bit played out. I think I'll go home. Thanks for everything.'

When Simons was gone, Séamus realized how tired he was. He needed to keep going. As he walked along the street, he phoned the New York hotel once more. Mr Schneider and Mrs Novacek had not returned. No reason why they should have. He needed a better contact number for them. Had there not been an Internet café once at the top of Dawson Street? He walked to where it had been, and had gone. Instead, a kitchen design shop proposed its gleaming wares. He crossed the road and entered Stephen's Green, the lush Victorian plantations instantly taking him back to his first days in Dublin. It was late afternoon now. He tried to breathe deeply, to relax, to clear the jitters and twitches from his badly extended nerves. The place was undeniably lovely. The sky was clear. As he walked through the classical centre of the park, two civil servants from Justice came walking towards him, deep in mutual conversation, and walked on by without recognizing him, although he had worked with them for years. Not pretending: Séamus really was forgotten, despite the efforts of the *Gurrier*. Freedom, of a sort. He kept going, passing by office workers dispersing towards their homes, immigrants relaxing on park benches, children running, mothers with buggies. These people paid not the slightest heed to him. Humanity, it struck him, can be as soothing as the sea: crowds can still the turbulence, the feeling that something hopelessly urgent needs to be done, but that it is already far too late. The three Fates were still guarding the entrance to the park near Earlsfort Terrace. A present from the grateful German people for Irish aid generously sent at the end of the Emergency.

And there, at the end of Leeson Street, was a new Internet café. He spent fifteen minutes browsing under the watchful eye of a young man wearing a black T-shirt stencilled NEXT QUESTION? 'Consultancy International' was too generic a search. There seemed to be many organizations bearing variants of that title in their names. None of them mentioned Senator Hinckley. He jotted some likely-looking telephone numbers on a sheet of scrap paper. Then he tried searches linking 'Consultancy International' with 'Guido Schneider', but before he could properly explore his search results, the young man confided that the shop was closing for the day. Séamus stood up, paid and left. Walking along the street, he used his mobile phone to try the numbers he had found. The London numbers rang unanswered, while puzzled receptionists in Chicago and Houston searched fruitlessly for Schneiders in their databases.

He was at a bus stop. He stopped. A 46A bus appeared, loaded to the ground. Crowded as it was, it probably would have sailed by, but some passengers wanted to get off. Séamus climbed aboard. The bus lurched through stop-go traffic to Donnybrook. He walked past the end of his street. Everything seemed quiet. Hungry again, he kept going until he noticed a restaurant sign on a street he remembered as dark and filthy. Now it was stylish, the restaurant entrance bright and welcoming. He ventured in. 'Early bird?' the waitress asked. He supposed that he was. The other diners at this hour were mostly old ladies, which probably meant that prices would be low by Dublin's extortionate standards. They sat him in a corner of what looked like an old school hall from the fifties, decorated like a nightclub from the seventies. He ate vegetarian food, not wishing to crunch through sinew and flesh after what he had last seen of Oliver Cregan. It was palatable. He ordered a half-bottle of wine, regretting his choice when it flowed like blood, but it did him good all the same. He felt guilty about frittering his day, wasting Peter Simons's time – he had failed even to get Simons past the gate of King's College – but then an idiot teenage voice in his brain said, Hey, Joyce, so you've accomplished nothing, is that so bad? Hey, man, you've been hit on the head, it's nothing to be ashamed of, failure is normal. He wanted to find that voice and strangle it. It was worse than his German psychologist.

He walked home. There was no Garda car on the street, no sign of surveillance or intrusion. He was forgotten. He went upstairs to the bedroom, undressed, lay down, arranged the blankets around him, put his head on the pillow and fell asleep as though stunned by a sudden blow.

9

Andrew O'Neill confessed in a fake Norwegian accent to the murders of both Cregan and Hynes (the latter having perished at a freak fire in the hospital). Shaking the snow from his long grey hair, O'Neill revealed that he had been hiding out in the Phoenix Park, subsisting on hazelnuts and reindeer flesh. Even as he listened, Séamus knew this must be a dream, though Heidi refused to agree.

Woken by a burglar alarm in the neighbourhood, he went downstairs, turned on the lights, found cleaning materials in the kitchen and began to scrub. This in emulation of Heidi, whose cottage and flat might be threadbare by comparison with Theresa's comfortable decor, but reflected Prussian standards of hygiene. He scoured the kitchen worktops, poured water on the floor to help dilute the blood. The kitchen was bigger than he remembered. Three men were seated on a low stage at one end of it, watching him without blinking. They had a roving spotlight, and shone it like a flashlight into the dark corners where spiders hid from his detergent, where the mop had yet to penetrate. A bird punched Morse code into the air in a high monotone, like a pedestrian-crossing indicator for the blind. Theresa appeared, carrying a tray with a steaming teapot and one of her favourite chocolate cakes. It appeared to be made of livers and kidneys. He woke up.

The burglar alarm was real. Dawn was creeping like a thief.

He still felt sore, as if Cregan's wounds marked his own flesh. Without warning, the alarm stopped, leaving behind a pulsating silence.

And the Morse code he had heard in his dream? A text message? He checked. 'Please await instructions. Taking action. Guido.'

He went downstairs, opened the front door. The street was empty.

Friday

I

Next time Séamus woke it was with a comforting sense of perspective regained. Daylight had reinstalled its customary façade. More than a day separated him now from the night of the murder, and he was still alive, so far as he could tell, although he was sore in unexpected places – his leg muscles, his feet, his shoulder blades. He drank water from the kitchen tap. Found the telephone directory. The King's College switchboard was not answering. He remembered Vice-President Millington's business card, still in his pocket. He dialled the direct line shown on the card and found himself talking to Millington himself. The Vice-President expressed regret that he had not received the College's hospitality last night, confirmed the story of the missing chalice, informed him that Oliver Cregan's body was likely to be released for burial within the next couple of days and assured him that his own personal effects could be collected at any time, unless perhaps he might prefer to have them delivered to another address? It was regrettable that the police had not seen fit to release the effects when Séamus had visited the College on the previous day. Regrettable.

'I'll come and collect.'

'We look forward to seeing you,' Millington said. 'And I would personally be delighted to invite you to lunch early next week, when things have settled down. Delighted.'

He thought of trying Guido's American number again. No. Far too early.

The phone rang in his hand. It was Peter Simons. 'What are you doing this fine morning?'

'For a start, I'm going to collect my stuff from King's College.'

'I can drive you. It's almost on my way. I'll be heading north to Belfast. Had breakfast?'

'There's no food in the house.'

'I'll pick you up.'

2

Over coffee and toast in the Ranelagh Hotel, Simons disclosed snippets from stories he was currently investigating. If what he said was true, Ireland was run exclusively by racketeers. This did not tally with Séamus's experience. Still, Simons was fun to listen to, and Séamus began to relax. He could even think of Cregan's twisted corpse without feeling physical shocks run through his stomach. The colours and shapes of the memory were growing less lurid in his mind.

Simons had found an address for Patrick Connolly in Howth. Not listed in the telephone directory. Ninety per cent reliable. They could drive out together at the weekend.

He paused in the lobby to buy a complete set of newspapers. 'Here,' he said, as they got into the car. 'Take a look, see if you're still famous.'

As they drove, Séamus wrestled with the newspapers. King's College was slipping from the news, but still received two inside pages in the *Courier*, which launched a systematic assault on the late President's reputation. Anonymous colleagues, students and acquaintances were quoted to the effect that Cregan's tenure had been uniformly disastrous, his so-called reforms ill-considered and vacuous, and his practices of favouritism verging on the corrupt. Some of the more ringing phrases in the report sounded like vintage Quaid.

According to the *Courier*, friends of the deceased claimed that Cregan had been a cocaine user, and that the pathology reports, expected shortly, would confirm this rumour.

'Just as I said, you can't libel the dead,' Simons remarked. 'What are they saying about you this morning?'

'I don't seem to figure in the *Courier*,' Séamus said. In the *Gazette*, he found Trixie Gill reporting on Student Union protests at the suspension of classes at King's and profiling some personalities connected with the case: President Oliver Cregan, whose meteoric career as a leading proponent of modern business culture in higher education had been so brutally cut short; Acting President Conleth Millington, who had once been tipped as a possible nominee to the Irish Senate; Inspector Michael Dineen, whose recent investigation into the Ailesbury Road murders had been widely praised; and Séamus Joyce, former drugs supremo turned management consultant, whose arrival in King's College had been followed by the President's death. The sources of Joyce's wealth were under scrutiny from civil service pension authorities, Trixie Gill's article alleged, before listing some of the houses where Séamus had lived in Dublin, falsely suggesting that these had been purchased out of his own funds. Recently, she stated, Joyce had moved his assets offshore, and had at least two homes in Germany. Her piece was accompanied by a flattering photograph of the Donnybrook house, including half of the house next door. €*900,000 pied-à-terre*, the caption read.

'Trixie as ever,' Peter Simons pronounced. There was a chirping sound, and he put a mobile phone to his ear, listened, grunted, closed the phone, turned apologetically to Séamus. 'These people, they pay me a salary, they seem to think that gives them the right to interfere with my day. I've got to go and cover a building accident at the Kilimanjaro, before heading north.'

'Kilimanjaro? Another new hotel?'

'No. Flat complex overlooking Leixlip. Nothing to do with

Forde. Scaffolding collapsed, a few brickies off to hospital. The unions are revolting. I'll drop you at the campus on my way.'

3

The gates of King's College were still closed, but this time the security staff had been instructed to let Séamus through. Simons was pleased. 'I wouldn't have made it this far on my own,' he said. When they pulled up in front of the President's House, that impression was confirmed. Emerging from the house, Sergeant Kyne lit on him with her blazing blue eyes. 'Simons! Who let you in? For God's sake!'

'Joyce's trusted driver,' Simons protested. 'Soul of discretion.'

'You'll have to leave at once.'

'Have we met?' Simons asked. 'If so, nice meeting you again. Sorry I can't stay. Be in touch. Have a nice day.' He slumped back into his little car, engaged the gear, pulled away noisily.

She turned to Séamus. 'We'll get your bag for you, then.'

Dineen himself had emerged from the arched entrance to the main quadrangle, holding a sheaf of papers. The thin policeman who had come to the hospital was carrying Séamus's overnight bag. Séamus wondered why they had removed the bag from the President's House. The papers in Dineen's hand were large photographic prints. The top one, at least, was so dark as to be illegible.

'Your bag,' Dineen said, motioning to his sidekick to hand it over.

'Thanks. Any news?' Séamus took the bag. He did not ask whether it had been searched.

'No news,' Dineen said.

Séamus hoisted the bag's long strap over his shoulder and turned towards the main College building.

'Where are you going?'

'To call on Quaid.'

'Afraid you can't. We'll have to ask you to leave.'

'He sent his driver away,' Kyne said, and blushed bright red. Séamus did not reveal that the mistake had been hers.

'What's this?' he asked Dineen. 'Is the whole College a crime scene?'

Dineen stood closer, answered quietly. 'I'm running an investigation, and I don't need consultants making their own alternative enquiries.'

'Is this something personal?'

'No. The other experts have been packed off home to England.'

'May I speak to Millington?'

'I'd really prefer if you didn't.' Dineen's tone was confidential. The other two stood back, and he continued even more quietly. 'I like to keep my work free of influence.'

'I think I know what you mean. But I don't try to use improper influence.'

'That's not what I said. You're an insider, Séamus. Man from the Ministry. The inside track, far from the coalface. I don't know where I stand with you.'

Séamus was surprised by Dineen's meditative tone and his oddly vulnerable form of words. Which part of his own soul was he supposed to bare in response? He said nothing.

'People say cops are corrupt,' Dineen continued after a moment, as though this gambit followed on from what he had been saying.

'Most aren't,' Séamus said. 'And I've never thought that.'

'Well, I've known good and bad,' Dineen said. 'Guys who try to make an extra few bob. Little scams, little deals, private business, property. Some do nixers as security men. Under Cregan, this College farmed out security to a private firm, partly staffed by off-duty cops, partly by retired criminals. I don't like it. But for every bad cop, there's five or six good ones.'

'I know. And it can be a hard life.' He thought of Guards

ringing doorbells on Sunday mornings to tell parents their sons have died in car crashes.

'Why should cops be singled out,' Dineen insisted, 'when others get away with murder?'

'And that's how you see me?'

'Not necessarily,' Dineen said quietly. 'I've been to visit Patrick Boyle.'

So that was it. As always, Séamus got a momentary flashback to the terrifying policeman who had attacked him after he had got the evidence against his Minister, Richard Frye. The image of the masked Goliath at the bedroom door in the hotel was never going to bleach from his memory. Likewise the shame and guilt he felt at injuring the man in self-defence. Even now he could hear the slight crunching noise when he had dropped the television set on his head. Was it the noise of plastic, or of bone?

'Boyle?' he said as casually as he could. 'You recognized him from Millington's description? When he claimed he'd told a detective about students making drugs?'

Dineen nodded. 'Red face, rough skin. Sounded like Pat, didn't it?'

'Maybe.' Séamus wondered why he was expected to assume familiarity with Boyle.

'Since he was fired from the force,' Dineen continued, 'Pat's living in the North Strand. The house is falling into ruin, the window frames don't fit, the walls are starting to peel, they've had the little garden coated in tar. And Pat used to be house-proud.'

Séamus was surprised at the elegiac note in this recital. He would have thought a criminal thug like Boyle anathema to someone of Dineen's sort. How well had they known each other? He said nothing, but Dineen was aware of his lack of sympathy. 'Pat spends his days staring at the television in a tracksuit that's falling off him. Wasting away. Unrecognizable. His wife has gone awfully heavy. Barely gets out to the shops.

She can't drive, of course, and he's not allowed since his head injury. The tyres are flat on his car. They have tenants in the house who play music and won't keep up with the rent.'

He stopped, drew breath. 'Would it have been better if I'd let him kill me, then?' Séamus demanded at last. Once again he saw in his mind's eye the black-clad Boyle bursting into his hotel room, throwing him around as though he were made of straw. The shock of that encounter was mixed in his mind with the feeling of helpless play. Cat and mouse. That was what he hated about physical violence. It reduced you to childhood.

Dineen shook his head. 'Pat's claim is that he was trying to stop your friends gaining control over the Dublin drug market. You injured him, you blackened his name. Now Pat is on disability, and he won't get the full pension because people believe he was a criminal.'

'Correctly, in my opinion. I'm sorry I hurt him, all the same. I was defending myself. I phoned an ambulance, remember?'

Dineen looked at him. 'Maybe you don't know your own strength. According to Pat, your friends in the drugs trade are doing well.'

'I don't have friends in the drugs trade.'

'He says they're everywhere now. They even have a foot-hold here in King's College.'

'Which is why you were calling on him, I presume. Did he ever pass on Millington's suspicions that drugs were being made here?'

Dineen looked grim. 'Decko Dowd can't find any record of a report from Patrick Boyle. Pat says Decko would say that, because he's always been against him.'

'I'd believe Decko.'

Dineen nodded imperceptibly, almost involuntarily, like a tennis player acknowledging an unreachable passing shot. 'Come on, I'll drive you into town. I've got a meeting in Harcourt Square.'

'That's near enough to where I'm going. Can you drop me at the National Gallery?'

4

On the Liffey quays, Dineen slipped into the bus lane, drove for a while in silence. Then he looked over at Séamus. 'Of course I told you none of that.'

'It's OK. I worked in Justice. All secrets go to the grave. And I heard about Patrick Boyle years ago.' There was no need to specify what he had heard. Boyle's unsavoury reputation must have been even better known in the force than in the Department.

'Henrietta suffers from depression. Pat's wife. She was doing all right. He had her taking her medication, until his injury. He was laid up for weeks in Cappagh, and she went to hell. They have just the one child, a boy, in New Zealand. Not much of a life.'

'Look.' Time to be blunt. 'If I hadn't fought back, I'd be dead.'

'Some don't agree. Boyle's a rough diamond, but he never killed anyone. You overreacted.'

'Maybe,' Séamus said. 'But if Boyle had handed me over to Billy O'Rourke, what would you give for my chances?'

Dineen said nothing this time, but later as they swung over O'Connell Bridge, he asked, 'Who do you think is attacking people in King's College?'

That sounded like a genuine question.

'You really want my expert opinion?'

'Yes, I do.' Dineen sounded almost friendly. His lament for Patrick Boyle seemed to have cleared something out of the way.

'All right,' Séamus said. 'The murder of Oliver Cregan could have been done by almost anybody, man or woman,

224

provided they were desperate enough. That was a frenzied attack, whereas whoever hit me knew exactly what they were doing. The attack on Hynes falls somewhere between those two attacks: extremely violent, yet with restraint enough to avoid killing him. Whoever hit me is almost certainly the one who beat up Hynes. So my first question is, can you link the three attacks, on the President, Hynes and me? Who could have been there at the relevant times?'

'Could be two different people,' Dineen said. 'Or more than two.'

'With the same modus operandi?'

'The second attack might have been a warning.'

'To Hynes, or to me?' Séamus asked. 'Am I a suspect?'

'You could have killed the President, and then been attacked by an associate.'

'Far-fetched, to put it politely.'

'Stranger things have happened,' Dineen suggested lamely.

'Only in books.'

They were moving through heavy traffic south of the Liffey. Dineen reached out and clamped a flashing light on to his roof, then touched the siren to clear space on the road before them. 'No further thoughts?'

'Not at the moment,' Séamus said. 'I'd need some facts. Do you have any to spare?'

'Nothing useful.' There was no hostility now. Dineen gave a rueful grin. 'I'm finding out about their little gripes and disagreements, and the scams that go on, but there's nothing that would cause violence on the scale we've seen. No grounds for murder. I could spend weeks finding out why Professor A thinks Professor B is a fraud and a charlatan, but that wouldn't bring me any closer to a solution.'

He fell silent. They were coming into Merrion Square.

'Until we meet again.' He stopped the car. 'I'll find you if I need you. That Nokia you bought in Pócafón – leave it switched on. If you need to contact me, here's my number.'

He handed Séamus a card, watched him stow it in his wallet.

'How do you know about my phone?'

'Pretty sharp boys and girls in our computer section. Don't forget your bag.'

5

The office of the Civil Service Pension Authority's Special Cases Commissioner was close at hand. Séamus rang the doorbell of the tall house in Upper Mount Street. There was no reply. He rang again, and waited. The door opened and an old man appeared. He was spindly, gaunt, respectably dressed for a different time of year. His hearing-aid was of an antique design, bulbous and pink. His white shirt was as dirty and crumpled as his white hair. His maroon tie, inexpertly knotted, proclaimed his membership of a golf club that had long since been sold off for housing development. His sludge-coloured gabardine raincoat was torn at the pocket.

'Mr Muldoon?'

The tall old man looked unsure for a moment, then said, 'Yes?' His voice was almost human, like the chirping of a burglar alarm or a bird.

'I'm Séamus Joyce. It's about my pension.'

Diarmuid Muldoon peered at him. The old eyes slowly filled with understanding. 'You're one of our cases. We have to be careful, you will appreciate.' There was nothing personal in this statement.

'I made an agreement when I left the service. It has yet to be honoured.'

'That was less than a year ago, I think,' the commissioner said. 'Anyhow, we can't discuss individual cases, you will appreciate. Lunchtime, I think, isn't it, yes. Good day.' And, with a polite smile, he tottered down the steps and set off along the pavement like a poplar tree on a windy morning.

'Thank you,' Séamus said to the retreating raincoat. His enemy was not poor Diarmuid Muldoon, but whoever had submitted the case to his jurisdiction.

6

At the drab office building in Clarendon Lane that housed Patrick Connolly's organization, Séamus pressed the bell, and waited.

The clicking of high heels behind his back alerted him to the arrival of a red-headed woman, poured into a black jersey dress. She wore black patterned stockings, black ankle-boots and a necklace of polished jet. The effect was stunning. She was almost as old as Séamus, but considerably sexier.

She produced her keys from a black pocketbook that also contained a striped paper bag from Au Bistro, the French slimming food emporium on Wicklow Street. 'Waiting for me?' she asked.

'For Mr Connolly.'

'Who's looking for him?' She cocked her head invitingly, bright red lips pursed in pleasant anticipation. Her voice had a slight American tinge.

'Séamus Joyce.' Even as he said the words, Séamus braced himself for rejection.

'Ah.' She looked him up and down. 'The man with the short memory. Do you recall me telling you to get lost some time recently?

'Yes,' he admitted. 'But I need to speak to Pat Connolly.'

'He won't be talking to you.'

'Why not?'

'Ask Hinckley.'

'Sorry to be a nuisance,' Séamus said. 'Did you hear about the President's death?'

'Yeah.'

'Could you ask Mr Connolly to contact me?'

'Nope. They paying you for this?'

'I believe so.'

'Get it in cash.' She turned the key in the lock.

'Did they fall out with him?'

'You could say that.'

'May I leave a message?'

'No, you may not.'

She stepped inside, closed the door.

He bought a triple-decker in the Big Thick Sandwich Company on Stephen's Green, carried it home to Donnybrook in a taxi. A small suitcase was standing in the living room. He recognized it, having lately watched it being packed. And in the kitchen, reading through the King's College documents that he had previously left on the table, fresh from New York or wherever she had been, was Heidi, radiant in white shirt, white trousers, white shoes, with a red and green silk scarf he had never seen before. Purchased in America? No sign of travel: everything about her was bright, from her white-blonde hair to her white tennis shoes. Smaller and lighter than he remembered. She stood up, looked at him with an unsettling gaze of maternal desire. 'We should never have sent you on your own, Séamus.' She sounded guilty. 'Guido was so concerned. He has spoken to several people in Dublin.'

'Not to me, though.'

Heidi smiled her crooked smile and stood back, holding Séamus's hand lightly in her slender fingers. 'I would have come yesterday. I was out of reach, and then they routed me through Frankfurt. When I phoned King's College from Dublin Airport, they said you were already on your way home.'

'How did you get into the house?'

'It's not so difficult. Somone showed me how to deal with locks. Quite nice, I must say. Very completely furnished, for a rental place.'

She glanced around the room with its over-emphatic decoration. He saw it for the first time through her eyes. It was as if he had imported her into a cluttered corner of Theresa.

'Why don't you sit down and rest for a moment?' she said. 'I will prepare something to eat.'

8

He sat up. A turf fire was smoking. The smell brought sharp memories of childhood.

'Guido is on the phone.' Heidi was holding it towards him, stretching her arm like a fencer.

He must have fallen asleep, yet again. She had massaged his head, finding springs of relaxation deep in his muscles.

Guido's tone was raised above its normal grave pitch. 'We owe you an apology, Séamus. We placed you in the line of fire.'

'I'm surviving.'

'If Senator Hinckley had been aware of the danger, I am sure he would never have wished –'

'Does he know what's going on?'

'Broadly. Given what has occurred, he will be even more interested in your views on King's College. However, my first task is to assure your safety. Therefore, you may leave this assignment at any time you like, and go back with Frau Novacek to Germany. We do not require you to carry on. If you "jump ship", it will above all not affect our relationship with you.'

'I'll stay.'

'Luckily, you have Frau Novácek to preserve you from harm. It has been good talking with you, Séamus.'

The communication was concluded. Guido had voiced his concern.

Séamus handed the phone back to Heidi. She passed him a cup of black coffee, by way of exchange. He sipped it and gradually began to come down to earth, in this house where he had never lived, but which he owned. His property. His stake in the country. Could Heidi live in Dublin? He thought of the places she knew. The house became unfamiliar: too domestic, too foreign.

'There is a quite clean electric kettle,' Heidi said, 'and all the kitchen appliances one could desire. Your local supermarket, Donnybrook Fair, is fine. A real delicatessen. I threw out that sandwich you bought. It was not very interesting.' She had produced a light lunch, and now she watched him as he ate. She was not hungry.

'I think you need more rest,' she said.

9

As things turned out, rest was not exactly what Heidi had in mind. Her plans included sex and conversation. First one, then the other. The extraordinary thing was that Heidi seemed to need him even more than he needed her. He felt strong and protective, as though healing some ancient hurt.

She made him recall, in minute detail, what had happened since he had left New York. People, places, times. He could see her making sequential sense of it all. He started to tell her about Fionnuala, then stopped. Better to leave that for another day.

Heidi asked him about Dublin, and the years he had spent moving from house to house. She seemed fascinated by the dull details of his life.

She told him of her own travels during the week: she had been doing a work-related errand – a favour for colleagues in the Permanent Liaison Committee – in the Washington area, then had gone off to visit old friends from her previous life. They were retired now, and living in the Blue Ridge Mountains. A couple who had worked in East Germany, before the Wall came down. These days, they were making violins. Guido had spent many hours trying to contact her after news of Cregan's murder had reached New York.

'Take me out,' Heidi said, rising from the bed like a mermaid. 'Show me the sights.' She disappeared into the bathroom. Séamus sat on the edge of the bed, stood up, regarded his own naked form in the bedroom mirror. He wanted to call out, to ask what on earth a woman like her saw in a creature like him, but instead he pulled in his pudgy stomach, straightened his craning head, tried to look like a real man. The effect was more Sancho Panza than Don Quixote. He turned sideways; the view was not greatly improved. He knew that real men are not supposed to fret about looks, whereas women of all ages are entitled to complain, verbally and in print, about how much they hate their bodies. The slightest bulge or asymmetry is good for a paragraph. Why should he not do the same? Bodily self-loathing had been one of the mainstays of Theresa's life. Her dislike of seeing her own flesh in the mirror was the reason why she had stopped getting fully undressed in Séamus's presence. Which was nonsense: Theresa had looked quite wonderful in her skin, whereas Heidi, to be frank (which he did not plan to be), was never so lovely as when standing by her cottage door in Germany, wearing her voluminous white nightdress. Séamus himself, he decided, was seen to best advantage in a pinstriped suit, preferably in a situation of low lighting.

Heidi gave a low wolf-whistle. 'Mister Universe.' She had entered the room noiselessly. 'When we go home, you can join my gymnasium. More work is needed at the level of the shoulders and mid-section. The legs are already satisfactory.'

10

In Donnybrook News, they bought the evening papers. 'I want to see where you spent your youth,' Heidi said, suddenly waving down a taxi.

'Youth?'

'The houses where you lived when first you were married.'

He held the taxi door for her. 'Ringsend, please,' he said to the driver. 'We'll start at the beginning.' A few drops of rain were beginning to fall. Heidi produced a mirror from her handbag, began to touch up the dark lines of her eyebrows. He had never seen her do that. A strange new form of intimacy.

The *Courier* led with news of another murder, committed by a husband who had stabbed his wife to death before driving himself off the end of a pier in County Galway. A closer reading revealed that this horror had taken place many months earlier, the news factor being that the *Courier* had obtained photographs of the couple's three children, now in foster care. An inside page, headed DRUGS LINK DENIED IN COLLEGE DEATH, quoted Derry McKinley, on behalf of the King's College board, dismissing a rumour that hallucinogenic drugs had ever been manufactured in the College's old chemistry labs. The presence of former drugs agency chief Séamus Joyce on campus at the time of President Cregan's murder was pure coincidence, McKinley claimed. The *Evening Herald* had nothing on King's, and led with the news that a call centre, employing three hundred young people in a Dublin suburb, was to be axed by the parent company in Atlanta. The jobs would relocate to Bangalore.

The Ringsend house looked tiny when they reached it, although once upon a time it had seemed almost spacious. Theresa had even considered taking in a lodger. Heidi made him walk her past the house and buy her a kiwi granita in

Beyond Juice, a squeaky-clean new healthfood bar on the corner of Irishtown Road. She was carrying her mobile phone in her hand. They had not brought umbrellas, and caught a few drops of rain before climbing back into the taxi. Séamus explained to the driver that he was revisiting old haunts, and after Ringsend he directed the taxi to Rathmines, then Harold's Cross, Rathgar, Dartry and Windy Arbour. In each case, he remembered exactly where to go. She opened the car window every time, stared without embarrassment. Once, there was a small child staring back. The increasingly large houses he had shared with Theresa had been further adorned in the intervening years: one had gained wrought-iron gates, another a new cobbled driveway on which a Lexus and a Porsche were parked. All had burglar alarm boxes. He omitted Glenageary from his tour. Theresa was still living there, it was too far out of town, and little of the house could be seen from the road. Heidi accepted his excuses. Instead, he asked the driver to take them to Stephen's Green, where he pointed out the hideous Justice Department building. 'It has somewhat the style of our own police establishments,' she remarked.

'Surprise, surprise,' the driver said.

'Which are the best shops in Dublin?' Heidi asked him. 'We have to buy a jacket.'

'For him or for you?'

'For him.'

'Grafton Street's the only place for him,' the man replied. 'I'll drop you on Dawson.'

Heidi added a generous tip to the fare, clipped the receipt into her wallet. 'Guido will refund our costs.' She was still carrying her mobile phone in her hand, as though expecting a call.

He let her lead him into Brown Thomas, where she bought him an assortment of fantastically priced underclothes, shirts, ties, corduroy trousers and a Harris tweed jacket. He would never have spent that kind of money. She paid no attention to cost, but carefully stored the credit card receipts. He remembered expeditions to draper's with his mother when he was a small boy, the brown paper parcels tied with string. Heidi liked clothes, kept them neat, never bought new things without carrying a consignment to the charity shop. He imagined her as having learned thrift when young.

As they made their way back up the pedestrian street, laden with paper bags, the rain set in: a sudden shower that darkened the sky and looked just a little like the beginning of the end of the world. They took shelter in the doorway of The Deep Ravine, where they were joined moments later by a lurching figure, clutching a sodden cigarette which he was attempting to revive by sucking it voraciously. Séamus's heart sank when he recognized him: Donie Browne. Donie had been a civil service messenger. Sadly, the recognition was mutual.

'Séamus, me ould flower! How's the form?' Donie's stage whisper was barely louder than the intakes of cigarette-shortened breath that punctuated it. 'What are you up to, sloping off – at this hour of day, hah? Office hours still in full swing. As they say.' He was gasping for air, could only issue burst transmissions. 'Or – did I hear – you were after retiring? Leaving Sal on her tod? I hear the new Minister – is all over – the same Sal.' Donie's familiar manner had always set Séamus's teeth on edge. Slow in the performance of his official duties, Donie had always been quick to trade gossip.

'I'm out for a healthy walk.' Séamus smiled at the rain.

This attempt at a light response failed dismally. 'Go on! Get out of it! Healthy walk, on the day that's in it?' Starved of air, Donie could no longer manage much volume, but made his feeble voice even more raucous to signify added emphasis. 'Get away! Didn't I hear you moved to Germany? And is this your lady wife? As they say.' Donie took another drag on his drowned cigarette as he inspected Heidi from top to bottom.

'Just a friend,' Heidi said with a blank smile.

'Dónal de Brún,' Donie said. 'Pleased to meet you, Missus. As they say. Hope I haven't interrupted your purchases?' He leered at the lingerie display that filled the windows of The Deep Ravine.

'Today we buy menswear,' she replied.

'And what are you doing yourself these days, Donie?' Séamus enquired politely. 'Still with the Department of Justice, Equality and Law Reform?'

'Not on your Nellie. Fecked off before Christmas. Took the package, got out early. Says you. Still young enough – to enjoy me old age, wha'? So you're shopping, are you? You're not the only one. Did you see me rig-out?'

He was wearing a rather loud suit with a black and tan houndstooth pattern. It looked as if he had run it up himself on a sewing machine. 'Off to the Clarence,' he confided. 'Job interview.'

'What's the job?'

'Some Yankee start-up. Healthcare, you know? They want a community liaison officer. Keep the local lads – from burning the place down, know what I mean? If you want to get on, that's what it takes. But you've got to be up to it. And you've got to be into it. If you're not on the ball, you're out on your ear. As they say.' He winked at Séamus. 'So, still in touch with the old gang?'

'Not really.'

'In the doghouse, are we?

'No.'

'You worked with Billy O'Rourke, didn't you?'

'For a few months.'

'Never been found. They say he's dead.'

'Is that so?'

'Hope so. That man really got up my nose. Came on the outing last summer. Which he was not supposed to, in actual fact, but he was sparking the club secretary. We were down in Killarney, knocking back a few Jamesons. I got off with this fabulous bird. Young one. Chatting her up. I was shifting her, we were all set, only Billy has to let out – that I'm a married man. Feckin' eejit. Your one was off, like a scalded cat.'

Séamus said nothing. Donie interpreted this as a hostile comment. 'Oh, fair enough,' he conceded, 'but Billy was supposed to be, you know, my friend. Wasn't he? And he drops me in it, like that? I was never so pissed off. Speaking of which, are yiz on for a quick one? As they say.' He included Heidi in the invitation.

'He means a drink,' Séamus explained.

'No, thanks,' she replied.

Séamus looked at Donie's unsteady stance. 'Strong coffee might be the thing, before the interview.'

'Ah, not at all. Them entrepreneurs, they're into their Bacardis and their Camparis. You got to be able to put it away. As they say.' And, waving goodbye, he hobbled across the street and ducked into Neary's pub.

After a few minutes the rain thinned, then stopped, and a watery sun began to break through the clouds. Séamus and Heidi walked slowly towards the Green. In contrast to Donie's physical grossness, she seemed ephemeral, too brittle to survive in the world of weights and measures. A butterfly? Séamus remembered the Wordsworth poem he had been made to learn: 'A lovely apparition, sent to be a moment's ornament.' That was the poet's tribute to his wife, who he finally comes to realize is a machine, travelling between life and death. Just the stuff for schoolboys to learn by heart. Heidi's lightness was a kind of strength. Séamus would sink into the earth; she would float.

'When he said "on your ear",' she asked, 'this also can mean "intoxicated"?'

'Yes. We have many synonyms for that condition.'

'The Irish are famous drinkers. Apart from you.'

'Apart from me.' That had been one of his failings, in

Theresa's eyes. Insufficient drunkenness. Lack of violence. Not a real man.

With sudden urgency, Heidi crossed the narrow street and accosted a young woman who was waiting on the corner with a vacant expression. 'Who sent you, please?' she asked.

'Hah?' The young woman looked bewildered. 'Who're you?'

Séamus, who had followed Heidi, felt himself shrivelling.

'I've never seen youse before in my life,' the young woman protested.

Heidi flipped open her mobile phone and thumbed through a little gallery of photographs, taken in the newsagents at Donnybrook, on the street in Rathmines, in several departments of Brown Thomas. Each of them included the woman, sometimes wearing a cap, sometimes bareheaded. 'We lost you in Donnybrook,' Heidi said, 'when we got into the taxi. I don't have you in Ringsend. I am not sure how you picked us up again. Satellite tracking, perhaps? Are you with the police?'

'God, no.'

'Who is your client, then?'

'I can't tell you that.'

'Who's your employer?' Séamus asked.

The young woman hesitated, shrugged. 'It's a company called Clarendon Investigations.'

'Beside Connolly's office,' Séamus said. 'In the same laneway. Too much of a coincidence.'

'You've been annoying her,' the woman said.

'The redhead? She's easily annoyed,' Séamus replied.

'I am glad we have settled that,' Heidi said, clipping shut the clamshell cover of her mobile phone. 'We are going to dinner now, and we wish to be alone.'

Saturday

I

His bed was empty. Coffee vapour confirmed her presence. And he could not remember a thing from his dreams, if any. It was as though he had died. Released from the daily rehearsal.

He felt diminished by Heidi's return. A good feeling. Also, doubly foreign. This was not his place.

Dublin had always been a problem. From second city of the British Empire, bigger than Calcutta, it had shrunk to being the capital of the Irish Free State. On first arriving from the country, Séamus had tried to identify with the place. Marriage to Theresa, first-generation English, had complicated that, but it was a dubious enterprise in any case. Rural Ireland distrusted all towns with a population of over 500, and was leery of Dublin, with its hordes of jackeens, shoneens and West Brits. Moreover, nationalist Ireland's proud tradition of resistance to foreign administrations had been seamlessly extended to resisting its own elected government. The nation's capital was, by definition, a centre of oppression. This created certain ideological strains in the breast of a civil servant, not least because the civil service, theoretically faithful to the myth of Irish Ireland, was in practice devoted to continuing the finest values of British administration. Over time, Séamus had come to the conclusion that this was the right thing to do, as the inturned, inbred Ireland that followed what he privately came to call the War of Pseudo-Independence had desperately needed the discipline of an external standard of conduct, however inadequate, to save it from imploding.

He had made his peace with Dublin, had been grateful for the limited space it had left for some kind of personal life. The growing influence of Europe had introduced a different sort of empire, more benign, more Austro-Hungarian. The Irish administration had finally evolved new skills, had transcended its colonial past so successfully that Ireland was now an enthusiastic colony of the United States of America. Which was, once again, an improvement. Television, immigration and travel had reshaped the Irish consciousness, transforming the nation into a slightly cosmopolitan place. The Dublin to which Séamus had previously become reconciled no longer existed. Even the food was different. Once, the choice had been shabby stodge or snobby stodge. During his student years he had taken Fionnuala to dinner in a place with dim chandeliers and greasy Paisley-patterned carpets, to be served boarding-school mashed potato by an unwashed waiter in black tie and tails. Dublin restaurants then had been no better than the Royal County Hotel back home. Garlic and herbs were the work of the devil.

If Dublin had adapted to the presence of aliens like Heidi, then Séamus was no longer at home here, and he might as well move to Germany and have done with it.

King's College was a long way away.

Had somebody called his name just now?

He was going to sell this house.

These variegated thoughts, some familiar, some new, had flashed through his head in a matter of seconds, as sequential and fragmented as news headlines traversing an electronic display. The last idea – selling the house – seemed perhaps worth preserving.

Voices in conversation rose from below. He quickly put on some of his new clothes, splashed water on his face in the bathroom. They watched him descend the stairs. On the glass-topped table, croissants and jam and newspapers.

They made a perfect couple: Mike Dineen, big and muscular; Heidi, light enough to float. Her hair was catching the light reflected from the window ledge. Something in her pose took her momentarily out of time, fixed her like a digital image. At once, that image conjured its opposite: Theresa when young. Theresa's softness was her disguise, her shield. It had stopped her taking hard decisions – such as jettisoning Séamus when he had first been revealed as a mistake.

Not that people did, in those days. One put up with things. Later, when separation and even divorce had become socially possible, Theresa had already opted for separate lives and a string of affairs. An Irish solution to an Irish problem, as someone once said.

Dineen sipped his coffee warily, as though it might have been poisoned. Heidi handed Séamus a glass of orange juice and a plate containing a large croissant. He glanced at the open newspapers. The *Irish Times* had an obituary of Oliver P. Cregan. The *Dublin Morning Courier* led with a stabbing in Limerick. The *Gazette* mentioned the condition of John Hynes, still in intensive care but expected to live. The author of that report, Trixie Gill, recalled that payment of Séamus's pension was being delayed pending a full review of his personal assets, and alluded to the seemingly unstoppable rise of something she called the East Side gang since Séamus had first taken over the reins at the Irish Drugs Enforcement Agency. Séamus had never heard of the East Side gang and suspected that they were a figment of Trixie's imagination.

Séamus drained his glass. Heidi passed him a cup of coffee. Dineen spoke: 'Surprised they're still spinning against you?'

'Yes. Why would they bother?'

'Look at it from their angle. Richard Frye was dumped in the heat of an election campaign. If you had exposed him at any other time, they would have brazened it out. He's waiting to claw his way back, but it could take years. If his friends can discredit you, that will speed things up.'

'But I don't cause trouble,' Séamus objected. 'I'm yesterday's man.'

'They can't be sure of that. Now, I've got something to ask you. It's personal to yourself.'

'I will go to the kitchen,' Heidi said. She closed the door behind her.

2

Dineen opened a cardboard file. Like a gambler dealing cards, he distributed across the carpet a sheaf of monochrome photographs showing the guest bedroom in the President's House. Séamus's arrival was recorded, then his return in the afternoon, and finally Fionnuala coming into the room at night, and what had happened on his bed. During this last sequence, Séamus could hardly be seen, but the view of Fionnuala was explicit enough.

'You know this lady,' Dineen said. He was embarrassed.

'Yes.'

'You never told us about this.'

Séamus stood up, crossed the room, opened the kitchen door. 'There's something you need to look at,' he said.

When she saw the pictures, she gave a low wolf-whistle. Dineen looked surprised. She picked up the most compromising image and examined it critically. 'He is not making the best of his opportunities, I must say. Have you brought a magnifying glass, Inspector?'

Dineen said nothing.

Séamus asked, 'What purpose do these pictures serve?'

Dineen looked at him. 'Evidence of timing, and motivation. See the time stamped in the corner? This was just before the President was killed. Everyone tells me you were close to this lady.'

'Long ago,' Séamus said.

'Not close enough, I think,' Heidi observed. She replaced the photograph carefully on the floor beside the sofa. 'Is there a sequence? Am I missing the best part?'

'And several people have informed me' – Dineen was doggedly serious – 'that she was close to the murder victim.'

'What strikes me,' Heidi said, 'is that Séamus is not very active in the situation. Which impairs the value of the resulting pictures.'

'What do you mean?' Dineen was growing frustrated.

'These pictures were made for a purpose, Inspector. The woman waves to the camera. She is quite photogenic, I must say. Posing like a water-nymph. *Die Lorelei*, perhaps. You could put her on the cover of a holiday brochure, for the over-sixties.'

'Do you think these photographs were made for blackmail purposes?' Séamus asked. 'Where did you get them?'

'The President's House,' Dineen said, 'was rewired. Cables going through the walls, linked up with cameras, microphones. The cameras can be controlled by switches or left on automatic. Whatever they pick up comes down to a server in the President's basement.'

'And Fionnuala knew that?'

'Haven't asked her.'

Heidi sniffed. 'Why not, Inspector? Why did you not ask her?' She stepped back from the pictures.

Dineen ignored her question. 'I'm doing you a good turn, Séamus, alerting you to this. Somebody outside the College is harvesting information. The President's server is networked to a machine in the United States, in Arizona. We'll get the exact address by tomorrow. And if it's a computer geek or an IT company over there, they've probably got links back to Ireland.'

Séamus instantly thought of McKinley, who had set up the meeting with Fionnuala in the restaurant. McKinley, or his associates, had already been involved in publishing pictures of Séamus's father. These new pictures were probably too hot for most Irish newspapers, but with the *Courier* such considerations might not apply.

'Have you heard of anyone planning to publish these?' he asked.

'No,' Dineen said. 'Not yet. We obviously take an interest, day by day, in what the news media are planning to say about King's College, because it can affect our work, and because I have to spend my own valuable time thinking up answers to media questions. Some investigations, both here and abroad, have been ruined by leaks and press speculation. Which is why we have our contacts. We keep our ear to the ground. So far, nobody seems to be talking about these pictures.'

'If the *Gurrier* gets them,' Séamus said, 'they'll be published. Thanks for the warning.'

The Inspector did not acknowledge his gratitude. 'Now I need to hear your explanation of what happened.'

'Nothing happened. She turned up when I was going to sleep.'

'Does this sort of thing happen to you often?' There was an edge of mockery in the Inspector's voice.

'Mr Dineen' – Heidi suddenly raised her voice – 'will you kindly leave our house?' She advanced on Dineen, quivering with sudden rage. Dineen flinched at the speed of her movement, glanced up to meet her eye, started to scoop the photographs from the floor. Séamus froze.

'I'm going.' The Inspector gathered up his photographs and stuffed them into the cardboard folder, never taking his eyes off Heidi.

'That is a good decision,' she said, opening the door to let him out.

As his car engine started, she crossed the floor and picked

up the single photograph she had flicked under the sofa with her foot.

'A souvenir?' She handed it to Séamus. Her smile was slightly dangerous. 'Really, you should bring it back to your old friend.'

Séamus glanced at it again. It showed Fionnuala from the back. How many men in King's College had seen her like this, loose hair tumbling down, right arm flung out like a child launching a yo-yo? Better not ask.

He looked at Heidi. 'Why are you not angry?' Even though innocent, he expected at least some blame, or a flattering show of jealousy.

Heidi shrugged. 'The honeytrap was a technique much favoured by the German Democratic Republic. The woman is not a convincing performer, I must say.'

'Nothing happened.'

'That is quite clear. Now,' she continued, 'I guess you will be wanting to consult with McKinley.'

'He gave me some phone numbers,' Séamus remembered, 'in the restaurant on Wednesday night.' He went upstairs, found the card in the pocket of his torn blazer. No answer from the Billings agency. He tried McKinley's home.

3

'For the good of the College,' McKinley said after a silence. 'No other agenda. I have always acted above board. I did not "set you up", as you say, with that woman, Miss Fagan.' His breath was short, as though he had been interrupted while doing his fitness exercises. 'I have no connection with any photos. I strongly disapproved of President Cregan's use of surveillance cameras. I told him so myself. More than once. I would never use the output from such a device. It's a violation of a lady's privacy, that's what it is. Of course those photos are not going to end up in the *Courier*. Don't be silly. Who showed them to you?'

'Have you seen them yourself?'

'Certainly not.' But he sucked in his breath at the end of the phrase, as though trying to swallow the lie.

In the background was the sound of a hesitant performer, perhaps a child, picking through 'Für Elise' on an adenoidal piano that needed to be tuned, mingled with the more distant whine of a high-pitched vacuum cleaner.

'You sent me home with Fionnuala. Why?'

'Never asked her to get into your bed, for God's sake!' McKinley protested. 'Have dinner, yes, have a drink, drive you home. That's all. We wanted to be friendly.'

'Why?'

'You were an unknown quantity. We knew why you had been sent, who was behind you, but we didn't know what line you might take. Cregan was afraid you might be disloyal to the College.' McKinley was talking too much, accumulating words like a dyke against his troubles. 'Hinckley is a bloody shark. Of course King's has its problems. In Cregan's view, that didn't mean we deserved to be turned into part of a foreign chain. He wanted to preserve our independence. As a board member, I supported him in that. Which doesn't mean I would ever condone improper means. Anyway, I'm sure Oliver Cregan had no intention of publishing the photographs. He was trying to get a handle on you. What he did was *ultra vires*. It was wrong.' He stopped, as if shocked by his own moral absolutism.

'Why should you care about the independence of King's College?' Séamus asked. 'What's your interest in it?'

'It's not about the money, Séamus. Surely I'm allowed to feel some allegiance to my alma—'

'Tell me,' Séamus interrupted, 'what exactly is wrong with Finer Small Campuses?'

McKinley sighed. 'They plan to commoditize Irish higher

education for their private gain. In return for a derisory investment, they aim to colonize our national resources. That's not right. We're not a banana republic. An education system is not like a copper-mine in Chile. Oliver Cregan didn't see why they should get away with it.'

'Did he blackmail the other consultants, too?'

McKinley chuckled. 'No need. Finer Small Campuses hired you. We hired the other guys. And consultants tend to write what their clients need to hear.' Despite his initial disadvantage, McKinley was regaining control of the conversation. 'It's doggy out there, Séamus.'

'Doggy?'

'Dog eat dog. Cregan was trying to defend his turf. Call him paranoid, but then look what happened to him.'

'Were you working for Cregan or Forde?'

'What difference does it make?'

'The Americans are interested in an educational partnership. But King's is also a development site. Forde wants to get the best property deal he can, whether or not the Americans gain control of the College. Forde has investments to protect. He's up before the tribunals. What's your connection with him?'

'We've handled his press releases. That's a matter of public record. All strictly professional. Billings is an ethical firm.'

'And your link to Cregan?'

'The same. Purely professional.' A pause. 'Oliver was obsessed with information, poor man.'

'Who installed the cameras in his house?'

'Guys from a security firm. On their day off.'

'Off-duty cops?'

'Some of them. Are you going to discuss these pictures with Fionnuala?'

'Yes. You've been most helpful. By the way, do you control the *Gurrier*?'

'Control? Me? No. Shareholder. Minor.'

4

During this conversation, Heidi had changed into a tight black top and well-cut black trousers that made her look, at first sight, like a twenty-year-old Dubliner going for her first job interview. She had also produced a duster and a little tin of polish, with which she now began to buff the brasses on the front door. Was this part of her Teutonic desire for cleanliness? He did not remember the obsession as having been quite so bad. He offered to help. She waved him away. He poured her another cup of coffee, which she declined. Her phone buzzed. She clicked it on, spoke briefly in German, stepped out on to the pavement to continue the conversation. When she returned, she reported to Séamus: 'That was Guido. Special meeting of trustees and council this afternoon, thirty minutes past two. Senator Hinckley is invited to send an observer, and he has nominated you. I will see you later.'

'First I want to give the photograph to Fionnuala.'

'Good idea.'

'Would you like to come?'

'No. You can handle this on your own. And I feel I have seen her quite extensively already.'

He transferred his credit cards, cash, pens and diary to his new Harris tweed jacket, and put the incriminating photograph into a large envelope that had contained a junk mail offer addressed to the previous tenants. By the time he came downstairs, Heidi was standing at the door, her mobile phone in her hand. She had tidied everything away. The living room was preternaturally neat, like a showhouse or a funeral home. She handed him a piece of paper containing Fionnuala's address and phone number. She had transcribed the information from the phone book. 'We must find you a taxi, and I think I will need to do some shopping.' She was holding a small supermarket bag, which appeared to contain the King's

College documentation that he had been given before Cregan's murder. She was invading his work. He could hardly object.

She linked arms and escorted him along the street to Morehampton Road. He felt like a prisoner under guard, unable to resist. Where was she going in her black business clothes? To visit a lawyer, from the look of her. A taxi appeared, and stopped at her command. She kissed him lightly, slipping her lizard tongue between his lips, and opened the taxi door with ironic deference. He climbed in. She stood and watched till he was out of sight.

Fionnuala's address was off the North Circular Road. He had never heard of the street, but the driver knew it well. Traffic was heavy but flowing; they were quickly on the Liffey quays. There, however, they got stuck. He was hungry again. Since Wednesday night, his body was following new rhythms. Twice, he tried phoning Fionnuala. The line was engaged. He wondered what Heidi might be thinking about him now. Her first amused reaction might have given way to anger. He imagined her thinking him a bit old to be caught out like this. A bird with greying feathers should be able to avoid a honeytrap. He wanted to phone her too, but restrained himself.

The house, when they finally reached it through bottle-necked traffic, was a drab red-brick with a small front garden, part of a narrow terrace close to the edge of the Phoenix Park. Close enough, in fact, to walk to King's College in fifteen or twenty minutes. He supposed that Fionnuala drove to work because walking across the Phoenix Park might not be such a good idea for a woman, especially when returning late in the evenings.

Her street was lined with silent ranks of parked cars on either side, not unlike his street in Donnybrook. Marriage to Theresa had removed him from little streets like this, until now.

He pushed his way through the garden gate and pressed the

plastic doorbell, which chimed like an airport announcement. When she opened the door, it was clear that she knew why he had come. McKinley must have warned her. Hence her phone line being busy just now. He handed her the photograph. 'Yours to keep.'

She blinked. 'Please, come in?'

The orderliness of Fionnuala's room at King's College had given no hint of her domestic life. The hall was in a mess, with books and bags strewn across the sisal matting. A single bulb cast a weak light from within a mother-of-pearl shade. A patch of peeling wallpaper was partly covered by a framed photograph of a king's head from a gothic monument. The frame was hanging askew.

Fionnuala trudged before him like a circus animal that has seen better days and may shortly be destined for cat food. He followed her three steps down into the kitchen extension, where uncleared dishes cluttered a wooden table and stained tea mugs were ranged on a discoloured worktop. The doors of the kitchen units were skewed on their hinges, as though deliberately damaged. The door of the dishwasher was twisted open. Loose sheets of typescript were strewn across the floor. There was a broken glass panel in the French window leading out into the back garden. The place looked as if a low-intensity bomb had been detonated in the vicinity.

'As you can see, we've had a break-in.' Noticing his surprise, she blinked. 'It's not my usual standard of housekeeping, Séamus.'

'When did it happen?'

'In the past couple of hours. We were out. Haven't even phoned the Guards yet. Don't know if I'll bother. Sit down. Red wine.' A statement, not a question. She rinsed a glass. The bottle was already open, and partly drunk, as was Fionnuala. She started to pour for him. 'That's enough,' he said.

They sat on wooden chairs. She looked at the photograph

again with a slightly appraising eye, then turned it face down. 'How can I explain this?' She drank deeply.

'Overwhelming passion?' He sipped from his glass, put it aside.

'I'm sorry,' Fionnuala said as if she meant it.

'When we first met on Tuesday, you couldn't wait to get out of your room.'

'You don't know the pressures, Séamus. That day you came to my office – Tuesday, was it really? – I was so happy.' She shook her head. 'Then I got a hysterical call from a man I'd befriended. Someone told him you and I were –'

She blushed. It suited her.

'Which we definitely weren't. Who was this?'

'Paddy De Soto. English Department. His wife died last year. I went out with him a couple of times to cheer him up. He became obsessive.'

'Was it Quaid who said I was with you?'

'Why do you ask?'

'He had been teasing me about you that morning. Also, he would see his Head of Department as a legitimate target.'

She nodded. 'I had to drive Paddy home. He would not believe me. He would not calm down. I had to stay with him half the night.'

'Better not show him the photograph, then.'

Fionnuala coughed. Swallowed more wine. Shuddered again, as though the wine were rough vodka.

'And the second man who phoned?'

'I don't remember that.'

'It was after you'd left. He warned you to stop the tittle-tattle. Country voice. It's on your answering machine.'

'I haven't listened to my messages.'

He changed tack: 'So, apart from passion, what brought you to the President's House on Wednesday night?'

She sighed. 'It's complicated. After Andy's dis-appearance –'

'O'Neill?'

'That's right.' Another sigh. 'After Andy's disappearance, he turned against me.'

'You mean Cregan?'

'Yes. Oliver turned against me. It started with the medieval remains, the Abbey foundations and so forth. Andy had been convinced that the Forde Centre building works were going to destroy them.'

'Jeremy Quaid told me about his digging.'

'Yes. Oliver was angry, but Andy insisted that Maxwell had hired the wrong firm of archaeologists for the site survey. I supported him in that. None of us had been consulted. They were cronies of Maxwell. Andy refused to back down. If he picked an argument, or decided something was wrong, he would follow it to the bitter end. Ever since his days in Zimbabwe, Andy did what he thought was right. Whatever the consequences. That's why he had to leave the priesthood.' She looked at Séamus as though he might wish to question O'Neill's bona fides. He nodded reassuringly, as though he understood and accepted everything.

'Before he disappeared,' she went on, 'he had found there was no danger to the old buildings. Or so Oliver said, and Martin Forde heard much the same from Andy's young research assistant, Ronan Gannon. Andy and Ronan had found that the Forde Centre was being built on the old abbey farm, which has no significant remains from the medieval period. I didn't know what to believe. I had heard Andy saying there were some remains of a holy well near the Temple of Remembrance, which got built over the remains of the abbey's chapter house. I asked Oliver about the well and suggested further excavations, to see if there was anything left that could still be preserved. Oliver turned away from me. He could be vindictive.' She stopped, drank more wine.

'Go easy on that stuff, Fionnuala.'

'You're right.' She put the glass down. 'I'm under pressure.

So that's how it happened.' She looked at him as though she had provided a full explanation.

'Getting into my bed with me was your way of making peace with Cregan?'

She did not seem to hear the question. 'We had been close, but Oliver no longer trusted me.' She frowned. 'Being President was everything to him. Maxwell had ruined us, literally pawned the College silver –'

'When you say "literally" –?'

'Yes. Literally. The tableware. Figuratively, too. He'd given away far too much to Seán Forde.'

'That seems to be a common failing.'

'Yes. President Maxwell compromised our independence. He was coming to the end of his term of office. He was grooming one of his favourites to succeed him, and then, when he had to resign prematurely, there was a real fight over the succession. Oliver, to get elected, promised far too much to the Americans, too much to the government, too much to his colleagues. Everybody was to get something. Two rival professors – Paddy De Soto and Magnus O'Toole – had both been promised the Vice-President's post, and in the end it went to Conleth Millington. You see, Oliver had promised Millington a new science building, although he must have known there was no money to build it. The vice-presidency was a consolation prize. Oliver had never admitted how much of the new College properties Forde already owned. He kept talking about having a source of matching funds. That was pure imagination. Hinckley must have realized the deal wasn't going to happen.'

She stopped. He had let her talk without interruption, but she knew that she was not answering the question that was most on his mind.

On the dirty gas stove, a metallic kettle sang, unaccompanied. It was a long time since he had seen such a kettle. The age of plastic had not yet conquered Fionnuala.

Still he said nothing. She coughed and asked quietly, 'How did you come by that photograph?'

'Inspector Dineen showed it to me. Along with others.'

'Oliver would never have made them public,' Fionnuala said, as though that were an important fact to be established. 'Oliver was not an evil man. He did not deserve what happened to him. He might have let you know he had the pictures, to influence your report for Senator Hinckley. But he would never have published them. I'm sure of that. And because I had helped him, he might have hesitated to move against me.' She took another drink.

'Why should Cregan want to move against you?'

'I'd supported Andy in raising questions about the building projects. He couldn't forget that. Forde's people – especially Stanihurst, the site manager – disliked Andy, so I was on the enemy list too. They even saw something sinister in my taking Martin to live in my house. Our relationship is completely proper.'

Séamus said nothing.

'Oliver was terrified,' Fionnuala continued, 'that I'd embarrass the College and cause problems with Seán Forde. And you can imagine how vulnerable my position has been. I've been acting director of the Medieval Dublin Centre since Andy's disappearance. There's been talk of closing it down. I've never had a proper job. Every post I've held has contained the words "temporary" or "acting". I've never been fully accepted. And now the pressure has got infinitely worse.'

She needed his approval. There was a sense of something unsaid. He wished that he could help, but bitterness welled up within him. 'You were proving your loyalty, then, on Wednesday night?'

'That's unfair,' she protested. 'Motives are not so simple. At least, mine aren't. You of all people should know that. I was reminding Oliver of my existence. I needed to get back into his house. Into his life. But apart from that, what

I said was true. You and I, we'd missed our chance, years ago.'

'In the days of Gaskell.'

'Don't be cruel, Séamus. Harold Gaskell took advantage of me. I don't want to go into all the details. Not everything that happens should necessarily be told.'

There were tears in her eyes. It was mostly the wine. He wanted to comfort her. He stretched out his hand. Hearing a sound behind him, he twisted around to face the bull-like young man he had first met outside Fionnuala's office: Martin Forde, standing in the open doorway to the garden. He looked angry and frightened. There was blood on his fingers.

5

Fionnuala rose and reached for a tissue. 'Here, Martin, let me clean your hand.' She took him by the fingers and led him to the tap. She poured a trickle of water on to a tea towel, dabbed at the blood with the dampened fabric.

'It's all that glass,' he said, distractedly. 'I thought I heard him again, at the back fence.'

'Martin disturbed the burglar, earlier this morning,' she explained. 'I'm sure he's gone long ago. They don't usually hang around. You two have met, haven't you? Séamus? Martin?'

The young man glanced at Séamus with apparent disdain. 'The American envoy, surely.' He spoke in a lilting Mayo brogue as though performing in a centenary production of some Irish classic play: 'The grand plenipotentiary of the Finer Small Campuses of the Western World. It's power they're seeking only.' He frowned. 'Too true, actually.' He had reverted to his previous accent. 'They'll take over the College, or whatever's left of it after my father.' There was a slight hesitation on the last word.

'Seán Forde.'

'Yes. My father. Seán Forde. As you say.' Martin spoke the words with shame and pride. 'I am the son of a great man.' He stood to attention. 'I'm entitled to preferential treatment and a brilliant career.' Somehow the irony failed.

'What exactly are my Americans planning to destroy? The remains of the medieval abbey?'

'No! The College. The country. Never mind the abbey.' His voice was too loud, too certain. 'The abbey remains were mostly destroyed when the King's quadrangle and cloisters were built, nearly two hundred years ago. Regency vandals. And the College chapel. Educational Goths. Now my father's people are going to wreck whatever's left of the chapter house, but even that was mostly ruined in 1863 by the Victorian Visigoths who threw up their Temple of Remembrance. No, it's not just the buildings. It's the money god. It's the decadent times we live in, darlings. It's the price of everything, the value of nothing, and they want us to cheer.'

During this booming speech, with its flashes of fragile wit, Martin kept checking the reaction in Séamus's eyes. He seemed to sense that he was failing to communicate his meaning, if indeed he had a stable meaning to communicate.

'Did you help Andrew O'Neill in his excavations?' Séamus asked.

'Must I answer your questions?' Martin asked. 'Indeed and I must, for you are the great investigator from beyond the seas.' He gestured at Fionnuala. 'She tells me you're very important.'

'Not really. I'm just trying to understand what's happened. Did you see what Andrew O'Neill was doing?'

'No. That was mostly Ronan. They worked together. They were close. Ronan wouldn't say what they discussed. He kept Andy's confidences. He was loyal.'

Martin's speech was too insistent, his voice a little too quick. He assumed that his listener was already tuned into each new topic, leaving no need for modulation. A young person's fault, although shared by such oldsters as Jeremy Quaid and certain other teachers that Séamus had met in his time. How old was Martin? Rather than a young adult, he was an enormous child.

Fionnuala was saying nothing, but watching to see how Séamus was judging Martin. He sensed that this was important to her.

'In the end,' Martin went on a little more quietly, 'Andy found he was wrong, and he was big enough to admit it. He told the new President that my father's people weren't building over the medieval part at all. They might have been, you see. The archaeologists' survey was full of stupid mistakes. But it made no difference. My father's in the clear, as usual.'

'I think he's a good man,' Séamus said. 'I don't believe he's out to destroy things.'

Martin laughed. 'So you're in his pocket, too?'

'No. Just calling it as I see it.'

'You don't know what he's done.'

'Ease up, Martin,' Fionnuala said. 'Your father isn't destroying anything. He's giving new buildings to the College for less than they cost to build. He's being generous.'

Martin looked at her with the amused pity of the young for middle-aged delusion. 'My father is muscling in. That's what he's doing. As always. You're easily fooled, Fionnuala. And yes, you need to break out. Let me take you away from all this.'

She nodded. 'So long as you can find your passport, Martin.' She turned to Séamus. 'He's taking me to Córdoba,' she said. 'I want to see the mosque.'

'Wonderful,' Séamus said, although he had never been there.

'They built it when we were making the Book of Kells. When Charlemagne was angling to be crowned Holy Roman Emperor.'

'When builders were builders,' Martin said. 'Yes, Fionnuala, we shall travel far.' He swung his right arm slowly in a wide gesture, taking in the chaotic kitchen, the scattered papers on the floor, the broken cupboards. 'Away from all possible embarrassment. My dear father will be up before the tribunals next week, you know.'

'I know,' Séamus said. 'That doesn't mean he's done anything wrong.'

'Oh, does it not? I hadn't realized. Well, how's it going to sound if he's been destroying a holy well, obliterating the last traces of a medieval chapter house, wiping out some of the last remnants of medieval Dublin? How's that going to sound? Do you think he'll get a hard time then? Would he get his name in the paper?'

Séamus raised his hands. 'Who knows? Depends on his lawyers, I suppose.'

'Oh, he has the very best. Believe me.' Martin smiled. 'A Forde can always afford the best.' His eyes twinkled with childish pleasure. 'No matter what we've been up to.' He stopped abruptly, stood up.

'Please wait,' Fionnuala said.

'You have a protector.' Martin looked down at Séamus. 'You don't need me.' His look suggested that anyone as decrepit as Séamus would be little use in defending a lady. It was as if he had not decided whether his own identity was based on mental agility or physical strength.

Séamus looked up at Martin. Martin was tall, broad, of athletic build, with the same awkward stance as old Forde, yet he had nothing to match the old man's commanding presence. There seemed to be more of him than he knew what to do with, whereas on first meeting his father Séamus had had the feeling of an integrated being, body and soul. He reminded Séamus of a collie pup belonging to his brother Daniel that had fetched up, in the distant past, under the wheels of a lorry on the back Dromahane road. Séamus asked, 'You were in charge of the mace, weren't you?'

'Please.' Fionnuala's voice trailed away.

'You know I was. So what?' Martin was trying to be nonchalant, but the question was painful to him.

'Who do you think removed it from the storeroom?'

'I don't know,' the young man said, his voice quickening again. 'I had nothing to do with it. The Guards took my fingerprints.'

'That doesn't mean anything, Martin,' Fionnuala said, as though speaking to a small child. She turned to Séamus. 'Please stop. Let's all have something to eat.'

'I've got to get going,' Martin said, moving suddenly across the room.

Something about the young man's heavy footfall stirred a subliminal echo in Séamus's mind. He stood up, blocking the steps leading to the hall. 'We need to talk,' he said. 'You and me.'

Martin Forde reached out, pushed Séamus aside with blood-stained fingers. Séamus steadied himself against the table. Martin shouldered past him to the hall, flung open the front door. Séamus followed. Martin did not look back. There was the sound of a car door slamming, then an engine starting up.

'Damn!' Fionnuala was standing in the hall. 'He's not insured.' Her exasperated look was laden with affection. They walked back to the kitchen.

The physical bulk and strength of Martin Forde, contrasting with his childish distress, stuck in Séamus's throat. He imagined a small boy being told that his mother had met her death. Drank like a fish, the former Lord Mayor had said. Had Martin heard the same words? Who could fix such pain? Time heals, but childhood is forever out of reach. What did Martin see in Fionnuala now? A surrogate mother to put him to bed?

'Why would Forde's son choose Medieval History?' he asked to distract himself from his thoughts. 'And why come to King's College, of all places? Because his father had some connection with the place?'

'Some connection, yes. But you've got it exactly the wrong way round.'

'How's that?'

'You mustn't jump to conclusions, Séamus.' Fionnuala was pleased to put him right. 'Seán Forde came to the College because of Martin. And Martin insisted on coming to study here because of his mother. Of course, you remember Mary Kate.'

6

'Mary Kate?'

There was a moment of incomprehension. Then, as if a trigger had been touched in his brain, Séamus was catapulted back into his student days, when he had sat in a large lecture hall looking at Fionnuala, and between them, geometrically positioned along a straight line midway between his eyes and the dark cloud of Fionnuala's hair, sat Mary Kate Gilligan. A feckless, good-hearted girl born in the wrong century, all idealism and concern, coupled with an almost complete disregard of her studies and any obligations they might bring. Mary Kate was in college to have a good time, and also to better the state of humanity, whichever came first. Slow to rise in the mornings, she tended to arrive late even for afternoon classes. She always spoke her mind, intervening audibly in lectures and tutorials, whether or not she knew anything about the topic of the day. She seemed immune to embarrassment, unaffected by criticism. Even the most forbidding teachers responded to her with warmth. She had been a good friend to Fionnuala, had even acted briefly as a go-between in Fionnuala's relationship with Séamus, while breathing not a word about Fionnuala's simultaneous entanglement with Gaskell. Six weeks before the final examinations, Mary Kate had been taken to hospital with alcohol poisoning. Séamus had not fully realized the epic scale of her drinking, exceeding even her considerable absorption capacity. Instead of returning to take her finals in the following year, she had gone off to work in London and had later married a builder. That much he had heard.

'Mary Kate's his mother?' As he asked the question, half of Martin's physique fell into place. Also his impulsiveness.

'Martin takes a lot from Mary Kate,' Fionnuala said as if reading his thoughts. 'He has her look, and more than that. Sometimes, when he turns his head, it's as if she were going to speak. She will have been dead fifteen years this autumn.'

'The present Mrs Forde being her replacement.'

'Lovely Lucy.' There was no malice in Fionnuala's praise. 'Lucy is not all that much older than Martin. Beautiful child. Beautiful old woman, if she lives that long. Seán Forde was widowed three years before he met her. She's a complete contrast. Poor Mary Kate had let herself fall apart.'

Fell over a cliff, the politician had said on Wednesday at the degree ceremony. Séamus had not imagined it then as something actually happening, but now that he knew it was Mary Kate, he could see her heavy shape upending into the void, as surely as if he had pushed her himself.

'From the drink?' he asked.

'Who knows?' Fionnuala pushed her glass away. 'She drowned.'

'Was it suicide?'

'Accident. That was the finding. Martin blames his father. He was a child. He knows nothing about it.'

'Why does he blame his father? Does his think he killed his wife?'

'Or that she took her own life because she was unhappy in her marriage. But Martin doesn't seem to distinguish between murder and suicide. At the time, he was far too young to understand what had happened. He seemed at first to get over her death. Did well at boarding school, and later as a student here in King's. He signed on for a postgraduate degree but never got started. He dropped out completely. He'd become obsessed with remembering his mother. Only her death, not her life. I've tried to tell him about Mary Kate when she was young, before her troubles got out of hand, but he won't listen.'

'He seems to be under some strain now.'

'Yes, he is extremely stressed.' Fionnuala's tone was urgent, as though Séamus could be persuaded to provide a solution to the problem. 'Andy's disappearance and Ronan's death affected him badly. Martin tends to blame people when things go wrong. There has to be someone to blame. Accidents are not an acceptable explanation. Mary Kate's death was also reported as an accident. She was going to leave her husband. Martin is haunted by something she said: "I love your father more than anything in the world. I'd die for him." Apparently she said this several times, before she died. He was eleven years old. He keeps repeating it. He has the notion that she gave up her life in some way.'

'Not a very helpful remark to make to a child.' Séamus felt an unaccountable surge of irritation that Mary Kate's emotional incontinence was still causing trouble, all these years after her death.

Fionnuala shook her head, as though casting out his judgmental comment. 'We don't know what she was going through. Yes, Martin has had a hard time.'

'What did he do when he dropped out?'

'Took menial jobs on building sites, here in Ireland, in Britain, in America. Got into arguments. His family have had to rescue him once or twice. We persuaded him to come back here when History was reorganized.'

'When Andy O'Neill was appointed.'

'That's right. Andy helped me to supervise him. He thought well of Martin, even interviewed him for a research assistantship. But Martin was barely starting his doctorate, and Ronan Gannon had already finished his. Martin was upset, but he didn't give up. Then his father decided to take over the College. That was unfortunate, if you like.'

'Is he still in contact with his father?'

'From time to time, when he can stand it. He still has a room in their house, but mostly I look after him. He's making progress, in spite of his family. But it's a delicate balance.'

'What's wrong with his family?'

Fionnuala leaned across the table, placed her hand on Séamus's arm. Still the slight tremor in her touch. 'Martin says they're not natural. That's unfair, but there is something monstrous about them all the same. Lucy is too young to be a mother figure. Seán Forde is too big. He's a megalomaniac. He's not built on the human scale. That's why he can do those big projects. He's like a medieval abbot, the sort who could build a monastery, plan an estate, organize a district. The peasants working in their fields twenty miles away would grow what the abbot wanted them to grow, marry who he wanted them to marry, think what he wanted them to think. Forde is one of those. It used to be cathedrals, now it's shopping malls. These are democratic times, but Forde and his kind can still get inside people's heads and prescribe their lives. They lay out the roads for us to drive to their shops, in cars they sold us, to buy their goods. Martin hates that. He doesn't want all traces of people's familiar lives to be wiped away. Martin's a real historian. He knows the pattern of the past.'

'Why are you telling me this?'

'Because I know you'll be interested. And you need to understand, if you want to work out what's happening here, why I can't upset the balance of Martin's life.'

'And why am I not fighting with you, Fionnuala, after what you did to me?'

'Because we go back a long way, Séamus.' And in the old

cliché he saw a grassy path winding away towards distant blue hills.

7

Heidi's phone was powered off, or else she was out of range. After several attempts to contact her, Séamus gave up.

The King's College meeting was in the same assembly room where the honorary degree ceremony had taken place, and where Séamus now seemed vaguely to remember the echoes of table-tennis tournaments and debating competitions from his so-called youth. Things had been rearranged since Wednesday. There was a long table on the podium at the top of the room, draped in green baize, and a bunch of lilies in a stand. At the centre of the table, behind a handwritten card that read ACTING PRESIDENT, sat Millington in a spotted bow tie, flanked by other worthies, all male. One was McKinley, looking solemn. He had changed his suit for a dark-blue pinstripe. Beside him was a tweedy leprechaun whom Séamus recognized, having seen his photograph and potted biography in the latest President's Report: he was a retired civil servant from the capital grants section of the Department of Education, who had joined the board in the past year. Next to him sat the rabbit-eyed former Lord Mayor, whispering convulsively in his ear. Near the end of the table, Seán Forde brooded apart.

Séamus and Fionnuala had walked over from her house, like old friends. Keeping to the roads, it took longer than he had guessed from reading the map. She had cooked him a terrible omelette. She herself had eaten almost nothing. She separated from him at the entrance to the assembly room. Walking away, she became a different person.

There were other faces which meant nothing to Séamus.

The rest of the hall had been packed with rows of plastic chairs, mostly occupied now by swarms of academics, chattering excitedly to each other, forming sub-swarms within themselves. Student representatives, including Fergus Kilpatrick and the *King's Chronicle* photographer, huddled near the door. The uniformed boy from the President's House, whom Séamus suspected of stealing his mobile phone, looked into the room and held a whispered conversation with Kilpatrick before tiptoeing out like a mangy cat who has successfully raided a deposit of chilled sardines.

Séamus went to sit in a quiet corner. Fionnuala was standing nearby, but did not meet his eye and presently moved away to join two other women on the far side, by the window. Quaid swept in from a little door at the back of the stage, surveyed the scene like a conqueror, trotted down the steps from the podium, traversed the room and parked himself next to Séamus.

Damnation.

Quaid raised an eyebrow. 'Pleased to see me?'

'Naturally.'

Burren came and sat halfway along the same row. He looked healthy and relieved, like a man bouncing back from a poisonous disease. Séamus presumed that the poison might have been called Cregan.

Millington stood up, sounded a gong, beamed his light-house smile over the crowd.

'Dinner is served,' Quaid audibly remarked.

'We are gathered on a sad occasion,' Millington began. 'Our President has been taken from us in the most appalling manner. His personal assistant, John Hynes, has been savagely assaulted. Savagely. However' – he held up a pink palm – 'the second assault has not proved as serious as had at first been feared. I am sure we all wish a speedy recovery to one of the College's longest serving and best-loved retainers.' There were loud murmurs of polite assent, under the cover of which Quaid, leaning closer to Séamus, enunciated in the tones of a radio announcer: 'RETAINER – *noun* – American word meaning corset or truss, *circa* 1932.'

'A sad occasion,' Millington repeated, 'but also a moment of crisis. As Professor O'Toole reminded me over lunch just now, the Chinese pictogram denoting "crisis" is the same character that signifies "opportunity". Even in the midst of grief, we must take action to survive – not just survive, but prosper – and we must do it now. I hope I can rely on the support of all members of the College.'

'Some hope,' Quaid said in an operatic sotto voce to Séamus. The murmurs of assent were in fact noticeably lighter than the previous set.

'This meeting is held to inaugurate a brief interregnum,' Millington continued. 'A brief interregnum,' he repeated, 'before our affairs are once again settled into a sound and steady course. We need to establish our ground rules. The proposed format for the meeting is as follows: Matters of Information; Procedures; Review of Finances; Offices and Appointments; Strategy Going Forward. Is that agreeable to all? Yes? I hope these ground rules will be agreeable. Everything that we do must be predicated upon sound principles and procedures. Oh, and before I go any farther, let me say straight away that the difficulties in using College facilities that we have experienced will cease from this afternoon. The difficulties will cease. We have reached an understanding with the Civic Guards, or should I say An Garda Síochána. Normal access to your rooms and offices will be possible without let or hindrance during working hours, and later by arrangement with the security staff. Access to the grounds for students and even for the general public has also been restored. And classes will resume from Monday morning. Needless to say, College activities will be suspended on the day that President Cregan's funeral takes place. The day of the funeral is not yet known, but it is likely to take place on Wednesday or

Thursday, rather than Monday as previously announced, erroneously I fear, in the *Irish Times*.'

Millington's voice was getting louder, his delivery more emphatic, his reiterations more frequent. Séamus got the uncomfortable feeling that the Acting President's introductory remarks were about to blossom into a fifty-minute lecture. He was wrong. There was an interruption. An ancient patriarch staggered to his feet. Amidst a deferential hush, he turned his face to the light and emitted his inaudible advice that what was *chzkizzly* required at this *chzkinktzh* was above all *thngzh* a sense of *pzz gzzt ckazzkp* and *unzhzhng* attention to *ckazzkp gzzt pzz ckizzkp gzzt trzdizns*. Exhausted, he collapsed out of sight and was thanked by Millington for making the effort to be present and for being a living example of devotion to the College.

'How insensitive!' Quaid hissed. 'Man's a dying example.'

'Excuse me! Excuse me!' A thin, querulous voice piped up behind Séamus's right ear. 'Status and remit of this meeting, please? Is this a proper meeting of the board? Are we properly constituted? Is everybody entitled to be here? Are there minutes of the last meeting? Why have they not been circulated?'

'Thank you, Professor Moriarty,' Millington said. 'I should have clarified the position. Thank you. This is an emergency special joint session of the board and trustees, meeting in open forum with members of the academic staff and some outside observers representing interests currently involved with the College. Thank you.'

'Excuse me! Excuse me!' cried the same voice. 'Seven days' notice has to be given of any meeting. This is not a properly constituted meeting. I demand that we disperse forthwith.'

'Why don't you show us the way?' Burren barracked.

'No, no,' Millington said. 'Everyone is most welcome to be here. We did send an email yesterday, and of course we can have another meeting in seven days' time if it is felt that there are formal decisions requiring to be ratified at such a meeting. Professor Moriarty's contribution is highly valued – highly valued – and we hope that he and all of you will choose to stay.'

'I have no intention of staying,' said Moriarty, sweeping up his papers and making for the door, 'at an improperly constituted gathering.'

'What are those papers you have?' the rejuvenated Burren loudly enquired. 'Why didn't I get any?'

Moriarty stalked from the room, a procession of one.

'If everybody else is staying,' Millington began after a moment's silence, 'and if the proposed format is acceptable, I would like to outline the current arrangements for the College governance. According to the statutes, as Vice-President I am expected to carry on until a new President is chosen. My hope and expectation is that this will happen within the next few months, so I won't be asking for your indulgence for too long. That is my hope and expectation.'

'Months? Did he say months?' grumbled a bass voice from the other side of the room. 'Why not weeks?'

Millington showed the faintest sign of annoyance. 'Because, Professor Granger, council and board must determine the parameters for the new incoming president, and once those parameters have been determined, the normal advertising, shortlisting and interviewing procedures have to be gone through. We cannot proceed with greater haste until the death of President Cregan has been fully investigated.'

'Shortlisting? Interview?' Burren was outraged. 'For your information, Professor Millington, Presidents here have traditionally been chosen by open candidature. I am not aware of any decision to alter that tradition. In my opinion,' cried the newly confident and assertive Burren, 'we ought to go back to election by simple majority, as we had in the old days. None of these search committees operating behind closed doors, and favoured candidates being presented for rubber-stamp ratification.'

Séamus wondered why Burren was speaking so freely. He obviously felt no fear of the contents of Cregan's safe.

'The open election system, excellent though it is, started only in our recent history,' Millington replied. 'Previously, we had a system of direct government appointments. That is still the case with the Higher Education Authority, which stands at the very pinnacle of educational planning in this country. It is even the case in some Oxbridge colleges, I do believe. Other leading Irish universities,' he continued, 'are tending towards a competitive appointment system for their top jobs. One must question whether the open election system is appropriate for the current climate, with all its competitive pressures, the need to find able candidates, the requirement that management be detached from –'

Millington's well-rehearsed disquisition was interrupted by several contending voices, which obliterated each other, so that Séamus could not make out what, if anything, was being said. One voice eventually soared above the chorus. 'Wherever the great universities of the world are under threat,' it began in a fine tenor, 'scholars must take a stand for fundamental values. These may be defined –'

'Oh, do shut up, Wellesley!' Burren again. 'We don't have time for your party piece.'

'Am I not then to be heard?' Séamus identified the speaker, a greybeard with half-glasses and a ragged corduroy jacket.

'Later, Dr Wellesley,' Millington said in conciliatory tones. 'Later.'

Wellesley slid slowly back to a sitting position.

Close to the front of the hall, a pudgy old man tottered and swung to face the audience. He had a tuberous nose, a hairless domed head and prominent ears. He was clad in dark respectable suiting, in a style some thirty years out of fashion. 'If I might be allowed to suggest an eventuality,' he boomed in deep contralto tones, 'I would like to suggest that, in the interests of continuity and to preserve an atmosphere of neutrality, it might be appropriate to consider the reinstatement of a previous President to act *ad interim* as Regent of the College while the present disruption is being restored to a state of normality. I refer to myself, if I may do so without incurring the charge of immodesty. I would be more than willing to serve, should the need arise, as temporary leader of our academic community, for a period of time not exceeding six months, or a year, if need be.' He sniffed vigorously through his potato nose. There was a silence.

'That's President Maxwell, arisen from the grave,' Quaid explained to Séamus. 'Not content with reducing the place to gibbering chaos for seven years, he wants to come back and repeat the trick.'

'My confidence in Conleth Millington is a matter of certainty,' Maxwell continued. 'I merely wish to offer to serve the College at this time when an authoritative figure may be helpful in maintaining the quality –'

'Thank you for your offer, President Maxwell,' Millington said, 'which is much appreciated, and I'm sure the board would be happy to –'

'Would this mean,' Quaid called out, 'that we'd get our silverware back from the pawn?'

Maxwell rounded on him, switching his tone to a fish-seller's catcall: 'Well, if it isn't Jeremy McQuaid, the Archbishop's third cousin! Appointed before my time, I'm glad to say.'

Quaid turned red with fury. 'He was not my cousin!' he finally managed to say. 'I will not be associated with that nancy candle-snuffer –'

An outburst of condemnatory noises, including the words 'shame', 'retract' and 'uncalled-for', drowned the rest of Quaid's diatribe. He was shuddering with rage. Had he changed his name? He did not particularly resemble the late Archbishop John Charles McQuaid. Séamus remembered old newsreels, the swish of lace, the incensuous atmosphere of the Ireland of his youth. It was true, he supposed, that the peculiar brand of prurient vigilantism favoured by Archbishop McQuaid, which had stifled Irish life for much of the twentieth century, had featured certain frilly elements of high camp, perhaps slightly exceeding the hermaphrodite norm of the times. Quaid's homophobia was, however, unexpected.

'Thank you, President Maxwell, for your most generous offer,' pink-faced Millington continued when silence descended once more, 'but unless the meeting is of the opinion . . .' His voice trailed off. The meeting was not of the opinion. Maxwell waited, hovered, subsided.

Séamus was appalled by the general air of drift. If this was how King's College coped with a crisis, it would not survive very long. He had heard it said that academics tended to argue to a conclusion rather than to a decision; these ones seemed incapable of doing even that. Millington lacked the standing to control his hydra-headed colleagues, and none of the other speakers so far seemed able to fill the gap.

'If I might chip in here,' yapped a tiny mousy man sitting close to the top table. Leaping to his feet, he repeated his exordium: 'If I might chip in here, I feel that reverting back to our previous leadership, excellent though it undoubtedly was, could be seen outside these hallowed walls as a retrograde step. It is important now that the College shows itself capable of progressing with regards to its current staffing resources at the present time and going forward. Personally, I offer my unstinting support to Professor Millington today as interim Acting President, pending the prompt selection of a suitable long-term successor to the late, and indeed lamented, President Oliver Cregan.'

'That's Professor Smugprick,' Quaid hissed to Séamus. 'Juvenile psychologist in our so-called Education and Training Department. Fancies himself as the next Big Chief. He's too small to have beaten Ollie to pulp with St Malachi's mace, but he could have hired a man to do it for him.' Quaid was beginning to recover.

Millington beamed his thanks at the new speaker, who scanned the room with a long triumphant gaze and continued, 'The selection of Oliver Cregan's successor is essential for our future going forward. We live in a competitive environment, where excellence is key. Tough strategic decisions will need to be taken if we are going to become a credible magnet for inward investment. We need to shape up, grow the student body, play to our strengths, seize our opportunities with both hands. We need a truly impactful leader with the correct skill-set.' He paused with the quiet satisfaction of one who has said something new and significant. 'We need a new and improved mission statement. I have a simple but challenging suggestion: "King's College Dublin, Where Learning Rules".'

Quiet groans were heard at the back of the room. Professor Smugprick resumed his seat.

'What's his real name?' Séamus, despite himself, quietly asked.

'Nobody knows,' Quaid replied. 'Smugprick seems to suit him.'

'Is anyone designated to take minutes?' This from a businesslike woman with grey hair in a bun. 'In case we wanted to refer to our decisions next time.'

Burren was indignant. 'Stop talking sense, woman!'

Millington held up a finger. 'Now, Bridgeen, this is an assembly, not a formal meeting. No minutes are required.'

She shrugged and sat down. 'Head of Irish,' Quaid explained sotto voce to Séamus. 'Lord knows how we ever employed her. Sound knowledge of her subject. Publishes good work. Supports her colleagues. Runs a coherent degree. Believes in teaching the students. Loser.'

Millington called on the new bursar to address the meeting. The new bursar wobbled to his feet. He was a convex man, with luxuriant grey curls and black eyebrows that met in the middle. His rolling eyes swivelled around the room as though he were watching an invisible trapeze act suspended over the audience. He settled some papers on the lectern and announced that the College was in a state of major, major disarray. This, he explained, was a transitional period. The College was heavily committed to a large number of building projects. There was currently a threat that some of these might be held up over planning issues of a technical kind, and this in turn increased the College's considerable pecuniary exposure. Deficient government support for certain core activities was continuing as a feature of the entire university sector – there had been a major, major cut in the previous two years – and consequently King's College was critically underfunded in many of its current academic undertakings. The shortfall was partially being made good by fees paid by students originating from outside the European Union, but with the terrible, terrible circumstances of the President's death, there was already talk of a number of these students withdrawing, even in the middle of the academic year. It was particularly worrying that some of the media had chosen to report what had happened in an irresponsible way, and it could only be hoped that the College did not suffer a haemor-rhage of United States or other non-European Union fees as a consequence. This was a time for fiscal rectitude.

'Rectal fiskitude?' Quaid interposed.

The new bursar, oblivious to Quaid's intervention, called upon line managers – heads of departments, centres, units and sections across the College – to be extra-vigilant in containing costs on all activities. Excessive use of electricity at peak times, or a failure to switch off computers when going home in the evenings, could lead to sudden blackouts and consequent losses of data. Colleagues should confine them-selves to one cycle of the hand-drying machines in the campus toilet facilities. He particularly appealed for a sparing use of photocopying facilities, warned of the pecuniary dangers of copyright infringement and announced an embargo on the purchase of envelopes until further notice.

As the bursar sat down, Quaid remarked to Séamus, 'Now you see the calibre of our officer class. That man used to be head of games. Not numerate. Semi-literate. Plucked from obscurity and named financial supremo, being guaranteed to offer little resistance to Cregan's little scams. No wonder the chief accountant has adjourned to a nerve clinic.'

'I wish to welcome the positive prospect –' Henry Kissinger growled in his grinding panzer voice. Séamus turned to see this unexpected intervention. But it was not Kissinger. It appeared to be a female. Did the old warmonger have sisters, or aunts?

'Dr Mardersteig.' Millington beamed nervously. 'We are always interested to hear your –'

'The positive prospect which confronts us!' She had risen from among the seats in the middle of the hall. As Séamus had been told, she did indeed look exactly like Tenniel's illustration of the Red Queen out of *Alice's Adventures in Wonderland*: squat, malevolent, misshapen. She pressed on with greater loudness: 'As we enter a new era in the wake of President Kriegen, we may grasp the new chance to set standards of behaviour for the College. We must stamp out corruption, the custom of abusive relationships with staff and students, male or female, who could –'

'That is out of order, Dr Mardersteig,' Millington pleaded. 'It is entirely inappropriate to –'

'Behind President Kriegen' – the grinding voice sank lower, like an earth-mover running out of diesel – 'sinister forces were at work.'

'Thank you, Dr Mardersteig. That will do.'

'It will not do. A property mogul is planning to use our College grounds for commercial buildings including a luxury hotel.'

'Dr Mardersteig, I have to remind you that there is a court order barring –'

'I will not be gagged, Mr Millington. If this private undertaking is allowed –'

Two huge security men converged on the professor. Seeing them approach, she turned to face the stage once more. 'By what authority, Mr Millington, do you pretend to have me removed? Has the meeting perhaps taken a vote?'

Millington was clearly perplexed. Since he had not previously challenged her right to attend the meeting, it was awkward for him now to have her ejected. 'You may stay,' he conceded, 'so long as you keep a civil tongue in your head. We are here to discuss the way forward, not to indulge in recriminations.'

'Recrimination,' she replied, 'is a fitting answer to what has happened. I see President Kriegen's ally, Forde, sitting up there as though he owned the campus.'

'Balderdash!' The speaker was a tall thin quivering man of advanced years. He had risen to his feet and towered over those nearest to him like a heron perched on a rock. 'Balderdash! I said at the time, when Mrs Mardersteig was appointed by President Maxwell, what a stupid idea it was to import a foreign woman to this university, where positions of responsibility have traditionally been held by men of judgment. Our former President, sad to say –'

Maxwell rose, purple with rage. 'If this is to be the level of debate –' he began, flailing his arms like a man setting out to lasso a buffalo.

'I call for the ejection of Mrs Mardersteig and former President Maxwell,' said the tall quivering man. 'These ex-employees have nothing to contribute to –'

'Motion denied,' said Millington firmly.

'Put it to the vote!' called the quivering man.

'Very well,' said Millington wearily. 'All those in favour of requesting Dr Mardersteig and President Maxwell to leave the assembly, please raise your hand.'

A dozen hands were raised. More than twice that number voted to oppose the expulsion. The rest abstained. Millington declared the motion lost. A jubilant Gudrun Mardersteig proclaimed, 'I then call upon Mr Forde to cease interfering with the College. I call upon the police to investigate his tax affairs.'

'Silence!' Millington spoke with a surprising degree of volume and vocal control. 'The fact that you are allowed to remain does not entitle you to abuse other participants. Kindly resume your seat.'

'I will not,' she shouted back. 'I go to the police to demand they investigate these profiteers who can buy university presidents, who can buy degrees for their wives, who can buy jobs for their offspring. I have here a newspaper article which reveals that another of these outsiders is connected with the drug traffic.'

She made for the door. Her former colleagues fell back silently to let her pass.

Séamus felt a wave of pity for this combative creature. An ebullient loner, she would never be at home in the world. He was also aware of faces turning towards himself. He breathed in through his nose, and kept his mouth shut.

'What happened to Connolly?' a man's voice demanded, but nobody took up the cry.

'May I assume,' Millington pleaded, 'that the sense of the meeting is that I have the support of colleagues to carry on this interim administration?'

There was a murmur of assent from approximately one-quarter of those present.

'Thank you so much,' Millington breathed. 'I am sure that we would all wish to avoid doing anything that might further damage the public standing of King's College.'

'When you say "all",' said the quivering man, 'I presume

you are not including those commercial interests at the top of the room, who couldn't –'

'Just one minute.' Old Forde had risen to his feet, near the front of the room. 'Could I make a point?' he asked Millington.

'Certainly, Mr Forde. Do please go ahead.'

'Most of you know who I am,' said Forde. 'I've been accused of a fair few things in my day, sometimes by people who haven't a bull's notion of what they were talking about. I've rarely met the level of ignorance of some of the comments here. Not one of the people who spoke against me has ever met me. If they would like to meet me, I'll be happy to arrange it. I didn't come here to take over your university. I've got enough problems without that. As far as I can see, anyone trying to take you over would want to be some class of a martyr. I respect the work you do. I never went to the university myself. I'd like to see the next generation get a better chance than I got. I'm proud to be associated with King's College, in partnership, as we develop some of the new properties around the periphery of the campus. That sort of development can help to pay for a lot of things. The government is not as generous as it was ten years ago. You have to have the buildings, you have to have the facilities, in order to do the work. I'm happy to come in on that. If you people choose to teach German, or Greek, or Mathematics, or Irish Literature, that's nothing to me. It's your business, and you know how to do it. You talk about external forces trying to take you over. The only force that's trying to take you over is an American chain of private colleges. Talk to their man' – Forde pointed at Séamus – 'if you're worried about being taken over.'

Séamus said nothing.

'I should have mentioned at the start,' Millington interposed, 'that nothing that is said here is intended for publication in the media.'

'You should,' was Quaid's tart comment, 'but it wouldn't make a blind bit of difference.'

A military-looking lady sprang to attention. Her eyes glittered behind gold-rimmed spectacles. 'Have you never heard of freedom of information, Professor Millington? The people have a right to know what is said. The people's taxes are paying our salaries, and they are entitled to know what we decide.'

Millington raised his hands to his head in an involuntary gesture.

'Through the chair,' coughed a voice behind the table. 'Through the chair.' It was the tweedy former civil servant who had been nominated by the government to the College board. 'If I might be heard. If I might come in –' Why was his voice familiar? Where had Séamus heard it recently?

'That's Master McGrath,' Quaid whispered audibly into Séamus's ear. 'The only civil servant named after a greyhound.'

'Come in, come in, for God's sake!' sang a voice from the back.

'If I might come in here,' the former civil servant said, 'through the chair, there is a place for confidentiality in the deliberations of any institution. It is not a thing that the public has to be informed of all the options considered at a meeting. It's decisions, not discussions, to which the public is entitled to. And if I might make another point, if I may, through the chair, what I'd like to say is the Minister would have an amount of disquiet over the argumentative nature of the arguments that's going on here –'

Burren rose once more to interrupt. 'Do you want us to wear muzzles, Mr McGrath? We might as well go home.'

'Be off home with you then, and bad cess to you,' the retired civil servant replied. Séamus realized that McGrath's voice was familiar because he had heard it on Tuesday afternoon, speaking into the answering machine in Fionnuala's office.

Millington finally took control. 'At this stage, indeed,' he said, 'we might consider adjourning. This assembly was called to mark the events that have occurred and take stock of the situation. Your contributions have been most helpful.'

'Can't do much stocktaking in the dark,' the military lady snapped. 'We all know what will happen next. Once this meeting is over, the College board and their cronies will retire to a quiet room and decide our futures without consulting us in any real way. When a forum becomes democratic, real power shifts elsewhere. As history teaches.'

'Well, I am not prepared to tolerate that,' said another woman. 'I call upon like-minded colleagues to meet in the senior common room and agree on a common strategy.'

'The meeting is closed,' Millington pronounced. It seemed a popular move.

8

Murmuring groups were shuffling towards the door. Fionnuala walked past Séamus as though she did not see him. She was surrounded by women. Smugprick clicked purposefully towards him. 'Mr Joyce? Professor Magnus O'Toole.' He held out a firm little claw to be shaken. Séamus tried to unlearn the sobriquet he had previously been given for this self-assured little man. 'Good to meet you, Séamus,' O'Toole continued. 'We admired your work at the iDEA.' He spoke with passionate sincerity, looked up to Séamus, checking the response, and continued: 'We're going to need good counsel from our allies and associates, going forward. This has been a shocking week. We have got to come out of it stronger. I want to hear words like "excellence" and "innovation" and "competitive" and "synergy", and I didn't hear them today. We've got to play to our strengths. I want to build partnership and leadership. That's the vision I have for King's.'

'My auntie had a vision once,' Quaid mused.

McGrath, the civil servant, tapped O'Toole on the shoulder. The little man was drawn away, apologizing profusely to Séamus as he disappeared among the thinning crowd. Quaid looked utterly morose. Séamus detached himself. Moved away in the opposite direction from O'Toole, walked out through a doorway and a shadowed arch, into the College grounds. It was a clear afternoon. The unfinished Forde Centre, catching the light from the west, looked like a Norman fortress among the Victorian and Edwardian red-brick buildings which it had come to dominate.

The noise of building work was temporarily stilled.

Across the green lawns a bright yellow bulldozer was moving towards the clump of young trees that surrounded the Temple of Remembrance. It was rolling too fast, as though it had escaped from the building site. Instead of deviating when it came to the young trees, it plunged at the first one in its path, began to push it over. The tree was a slim birch, spindly and vulnerable. Perhaps part of a landscaping project, it was of a more recent vintage than the venerable oaks and chestnuts that staggered in long majestic lines across the grounds. The bulldozer nudged the slender birch and pushed against it until at last it toppled backwards like a soldier caught by gunfire. Roots, torn from the ground, straggled around the bulldozer, which was already backing off, and wheeling around, and attacking a second tree.

A man in blue was running towards the bulldozer, waving his arms. He was shouting, but it was too far away for Séamus to make out his words. The man in the bulldozer cab, Séamus could now see, was Martin Forde, sitting upright and manipulating the levers as the shovel mashed into the branches of the second birch. The engine roared, the wheels moved forward, the second tree went down, scarred and flayed.

The man in blue was waving his arms in front of the

machine. The bucket almost grazed his head as it swung around, and Martin Forde plunged towards a third tree.

People came running: men in yellow helmets converging on the bulldozer. They were in time to save the third tree. Martin Forde, finding himself surrounded, jumped from the cab and ran stumbling into the distance. Two men ran after him, slowed down, stopped.

A group of academics from the assembly, including Millington, were standing at the edge of the great lawn.

'We waited for those birches since the old elms had to be felled,' said a grey-bearded man beside Séamus. 'The birches were better. They stood in the right proportion to the Temple.' It was as if he were referring to something that had happened long ago.

'Young Martin,' said careworn Agnes Lambe from the accounts department. 'I would never have expected it of him.'

'He waited till we'd left the meeting,' another woman said. 'He wanted an audience for his vandalism.'

'Sick,' said a solemn girl in a black smock. 'Sick-sick-sick.'

'What was his point?' Agnes Lambe wondered.

In the distance, Martin Forde drew clear of his pursuers. He shouted something that Séamus could not hear.

'Somebody get me Mr Stanihurst,' Millington commanded.

The pale boy from the President's House was there. He produced a phone from the breast pocket of his uniform, tapped in a number, passed it to Millington. Millington spoke urgently, demanding instant repairs, asking if the trees could be levered back into position. As Séamus watched, the bulky form of Stanihurst emerged from behind the Forde Centre, holding a mobile phone to his head, jogging across the open ground towards the damaged trees with the quick deliberation of a soldier. Afternoon sunlight flashed from his spectacles, making him look twenty years younger. It came into Séamus's mind that if Forde was like a medieval abbot, as Fionnuala said, then Stanihurst was his steward, ready to do whatever was required to keep the serfs in their place and save the sum of things for pay. The sum of things: whose phrase was that? Some old out-of-copyright poet. Yes, it was A. E. Housman, whose works Séamus had read on this very lawn, preparing for his second-year exams.

Millington handed the phone back to the uniformed boy and set off to meet Stanihurst near the Temple of Remembrance.

There were names of the dead from the Crimean War on a marble plaque in the temple, Séamus remembered. He had seen them in his student days. Adamson, Bergin, Bermingham, Broadbent, Canavan and a dozen more. He could reconstruct most of the list, given time. He remembered reading that more than 7,000 Irishmen had perished in that conflict. What on earth had it been about? Séamus had grown up in an Ireland committed to commemoration, but even fonder of forgetting. King's College graduates had served in the Crimea in the 1850s, and had died there, some of them at much the same age as Martin Forde.

To tear up trees is a sacrilege. Groves of trees have been venerated for longer than churches or temples.

Martin, meanwhile, was trotting away unchallenged into the distance. Séamus trailed far behind him. Martin was faster than he looked. He reached a boundary fence, climbed it, jumped down on the far side, headed away across the open grasslands of the Phoenix Park, never once looking back. Perhaps he knew that nobody would follow him. Isolated by his position as the son of a great man, he was like an explorer lost in some unpeopled veld.

Séamus changed direction, made his way towards the College gate. The Forde Centre now stood between him and the temple, so he could see nothing of the aftermath of the earlier scene. Cars were beginning to pull out into the avenue, some driven by academics who had attended the meeting, but nobody stopped to offer him a lift. Trying not to be resentful, he reflected that this might be because they imagined that he had his own transport. After all, Finer Small Campuses controlled unlimited wealth, and the image of Séamus Joyce plodding down the long driveway, with nothing between him and the road but the thin soles of his good shoes, did not fit.

The ground was rising slightly, and he got a clear view out across the expanse of the Phoenix Park: green nature so copious, so persuasive that it almost obliterated the fact of being contained within city limits. There were trees enough to impede the vista, making the undulating parkland seem even broader than he knew it to be. One could only marvel at the vision that had led planners of great cities in centuries past to lay out green spaces such as this – Central Park, Regent's Park, Villa Borghese – to negate their surroundings and create a fiction of freshness and solitude, a place of light and darkness.

In the distance a herd of deer flowed like flamingoes, their spindly feet too insubstantial to be seen, so that their bodies seemed to float in one wavering band of light brown, past the signs erected by the Board of Works: CULLING IN PROGRESS.

The deer reminded Séamus of academics arguing their way to oblivion. He realized that for no reason at all, he felt rather fond of those people who had met in the Assembly Room, with their titles and principles and their strange mixture of knowledge and naivety, and he wanted somehow to protect them, much as a child extends a protective arm around a group of grubby teddy bears when the light goes out.

He looked back over his shoulder to see, under a canopy of clouds that were purple to the east but reddened on the western side, the slate-blue basin of the Dublin Mountains, seemingly close at hand. A sign of impending rain? One never knew where one stood with the Irish weather. Why on earth had he not appreciated the beauty of this place when he had studied here long ago?

He imagined Fionnuala talking now with indignant university women in the senior common room, and was doubly glad that he had managed to block publication of her photographs, at least for the time being.

He switched on his mobile phone, tried Heidi's number. Still out of reach.

He was almost at the College gate when a compact Isuzu jeep came trundling by, slowed, did not stop. The pale boy from the President's House sat at the wheel. The vehicle was not new. Perhaps it was the property of King's College, used by security staff to patrol the perimeter. Or perhaps not. Séamus watched it turn outside the gates and set off through the park towards the city.

Wheels scrunched to a halt: Inspector Dineen, in a beat-up sludge-hued Mondeo that looked for all the world like an undercover police car. The passenger window slid down.

'Hop in. Unless you're too proud.'

Séamus got in.

'Seat belt,' Dineen said.

'I always wear a seat belt.'

'Tell me what happened at the meeting.'

'Is that why you're offering me a lift?'

'Precisely. They train us to be kind to informants. What happened?'

'Nothing much,' Séamus said. 'They don't know what to expect. They seem to think they're in imminent danger of being swallowed up by my American friends, failing which they feel they have already been swallowed up by Mr Forde the developer, despite which several of them seem to want to be the next President, while others are content to score debating points and tear strips off the management.'

Dineen nodded. 'Headless chicken fever. I've seen it before. When they closed the shoe factory in our town, the public speakers came out of the woodwork. We could have entered a competition.'

Séamus said nothing. Dineen said nothing. In their silence, Séamus thought he could discern the outlines of an unspoken truce.

They had reached the main road leading through the park into the city. The Isuzu was in front of them. The driver was jigging from side to side in his seat, checking his mirror.

'Don't look now,' Dineen said, 'but I think we may have been spotted.'

'By that creature?'

'You know him?'

'Works in the President's House with John Hynes. Jamie?'

'That's right. Jamie Roper.'

'He's the one I suspect of stealing my phone. And I noticed him earlier talking to a slightly sinister mature student who helped the *Gurrier* with their first story about me. Fergus Kilpatrick.'

'So you're prejudiced against Jamie.'

'Afraid so.'

'Good instincts. You might have made a policeman.'

The traffic began to move, and the little square vehicle lurched forward. Instead of following it, Dineen swung his car to the left and took the direction leading north towards Castleknock.

'Where are you taking me?' Séamus asked.

'Looping around,' Dineen said. 'My local informants have been telling me about Jamie. He's supposed to be making a delivery to Temple Bar one of these days. Since we're travelling in the same direction, I'm going to tail him, but not too closely.'

He swung the car in a squealing arc and retraced his path in the direction of the city. There was no sign of the Isuzu, but as they came down to Parkgate Street they picked it up again, ten or twelve cars ahead. 'As long as he didn't see us make that turn,' Dineen said, 'we're oxo. You don't mind me taking you out of your way?'

'If it's in the interests of law enforcement, how could I possibly object?'

'How indeed?' Dineen switched on the radio, which gushed with news of Saturday sports fixtures. They drove into town along the quays, through relatively free-flowing traffic, until the Isuzu eventually turned right across the river, doubled back and found a parking space. Jamie Roper climbed out. Dineen managed to pull in well behind the Isuzu, and sat motionless until they saw the boy rounding one of the corners into the little streets of Temple Bar.

'And they're off.' Dineen sprang from the car and strode along the pavement. Séamus hurried after him. Dineen turned and locked the car with his remote control from a distance of twenty feet. 'You don't have to follow me,' he said to Séamus. The boy was disappearing at the far end, turning right. He was walking at a great pace.

Drawn by curiosity, Séamus found himself almost running to keep up with Dineen. The Inspector moved smoothly, with the sureness of one who knows his way. He took a left, a right, then another left. They were standing at a tall yellow building. Over the door was written, in brown straggling paint, 'The Yellow Leaf'. It was a pub. There were smokers outside in the street, huddled against the fresh air. Dineen walked among them, pushed the door, marched into the bar.

9

The Yellow Leaf reverberated with piped music. Flags, photographs and beer-related forgettabilia hung from the nicotine-stained ceiling and yellow walls. A cheerful hen party of young Englishwomen was camped at one end of the bar, while a group of men in Welsh rugby shirts – not quite classifiable as a party – occupied the far corner. There was no sign of the boy. In this crowd, he might simply have got crushed. Perhaps he had found a new existence in two dimensions.

Then they saw him, talking quietly to a thick-set man at the end of the bar: a man of uncertain age, pasty-faced and with the indoor strength of one who has not taken the air for a long time. The boy handed him something and the fat man moved, having noticed Mike Dineen. He pushed drinkers aside, making for the swing doors into the street. Before he could reach them, Dineen had a hand on his arm. The swing doors burst inward, and a pair of beautiful men with curly gold hair, wearing leaf-green rain-jackets, seized both Dineen and his victim, turned them smartly around. One began to frisk the pasty-faced man, while the other pinned Dineen's arms to his side. Dineen said nothing. The two men looked bright, their faces shining, like twin brothers playing on a winning team. A familiar voice boomed from the other door of the pub: 'Is it yourself, Mike? Nice company you're keeping.'

Decko Dowd was rolling his eyes and laughing, with a huge hand clamped firmly on Roper's arm. 'That's the end of your gallop, Jamie me lad. We have you.' The boy turned and stared at Séamus with his pale eyes, like a cat surveying a bird on a low branch.

Other men had blocked the doorway behind Séamus. The drinkers looked around, interested but not unduly alarmed. No obvious violence had taken place.

Decko called out, 'Gabriel, you done a grand job, but maybe you should let go of Inspector Dineen all the same.'

The golden-haired policeman was mortally embarrassed. 'I should have known you, sir,' he said to Dineen.

Dineen shook himself like a dog shedding fleas, and turned to the boy. 'I reckon you're Decko's personal property now, Jamie. You might have been better off getting arrested by me. Declan Dowd is a terrible hard man.'

Roper looked around with dead eyes, saying nothing.

Decko reached into the boy's pockets, fumbled, withdrew his hand. 'You must have handed it over,' he said, pushing him against the bar.

'Who are you?' Roper was incredulous. He stretched out his empty hands, the scene frozen like a second-rate genre painting.

When he moved it was sudden. He punched Decko under the ribs with his left fist, a vicious upward jab. In his right hand was a tall-necked beer bottle, the end of which he broke with one expert flick against the beer-taps. Decko crouched backwards. The boy swung the broken bottle in a slow arc as customers shrank away from him, and then darted for the far door. Séamus skipped out of the way of the swinging bottle, and was amazed to find himself toppling a barstool into Roper's path. The boy tripped, upended himself on the floor, smashed the remains of his bottle on the boards. One of the Guards sat heavily on his back.

Dineen laughed. 'Have-a-go Joyce.'

It was only then that Decko Dowd recognized Séamus. Pure happiness spread across his honest face. He looked like a man who has won a small but well-deserved prize at a charity carnival. 'Séamus! Got your message. Must talk.' Still winded, clutching his stomach.

The barman came out from behind his counter and spoke respectfully to Decko. 'I don't know why you're here, sir, but there's nothing going on in this bar that we're aware of.'

'Yeah,' Decko said. 'See no evil. Tell the tourists to clear out. Regulars stay put.'

The barman hesitated, then went off shuffling around the tables, muttering to some of the customers standing at the bar. People began to make for the door, some relieved, some truculent. It was not good for business.

Jamie Roper was helped to his feet, then handcuffed. His arm held tightly by his golden-haired captor, he hobbled to a barstool and sat up on it. He seemed to be moving with genuine pain and difficulty. He looked younger than before – almost a child, in fact.

The Guards had hauled the pasty-faced man back into the centre of the room. Decko stood straight in front of him, reached in his pockets, pulled out two clear plastic bags full of pills. 'Taking your medicine, Liam?' he asked.

'I know nothing about those,' Liam said. 'Youse put those in my pocket.'

'Did I? I've got witnesses. Mr Joyce here, former head of the iDEA, will swear he saw me reach in your pockets and find those things there.' He turned to Séamus. 'Won't you?'

'If necessary,' Séamus said, unenthusiastic at the prospect. He should have stayed in Germany.

The green-jacketed Guards made a sudden move, seizing a smartly dressed woman as she made to step outside the door. She shrieked distressed obscenities, but they clamped her by the arms and dragged her to the bar.

Another young woman, dressed in faded denims, approached the group. Séamus assumed she was a friend of the captive, about to make a protest. Instead, she ran her fingers expertly over the other woman, dug into the belt at the top of her tight skirt, pulled out a small plastic package of white powder. 'You should have dropped it, Marion,' she said.

Everyone else had left the premises. The barman was standing uneasily, watching. The smartly dressed woman rounded on him. 'You needn't think you're going to get away while the rest of us go down,' she said to him. 'Guard, he stores the stuff under the towels.'

'Is that a fact?' Decko went behind the bar, lifted a pile of towels, picked up some tiny packages of white powder between finger and thumb.

'Marion must have put them packages there,' the barman said.

'Keeping just the one for herself?' Decko laughed. 'We're

going to have the licence. I don't think your investors are going to enjoy that.'

The barman froze.

'A limited company,' Decko remarked casually to Séamus. 'Owned by respectable criminals. Very well connected. They're not going to like this.' He began to chuckle. 'Their fine friends aren't going to like it either. In fact, we're going to be accused of all sorts of bad things.' His eyes were twinkling. 'Which is why I've taken personal charge, in spite of my exalted position. It's good to be back on the job.'

'When can we go?' Dineen sounded impatient.

'In a minute, Inspector,' Decko said. 'We won't detain you. A statement would be nice, though. Seeing as you nearly screwed up the operation.'

As Dineen's statement was being transcribed by the young female Guard, Séamus took Decko aside and spoke quietly. 'Quick question? Off the record and unattributable.'

'Go ahead.'

'I'm in King's College these days –'

'I heard.'

'And Mr Forde's wife –'

Decko rolled his eyes.

'– asked me for advice.'

'Give it to her, my boy.'

'Her husband is being put under pressure. She's worried. Somebody attacked him years ago and ended up hurt.'

'What kind of pressure?'

'Not sure. An attack on a security man at Forde's building site in Kinnegad. Site foreman says he fell off his scooter, but apparently he was shot in the leg. Mrs Forde says the Guards won't take it seriously because the security man owed money to a drug-pusher. Do you know anything about that?'

'Heard of it,' Decko said. 'Not drugs, actually. So far as we know, there's a protection racket targeting that particular site. Sorry, did I say protection racket? I mean, of course, a community policing and anti-drugs movement run by certain public-spirited boyos who are after retiring from the fight for Irish freedom. These boyos may or may not have been acting on allegations made by Patrick Connolly. Do you know who I'm talking about?'

'Formerly of the King's College board?'

'That's the one. You're his replacement, they tell me.'

'Sort of.'

'Connolly owns land in Tullamore. He got planning permission to develop it. Educational use. The place was a convent up to five years ago. Saint Gobnait's. Rumour is Connolly wanted to start his own university.'

'You hear everything, don't you?'

'I'm a terrible man for gossip,' Decko conceded. 'Or intelligence, as they call it. Though I was never accused of that.'

'Why on earth would Connolly want to start his own university?'

'Can't sit still, that's why. Tries his hand at things. Laundry, catering, betting shops, moneylending. We keep an eye on him because those kinds of businesses sometimes get used for money-laundering. Anyway, Connolly's university project fell through, and he's stuck with his convent. Can't get it zoned industrial. We think he has a grudge against Forde.'

'Mrs Forde's worry was that her husband's site manager, Stanihurst, was planning to deal with the protection problem himself.'

'She's right to be worried. Stanihurst's a scary guy. Former soldier of fortune. Broke the arm of a nice young man who tried to offer him protection on the King's College site. Forde himself is a pussycat, they tell me.'

'Would you talk to Mrs Forde?'

'I can put her on to a man I know in Special Branch. We certainly don't want Stanihurst taking action. Our freedom fighters are sensitive folk, and they don't deserve Stanihurst.

They sometimes forget how peaceful they are. Do you have a number for Forde?'

'Just for his wife.' Séamus produced Lucy Forde's visiting card from his wallet, and handed it to Decko.

'That's the ticket,' Decko said. 'I'll give her a call. Do you have a mobile number yourself?'

Séamus recited it from memory. Decko wrote it on Lucy's card, which he pocketed. He turned to Inspector Dineen, who had finished giving his statement. 'Right you are, Mike. Thanks for your help. And if you ever need any help in sorting out the King's College cowboys, just give me a call.'

Mike Dineen was stiff with annoyance as he led Séamus out into the pale evening sun. Jamie Roper was being escorted to the police van. His face was clenched with pain. His left leg failed at every step. Séamus kept expecting him to make another dash for freedom, but the injury was real. The boy was temporarily maimed.

Dineen stalked back to the Liffey quays to retrieve his car. Now Séamus realized why he had managed to find a parking space so easily. His car was in a clearway; clampers had attached a Denver boot to one of its wheels.

Dineen tapped on his mobile phone and began to snap at the person on the other end of the line. It appeared that he was being asked for his credit card number, which caused him to make abusive comments about the telephonist and the company that employed her. At last he capitulated, recited the credit card number and stipulated that he expected them to come and undo their work within ten minutes.

'I'll make my own way home, then,' Séamus said. He sensed that Dineen had had enough of him for the time being. There was no reply. He went looking for a taxi. While waiting, he tried Lucy Forde's number, still the only one in his mobile phone's address book. He got her answering service, and mentioned that Declan Dowd would be in touch.

10

The news bulletin on the car radio led with three boys from a provincial boarding school, arrested while purchasing a wholesale consignment of Ecstasy from a dealer in Blackrock.

'They're all at it,' said the taxi driver.

'Who?'

'Students, schoolkids, they're all on drugs. Question is, where do they get them?'

'No shortage of distributors, by all accounts.'

This rated an ironic glance. 'You'd know,' the driver said. 'Saw your photo in the paper. So who killed your man?'

'Anybody's guess.'

'I do sometimes drive students out from the College to collect the stuff,' the driver continued. 'Or maybe deliver it.'

Séamus looked at him. 'Deliver drugs?'

'That's what I reckon. Rich lads calling on a block of flats, carrying a leather briefcase, staying ten minutes, then back to the College, paying me out of a wodge of rolled-up notes – it's hardly prayer books for the Legion of Mary.'

The radio news rolled on to the planning tribunals, where morally flexible developers, bent politicians and complacent or incompetent planners were hauled through a process designed to suggest that they really ought to be thoroughly ashamed of themselves. At first it had provided wonderful entertainment for the populace, but as the tribunals dragged on, year after year, resembling more and more the work of the Military Armistice Commission in the decades following the temporary truce in the first Korean War of 1953, boredom had inevitably set in and issues of corruption had become so segmented in people's minds that they no longer had any visible effect on political preferences. If anything, this was a new form of Saturnalia, where the great were ritually disgraced and the least influential of the most obviously guilty were slapped on the wrist, but no lasting change was envisaged. As time went by, it also became tacitly accepted that those selected for punishment were merely a peculiarly inept or brazen subset of the kleptocracy. Outlandish acts of transparent perjury were left unsanctioned. An example was made of a few malefactors, while their successors were left free to carry on in much the same old way. A charming feature of the new culture of revelation was the righteous certainty of several kleptocrats and their loyal sidekicks that they had been morally entitled to steal as much as they could conveniently pocket over the years, and that it was both impolite and unpatriotic to question their techniques of self-enrichment.

The episode currently playing on the taxi driver's radio featured a dramatic reconstruction of the evidence of an indignant magnate, protesting his innocence or ignorance of various bribery and tax evasion episodes. The man was blessed with a rich Cork accent, which the actor reproducing his lines rendered with glorious musicality. At the end of the item, the reporter mentioned that the star of the following week's tribunal proceedings was to be Seán Forde, who had alleged that his proposed redevelopment of an inner-city area had been held up by his unwillingness to pay bribes to a former Minister. Mr Forde was currently involved in extensive developments along the banks of the Liffey close to the Phoenix Park. He was seeking planning permission for a major hotel and conference centre with outlying accommodation in the surrounding area, and was known to have financed a major building project in King's College Dublin, adjacent to the area he wished to develop.

'They're all at it,' the driver said again. 'Saving your presence, sir.'

Heidi's phone was still switched off.

Séamus paid for his taxi ride with small coins, fumbled for his door key.

11

Red curtains dragged across the floor, the sofa gutted, its stuffing spilt like the entrails of a fish. Venetian carnival masks torn from the walls, lying trampled on the ground. A shelf partially ripped from its moorings, revealing pink paint underneath. The television set face down, its back smashed open. Kitchen equipment scattered across the living room. Drawers strewn around the floor, empty. Of course they were empty. The tenants had left months ago. Closed, the drawers had looked full.

This devastation he took in at a single glance, while standing at the open door.

The taxi had pulled away.

He found Dineen's card, unlocked his mobile phone, closed the door, tapped in the phone number.

'Yes?' Dineen did not sound pleased.

'We've had a break-in. My house is trashed.'

'I'll get someone. Wait in the street. Don't touch.'

'Thanks.' But he could not wait. He had to know.

He stepped inside, dread gripping his stomach, switched on some lights. In the kitchen, crockery and glass were shattered on the floor, the oven and refrigerator open.

With a sinking heart, he climbed the stairs. The bedrooms were awash with torn fabrics and stuffing from disembowelled mattresses, exploded duvets, pillows. His travel bag and Heidi's had been opened, emptied.

He steeled himself to glance at her, lying on the bathroom floor, throat cut from ear to ear.

Not there.

Where, then?

He searched again through mattresses, bedclothes, cut his wrist on a protruding edge of metal.

There were two built-in cupboards in the upstairs bedrooms. The first was empty, the second also empty. He licked blood from his wrist, wondering whether the metallic taste came from the metal that had scratched him, or from his own veins.

Nothing to be found in the cramped scullery behind the kitchen. The tiny back yard was empty. Its few straggling plants, emerging from between concrete slabs, were too wispy to hide a corpse. Even a very small corpse.

He lifted the curtains from the living-room floor. Nobody lying there.

Hearing a car pull up, he went to the front door. It was not the police, just an elderly man coming home to a cottage across the street, where he was greeted by an elderly woman. They looked as if they had lived there for ever. Their car was twelve years old.

He stepped outside, stood on the pavement. The cut on his wrist was little more than a scratch. He was shaking, not from the cold. There was a light breeze. Neighbours walked quietly by. Everything was normal.

An unmarked car accelerated along the street, its headlights set to full beam. It jolted to a halt, and two young men got out. 'You the guy phoned Inspector Dineen?'

He explained what had happened. They went inside. He stood in the street, breathing deeply, then followed them.

'See here, sir? They came in through the kitchen door. See where it's been forced? Back wall out there is easily scaled.' One of the two detectives was the spokesman. The other bounded upstairs, poked around noisily.

'We can get people to take fingerprints,' the spokesman continued. 'For all the good it will do.'

'Would you help me search?' Séamus asked.

'For what, exactly?'

'My partner has been out of contact all day. I can see no sign of her.'

'I wouldn't worry. Look at this mess. It's a break-in, not a physical attack. You'd have more of a focus. Still, we'll take a look.' The two men made a good show of sifting quickly through the chaos, opening cupboards, looking under beds. 'Not a sausage,' the spokesman said. 'We'd better be off. The lads will be along in the morning to do fingerprints. Don't touch the kitchen door. Will you be all right now?'

'Yes. Thanks very much.'

They got into their car and were gone. Séamus looked around him. Neighbours were watching. Another old woman smiled at him, standing in her own doorway. Strangely, there were no children on the street. This must be a place for yuppies and the elderly.

His scratched wrist was starting to bleed again. He washed it under the kitchen tap, then checked in his pocket for the key, pulled the door closed, wandered away. In his hand was his mobile phone. Silent.

12

On the main street, he was starving. Shock, presumably. Walking too slowly. He tried to speed up. A green neon cross marked a pharmacy. They sold him a box of Band-Aid. He stuck the biggest bandage on his wrist.

His visit to the house had taken less than thirty minutes. It felt like a lifetime. He would be glad when this day was over.

He came to an Indian restaurant. Breathing better now. Pocketing his phone, he ordered a starter and main course, sat at a little table on his own, waiting. Not only for food, but for something else. Heidi's sudden appearance and disappearance had projected him into a newly unfamiliar world. The other diners were living on their separate planets. Séamus was drifting towards some warped crevice of the universe where life and death were the only questions left to be decided. Yet he looked normal to them, and they to him.

Which of these diners was incubating the tumour that would soon lead to the operating table and the anaesthetic needle? Which couples were starving each other of what they really wanted? Normality is denial.

Food came and he forced himself to eat, driving out morbid reflections and gaining hunger with every mouthful. He took his time over the main course. There was no hurry to get back to the house. He might spend the night in a hotel. Heidi could reach him through his mobile phone.

He drank another glass of water, ordered coffee and an Indian dessert. The sugar would do him good.

The phone in his pocket began to vibrate. He took the call. Not Heidi, but Mike Dineen.

'Everything OK with you, Séamus?' Dineen sounded happy.

'Yes. Thanks.'

'Sorry I couldn't get there myself. Too busy. All down to your tip-off.'

'What?'

'We've picked up Fergus Kilpatrick.'

'Because I saw him talking to Roper?'

'That's what put the idea in my head. We knew a consignment was due, and the amount of stuff Roper was carrying told us it could be a big one. Kilpatrick had a sports bag full of pills, and he was high as a kite. He knows we've got him, so he wants to be helpful, but he's scared to give me the name of his main supplier. Instead he told me all about your crimes and misdemeanours at the iDEA. When you ran the drugs agency, your friends in the trade got a free run.'

'And so on and so forth. The usual rubbish.'

'It's always good to hear the gossip from the fringes of the drug trade. Amateurs like Fergus. Not that they don't do damage. A King's College student died last year. Overdose. Makes the headlines for a day, then everyone forgets, except for the family and people like me and Decko. Anyway, we're gradually coaxing Kilpatrick on to more fertile ground. He's hinting he knows who killed Cregan, and Gannon, and O'Neill, to say nothing of Shergar and Olof Palme. If he keeps blabbering like this, it's just a matter of time before he starts telling the truth. He claims the key to the Cregan murder lies in the O'Neill and Gannon case. I suppose he could just be right.'

'Any reason, other than the connection with King's?'

'Don't knock coincidence, Séamus. Sometimes it's all we've got. Talk to you soon.'

It was an odd phone call. He had never heard Dineen so forthcoming. He wondered why. There could be some hidden agenda.

Dessert came, and coffee. His phone began to vibrate once more. He pressed the green button and heard a woman clear her throat. Heidi.

'Hello?'

Not Heidi.

'Who is this?'

'Lucy. Lucy Forde. Is that Séamus Joyce? I need your advice again.'

'For what it's worth.'

'I spoke to Declan Dowd. He's very kind. We've received further threats, unfortunately. My husband wants to talk to you before contacting the police. When can we meet?'

'As soon as you like. I'm in Donnybrook.'

'Where exactly?'

He read the name of the restaurant from the menu.

'I know just where that is. I need to speak with you privately, before you see my husband. I'll send someone to collect you. It should be less than twenty minutes.'

He called for his bill, paid, waited at his table. Outside, nightfall was coming. Earth was draining Europe's light and pouring it across America. Heidi's cottage outside Aachen would be in darkness by now. The birds would have fallen silent. His wrist was no longer sore.

A Jeep Cherokee came gliding to a halt on the double yellow line across the road.

13

Derry McKinley slipped down from the driver's seat, trotted over to the restaurant, opened the door.

'At your service.' Unfazed by the transparent depths of his various treacheries. 'She sent me to collect you.' He appeared surprised by the cool reception, but prepared to forgive.

'Who?'

'Lucy, of course. Her wish is my command.' He managed a rueful smile, which made him look like a vampire at sunrise. 'She is the wife of a major client.'

Séamus left too large a tip. The desire to be remembered.

McKinley held the restaurant door, then opened the door of his jeep. Séamus climbed in. As they swung from the kerb, Séamus asked, 'Where to?'

'Killiney. They've bought themselves a mansion. Beautiful sea views, extensive grounds. Room for a dozen luxury homes. If only they could get the planning permission.'

Séamus said nothing. McKinley pushed a button and the sound of Sidney Bechet's clarinet filled the vehicle. Séamus suspected that this music had been chosen for his benefit, probably following extensive consultation with Rocky Burren on the subject of Séamus's musical preferences.

'Did you hear they arrested a student from King's? Mature student. Editor of the *Chronic*?'

Séamus said nothing. Clearly, McKinley had rapid sources of news.

They proceeded through Booterstown, Blackrock, Seapoint,

Dún Laoghaire, and then along the coast past Sandycove towards Dalkey, while Bechet played melodies of Picardy and Antibes, sang of Madame Bécassine and Buddy Bolden. McKinley maintained a benign silence.

'What's worrying Mrs Forde?' Séamus finally asked.

'Crude physical intimidation. Very distasteful. Guys wanting protection money. Said they'd have her husband shot one morning when he's walking the dogs along Killiney beach. Lovely dogs they have. Ridgebacks. Hunting animals. Not that Seán hunts. Somebody knows his daily routines. Stanihurst, for personal reasons, is highly averse to doing deals with "terrs", as he calls them. He is apt to take the muscular approach. There's the danger of overreaction. Seán Forde is very fond of Stanihurst, and it would be a shame if he blotted his copybook. So that's the physical threat. Then there's the blackmail.'

'Yes?'

'I'll let her tell you herself. But you've probably heard the old story about Seán's first wife, and the tragic accident.'

'She fell over a cliff.'

'That's right. Of course, it's easy for people to suggest otherwise.'

'They'd need evidence.'

'Yes, well, there was discord in the home. She had a drink problem.'

'I remember. Mary Kate and I were in college at the same time.'

'Of course you were! Contemporaries. How could I have forgotten that?' The road started to climb.

'Mary Kate went to London,' Séamus said. 'I'd never heard about her death, nor even who she'd married.'

'Seán Forde is a saint,' McKinley said. 'What that woman put him through. She should have been grateful. She was cleaning toilets when he met her. He had a drink problem himself when he was young. They dried out together. He stayed off the sauce. She used to relapse. Nearly burned the house down. Wrote off the family car. He stuck by her. Fifteen years since she died. The boy was young. He took it hard.' They were on the winding roads of Killiney Hill. McKinley was negotiating the curves gently. Darkness was thickening.

'How do you know all this?' Séamus remembered the easy acquaintance that this man had claimed with his own father. McKinley was a trader in other people's lives.

'I knew the two of them before she died. Long time ago. I was fundraising for a political party. Seán was making his mark. Big man, big projects. He was having a hard time with poor Mary Kate. Got to know him better later on. I was one of the select few invited to his wedding with Lucy. Lovely girl. She's good to that boy. Doesn't try to be his mother.'

'Just as well. She's not much older than him.'

'You're being gallant, Séamus. She looks younger because she's married to an older man.'

That was possible, Séamus knew. Some younger wives adopt the age of their husbands, while others react to the age gap by staying heroically young. When her mate dies, such a woman lapses into her real age like a hero falling from a horse. The trophy wife, the graduate student, the secretary trapped in her cage of youth, to be released one day into the afterlife.

'What age is Lucy, then?'

'Thirty-six at the last count. Still a child.' McKinley swung through open gates, the word REICHENBACH neatly lettered in black capitals along the curving white wall. 'Used to belong to a Swiss financier,' he said as he drove along the gravelled driveway towards the front of an imposing house that revealed more of its size as they approached. The driveway was flanked by glowing lamps, and as the sweeping headlights showed, the grounds were rich in flowering trees, with sloping lawns, herbaceous borders and shrubberies. The house front was dark, unsighted. McKinley stopped, stepped out, carefully closed the driver's door. 'Here we are. *Ne plus ultra.* We've got to go to the side-door. Tradesmen's entrance.' He gave a little laugh.

Séamus followed his footsteps down the gravelled path. Rounding the side of the house, he saw a great bank of grass falling away towards the sea. Blinking lights were visible in the distance: trawlers, tramps, ferries? Evening had sunk behind the hill. There was wind in the trees tonight. Shadows played around McKinley's snow-white hair as he pushed open French windows, pulled back heavy curtains and held them open for Séamus to walk past him into a cavernous drawing room, punctuated by Corinthian pillars, gold-framed portraits, heavy furniture arranged in separate enclaves. Floorboards creaked underfoot. Weak light leeched through an open door halfway along the opposite wall. McKinley led the way, moving diagonally among sofas and armchairs, in through the door, down a wide staircase flanked by a set of complex geometric designs, painted in grey on tiny unframed squares of canvas. 'Lucy's work,' McKinley said. 'Very challenging.' They had reached the basement, and a dark corridor. Through another door he saw, seated on a sofa in front of a flickering television set, Seán Forde and Stanihurst. McKinley ushered Séamus into the room, followed him, clicked the door shut.

14

Forde picked up the remote control, and the television picture died. Nobody spoke.

Séamus saw his own reflection in the rippled plate glass of the window. Outside, unbroken darkness. Inside, the only light came from a standard lamp beside the sofa.

'Where's Mrs Forde?' Séamus asked.

'In another place,' Forde said.

'When will she be here?'

'Later.' Forde was embarrassed. 'We've got questions for you, Mr Joyce. Sit down.'

Séamus sat on a straight chair. 'I came at your wife's request.'

'You've got to answer us first.'

'What do you want?'

'We need to know what you know,' Stanihurst said, standing up. The room grew smaller. The ceiling was low, the walls thick as a dungeon.

'And what you've done,' Forde said, sitting and staring at Séamus like a judge about to pass sentence.

Stanihurst was dressed in a blue denim suit. It was probably intended as his weekend 'smart casual' outfit, but the effect was more military than leisurely.

McKinley coughed. 'Seán is feeling sensitive, Séamus. He's testifying before the tribunals next week. His solicitor was out here this afternoon, and one of the top barristers in the country. We've already had to take out two injunctions to stop malicious newspaper reports.' He held up his hands, fingers splayed as if trying to stop a flying football.

'Not in the *Courier*?'

'No, not the *Courier*.'

'What's it got to do with me?'

'It appears' – McKinley shook his head – 'that some of the materials may have emanated from your Americans. Also, as I mentioned earlier, there has been physical intimidation.'

'I know nothing of that. The Americans are not my employers. I am merely doing a consultancy report for them. I don't use improper means.'

Stanihurst approached, leaned over Séamus like a tower under a cloudy sky. 'We need to know your agenda.' Again, those traces running through his accent, like mineral streaks in rock. Ireland, England, something sharper. Australia? South Africa? 'You've upset people. You've disrupted our work.

There are people snooping. We're heading them off. We don't like being taken for a ride.'

The same sentiment had been voiced by Connolly's red-headed woman, in much the same words. Everyone involved with King's felt cheated.

Séamus kept a neutral tone. 'Can you be more specific?'

This did not mollify Stanihurst. He started pacing the room with irregular steps. 'You're the one,' he said, 'who needs to be specific.' His voice was too loud. 'We've all got people to protect.'

'There's no mystery about why I'm here,' Séamus said quietly. 'Senator Hinckley sent me. Didn't even mention your involvement. In fact, he said nothing about building or development.'

'We find that hard to believe,' Forde said. 'What did he tell you about Cregan?'

'Nothing.'

Stanihurst stopped in front of Séamus, glaring down. 'And what did Cregan tell you about us?'

'He talked more about himself. He was going to do great things for the College. We didn't get into detail. I was to meet him on Thursday.'

'What was the document he handed you after the graduation ceremony?'

'His general ideas about academic reorganization.'

'That's all?'

'That's all.'

'You've got documents relating to us, haven't you?'

'No.'

'Will you show me the document you received from Cregan?'

'No.'

'Why not?'

'It's confidential. It contains people's names and private business.' Cregan's plan to dismiss Paddy De Soto, for example. He realized now that Cregan had made a special point in giving him the memo at the conferring ceremony, so as to suggest some secret understanding between them. That was the way Cregan had operated. He had lived by innuendo.

McKinley shuffled uneasily. The door opened behind him and Martin Forde came into the room. 'Found it,' he announced. 'In my bookcase. Pilar must have thought it was a book, on account of having pages in it.' He did a double take when he saw Séamus. 'How now, brown cow! You here? I thought you said you weren't in my father's pocket.'

'What did you find?' Stanihurst asked Martin. 'We didn't know you were here.'

'Walked up from the DART. Healthy exercise. Good for the joints. What did I find? My passport. We're off to Spain, Fionnuala and me, for a chaste honeymoon, far from talk of tribunals. I imagine the news media will be all excited about the chapter house, now that I've exposed its foundations.'

'You feel proud of yourself, do you,' old Forde asked, 'for destroying those trees?'

'All in a good cause, dear Father. Exposure. The light of day.'

'Don't be silly, Martin,' McKinley said. 'They have other fish to fry.'

'I was being ironic,' Martin told him.

'We've got things to discuss with Mr Joyce,' Stanihurst said in a patient voice.

'Oh. I'll just run along, then, shall I? I'll go play with my ball.' Martin left the room, slamming the door like a child. Séamus said nothing. He looked up at Stanihurst, glanced over at old Forde sitting motionless in his chair. Tonight he thought of him as old, by contrast to his powerfully built young son. Forde had clearly once been broad, and tough, but was beginning to shrink. He slouched like a man defeated, who does not think to rise again.

'Who's in charge here?' Séamus asked.

'Don't give me that, hey!' Stanihurst snapped. His breathing was noisy. 'I work for Mr Forde. I try to stop people taking advantage of him, ripping him off. I've been doing that for twenty-five years. He's the boss, you bet.' McKinley, in the background, nodded his head in assent.

Forde sat there, surveying the three of them. Sadness enveloped him like an invisible halo. 'We have some more questions,' he said.

15

'Did you tell Mr Quaid,' Stanihurst asked in a measured voice, 'that the mace used for the conferring ceremony was a fake?'

'Of course not.' Séamus shook his head.

'You're sure?'

'Absolutely. Why would I say that? I hadn't seen the thing in decades. It looked much the same, so far as I can remember.'

'And you've never seen anything else like it?'

'Of course I have. A mace is a standard ceremonial prop for mayors and councils. When the Queen opens Parliament –'

'Forget the Queen!' Stanihurst moved closer. 'Did you ever see St Malachi's mace in Senator Hinckley's possession?'

'No. I've met Senator Hinckley for one morning in my life. That was on neutral ground. He wasn't showing me his silverware.'

'Where did you meet him?'

'Two locations. A bank and a club, both in New York. Lower Manhattan. Financial district. I don't appreciate being interrogated like this.'

Seán Forde looked embarrassed. 'We're not doing anything wrong here. There's been an accusation of theft, a suggestion that I've been made a fool of, that the College has been defrauded, and we want to know the truth of it. Especially as it's mixed up with the murder of President Cregan.'

'Have you told the police of your suspicions?' Séamus asked.

'We need answers, man.' Stanihurst moved closer, bent down and gripped Séamus by the shoulders. He stared into his eyes. Behind his glasses, his eyes were big. The grip of his hands was powerful, but his pale blue eyes told a different story. They were empty except for a tiny spark of fear. Not physical fear. The man didn't seem to be built for that. This was moral fear. Stanihurst's breath was hot on Séamus's face. 'A private art collection? Place on Long Island? Big house in Sea Cliff? Upstairs room? Ivory chessmen? Egyptian grave monuments? Italian statuettes? Part of an Irish high cross? The original of St Malachi's mace?'

The pale blue eyes were searching Séamus's skull, as though hoping to see each of the named articles hiding in there. Séamus shook his head as the catalogue went on. Stanihurst's anxiety was palpable. He really did need answers to those questions.

Séamus let his breath out. 'None of the above. What on earth have you been told?'

Stanihurst relaxed his grip, stood back slowly. He probably had not intended to hurt Séamus. 'How do I know you're telling the truth?'.

Séamus shrugged his shoulders. Fresh pain spread to his neck. He made no reply.

'I told you Quaid can't be trusted,' Forde said sadly. 'Isn't that the truth, Derry?'

'Afraid so,' McKinley's voice had gone hoarse and soft. 'Quaid never spoiled a story for want of a few facts.'

Stanihurst turned on him. 'Why didn't you tell me, hey?'

'You never asked.'

'But he told the truth about other things.'

'Ah, well,' McKinley shrugged. 'If the truth will stir things up, Quaid is always happy to –'

'Shut your mouth!' The big man's voice boomed like a wounded animal. The echoing room seemed to bulge with the sound.

Séamus saw, in a flash, what the story might have been. Quaid had teased Stanihurst about the mace having been sold to Senator Hinckley. He had already told Séamus that the restorers in Switzerland had sent back a replica instead of the original mace. Séamus had not taken him seriously. For somebody with Quaid's malicious twist of mind, it was a short step from that allegation to fantasizing that the original had been sold on to Senator Hinckley. And, by way of corroboration, that Séamus Joyce had seen it in his house. Stanihurst, being a literal-minded man who worked in the real world, might have fallen for the story.

Could someone have killed President Cregan over that?

Nonsense. Too trivial a cause for such a frightful deed.

'Who cares about the mace? That can't be the –' Séamus stopped himself.

Stanihurst stood completely still, a shock passing through him like electricity. It was over in a moment. His eyes cleared again. 'The mace is a side issue,' he said quietly.

'I built them the big Centre,' Forde grumbled. 'Lecture halls, shops, audio-visual, gym, you name it. I'm building the residences. Happy to do it, too. I'm not making a penny out of it. You'll find that hard to believe, Mr Joyce. On a deal of this size, I'll normally expect to clear upwards of twenty million sterling. It's the way I work. But this time, because of my son, because of my wife, I was happy, I was proud to do the whole thing at cost. And I gave them the museum. The little display. Archaeological remains. I put up the money for a catalogue. St Malachi's mace. The old cross from the chapel. The other stuff they used keep in their little archaeological museum before it was closed down twenty years ago. I even bought back the gold chalice that used to be in their museum, that was sold off to a collector in the fifties. It cost me a mint, but that's no problem. There's another room that's going to be for Georgian Ireland. Silver, and the like. They can buy more, if they want. I'll give them money to stock the damn thing. The mace was only one part of it. If it's a fake, we'll get another one. I don't care if no tourists turn up. It's OK if the students just look at the stuff, realize where we came from. That we're not all made out of polystyrene. That we're not all in off the bog.' He stood up, as if lifted by his own words. 'I didn't like to hear about Andy O'Neill badmouthing our staff, accusing us, accusing Ricky' – he gestured at Stanihurst – 'of bulldozing through the place where the monks used to meet about their business, a place that should have been preserved at all costs. I didn't like to hear him saying we were breaking the law, destroying the origins of the place. I did not like that at all.'

'Who told you that?' Séamus asked.

'My son. He was the one got me worried about it.'

'But O'Neill had admitted he was wrong,' Séamus said. 'This is important. Listen. The Forde Centre is not built over archaeological remains. And the Temple of Remembrance is a side issue. It's not even your fault. Your son told me himself that the damage was done in 1863. It's at least fifty yards from the Forde Centre. You have nothing to reproach yourself with.' Séamus was trying to reason, but the old man's distress was unabated.

'Andy O'Neill,' Stanihurst said, 'called us criminals.'

'Poor Andy made a mistake,' McKinley interjected. 'But we all make mistakes. The man who never made a mistake never made anything.' He tried a little laugh. It stuck in the roof of his mouth.

'That's enough,' Stanihurst said quietly. McKinley drew in his breath.

Séamus kept silent, looked from one to the other. He seemed to be understanding less and less.

Martin came back into the room, stood beside Stanihurst, matching him in size and bulk. He looked strong enough to batter Stanihurst to the ground.

'Are you keeping this man here against his will?' he asked.

'We've got questions,' Stanihurst said. 'We need answers.'

'We'll dig if we have to,' Seán Forde said, sitting down again. 'We'll excavate the whole bloody site. We can rebuild the abbey if you like, Martin. Just show me where it goes. We'll do a replica of the whole place, if that's what you want. Why blame us? We didn't bulldoze your remains. You said it yourself.'

'Too many people drowned,' Martin said.

'Are we having this again?' The old man's eyes opened wide.

Stanihurst spoke gently: 'Stop tormenting your father, Martin. It's not fair. It's not right.' This was a different Stanihurst, full of affection.

Seán Forde looked up at Martin, his head haloed in white hair. Martin's huge hands clenched and unclenched. A painted scene swam into Séamus's memory: Abraham and Isaac. The good father, authorized to slaughter his own son for God's sake. The world, to its shame, is full of such sacrificial fathers. Here the son was the threat. Something was wrong with the picture.

He remembered Mary Kate's blowsy dramatic way of being. She was one of those people who wander through life looking for a way out. He imagined her lost in the labyrinth of herself, trying to find the thread. And now her son, lost in his own maze.

16

There was a sound of rapid footsteps, and the door burst open. Lucy's eyes were black, her movements angular. Martin stood back from the old man.

'What is this?' Her voice came out as a squeak.

Nobody answered.

'You agreed to bring Séamus to meet me,' she said to McKinley.

'I'm sorry for the delay,' McKinley said. 'They wanted a word with him first.'

'It was you,' she accused, 'that got me to phone him.' She turned to Séamus. 'I'm really sorry about this.'

'Thank you. I'll be glad to leave.'

'You're free to go at any time,' Sean Forde said. 'We owe you an apology for subjecting you to one of our family scenes.'

'You don't need my advice,' Séamus said to Lucy. 'You've got Derry McKinley.'

McKinley nodded, pleased.

'Can I at least drive you into town?' Lucy asked Séamus.

'I'll do it,' Stanihurst said.

'No, thanks,' Séamus said. 'I'll walk to the DART. Trains are still running at this hour, I presume.'

'I'll come with you,' Martin said. He turned to Seán Forde. 'Try telling the truth.'

'Goodnight, Martin,' his father said wearily.

Lucy, Seán, McKinley and Stanihurst watched as Séamus and Martin left the room. Séamus wondered if Martin had summoned Lucy. If so, he owed him a debt of gratitude. Only now did he realize the depth of visceral fear that his rational mind had been trying to mask.

Martin lingered on the stairs, looking closely at Lucy's geometric pictures. 'Beautiful, aren't they?' he asked.

'Oh, yes,' Séamus said, although in fact he thought they were devoted to the studious avoidance of beauty. Lucy had more than enough of that already.

They walked through the enormous drawing room to the French windows. Outside there were heavy feet on the gravel. Stanihurst had come around the back of the house and was walking quickly towards the gates. Martin took Séamus's arm and held him back in the darkened room. Looking out, through shrubbery and trees, the grounds of Forde's house could be seen sloping away, declining to the sea. Out in the darkness, the glimmering water shone in patches through the trees.

Lights came on outside: decorative lamps, sunken bulbs in pathways, then dazzling security beams cutting through the dark. McKinley came trotting into the room. 'Martin! Séamus! There you are.' He flicked switches. Chandeliers and spot-lights blazed into light. 'I'll be your driver, then.' He opened the French windows.

Stanihurst came back up the garden, shielding his eyes against the lights with one hand. Car headlights swung into the driveway, then there were slamming doors, loud voices. Tall men surrounded Stanihurst, before converging on the French windows where Séamus was standing with Martin and McKinley.

'What's going on?' Lucy's voice.

And Mike Dineen: 'Over here, please!'

Two men caught hold of Martin's arms as Dineen approached across the gravel. 'Martin Forde, I am holding you under Section 4 of the Criminal Justice Act for the murder of Andrew O'Neill. You have the right to remain silent. Anything you say may be recorded and used in evidence.'

Sunday

I

Séamus sat in the wreckage of his Donnybrook house. Dineen had not objected to his return. This place was no longer considered an interesting crime scene.

His telephone call to Fionnuala had been brief: 'Stanihurst is Martin's father, isn't he?'

'I suppose so. Yes. They don't talk about it.'

'Martin has been arrested.'

'Arrested? Oh God. For what?'

'Andrew O'Neill's murder.'

'That's impossible.'

'I was there.'

'Where?'

'Killiney. Stanihurst was shouting at me, Martin was shouting at Seán Forde, and I realized I had the wrong father.'

'Where's Martin now?'

'At the Bridewell Garda station.'

'Oh. I'd better go. Will you be there?'

'No. I've got other things on my mind.'

By which he meant Heidi. Still out of reach.

He called Dineen's mobile phone to ask for help in tracing her. There was no answer, no voicemail service. He tried again, and again, until he got an answer. Dineen was no longer genial. No time, he said. And no need to worry about Heidi. She would be all right. Séamus should concentrate on looking after himself.

His mind kept replaying the scene in Killiney.

We've all got people to protect, Stanihurst had said. A plea for understanding, or a threat?

He tried Guido Schneider's number, and got a voicemail announcement. He left a circumspect message.

He sat for a long time, then dozed on his ruined sofa.

At seven o'clock on Sunday morning, there was a gentle knocking at his door. He stood up. His mouth tasted like a curry factory. He opened the door. Blinking in the sunlight stood Lucy Forde. White-faced, black-haired, red-rimmed eyes circled with sleeplessness, she was living proof that beauty has nothing to do with happiness or well-being. 'I'm on my way home from the Bridewell. I've come to say sorry.'

'No need.'

'My family let me down.'

'You've had a bad night.'

'Yes.'

'Is your husband with you?'

'Seán asked Derry McKinley to drive him back to Killiney. His regular driver is on leave. Derry says Seán's asleep now.'

'Can I offer you some coffee?'

She stepped inside the door, and was aghast at the damage. 'Who did this?'

He shrugged his shoulders.

'Martin's house – Fionnuala's house – also had a break-in. Why?'

He had given some thought to the question. 'Looking for something.'

'What?'

'I don't know yet.' He put on the kettle. 'How are they treating Martin?'

'He's saying nothing. Refuses even to give his name, though Jack tells him not to be silly, he's hardly likely to incriminate himself by answering that question. Jack Drumm is our solicitor.'

'I've heard of Drumm. Quite an expert on the rights of

suspects.' Or so Séamus had gathered from hearing former colleagues in the Department of Justice cursing the same Jack Drumm, who had tilted the scales for some fearful malefactors.

Lucy moved her greasy black hair back from her face. She wasn't trying to be beautiful. It just happened. 'Jack is staying in the Bridewell for the night, and he was present when they questioned Martin. Around one o'clock, Martin asked to be allowed to eat, and they suspended questioning.'

'How long will they hold him?'

'We don't know. Martin's a gentle boy. We know he'd never hurt anyone.'

Séamus said nothing.

'Everyone's shattered. My husband, myself, Fionnuala, Ricky most of all.'

'Ricky being Stanihurst.'

She nodded. 'He doesn't let his feelings show. He used to be a soldier, and he thinks you should be able to stand anything without flinching. He was tortured during a war in central Africa, before he came to work for my husband.'

Séamus found a glass cafetière, poured boiling water over some of the ground coffee that Heidi had bought at Donny-brook Fair. He found two unbroken mugs, poured black coffee for Lucy and himself.

'Martin will be all right,' he said. 'With Jack Drumm breathing down their necks they'll treat him carefully. What evidence do they have?'

'According to Jack, it all started with someone called Kirk-patrick.'

'That must be Fergus Kilpatrick. A mature student in King's.'

She took a sip of hot coffee, pursed her lips and blew on the mug. 'This person describes himself as a friend of Martin's. He made a statement to Inspector Dineen, said Martin had confessed to him that he'd murdered Andrew

O'Neill because he hadn't been awarded a research assistant's post.' She gave something that was probably intended as a cynical laugh, but cynicism was not in her repertoire; it came out like a baby's hiccup. 'That's so ridiculous. Martin has an allowance from his father that's three times more than a research assistant gets paid. He was delighted when Ronan Gannon got that post. They were close friends.'

'Kilpatrick is an addict. Dineen caught him with drugs yesterday. His word is not going to carry much weight.'

She nodded. 'That's what Jack says. But then, later in the evening, Dineen got some images back from his computer section. Taken by surveillance cameras, the night that Andrew O'Neill disappeared. They were unreadable. It was too dark for the cameras. But the computer people worked on the images and brought up what they say are shots of Martin under a lamp standard, carrying a body.'

'How recognizable?'

'Jack says the shots are blurred. They could be Martin, or they could be O. J. Simpson. That's how he puts it.'

Séamus sipped his own coffee. 'Jack Drumm is a wily old bird,' he said. 'You can imagine a defence counsel hacking the evidence to pieces. Zealous cops, anxious to clear up an old case, tarting up a dubious image on the basis of a malicious story peddled by a drug addict trying to save his own skin.'

Lucy gave him a shy smile. 'I can just hear Jack saying that. You make it sound easy. But it doesn't help that Martin had just booked to go on an instant holiday in Andalusia. You know extradition is harder from Spain.'

'So the combination of these three elements catapulted Mike Dineen into action. The statement, the pictures, the airline ticket. Covering his back. He's going to look stupid if he's wrong, but he doesn't want to be accused of letting a suspect slip through his fingers. Did I understand that the trip to Spain was Fionnuala's idea?'

'Yes. She's worried about Martin. Says they both need a

break. She got him to book it for her sake, because he doesn't like to appear weak on his own behalf. He's very chivalrous. She takes a genuine interest in his welfare.' This was said defensively, as if Séamus, like everyone else, would have assumed that Martin was just another of Fionnuala's conquests.

'I understand perfectly. Fionnuala and I were both students with Martin's mother.'

This caught her interest. 'Mary Kate. What was she like then?' She held her breath.

He tried to be diplomatic. 'Full of enthusiasm. We were all fond of her. Not too well organized. A genuine spontaneity, but she wouldn't have had your strength.'

'I'm not strong,' Lucy said. 'I just live with strong men. My husband is old, but he still has the vision to achieve great things. And Ricky is indestructible. After spending the whole night at the Bridewell with us, he's straight off to our building site in Kinnegad.'

'Extraordinary.'

'Yes, isn't it?' Lucy looked genuinely lost in admiration. 'The men are working Sundays to get the project finished on time, and they have a brilliant foreman, but Ricky says they need him to show his face. I've never seen Ricky take a rest.'

'They sound like a powerful team,' Séamus said, although what he really meant was that Stanihurst and Forde sounded closer than a married couple. He looked around. 'I'd offer you a biscuit if I could find one.' He searched amid the debris of the kitchen. Heidi had bought heavy butter biscuits made by Bonne Maman. The package turned up, but it was torn open and there were no crushed biscuits around. 'I'm sorry,' he smiled, holding up the packet. 'My intruder seems to have eaten all our French *sablés*. Goldilocks comes to Donnybrook.'

His cheerfulness found no echo. 'Those are our favourites,' she said with great seriousness, 'though they are certainly not good for the waistline.' Even more solemnly, she put down her half-finished coffee and said, 'Time I was off. And we really do owe you an apology. Take care of yourself.'

He stood at the door and watched her dusty Citroën Picasso pull away in the silent street. There goes a good woman, he thought. But he had been wrong before.

His elderly neighbours were watching from their window. He went over and tapped on their door. They came out together.

'My house was broken into yesterday. Don't know if you saw anything.'

'Well, in a sort of a way,' the old woman said. 'I seen the big man looking out the window of your front room, a little while after you left in the morning. Didn't see him going in. Thought he might be a tradesman or something. He left by the front door. Nothing in his hands when he came out. Did they catch them yet?'

'I don't think so.'

'Of course, your one has been here most of the night.' The old woman gestured at a blue car parked twenty yards along the street. Sitting in the front seat was the young woman from Clarendon Investigations, whom Heidi had accosted in Grafton Street.

'I never noticed her,' Séamus confessed. 'But you're very observant. I've seen her before.'

'Isn't she very young to be a Guard?' the old woman said.

2

He needed to be gone from here. Would Heidi still know where to find him? He left a message on the answering machine in her cottage outside Aachen, outlining his current beliefs about the King's College murders, just in case he might not get the opportunity to explain them in person.

Mike Dineen's mobile was not answering. He left a message containing the registration number of the blue car.

A quick wash, a rudimentary shave, and he was ready to move out.

Peter Simons appeared at the door, unkempt, his jowls sprinkled with stubble. The effect was thoroughly disreputable.

'Fresh from Belfast,' he said. 'You're looking grim.'

'How was it?'

'Professionally, a total waste of time. Tedious terrorist propaganda stunt. But I caught up with some old friends. Had a good night. I drove straight back when I got a text message from my boss man. You know they nabbed Forde's son? To say nothing of the creep Kilpatrick?'

'Yes. I was there. Also a juvenile security man with a pocketful of pills. Why didn't you phone before coming?'

'You might have told me to fuck off. If I hadn't found you, I would have tried your mobile. But it's Sunday morning. You were bound to –' Simons stopped, looked around with wide-eyed wonder. 'Oh my! They've rearranged your sitting room. Anybody hurt?'

'Not that I know of.'

'Who's your furniture mover?'

'Don't know,' Séamus said.

'My spies tell me' – Simons watched Séamus closely – 'Martin was off to Spain if they hadn't caught him.'

'True.'

'Do you think he killed someone?'

'No.'

'Why not?'

'I have my reasons.'

'We are being coy this morning. How are the family taking it?'

'Not pleased.'

'Who's your source for that?'

'Can't say. Sorry.'

'What's the evidence against young Martin?'

'A statement from Fergus Kilpatrick.' He said nothing about the surveillance images.

'Sounds like bollocks,' Simons remarked. 'Nobody's going to believe a smackhead like Kilpatrick. So what's all this got to do with Séamus Joyce?'

'Professionally, nothing, except as it impacts on the involvement of Finer Small Campuses. Personally, it may turn out to mean rather a lot.'

'Why's that?'

'Can you take me driving again, please? To Kinnegad?'

Simons gave him a sharp look, nodded once. 'Let's go.'

3

In the car, Séamus explained what he wanted. He was not reassured by Dineen's complacency about Heidi. He needed to ask Stanihurst what he had meant by saying that we all have people to protect.

He was prepared to negotiate.

The mid-morning traffic was light. No commuters today. The blue car followed for a while, then turned off into a side road. Simons put on a cassette tape of Klezmer music as they cruised along the Liffey quays, drumming his fingers rhythmically on the steering wheel. His only form of exercise, he explained. Digital aerobics.

In profile, Simons's pudgy face seemed set in a natural expression of insolence. Even when he was doing something as innocent as steering a car in a straight line, he looked as if he was up to no good.

A few drops of rain began to fall, then the weather cleared again. A minor accident at the Red Cow roundabout snarled the traffic flow. After that, progress was quick. They got to Kinnegad in well under an hour. Séamus was feeling sick.

The Fern Valley building site was beside a brand-new estate of sharp white houses with easily maintained pocket gardens. Simons found a parking place. Dublin was not so much sprawling as scattering seedlings of itself across the countryside, propagating little pockets of suburbia that gradually overwhelmed the archaic towns they ringed. Outside every house was at least one car. Séamus envied the couples who lived in houses like these, with their hours of commuting and their crushing childminding costs. He wished he had children of his own. Even grandchildren. Why not? He was old enough, in theory. But his paternal feelings had tended to be misplaced. Billy O'Rourke he had seen as a sort of surrogate son at one time, and Billy, as things turned out, would have killed him.

They walked along a muddy road beside a green hoarding decorated with fern motifs. Against a light blue sky, three cranes swung like synchronized swimmers. Work was proceeding quickly, with materials being lowered to a rooftop where gangs of workmen were grouped.

According to Simons, this was going to be an office park and a big shopping mall, though nothing on the same scale as the mammoth installations at Liffey Valley, Blanchardstown, Tallaght, Dundrum.

Theresa had always been fascinated by retail developments, patrolling each new venture with gimlet-eyed attention. Theresa predicted which shops would succeed, which would fail. She was hardly ever wrong.

At the security hut, Simons asked to speak with the site foreman.

'What did you want to see him about?' asked the security guard. 'He's a busy man. So are we all. No slackers. Not even on a Sunday morning.' He himself looked cheerful and relaxed.

'Radio Free Dublin.' Simons produced a business card and handed it over. 'We're preparing a radio feature on safety on building sites. It's in the news, after the scaffolding collapse at the Kilimanjaro. We heard you'd had a worker injured here as well.'

'I'm the person you want, then,' said an English voice behind Séamus. The speaker was tall and slim, with wary eyes set in a watchful face. Almost as old as Séamus, but fit enough to be twenty years younger. He took the business card and read it. Hands too clean for a builder. 'Our colleague had an accident on his way to work. Fell off his Lambretta.' Classless voice. 'The site as such has a perfect safety record. We have skilled men from six or seven nationalities here – Poles, Lithuanians, Ukrainians, you name it – and we train them to operate best practice at all times. Wouldn't have it any other way.'

'May I speak to the injured man?' Peter Simons asked.

'Can't give out his address. Not without his consent.'

'Could you contact him, ask if he's willing to speak to me?'

'He's on leave. Convalescing. Statutory entitlement.'

'May I speak to some of his mates?'

The foreman gestured up to the roof lines where workers were unloading pallets of materials. 'Afraid they're hard at work. As they tend to be, for some reason, during working hours.'

'Perhaps we could record an interview with yourself, then?'

'Sorry. I don't talk to the media.'

'So who can I ask?'

'Safety questions go to our general manager.'

'Is he available?'

'No, you've missed him. What are we today? Sunday? Drop by about midday Tuesday. He'll straighten you out. He's proud of our safety record. Rightly so.' The foreman's walkie-talkie began to quack out a question full of complicated weights and numbers. He walked away, gesticulating to some-one on an almost finished roof parapet. The security guard's expression indicated that it was time to leave.

322

'He works them hard, all the same,' Séamus remarked.

'You'd think they were the bloody Inniskilling Fusiliers,' the security guard said. 'And the big fella, the generalissimo, marching up and down shouting at them like they were going over the top into the jaws of the German guns. He's brought extra troops this morning. Pulled them off his other site in the Phoenix Park, drove them over in his van. He was ordering them into the buildings like feckin' commandos, to reinforce the supply lines, as he said. He wants output doubled this week. Doubled! We'll be finished ahead of schedule, and I'll be looking for another job.' He dismissed them with a genial wave.

As they walked away, the cranes renewed their swinging, long chains twisting in the morning air.

Gravity was a thing of the past. Building had once been a matter of lifting heavy weights from the ground, tearing roots and sinews. Builders, like Séamus's own brother Daniel, were muscular men with compacted spines. Now, everything was dropped from the sky, like democracy.

There was a billboard listing architects, builders, subcontractors and consultants for the site, including Billings for public relations. A large coloured panel showed what the finished Fern Valley complex was going to look like, assuming that the cloudy Irish sky would meanwhile have given way to a monotone of Alpine blue. Séamus recognized the tall glass office blocks in the picture. He had seen them among Derry McKinley's papers showing future plans for King's College Dublin.

'Next?' Peter Simons asked, almost running towards the car. 'What's on your mind, Séamus?'

'Two possibilities. Martin killed O'Neill, and possibly Gannon and Cregan as well, in which case it's all over and I can relax.'

'And if he did not?'

'If he did not, and there's a credible security camera shot

of him carrying O'Neill's body, then he was carrying the body for someone else, or else the body was being carried by someone who looks like Martin, from a distance, in the dark, on a security camera.'

'I know.'

4

The blue Transit van was parked on the grass beside the Temple of Remembrance, its front end touching the builders' Portakabin that had been positioned there. As Séamus approached, he could hear the sound of digging. Together, the Temple, the Portakabin, the blue van blocked the view from all sides. Nobody looking out of the windows of the College buildings could see into that private place.

He walked quietly across the grass.

Stanihurst was stripped to the waist. His spade sank into gritty soil, came up with a load of earth and stones which he flung on to the mound by his side. He had already excavated to a depth of three feet.

Something glinted in the dark loam. A gold bracelet. Possibly part of a watch. Stanihurst picked it out with finger and thumb, laid it gently aside.

Heidi had once worn a gold watch.

Stanihurst looked up. 'What brings you here, man?'

'Coincidence. The Rhodesian connection. Once I'd worked out your accent. What did you have against McNeill?'

'Couldn't let the past lie down. What can I do for you, Joyce?'

'I'm looking for a woman.'

'She's not here.'

'Do you know where she is?'

'No idea.' Stanihurst seemed to be speaking the truth. Séamus tried to conceal his relief.

'It's over, now.' Stanihurst sounded resigned. He was going to accept his fate. He planted his spade firmly in the ground, stared at Séamus as though trying to recognize something. 'I did my best.' He shook his head, defeated. Séamus was still glad that Simons was positioned just around the corner, ready to summon help. 'You going to turn me in, hey?' Stanihurst asked.

'I don't know. What happened to Cregan?'

Stanihurst suddenly winked at somebody behind Séamus.

Séamus turned to look. There was nobody there. Stanihurst had him by the ankle.

For a big man, the speed of his lunge was amazing.

Séamus kicked free, lost his shoe, stumbled across muddy ground behind the Temple of Remembrance. Thirty feet away, Peter Simons stood in the car park, pressing the send button on his mobile phone. His Punto was parked farther away, on the grass. He had switched off the engine on Séamus's instructions and coasted for the last fifty yards.

'It's no use,' Séamus said to Stanihurst as the big man rounded the corner of the Temple. But Stanihurst had already traversed the short distance and kicked the phone from Simons's grasp. He felled Simons with a chopping blow to the head.

People in the College would hear, or see. But the place was silent, the windows blind. These days, students went home for the weekend.

Stanihurst ambled forward. Séamus backed away, around the corner of the temple. Stanihurst closed in. Once more they were beside the open grave. Séamus ran away across the mud, towards the Forde Centre. Stanihurst came after. In the distance were sirens, fading.

Across his field of vision limped Jamie Roper, still injured from the Yellow Leaf. Black ski hat, black clothes. Face covered in dirt. An ugly imp of darkness. Holding up a mobile phone, as though trying to take pictures with it.

Stanihurst hesitated, momentarily confused. Séamus, too, was amazed. Why would Roper intervene?

Because this was not Roper, but Heidi.

There was a wide pit at her back, part of the foundations of the Forde Centre's boiler house. Stanihurst changed direction and charged straight at her. He was going to throw Heidi into the pit.

She moved to one side. He grasped her elbow and she fell.

Stanihurst tripped over her, picked himself up, lashed out with a savage blow to stun her. His fist passed inches away from her head.

Heidi was on her feet, limping along the edge of the trench. Stanihurst circled around, closed in again.

This time she was cornered. She clutched at Stanihurst's huge hands, then fell over backwards, landing awkwardly. Stanihurst grabbed at her head, pulled off her ski hat. She rolled along the ground at the edge of the trench, bright hair streaked with mud.

She clambered to her feet, waving her hands and shifting from side to side like a child who has watched wrestling on television but is not quite sure how it is done.

Séamus was running now.

Still laughing, Stanihurst spread his arms wide. He was going to throw Heidi into the boiler-house foundations, then do the same to Séamus. He reached out with one enormous hand. She ducked. He reached for her again. There was a playful impudence in the way he fastened his fist on her thin forearm. The contrast between his bulk and her lightness was obscene. She stood no chance.

Séamus launched himself at Stanihurst's ankles. As if expecting the tackle, Stanihurst took one step sideways, kicked back casually, caught Séamus on the side of the head, shambled away like a great carthorse unaware that it has crushed a cockroach.

Séamus sprawled on the edge of consciousness. Raising

his head again, he could see Heidi slipping once more from Stanihurst's grasp, skipping away like a bird with a damaged wing. How had she concealed her limp so well, during all their time together?

Stanihurst closed in on her for the last time. She was a light squirrel in the talons of a hawk. As he caught her, she slipped and fell once more.

Séamus was a man thrashing in a nightmare. He tried to stand. Like a baby, his head was too heavy.

Stanihurst was poised above Heidi. She raised her knees in pathetic self-defence, clutching at the belt of his blue denim jeans. The big man spread his legs wide, bending down to scoop her from the ground, and Séamus could only watch in amazement as the mammoth weight of Stanihurst acquired a sudden lightness. Like a trapeze artist executing a mid-air cartwheel, he flew over her upstretched feet and sailed down into the deep shadow of the trench.

Heidi was on her feet, rock-steady. She gripped Séamus's elbow as he craned to look down.

Stanihurst lay sprawled at the bottom of the trench, a soldier from the Great War. His glasses were broken, his face was at peace.

'He will not die,' Heidi said. Why so sad?

5

Seán Forde sat at a big table in the interrogation room, his head bowed. Lucy, standing behind her husband's chair, rested her hands on his shoulders. Séamus sat beside Heidi on the far side of the room. Mike Dineen stood tall against the window. It was almost evening.

Dineen had spent much of the day taking statements. The Fordes' lawyer, Jack Drumm, had been working to secure Martin's release. Surprisingly, this was proving difficult.

Dineen's superiors had come up with the creative hypothesis that Stanihurst had allowed himself to be captured, by the unlikely combination of Séamus Joyce and his little woman, in order to cover up for Martin, the real culprit. Shortly before midday, Martin's period of detention had been extended for another six hours; according to Drumm, it was doubtful that the Guards would bring charges against him. They would have to let him go very soon.

Dineen cleared his throat. 'Good thing you didn't kill Mr Stanihurst, all the same,' he said to Heidi.

'Good thing he didn't kill her,' Séamus said. His fingers felt the bruise where Stanihurst had kicked him in the head.

'Not much danger of that,' Dineen said. 'A few months ago,' he explained to Heidi, 'a team of investigators was asked to collect some background on Séamus, his contacts and so forth. People were saying, maliciously, that he was mixed up with criminal elements and spies and what have you. Questions had been raised about paying his pension. So enquiries were made in Germany. Not that Decko bothered to share any information with the likes of me. Not until one o'clock this morning, when I consigned Fergus Kilpatrick to his tender care. We know you retired a few years back, Mrs Novacek. Of course you're still able to look after yourself and your family when the need arises.'

Heidi turned down the corners of her mouth. 'I was not always so fortunate.'

'In the past,' Dineen said, 'maybe your enemies were more dangerous.'

Séamus supposed that he should have pressed Heidi for details of her personal history during the months they had been together. He was glad that he had not done so. She would tell him in her own good time. Dineen's remarks merely confirmed what he had sensed subconsciously. He gave no sign of surprise, but changed the subject by turning to Lucy. 'Did you know it was Stanihurst?'

He had not meant this to sound like an accusation. Lucy blinked her brown eyes. Her reply was composed, like a well-rehearsed performance. 'I suppose I must have known. Ricky was angry with President Cregan. He believed they were working against us.' She stopped.

'He was a great man, you see,' Seán Forde said. 'Always loyal to me, except for the one time, with my first wife. He hadn't got over the wars. Always worked for us. Gave me everything. Didn't count the cost.'

'And fathered your son,' Séamus said.

Old Forde put his hand over his eyes. 'Never claimed him,' he said. 'He wanted nothing.'

'Loyally gave his flesh and blood.' Séamus meant to speak ironically, but it came out as a sort of declaration.

Forde nodded. 'That's about right,' he said. 'That's about it. Ricky used to say we made him. As true as fact. That's what he used to say. He was nothing, he said, he was ashes and we raised him up. Mary Kate and me.'

'She took advantage of him,' Séamus said.

'My fault. Couldn't have children, you see. As the boy got bigger, she came to hate me. Nothing to be done about that. She went back on the drink. I couldn't divorce her, you see, and the man she loved couldn't marry her. Mary Kate loved Martin. She did. It was me she couldn't stand. Took to poisoning me, bit by bit. I was in and out with cramps, heart problems. She was afraid to wipe me out in one go. That was her mistake. She'd never told me Ricky was the father. Of course I knew. I'm not simple. Anyway, it didn't matter. Martin was her son. That was good enough for me.'

'She left him with you when she went,' Séamus said.

The old man nodded. 'She was doing the best for him. I've thought about it, and that's what I think was in her mind. Accident or suicide: I don't know which, and I don't think she did, either. She knew I'd look after him, and Ricky would too. She knew he'd be safe. It was me she couldn't stand,

and herself, of course. After the hospital explained how she was poisoning me, I could have had her committed. I did nothing. That was the worst.'

'You couldn't have known,' Lucy said.

'If she'd left me, you see,' Forde said, 'she might have been happy. But I couldn't have let the boy go with her. It wouldn't have been safe. She wasn't fit. I'd have got custody. She knew that.'

Dineen cleared his throat. 'How many do you think he had killed over the years?'

'None while I knew him,' Forde said after a moment. 'Or so I believe. When I took him on, he was back from the wars. Always fought on the wrong side; for the whites in Rhodesia, then as a mercenary in the Congo. He was a big man, accustomed to command. I guessed he'd committed some terrible sins, but he was broken. He needed a chance and I gave him one. He paid me back with everything he had. Worked like a bloody horse. I put him in charge of a team of labourers, then I trusted him with a whole site. He was a superb organizer. Got the men on his side, the crafts-men as well as the labourers. He could be gentle as well as tough. Stanihurst knew what a man could do, and what he couldn't. He pushed them hard, but he'd look after them when they were in trouble. He came to stay in our house after that, when I was doing a big project in Birmingham, visiting the site every day. He put in all the hours God sent. Up before dawn, bed after dark, and he got the job done. I respect that.'

'You'll miss him, then,' Dineen said.

Seán Forde passed a hand over his face. 'I'm not a romantic type,' he said at last. 'I can make money. I can strike a deal. I can hire good men. I can't do the building myself. I was a lousy workman. Put a spade in my hand and I'm lost. But I had men like Stanihurst. He was the best of them. Not that he was a builder by trade. He'd never served his time. What he knew was the men. Better than I did. When he came on to a project, by God it moved. I could have done nothing without him. I think I'll hang up my boots.'

Lucy Forde ran her fingers softly through her husband's hair.

There was a knock at the door. Dineen was called away. Having heard from Jack Drumm about the case against Stanihurst, Martin had asked to see the Inspector. When Dineen went downstairs, Martin dismissed his lawyer and confessed to all three murders, with a wealth of persuasive detail.

The Grounds

I

Weeks went by before Séamus saw Senator Hinckley again. Caught up with mergers and acquisitions, the Senator wished to receive Séamus's report by word of mouth, rather than in writing. The broad implications of the events in Dublin had already been conveyed to Hinckley's office by Guido Schneider, who had come over to Ireland to work with John D. Provenzano on certain proposals that Hinckley wanted to have considered by government agencies.

Provenzano, whom Séamus had met at the degree ceremony, was Hinckley's enforcer. He was referred to by the Irish civil servants as Dr Provenzano, in mock deference to his honorary degree from King's College. Séamus had found himself drawn into the discussions, which were only tangentially concerned with the matter of King's. Hinckley had a whole range of business propositions that could potentially be of interest if the right subsidies and regulatory framework could be provided: information technology, higher education, prison administration, healthcare products. Provenzano combed briskly through these variegated fields with a number of different Irish officials, exploring possible areas of cooperation, jettisoning those ideas that were obviously not going to fly. He never wrote anything down. Guido, on the other hand, took copious notes, produced minutes, briefing documents and financial spreadsheets. Séamus sat in on several meetings under strict instructions to keep his mouth shut. Afterwards, Provenzano questioned him on what the Irish officials might have meant by what they had said. It was assumed that Séamus understood these people. Neither Guido nor Provenzano revealed what exactly Senator Hinckley's bottom line might be on any of the projects discussed. It seemed possible that they did not know.

Stanihurst was in custody, awaiting trial. His confession had proved even more convincing than that of his son.

Séamus and Heidi returned briefly to Germany and picked up some of the threads of their domestic life. Then, on the day when Hinckley was scheduled to come to Ireland, they met Guido at Gatwick, crossed to Newark on a Continental 767 and boarded Hinckley's Gulfstream II for the return trip. Hinckley had calls to make, people to see, but hoped to visit with them for about an hour in the course of the flight.

Séamus had learned a little more about the Senator when he finally got to meet Patrick Connolly. The proprietor of Padcon turned out to be an unappealing grey man with a metallic angle-grinding voice, who lived in a bleak house not far from Howth. The glamorous redhead from Clarendon Lane was, it transpired, his wife, and she it was who had hired the young woman in the baseball cap to trail Heidi and Séamus during their day in Dublin. Connolly considered himself to have been robbed by Hinckley, who had cut him out of the deal he had devised to transfer King's College to Tullamore, in the Irish midlands. This had caused him to leave the College board, and he still felt a strong need for compensation. He had also resented Cregan's attempts to blackmail him. He had warned Séamus not to be too impressed with Hinckley, who had never been a real Senator, having merely served one term in the State Senate of Virginia, many years before.

Although small when seen from the outside, the Gulfstream proved surprisingly spacious and quiet, and Séamus quickly stopped wondering how such a diminutive craft could cross the Atlantic. Immediately after takeoff, they were confined to the rear of the cabin, where they were welcome to amuse themselves with a selection of current magazines and to chat socially with Hinckley's stewardess and two earnest young skinheads – Jake and Daniel, one a linguist, the other a marketing psychologist – who claimed to have invented a better way of mining computer data to detect potential terrorist supporters among email users by triangulating the English syntax, health and education records and grocery shopping preferences of millions of individuals over a six-month period. Or so Séamus inferred from half-dropped hints. The two young men were not at liberty to disclose the details of their system, which suited Séamus fine, but were betrayed by their enthusiasm for its potential. They got to make their pitch for Hinckley's investment half an hour into the flight. Guido conjectured that they were not likely to be extremely successful if they blabbered to everyone about their project and insisted on 'inventing' things that were already commonplace and rather ineffective. They huddled with Senator Hinckley on a sofa. Séamus could not hear what they said, but he watched from the back of the plane. Their body language gradually subsided from eagerness to dejection as Hinckley began to lean back in his chair, visibly losing interest in what they had to say. In the days of the Italian Renaissance, he might have pulled a small lever to catapult them out of their seats and into the ocean. Instead, he merely signalled to his personal assistant that she could stop taking notes, leaned forward, shook hands cordially with the two suppliants and sent them back to join Séamus, Guido and Heidi in limbo.

'Chewed us up and spat us out,' said the younger of the two in disgust.

'Don't take it bad,' the stewardess said. 'If you made it this far, he's got to be interested. He remembers people. You won't lose out by talking to the Senator.'

Séamus listened to the steady note of the twin engines, and tried not to think of the ice-blue water six miles down.

He expected to be summoned forward at any moment. This did not happen, which left far too much time to think about the mystery of flight. He watched as Hinckley's personal assistant, a tall woman of the utmost gravitas, produced files to be read and letters to be signed. Her boss dealt swiftly with these papers, scribbling marginal notes and issuing instructions. She handed him a sheaf of computer printouts, into which he burrowed happily. Séamus was reminded of a prairie dog disappearing underground. When next he surfaced, it was to murmur a long memo into a recording device, which the senior secretary retrieved and started to transcribe, using headphones and a portable computer. The Senator then reclined, covered his eyes with a mask and fell asleep for a short while, after which he shook himself awake, stood and stretched luxuriously, came to the rear of the cabin, poured whiskies for everyone. Betraying no embarrassment, he struck up a fresh dialogue with the two computer wizards. He knew that they had worked in Menlo Park, where one of the Hinckley offshoots had connections with a niche software development company. He discovered some mutual acquaintances and traded gossip. A thought struck him. 'Let me grab a pen.' The stewardess passed him hers. He wrote a telephone number on the back of a business card and passed it to the man whom he had correctly identified as the leader of the two. 'Talk to Bill,' he said. 'Show him what you got. The whole nine yards. It's not for me. Some of it's close to stuff that's out there, but your system may contain new technical wrinkles. I don't have the knowledge. If I took it on, I'd be sued for copyright infringement by the data mining companies, plus I'd be screwed by the ACLU. But you can trust Bill. He has access. He'll tell you straight off how much of your stuff is fresh. Some of this they don't patent, which makes it tough for developers. If there's anything new in what you've assembled, they'll buy it, or they'll pay you to work it up. You don't have to worry; they'll respect your intellectual property rights. And they'll pay you for your time.'

The two men made noises of gratitude. Senator Hinckley invited them to fly on to London with him and meet some of his British contacts. 'I'd enjoy your company,' he assured them. Séamus found this hard to credit; he found them as congenial as a pair of caged rats.

Hinckley turned to Séamus and interrogated him at length on the personalities and careers of Ireland's political leaders, the foibles of past generations and the promise of the next. He had been briefed on these people, knew more about some of them than Séamus did.

Séamus was still enough of a civil servant to reveal little or nothing that he had heard privately in the course of his work; he would comment only on stories that were already in the public domain. Hinckley recognized this inhibition, lost interest in questioning him and started instead to explain a little more of his plans for the future of King's College Dublin. He spoke as though the others were not present, as though he were alone with Séamus. Some of what he said matched what Séamus had already gleaned from other sources.

The current visit was to give public effect to the outcome of negotiations recently concluded by John D. Provenzano. According to Hinckley, Provenzano was a born diplomat, despite his intractable manner, or perhaps because of it. In Dublin he had not only brokered a good deal with the Irish administration, but had also succeeded in restoring good relations with Patrick Connolly. Padcon was poised to expand its prison catering business dramatically in the United States.

As a result of John D's diplomacy, Hinckley himself was *persona grata* with the Irish government. In Dublin he was to meet the Minister for Industry, Trade and Employment and announce the creation of 200 computer-related jobs in Tallaght. His next appointment was with the Minister for Education and Science, to transfer the trusteeship of King's College Dublin into the great educational family of Finer Small Campuses, thereby removing yet another useless burden from the Irish taxpayer and marking an important step forward in Ireland's quest for global excellence.

With the mess that had been left in King's, nobody else was in a position to take it on. The public universities had problems enough of their own. The owners of a private Irish college had made a bid, but an urgent analysis by top government experts had determined that these people lacked the requisite experience. Finer Small Campuses was reckoned to be the sole credible bidder for an immediate sale.

Synergy was the keyword: there would be a new Department of Software Studies, meshed in with Hinckley's European software development team. Among other things, the new department would have an advisory role on ways and means of implementing the strategic objectives of Ireland's Information Age Development Plan. If all went well, it had been hinted that there might even be the possibility of a future link-up with Dublin's Digital Hub, across the Liffey.

Rumours that the whole campus was about to be decentralized to Tullamore had been scotched. There was indeed to be a second campus, located just fifty miles away in the historic town of Kells, County Meath, which coincidentally was in the constituency represented by the Minister for Education and Science, Mr 'Porky' Keeffe. The Kells campus, to be known as King's College Royal Meath, was to concentrate on attracting rural Irish students who could not afford Dublin housing prices. The finest teachers from the Phoenix Park campus would come to lecture once a week, so the quality of the Kells degree would equal the standards of excellence traditionally associated with King's. Professor Millington, designated to head up the Kells campus, was planning a new library building and had already launched one-sided negotiations with Trinity College Dublin for the return of the Book of Kells, Ireland's greatest medieval manuscript, to its proper resting place. So far Trinity College was being obdurate, but Millington had hopes.

The teaching staff were much relieved, Séamus knew. Kells was better than Tullamore. Most of the staff would not have to move house, although they might have to commute longer distances. There were cast-iron guarantees of employment for all academics and some administrators – sadly not including the accounts people, since Finer Small Campuses had a state-of-the-art revenue facility located in Malaysia, for all its colleges worldwide.

Séamus could see other potential advantages to the new plans. American postgraduates might well be attracted to the one-year MPhil programme in U2 Studies that had been announced for the Phoenix Park campus: an interdisciplinary venture between English, Religion, Music and Business. The provision of English composition training for all undergraduate students was also educationally respectable, in an era when functional illiteracy was spreading. The abandonment of the late President Cregan's structural reforms could only be good.

What Hinckley added to Séamus's existing knowledge was the sporting angle. This was the political and economic lynchpin of the entire project. The jewel in the crown, for the Kells campus, would be its distinctive Irish games programme. The country's first full professorship of Gaelic Athletic Studies was to be announced. A suitable candidate had already been approached. Under his leadership, historians, sociologists, political scientists, strategists and physiotherapists would train a generation of physically fit, skilled and culturally aware sportsmen and sportswomen to lead the county teams of Ireland. Politically ambitious students would be attracted to the course, given that the Gaelic Athletic Association epitomized all that was best in Irish life, and GAA players and officials tended to do remarkably well in Irish elections. The influence of King's College would grow; its future would be guaranteed.

Because the Kells campus was in the Royal County of Meath, the first emphasis would naturally be on Gaelic football. Indeed, a proportion of the generous football scholarships tenable at King's College Royal Meath would be reserved for natives of the county. There was obvious scope for sponsorship. The other leading Gaelic sports, hurling and camogie, would not be neglected, while a visiting chair of Australian Rules would ensure a strong international outlook.

Moreover, because it was Meath, space would be no problem. The limited extent of the Phoenix Park grounds meant that an expansion in Gaelic games had never been an option on the original King's College site. Other games could prosper there, however. As the old campus would house large numbers of visiting American students, it would develop a strong basketball programme. There would be heavy investment in premises, equipment and training. Again, the sponsorship potential was considerable.

These complementary sports investments, Senator Hinckley explained, were a winning business proposition. Just think for a moment. Dublin, where space cost money, was the wrong place for Gaelic games, but perfect for basketball development. Removing Gaelic and soccer from the Phoenix Park site would free up seven acres for quality apartment buildings, housing students during the academic year, tourists in the summer months. The profits would pay for space in County Meath for Irish students to study and read and play ball. 'Do the math, Séamus,' Hinckley urged. 'Basketball has the right footprint. Your Gaelic pitch measures one hundred forty-five metres by eighty-five, while a basketball court measures only twenty-eight metres by fifteen. You could fit twenty-nine basketball courts into one Gaelic pitch. OK, basketball has teams of ten, while your Gaelic games of hurling and football have teams of fifteen. Even so, the space per player in Gaelic games is about twenty times what you need for basketball. It's a slam-dunk.'

'And will the government allow you to sell development land in the Phoenix Park?' Séamus asked.

'Guess so. It's in a good cause. I'm using the proceeds to fund your native Irish sports in the Education Minister's own backyard.' Hinckley leaned forward. 'If this model works, Séamus, it could be the start of something big. We could rescue other Irish colleges, even some of your old failing universities in Europe, bring them into the big time. Now this is not a takeover. King's College will be run by a local man. Professor O'Toole has already moved into the President's House.'

Hinckley finished his drink, invited Séamus to move forward in the cabin and give him his personal report. 'Events have moved on, but you know, Séamus, I like to get the human story. You can tell me.'

3

This was what Hinckley had paid for. Séamus could hardly refuse. He would speak the truth, so far as he knew it. They reclined on a matching pair of swivel chairs. Heidi and Guido, at the back, were deep in conversation with the two software designers, but Guido glanced over from time to time to see how the client was reacting to Séamus's pitch.

Hinckley stared at Séamus through half-closed eyelids, absorbing what he had to say with total attention, throwing in occasional questions. Being the object of such close scrutiny was like being auditioned by some famous conductor with a view to a solo performance.

Séamus became aware that Hinckley had already assimilated some key facts in the case. This knowledge would have facilitated his recent negotiations, through Provenzano, with the Irish government. Knowing too much might have been a hindrance. Séamus's role now was to fill some gaps, not to start from scratch.

Much of the framework that underpinned his words came from Heidi. She had primed him for this interview, piecing the case together from all its different sources, guessing that Hinckley would prefer to hear the story from him, although she herself could have told it just as well. Heidi had a systematic mind, liked to get things straight. She knew what she knew, and what she did not know. That was part of her professional identity, her training: not just teaching fat men to fly.

In the end it was not one story, but three, linked by malign coincidence and a generous dose of stupidity. Séamus tried to put it into sequence. One of the roots of the problem, he suggested, lay in the character flaws of the late President Cregan: his habit of promising the same things to different people, coupled with an unfortunate propensity to blackmail and a disastrous tendency to half-believe his own fantasies. A second root cause was the idealistic but ill-informed desire on the part of the late Andrew O'Neill to preserve non-existent archaeological remains from the greedy maw of property developers. The most distant cause, and ultimately the most lethal, lay in the almost forgotten Rhodesian wars, back in the seventies, when Richard Stanihurst had been a white farmer's son pressed into military service against the guerrilla fighters of Joshua Nkomo and Robert Mugabe. How these three factors had combined to produce a string of recent murders, instead of remaining separate and inert, was an unanswerable mystery, as inscrutable as the mystery of why one young man comes home from a night's drinking with nothing worse than a mild headache, while another is drawn into a casual fight and gets kicked to death by a gang of jolly schoolboys. Fate, fortune and Cleopatra's nose will blow where they list. Without aspiring to the happiness of being able to determine the ultimate causes of things, Séamus took as the most convenient chronological starting-point the arrival of Andy O'Neill, some fifteen months back.

O'Neill, more a passionate enthusiast than a careful researcher, had come to King's College as Professor of History, having negotiated a six-month sabbatical to start his new job. President Maxwell, overawed at capturing such a distinguished chair-holder, was happy to concede this initial period of uninterrupted study, and the new President, Oliver Cregan, reluctantly went along with the arrangement. O'Neill was completing a book on Viking cities, to be published by one of Britain's leading university presses. (It subsequently transpired that the press in question was unaware of his plans.) He became interested in the remains of St Malachi's Abbey, as evidence for the development of satellite settlements in the environs of medieval Dublin. He had read the archaeologists' report prepared in conjunction with Forde's building projects, and noted some obvious inaccuracies that led him to suppose that the report might be generally flawed. Being an impulsive man and a late convert to the methodologies of medieval studies, he had jumped to the conclusion that the Forde Centre was being built over the heart of St Malachi's Abbey. Further documentary research, and his amateurish excavations, soon showed that he had been quite wrong about that. The main Abbey ruins in fact lay under the nineteenth-century College buildings, and had been irreparably damaged during the construction of the quadrangle and cloisters in 1832. Having started his investigations, however, O'Neill continued digging, in order to map out the boundaries of the Abbey farm.

At this point, Stanihurst became suspicious of O'Neill's interest in the Forde Centre. He confronted O'Neill as he wandered through the building site, warning him to stop interfering. O'Neill assured him that there was nothing in his findings to cut across the new construction plans, but then, as he reported in his memorandum, a trivial coincidence, something that Stanihurst said – a single word of Rhodesian army slang, nothing more than the word 'takkies', used to refer disparagingly to the old tennis shoes O'Neill was wearing as he walked through the muddy foundation trench – flashed O'Neill back to what had happened decades earlier when he was a young missionary priest, working to spread education and justice in southern Africa.

Shortly before the fall of the Smith régime, during the endgame of the Rhodesian war, there had been, among other atrocities, the massacre of a rebel company together with their putative supporters in a remote rural area. Men had been shot, women burned. Andrew O'Neill, already a radical opponent of the Smith régime, had spoken to witnesses of the massacre, read accounts of it in the newspapers and propaganda sheets, collected evidence and statements to send to a campaigning bishop. Among the materials he had assembled was a photograph of a huge bearded young man, slightly younger than himself, who had commanded the small platoon of Selous Scouts suspected of having performed the massacre. Meeting Stanihurst all those years later, even when they had both shed their beards and some of their other hair, he was unable to conceal the spark of recognition.

He said nothing at the time. Neither did Stanihurst. Following the meeting, however, O'Neill took a short break from medieval archaeology and threw himself into reconstructing the personal chronicle of Stanihurst. He used the Internet to check information sources, and through Justice Watch Africa he contacted a group of lawyers in Holland who were relentlessly preparing files on ancient war crimes, hoping to submit them to the International Criminal Court, if the correct conditions for ICC jurisdiction could be met. Alerted by a South African sympathizer who had infiltrated the Dutch group – or so it was presumed, as files on other cases had certainly been leaked and the South African was no longer traceable – Stanihurst discovered the extent of the evidence O'Neill had collected. He confronted O'Neill one night in his bedroom on campus, killed him and burned his papers.

'Overreaction,' Senator Hinckley commented.

With the dead body lying on the bedroom floor, Stanihurst sent an email message from O'Neill's computer, inviting O'Neill's research assistant Ronan Gannon to meet him at eight-thirty on the following morning to go swimming. He signed the email 'Andy', and closed the computer down. It was a portable computer, easily disposed of. Early-morning swimming was one of O'Neill's established habits. The message aroused no suspicion. He then buried Andrew O'Neill's body near the foundations of the restored Temple of Remembrance.

As one of President Cregan's favourites, Ronan Gannon had been housed in one of the new staff maisonettes that were beginning to appear on the edge of the campus. Stanihurst drove O'Neill's small car around to Gannon's place. He had a master key. He stunned the young man with a single blow to the back of the head, then drowned him in the bath, mixing some household salt with the water. He greatly regretted this second killing, although he saw Gannon as a rival to Martin Forde, and a bad influence on him. He removed Gannon's computer and back-up disks. He then drove to Portmarnock, walked into the sea carrying the body, released it into the waves. There was a strong offshore tide running at the time. He was back in his apartment by four o'clock in the morning.

'Apartment?' Senator Hinckley enquired. 'I thought he lived in a big house with Mr and Mrs Forde.'

'Most of the time. But he often rented rooms near the building sites he supervised. That way he could save commuting time and manage double shifts of workmen. For the jobs in King's College and Kinnegad, he had taken a small flat in Chapelizod.'

He had murdered the research assistant for what he believed were two good and necessary reasons: to cover his crime by creating the supposition of a body lost at sea, and because he suspected Ronan Gannon of being involved in O'Neill's researches into his own military past. O'Neill had been known to be hopeless with computers, yet the investigation into Stanihurst's past had been conducted using sophisticated computer searches.

The double killing paid off in yet another way: Ronan's death was accepted by some gossips in the College as being a case of suicide following murder. The story, purely conjectural but widely circulated, was that he had done away with Professor O'Neill, then drowned himself in a fit of remorse. His worship for O'Neill was legendary among the students, but it is a known fact that students sometimes kill their teachers, whereas the opposite rarely happens despite all provocation. So far, Stanihurst had been luckier than he might have dared to hope. The drowning story was believed, a culprit had been named, and the police investigation had been shoddy enough to avoid any unwanted revisionism.

'Now, you're going to tell me,' Hinckley said, 'that his troubles hadn't gone away.'

Séamus agreed that this was so. As summer gave way to autumn, Stanihurst realized that the problem remained unsolved. Haggling over delayed payments for some building work on the President's House, President Cregan dropped veiled hints that he knew something about Stanihurst's military career. Stanihurst began to suspect that Cregan might have had access to Andrew O'Neill's documentary evidence. The truth was even worse: one week before being murdered,

O'Neill had gone to see the new President and handed him a complete copy of the dossier he had assembled: *The War Crimes of Richard John Pole Stanihurst.* The title was arguably an exaggeration, but some of the content was gruesome enough.

Additional photographic evidence relating to O'Neill's burial, taken from College surveillance cameras, was stored not on Cregan's computer but on the normal College security system. The initial Garda investigation, led by one of Dineen's less competent colleagues, had downloaded the dark images but found nothing in them. They had never been sent for computer enhancement, until Dineen came to take charge of the Cregan murder case.

Fionnuala Fagan, O'Neill's lover, knew nothing of the Stanihurst dossier, but she knew that O'Neill had been to visit the new President shortly before his presumed drowning. She had seen O'Neill working on papers that he refused to show her, and she conjectured that O'Neill might have given Cregan some further evidence proving that the building works posed a danger to the old Abbey site. Fionnuala had become obsessed with the notion that these hypothetical documents might contain the key to Andrew O'Neill's disappearance. She half-suspected the President of being behind that disappearance, for reasons connected with the building works. She feared Cregan, but could not imagine him physically harming O'Neill. Physical violence would have been out of character for Cregan. Mental cruelty and manipulation were more his style. Had she had any concrete evidence relating to O'Neill's death, she might possibly have taken her suspicions further. As it was, she allowed them to fester.

O'Neill's evidence, if it existed, would probably be kept with other prized documents in the storage drawer under the President's bed. She knew the function of that storage drawer, being no stranger to Cregan's bedroom. She also knew that the President's House was covered by surveillance cameras, although his private quarters were not.

She made several half-hearted efforts to revive her former liaison with President Cregan. Her motives for doing this were not clear, least of all to herself. Cregan was reputed to have a new woman in his life, an American teaching in France (although the woman in question subsequently failed to show up at his funeral), and he did not relish the idea that old mistresses could enforce a continuing claim on his intimacy. Fionnuala was frozen out. She even began to worry that Cregan was planning to remove her from her job, as he had already done with another former girlfriend, and his vague commitment to make her Director of Equality failed to allay her fears, particularly after she discovered that he had made a similar promise to Ms Lola Sanchez of the former Spanish Department.

Things had come to a head with the arrival of Séamus Joyce, which occurred at a point when, as President Cregan hinted to Fionnuala, King's College faced bankruptcy, while he himself was drifting towards a potentially disastrous scrutiny of his stewardship. Needing to blunt what he perceived as the attack from America, he set Derry McKinley, his public relations consultant, to assemble material which might be used to discredit Séamus, and did his best to reassure Forde and Stanihurst that their interests were not under threat. Stanihurst kept insisting to Seán Forde that President Cregan must be in league with the Finer Small Campuses organization, planning to oust the Forde organization from the campus and to cheat them of the money owed for their building work. In this belief, Stanihurst could hardly have been more mistaken. Far from conspiring with FSC, Cregan had diverted American money to prop up other projects, and feared exposure and disgrace at the hands of Senator Hinckley. Such was the pressure that he even confided some of his fears to Fionnuala. FSC, he told her, were sharks.

'King of the ocean,' Senator Hinckley said. 'I can live with that.'

Even the mild and ineffectual Séamus Joyce, as emissary of FSC, was given honorary shark status. Cregan had heard from McKinley what a dangerous man Séamus really was, despite his drab exterior.

The inquisition by Finer Small Campuses had to be stopped. Hence McKinley's excessive efforts to discredit Séamus. Hence Cregan's desperate plea to Fionnuala to do something to compromise Séamus for the benefit of the surveillance cameras: to generate some evidence that could be used to soften his cough, should the need arise. Cregan had promised to conceal Fionnuala's identity in any use of the photographs: an absurd promise, given the nature of the evidence he hoped to obtain, but not out of character for Cregan.

Fionnuala reluctantly agreed to visit Séamus's room on the second night of his visit to Dublin, although she did not specify exactly what she proposed to do. She felt bad about the whole thing, as she afterwards told Heidi. It raised issues about her past. She claimed to feel some lingering affection for Séamus.

By malign coincidence, Jeremy Quaid, acting out of sheer spite, chose that same evening to inform Stanihurst of a rumour (entirely invented by himself) that Cregan had sold St Malachi's mace, centrepiece of the new Forde Centre Museum, and was planning to substitute a fake mace for the admiration of tourists. Stanihurst, sensing an advantage, tele-phoned the President, challenging him to disprove the rumour. He demanded to borrow the mace and have it examined on the following morning by a leading expert on Irish antiques, who acted as adviser to a jewellery store on Grafton Street. If Cregan refused this demand, all building work in the College would cease and the Forde organization would take out a court injunction to freeze the College's assets.

'Your Mr Stanihurst hang out much with jewellers?' Hinck-ley wanted to know. 'He doesn't sound the type.'

Séamus explained that the architect of the Forde Centre had invited this particular jeweller to a meeting about display cases and conservation facilities for the new museum. Stanihurst had met their expert adviser and had been impressed.

Hinckley nodded. Séamus continued the story: Cregan tried negotiating, claiming that he could not let Stanihurst remove the mace from the College premises, whereupon Stanihurst, losing all sense of proportion, went so far as to summon the President to join him later that night in the basement security store under the cloisters, and to have Fionnuala Fagan on hand as a medieval expert who could authenticate the mace, or at least explain to him why it might be authentic. Stanihurst knew Fionnuala because Martin lived in her house. He said that he himself would come around to the President's House at midnight to escort Cregan to the security store. Cregan should arrange for Fionnuala Fagan's attendance.

Normally, President Cregan would have rejected this preposterous demand. There were four reasons, in Heidi's opinion, why he had not done so. Séamus laid them out one by one. Cregan was physically frightened of Stanihurst. He knew that the mace was authentic, and therefore expected to score a psychological point over his tormentor. He was reaching a crisis point over the cash he owed to the Forde organization. And if they still could not reach agreement on the timing of payments due for the building work, he thought that he might be able to protect himself by showing Stanihurst the dossier O'Neill had given him.

'High risk,' Hinckley said. 'Cregan was too confident. He was used to dealing with professors. They don't cut up rough.'

Séamus continued his narrative. Fionnuala changed her clothes in the President's private bathroom, but had no opportunity to search the drawer under Cregan's bed, as he was pacing up and down in his room, planning what he was going to say to Stanihurst. She crossed over into the guest quarters, and was with Séamus when the doorbell rang: Stanihurst had turned up earlier than agreed, to escort the President to the storeroom under the main College building where the mace was kept. Hearing the bell, Fionnuala ran out on to the upper landing, whispering to Cregan to go ahead; she would join them in a few minutes. As Cregan left, she went into the presidential bedroom and quickly searched his store of documents, hoping to find the documents which could explain the disappearance of her former lover, Andrew O'Neill.

'This is like a French farce,' Senator Hinckley objected. 'Ladies with stopwatches.'

'She didn't find it farcical,' Séamus said. 'She was badly scared. You're right, though. The timing is essential. That's why I'm giving you the exact sequence, as close as we can reconstruct it.'

Although fatally stupid in his handling of larger issues, Cregan could be clever about some small things. He had of course made a second copy of the file which he had brought to his meeting with Stanihurst. And so, although the drawer contained no archaeological revelations, what Fionnuala found instead was more interesting: an extra copy of O'Neill's dossier on Stanihurst the war criminal. As she glanced through the closely typed pages, she knew at once why O'Neill had died, and who had murdered him.

In the President's bedroom, Fionnuala took that second copy of papers out of their cardboard folder, intending to make yet another copy. The copier in Cregan's study had run out of toner, so she got dressed and hurried over to the History Department in the main university building. She used the copier in the secretary's office – an agonizing process, as the copier took five minutes to warm up. There was no time to put the original back under Cregan's bed; she would try to do that later. She made her way down to the basement, expecting to meet Stanihurst with Cregan and say her piece about why the mace was authentic. The security room was unlocked; the mace was missing. Nearby, in the accounts office, she found Cregan, dead.

'Why did she not raise the alarm?' Hinckley wanted to know.

'She's not that kind of girl,' Séamus said. 'Apart from being worried about her own physical safety, her first instinct has always been for concealment. Also, she feared for the mental balance of Martin Forde. She believed that he knew, at some subconscious level, that Stanihurst was his father. She thought that his rejection of Seán Forde might have been made on the basis that he secretly knew who his real father was. To find that –'

'Enough analysis, already,' Hinckley said. 'More facts, please. I find them reassuring, even when they're made up.'

Séamus pressed on. Cregan had presumably tried to threaten Stanihurst by showing him the dossier in its cardboard folder. Stanihurst had seized this copy and stuffed it inside his shirt after beating Cregan to death with the mace. Investigators had found the bloodstained folder in Stanihurst's bank deposit box, and the bloodstained shirt in the washing machine in the kitchen of his apartment in Chapelizod. The stains were on the inside of the shirt, and had not been entirely obliterated. According to Heidi, Stanihurst should have used biological washing powder.

Hinckley shook his head. 'Killing the President was not a healthy reaction. Mr Stanihurst wasn't figuring straight. Thing in Rhodesia happened way back. They were never going to get the witnesses. He would have walked. We have to put these things behind us.'

This was a lesson that Séamus himself should have learned, concerning his own childhood and youth. He looked at Hinckley, trying to estimate his age. Too old for Vietnam?

'Yeah, I'm a veteran,' Hinckley said as though reading his thoughts. 'Caught the tail end of Korea. Never killed nobody.

I was lucky. Met boys who never got over Vietnam. Boys who never asked to go there.'

'Stanihurst was drafted into the Rhodesian Army. He was a farmer's son. He had to go. Then he volunteered for the Light Infantry, got mixed up in the dirty end of counter-terrorism.'

'Must've seemed the thing to do,' Hinckley said. 'Bad decision. But even guys who fight on the right side get mixed up in wrong actions. Mostly, foot-soldiers don't get held accountable.'

'Stanihurst couldn't take the idea of being accused, after all these years.'

'Sensitive guy?'

'On most things, no. On one thing, absolutely. The way I read it, Stanihurst needed to look good in the eyes of his son. Even if Martin didn't know he was his father.'

Hinckley nodded, almost sadly. 'Yep. He'd never claimed the boy. Should have spoken out. Misplaced honour. Sort that don't do no good.'

This comment suggested, among other things, that Hinckley knew more about the background to the case than Séamus was telling him. And this, despite Séamus's attempt to spell out the whole story in exhaustive detail. Once again, there was the sensation of being auditioned for the performance of a well-known piece. Conversations with great men tend to work that way. One feels judged.

'I've been thinking about Stanihurst,' Séamus said. 'He settled for very little in life. We do that as we get older. Content to stand at the sidelines. To be seen by his son as a good man, out of the corner of his eye.'

'It's not enough.' Senator Hinckley shook his head. 'Man needs more than that. Pin everything on a peripheral, you can't afford to lose it. Like Samson. In the end, your haircut costs you a darn sight more than it should.'

'I think he couldn't take the thought of Martin turning away from him.'

'Couldn't let go of the kid because he'd never held on to him. You a parent, Mr Joyce?'

'No.' That was the short answer.

'Well, take it from me. Letting go is something we all face. Enough of this homespun wisdom, sir. Marilyn, can we trouble you for some coffee?'

4

Séamus looked at Guido, chatting with Heidi and the two young men. Guido's part in Heidi's life, if any, remained obscure, but in recent weeks other elements in Séamus's world had started falling into place. His life in Germany had been investigated, at the behest of the Pensions Authority. The senior policeman sent to Aachen seemed to have discovered things about Heidi that he himself did not yet know, and which might in the long run be even more interesting than the King's College mystery or the defeat of Stanihurst. Which, he realized, she had brought about with finely calibrated cunning. Stanihurst was a trained fighter, a man of dexterity as well as huge physical power. In open combat he would have overwhelmed her. She had led him on, flapping and tripping and playing the easy victim, not letting him see her skill until it was too late. It had been touch and go. He must have felt a damned fool as he fell into the trench.

Séamus too had underestimated Heidi, had taken her as she had presented herself. Which was presumably how she preferred it. There are women like that.

He saw her looking at him now, from her seat at the back of the Gulfstream cabin, her face lighting up like a mother with her child. As if she had given him new life. And yet she needed comfort, which he would provide, playing the role of the strong protector. Their relationship had a new foundation, built on misfortune.

The junior secretary brought coffee. Séamus picked up the story from the murderer's point of view. Stanihurst had battered Cregan to death, and wiped his prints from the remaining stump of the damaged mace. Knowing Cregan as he did, he rightly suspected that another copy of the dossier might be concealed elsewhere. He left his victim lying in the accounts office, moved through the cloisters without meeting a soul, walked to the Portakabin where he kept a spare set of overalls. He put them on to cover his bloodstained clothes, and began to think of how to retrieve the documents that might incriminate him. The most likely location was in the President's House. He knew there was a safe in the basement. If he could not find the documents himself, he could force Hynes to help him. The first problem was getting across the campus. Knowing where the surveillance cameras were positioned, he was determined to leave no traces in their memory. But before he could approach the President's House, Hynes had come over to the cloisters, looking for Cregan. He wanted to warn the President that Séamus Joyce had left the house and was on the prowl. Hynes found the body and raised the alarm. Within minutes the police arrived, and for more than an hour there was too much coming and going in the area around the President's House for Stanihurst to gain access.

Meanwhile, Fionnuala too had changed her clothes. She had knelt on the floor to feel Cregan's pulse, searching for signs of life. Finding blood on her fingers and on her black dress, she worried that she might be accused of killing him, so she washed her hands in the ladies' room, went back to her own office and put on the loose denim smock that she kept in a cupboard for use on those days when she worked in the dusty cellars where the artefacts of the College's defunct medieval museum were stored.

She was trying to brace herself to make an emergency call, to summon help for Cregan just in case he might not be dead after all, but when she heard shouting, she knew that his body had been discovered. It was a huge relief. She had made her way to Quaid's room. She knew Quaid would protect her, because he loved her, and always had. At least, this was the conclusion that Heidi and Séamus had reached, on the available evidence, on the basis of half-buried memories and following a heavy-drinking interview with the no longer morose Dr Burren. In fact, Séamus suggested to Hinckley, it was probably Quaid's jealousy, sparked by Fionnuala's new overtures to President Cregan, which had caused Quaid to make up the story about the substituted mace, so that Stani-hurst would put the frighteners on Cregan. He had hardly intended it to lead to Cregan's death.

'Hell hath no fury,' said the Senator.

After the murder, Stanihurst had lain low in the College grounds for a couple of hours. Eventually, he worked his way around to the Servants' Lodge beside the President's House to catch Hynes and make him open the safe. Stanihurst had a slight hold over Hynes because of the drugs trade on campus, in which Hynes was marginally involved. Hynes had no pension, had gambled away his house, was working on well past retirement age at the President's pleasure. When he eventually retired or was dismissed, he would be homeless and indigent. He was still addicted to gambling. Hence his desperate need for extra cash, and his willingness to engage in questionable activities. Stanihurst regarded him as a man of straw, and felt confident that he could persuade him to hold his tongue.

The President's House was under guard, but as far as he could see there was nobody inside. Stanihurst guessed that the policemen guarding the downstairs doors and windows might be unaware of other access points. He cut off the power to the surveillance cameras, entered the Servants' Lodge, forced Hynes to lead him through the tunnel to the President's basement, opened the safe, and found nothing useful to his own case. Hynes, under duress, had revealed that the President maintained another cache of papers under his bed. Stanihurst had gone upstairs to Cregan's bedroom and found a cardboard folder identical to the one he already held, but containing no documents. He hauled Hynes into the President's private study on the ground floor, made him open the drawers and cabinets. Nothing was found. He switched on the President's computer and found some surveillance video recordings, which he erased. He missed the file featuring Fionnuala in bed with Séamus. Also, the older surveillance footage. He then escorted Hynes back to his own quarters and battered him almost to the point of death, but Hynes knew nothing, had nothing to confess. Stanihurst might conceivably have killed Hynes had he not been disturbed by Séamus. He had escaped from the Servants' Lodge as Inspector Dineen returned. His next step, in all probability, had been to return to his rented apartment in Chapelizod and wash his clothes.

As the hours went by, Stanihurst tried to guess who might hold another copy of the dossier, which now risked not only having him dragged before a war crimes tribunal and possibly being convicted of an ancient atrocity, but also implicating him in the deaths of O'Neill and Cregan.

For the first twenty-four hours he did nothing, but showed up punctually on site and worked harder than ever, keeping himself in plain view, even conferring with Inspector Dineen about traffic management for his lorries and the police vehicles. All the time he must have been suffering agonies of doubt. Who else might have received copies of the Rhodesia document? He guessed, correctly, that Fionnuala could have a copy: McKinley had informed him of her visit to the

President's guest room, and besides, she had been O'Neill's lover. He went through the filing cabinet in her College office, to no avail. She had taken the papers home and hidden them in the blocked-up fireplace behind her cooker hood.

His next target was the office of Patrick Connolly. He had conceived a violent dislike of Connolly, knowing his desire to have FSC take over the college and set up an outreach campus on the development site in Tullamore for which Padcon had already received outline planning permission. Connolly had worked out the brilliant scheme that FSC should sell off the sports fields at the Phoenix Park campus, but had failed to come up with a politically acceptable way of doing it. The land in Kells was to be purchased, with government subsidies, from the cousin of the wife of an influential junior minister. Padcon was left with the Tullamore lands, where the planning permission only covered educational purposes. Connolly was looking at a substantial loss. He had withdrawn from the board in disgust on learning that Kells was the favoured site. Feeling betrayed, he had turned against FSC.

Stanihurst wrongly believed that Connolly and FSC were still close allies of President Cregan, and might have shared in the evidence that Cregan had gathered against the Forde faction. During the night of the second day after the murder, he had therefore ransacked Connolly's office on Clarendon Lane. He had worked neatly, had worn latex gloves, had left no prints behind, but in his bedroom in Chapelizod was an ivory statuette of a bulldog, belonging to Connolly's wife. This tasteless hybrid was the only thing that had been taken in an otherwise fruitless burglary. Even the petty cash had been left untouched. Mrs Connolly demanded her bulldog back, and it was released into her care.

Stanihurst's next target was Fionnuala's house. By now he was growing more agitated, losing his finesse. Absenting himself from the building site at King's, he broke into

Fionnuala's kitchen to search for the dossier, and was pulling the place apart when he was disturbed by the return of his own son, Martin. He escaped unseen. But Fionnuala knew he had been there, and that he suspected she held the dossier.

Even now, why had she not gone to the Guards with her evidence? She was certain that Stanihurst was a killer, and even if this were not the case, she should have had no compunction about making him accountable for his past war crimes. On the other hand, she found him terrifying and did not trust the Guards to lock him up. What if he found out she had reported him? He would come and get her, whether at once, or after many years. Besides, there was her allegiance to Martin. Might she not be safer waiting to see if the Guards arrested Stanihurst, independently of her efforts? In short, Fionnuala's motives were as confused as they had been on all major decisions since Séamus had first come to know her. Hence her decision to light out for Spain.

Stanihurst's next target in his increasingly desperate quest for the missing dossier was Séamus Joyce, whose Donnybrook house he ransacked, to no avail. After that, the Billings Partnership received a visit.

Meanwhile, Inspector Dineen and his team were gathering evidence, analysing statements, collating records. Stanihurst was emerging as one suspect, but there were others. Fergus Kilpatrick, for instance. Jeremy Quaid. Burren. Séamus Joyce. If any of these had been arrested, Stanihurst might have been temporarily in the clear. If there had been enough gaps in the data that the Technical Bureau was gradually extracting from Cregan's computer records, he might have hoped to escape definitively. Sadly for Stanihurst, the Garda computer experts were doing a good job. They had retrieved a number of deleted files, and even enhanced some old surveillance video sequences from the night of Andrew O'Neill's murder. A man of Stanihurst's unusual size was dimly recognizable in several photographic images, and it was only a matter of time, they later claimed, before the net would have closed more tightly around him. In the meantime, Fergus Kilpatrick's false accusation against Martin threw them momentarily off the track.

For Kilpatrick's behaviour, several explanations were possible. Arrested while under the influence of drugs, he was naturally afraid to name his drug supplier, for fear of being killed. Failing that, Dineen enquired about what had been going on in King's, and offered Kilpatrick lenient treatment if he could help with some information. Kilpatrick was a friend and admirer of Ronan Gannon, O'Neill's murdered assistant, and half-believed a rumour that Gannon was murdered by Martin for reasons of rivalry.

After Cregan's death, Stanihurst might have been better advised to disappear at once. With his skills and connections, he could have removed himself from circulation, at the cost of tacitly admitting his guilt. He could not bring himself to take this step, which would have meant cutting himself off from his son. His natural love for Martin was probably compounded by the realization that he had committed three murders largely for the sake of his son's good opinion. And when he found that he had unwittingly caused Martin's arrest, he made one last desperate effort to set everything right.

What he did not realize, during the final hours of the case, was that he had been joined by a tracker even more skilful than himself. Heidi had noticed him loitering near the Donnybrook house on the morning after her arrival. When she had appeared at the door, he had pulled back. Her suspicions aroused, she left the house with Séamus, dispatched him to visit Fionnuala, and rented herself a black motor scooter from Ride of your Life on Morehampton Road. She then switched off her mobile phone and rode back along the street on the scooter, just as Stanihurst left the house after his brief rampage indoors. When he drove away in his van, she followed him to the Billings Agency, and later to King's

College. Loitering in the College, she found a public phone and contacted Guido Schneider. Having read O'Neill's obituary in the King's College President's Report, she knew where to point them. The computer gurus of Consultancy International started to trace Internet traffic to and from the Justice Watch Africa website in Holland. Her other phone call was to Clarendon Investigations, whom she hired to keep watch over Séamus that night. They would not be sharp enough to trail Stanihurst, but she thought they could probably handle Séamus.

As her own mobile phone remained switched off – electronic invisibility was essential – she later borrowed another phone from the young woman who worked for Clarendon Investigations.

On Saturday evening, she had followed Stanihurst to Killiney. Her worst moment had been when Séamus entered the house. She could see through the window of the downstairs room, but it would have been hard to intervene had Stanihurst attacked him.

Stanihurst's aim in digging up O'Neill's body had been simply to remove evidence that could have been used against Martin. His own DNA was probably so close to Martin's that a scientist could have used traces of his contact with O'Neill's body to wrap up the case against Martin. Or so he thought. Stanihurst admired engineers, but had no faith in chemists.

'Gotcha,' Senator Hinckley said. 'And Stanihurst's employers knew nothing?'

'Nothing at all. It's been traumatic for them. Seán Forde has withdrawn from the College. He's believed to have donated all his construction work for free, not even asking for his costs to be covered. He's taken a huge financial hit.'

Hinckley nodded. 'We'll do a deal.'

'In the end, people may see your arrival as the best available solution.'

'We try to help,' the Senator sighed. 'Does no one object to my philanthropy?'

'Some newspaper columnists, trade unionists, nationalists worried about Ireland losing its identity and having its heritage stolen by carpetbaggers.'

Hinckley spread his palms wide. 'You get what you get. It's been good talking with you, Séamus. You have exceeded my expectations, sir. You are looking at a satisfied customer.'

'Did I get the story right?'

Hinckley shrugged. 'Pretty much. Also, I guess your presence helped to move it toward a happy ending. OK, we're good to go.'

The story had lasted longer than planned. The pilot was already announcing their descent into Dublin.

The Death of King's

I

Passing through the VIP channel was, Séamus decided, quite the best way to experience Dublin Airport. Heidi and he stood aside as the official welcome party stepped forward. A few politicians and officials recognized him. One or two greeted him by name.

Choreography for the airport welcome and press conference was being handled, with considerable grace and efficiency, by the Billings Partnership, under the beaming direction of Derry McKinley. He hailed Séamus with unaffected pleasure, and explained (unasked) that the Billings Partnership had felt compelled to withdraw from the King's College account because of a perceived conflict of interest. They were now representing Senator Hinckley in all of his dealings with the Republic of Ireland. He was overjoyed to see Séamus looking so well after his ordeal and hoped he had enjoyed his flight. Those Gulfstreams were a marvel. Would Séamus be interested in joining the Higher Education Authority? The government was looking around for men and women with high-level administrative experience, and McKinley had of course mentioned Séamus's name to his old friend 'Porky' Keeffe. Could he pursue it further with the Minister?

Séamus had no wish to hit him. Violence is always sinful.

Senator Hinckley's visit lasted two days, during which everything went according to plan. There had already been a government announcement that, in view of the recent issues around King's College Dublin, an entirely new governance and management structure was required. The College board held a special meeting to sanction a deal whereby Finer Small Campuses of the Western World became majority owners of the College.

Some Irish students already enrolled for regular degrees at King's would be going to the new campus in Kells, County Meath, recently vacated by Nebraska Computer Peripherals Inc. Five scholarships were announced for the best and the brightest King's students to spend a summer semester studying basketball sociology at the FSC Education Innovation Center at Battle Creek, Michigan. Academics unwilling to work on the Kells campus were offered the alternative of early retirement. None took up the offer.

The Phoenix Park campus was designated as the principal residential facility for visiting students from the United States. The European Research Monitoring Agency of Finer Small Campuses, due to be established within six months, would also be based at the Phoenix Park, guided by a distinguished advisory committee under the experienced leadership of Harold ('call me Hal') Gaskell, who had been successfully wooed away from UKURQIA, the United Kingdom University Research Quality Improvement Association, following a misunderstanding involving his excellently proportioned secretary and a popular tabloid newspaper.

Senator Hinckley was happy. The European Roots to Education movement was the latest exciting trend in private college education, and Finer Small Campuses had got in on the ground floor. Given that Patrick Connolly was no longer available, Senator Hinckley announced a new board member of King's College: Professor Hart Stephen, recently named as International Ethical Investment Advisor to the Irish government.

The news got better in the weeks that followed. The independent Special Cases Commissioner of the Civil Service Pensions Authority took an objective and exhaustive look at Séamus's severance and pension entitlements, which he independently decided should be paid in full, with interest.

Séamus contacted the warehouse that had held his personal possessions since the break-up of his marriage, and arranged to have everything shipped to Germany. Heidi was willing to house half of his music collection in her country cottage, the other half in the new apartment which they proposed to buy together.

Before leaving Dublin for Germany, he made arrangements for the sale of his house in Donnybrook. While much of the furniture had had to be thrown out, enough remained to suggest a certain potential for gracious living. The estate agents boasted that they could easily obtain €750,000, without going to auction. They were negotiating, through solicitors, with a potential purchaser; Peter Simons claimed that the purchaser in question was Séamus's ex-wife, Theresa. Negotiations dragged on.

He decided not to bother suing the property management agency for their dishonesty. Life was too short. Peter Simons would make them pay in bad publicity when he got around to running his report.

Séamus had asked his solicitor to set up an anonymous charitable trust for the benefit of Mr Patrick 'Pimple' Boyle, into which one-third of the house sale price was to be paid. Bridie Morgan, the solicitor, said that she would cross that bridge if and when the house sale was ever completed, which she doubted, seeing the sort of shaggers that were involved on the other side. Séamus conceded that Boyle might be a criminal, but as it was he who had ruined Boyle and his unfortunate wife, he felt some responsibility towards him. Bridie riposted that he would need to get himself another lawyer if he really intended to go ahead with that load of codswallop. She could not be responsible for helping a client to cut his own throat. Anyone who did, in her humble opinion, deserved to be struck off.

The case of Hynes, confined to a wheelchair in a grim institution, was hardly less pathetic, but Séamus could claim no personal responsibility for that.

Séamus was not going to be short of ready money. Consultancy International had paid him well for his work in New York and Dublin, and placed him on a generous retainer.

Heidi and he were not yet spending much time in her cottage in the woods, because she was going through exhaustive medical investigations at the Universitätsklinikum Aachen, a hospital of staggering size and efficiency. This involved occasional overnight stays. Everything was paid for by her employee welfare scheme. There was talk of a mud spa holiday in the near future. Partners were welcome and would be accommodated free of charge. Meanwhile she insisted on blood tests and physical assessments for Séamus, pending a serious course of physical training. Never again must he allow himself to be placed at a disadvantage. Séamus wondered what lay behind these concerns, but thought it best to humour her. While she was out at work or in the university hospital, he spun the wheels of the exercise bicycle in her apartment, listening to recordings of her favourite master among Soviet cellists, Daniil Shafran. They got to the cottage at weekends. Summer was coming on, with the promise of heat.

There were literary repercussions from the King's College case. No fewer than three books appeared. The most successful was *The New Phoenix Park Murders* by Peter Simons, a sensational work that for two weeks reached number three on the Irish non-fiction original paperback bestseller lists. Gudrun Mardersteig's weightier tome, *Systemic Betrayal of the*

Values of the Academy in Europe and the United States, sank without trace. It was largely concerned with the failure of two other universities to recognize and reward her extraordinary talents. Séamus tried to read it for amusement, but found it painful. A bruiser bruised is a sad sight.

Jeremy Quaid's debut novel, *The Death of King's*, fell somewhere between the first two. It did well in university bookshops, despite a remarkably hostile review in *Prospectus*. Condy Moran, mellowed by his four-figure deal with a leading literary publishing house, had been kind in the *Gazette*. The embittered author, interviewed on *Arts and Minds*, was so unkind as to describe the *Prospectus* reviewer as lazy, stupid, dishonest and ugly. In his spoken as well as written style, Quaid had a tendency to oversprinkle his adjectives, often deploying them in threes, a habit he claimed to have picked up from the religious poetry of Saint Francis of Assisi. In the case of his comments about the *Prospectus* reviewer, the fourth adjective at least was certainly unjustified, as Quaid was unaware of the reviewer's identity and had no way of knowing how handsome or otherwise she or he might be. Former President Maxwell vehemently denied any connection with the review, which his friends photocopied and posted on College noticeboards. A barely concealed *roman à clef*, Quaid's novel was prefaced (unwisely, in the view of *Prospectus*) with an epigraph from Shakespeare's *Richard the Second* which sought to lend it a spurious air of distinction but which merely served to highlight the tawdry inadequacy of Quaid's own style:

> For God's sake let us sit upon the ground
> And tell sad stories of the death of kings:
> How some have been deposed, some slain in war,
> Some haunted by the ghosts they have deposed,
> Some poisoned by their wives, some sleeping killed,
> All murdered.

Séamus watched Heidi, in white, planting geraniums in window boxes all around her painted cottage, dappled in shadows like clouds of falling leaves.

Author's Note

In recent years, portions of the Irish higher education and research sector have been subjected to an extravagantly wasteful and debilitating series of 'reforms'. Inevitably, the fictional world of King's College Dublin has been affected by some of these satire-defying innovations. There is, however, no university in the Phoenix Park, and the persons, places and incidents described in this novel, which is a work of imaginative fiction, bear no relation to reality. (Reviewers will kindly refrain from quoting this last phrase.)

King's College Dublin was in fact invented by my late mother, the novelist and children's writer Eilís Dillon, whose *Death in the Quadrangle* was first published by Faber & Faber in 1956. There are some continuities between that novel and this, but *The Grounds* also takes cognizance of the sad decline in standards that has occurred in the intervening years. (Reviewers, please see above.)

My book, therefore, is not a *roman à clef*. It does not describe the current state of Trinity College Dublin, or any other seat of learning. The fact that characters in the work are equipped with various jobs, genders, physical characteristics and personal histories should not suggest that they are modelled on, or adapted from, real individuals sharing those or other features.

Rather than explaining some apparent anomalies of Hiberno-English – the variant usages and collocations of terms such as Garda, Guard and policeman, for example – I would ask the reader to take it on trust that this is how we deploy those terms over here.

Apart from the inevitable but truthful protestations of

gratitude to family members (notably the long-suffering Phyllis Gaffney), to my agent and philologist Jonathan Williams and my editor Brendan Barrington (at whose feet Monsieur Jourdain's philosophy master could profitably have sat), grateful thanks are due to Eithne Fitzgerald for advice on matters of characterization, psychology and real estate.

Needless to say, if any faults remain in the present volume, it seems to me that these people must take at least some of the blame.

CORMAC MILLAR

AN IRISH SOLUTION

'Millar … could do for Ireland what Dibdin has done for Italy'
Sunday Times

Seamus Joyce has got a few things on his mind. He has just been appointed Acting Director of iDEA, the Irish Drug Enforcement Agency. His wife is in hospital, dying of an unidentified ailment. And he is starting to question the purpose of his own existence. It's a tricky time at iDEA: an ambitious new Minister for Justice is anxious to secure a few big scalps in the Dublin drug trade, and Joyce is expected to put himself on the front line of the fight.

Soon he begins to suspect that the police, in league with the Minister, are bending the rules – and he still doesn't quite understand what the rules are. Why is money being paid into his bank account from an unnamed source in Liechtenstein? Why are his phones being tapped? And why are a troubled schoolgirl and a diminutive nun accusing him of being at the heart of a lethal conspiracy?

'Cormac Millar can write like hell' *Sunday Independent*

'An arch, sophisticated and thoroughly enjoyable crime debut that marks Millar as a talent to watch' *Irish Independent*

'Millar has a pleasingly black sense of humour and a keen eye for ambiguity' *Irish Times*

He just wanted a decent book to read ...

Not too much to ask, is it? It was in 1935 when Allen Lane, Managing Director of Bodley Head Publishers, stood on a platform at Exeter railway station looking for something good to read on his journey back to London. His choice was limited to popular magazines and poor-quality paperbacks – the same choice faced every day by the vast majority of readers, few of whom could afford hardbacks. Lane's disappointment and subsequent anger at the range of books generally available led him to found a company – and change the world.

'We believed in the existence in this country of a vast reading public for intelligent books at a low price, and staked everything on it'
Sir Allen Lane, 1902–1970, founder of Penguin Books

The quality paperback had arrived – and not just in bookshops. Lane was adamant that his Penguins should appear in chain stores and tobacconists, and should cost no more than a packet of cigarettes.

Reading habits (and cigarette prices) have changed since 1935, but Penguin still believes in publishing the best books for everybody to enjoy. We still believe that good design costs no more than bad design, and we still believe that quality books published passionately and responsibly make the world a better place.

So wherever you see the little bird – whether it's on a piece of prize-winning literary fiction or a celebrity autobiography, political tour de force or historical masterpiece, a serial-killer thriller, reference book, world classic or a piece of pure escapism – you can bet that it represents the very best that the genre has to offer.

Whatever you like to read – trust Penguin.

read more
www.penguin.co.uk